JAmes M. Owen

Aug 21, 2002

# No Time for Pilots

# No Time for Pilots

**James McMillen Owen**

Pentland Press, Inc.
England • USA • Scotland

PUBLISHED BY PENTLAND PRESS, INC.
5122 Bur Oak Circle, Raleigh, North Carolina 27612
United States of America
919-782-0281

ISBN 1-57197-186-6
Library of Congress Catalog Card Number 99-74222

Printed in the United States of America

*Dedicated to Bobbie, who does all the work around our place and put up part of her inheritance to pay for this foolishness.*

*Funny Wings: Navs, EWOs, Crows, Ravens, WOs, ROs, GIBs and YGTBSM crazies [Navigators, Electronic Warfare Officers, Bomber EWs, Reconnaissance EWs, Weapons Officers, Radar Operators, Guys in the Back Seat, YGTBSM (Don't ask. Don't tell.)]*

*Curtis E. LeMay, one iron-assed, tough son of a bitch. A stand-up commander whose Vietnam policies would have saved a million lives in Southeast Asia.*

*Pilots, last, but not least, to all you coordinated, farsighted bastards who flew big barn doors and didn't kill me.*

*I would like to offer special thanks to Rudyard Kipling and Charles Lutwidge Dodgson for their poetry and words used at the end of each chapter. It's up to the reader to guess who wrote what.*

*To Rowan and Martin and their inspiration for the dialogue I attribute to them although it was made up out of thin air.*

*To my friends and relatives who may see a part of themselves in my characters.*

• • •

# Chapter 1

## The Ohio State University

Sometimes I'm called J. R., that's short for Johnny Ropp. Been called Johnny ever since my great grandfather was alive. Back when I was learning to put one foot in front of the other, Grandmother called me J. R., so my great grandfather wouldn't get confused. Couldn't see why he would, what with me being only three and short. It was Mother who named me after my great grandfather. He was a surgeon in Sherman's Army on its march through Georgia, from Atlanta to the sea. My great grandfather killed more Yankees with his surgeon's knife than the rebels did with bullets. Maybe that's why he had more Confederate medals than Yankee ones. 'Course he said a Reb lieutenant gave them to him because he didn't saw off Johnny Reb's leg. Got called J. R. again in college, at Ohio State University, because we had one too many Johns in our dorm.

Now, I'm not too tall, or short, or fat or thin. I'm about right-sized for a sod bustin' Ohio farm boy, with wide shoulders and little feet. Stand about five-foot-eight, and hair? Kinda sandy brown, sometimes blonde, depending on what time of year it is. Age? Well, when I left college I was barely twenty-one. Now, turning twenty-one is important when you live in a state that can't make up its mind if its wet or dry. Turn twenty-one in Ohio, you can buy six percent beer instead of three-two. And hard liquor, too, if you have a taste for it, which I didn't. Not that I'd drink it anyway. Two whiskey sours and I'd upchuck supper.

Now, I'm not what you'd call your run-of-the-mill farm boy. Read one too many books in a dim lit attic. Gettin' smart kept me from being a pilot: all that readin' by dim light kept me from having twenty-twenty vision. Didn't have a choice, bein' a navigator or a pilot. And most pilots are so worried about their distance vision they won't read anything deeper than *Black Beauty*. As you can tell, I'm not short on conversation. When you spend half your life looking at the back end of sheep and the only one around to talk to is a Border collie, well, you catch my drift. Dogs listen all right, but, like pilots, they do have a short attention span and I wasn't cut out be a farmer. John Wayne was talking about farmers, not actors, when he opined, "Talk low, talk slow and don't say too much." My bein' able to read made me a candidate for a B.A. degree in American Literature at The Ohio State University.

Spent most of my growin' up at our Scioto River farm in Concord Township across from Bellpoint, a village so small we didn't have enough boys in school to field a baseball team. Didn't take long for me to realize I didn't want to be a farmer. Ever spread manure on a meadow on a hot, humid summer afternoon? I didn't want to spend another spring near a barnyard when the ground thawed, ripe with a full load of hog manure. Whew-ee! That smell is strong enough to drop a turkey vulture out of the sky. And as much as I liked my Border collie, Ralph, I couldn't stand the smell of one more sheep. I could run away, join the circus or go to the university, all things being equal. But for me there was no other choice. The Ohio State University was my ticket out. Don't know why they insist on putting a "The" before Ohio. Not like we'd ever be mixed up with those cave dwellers way up north, just below the glaciers, in Ann Arbor.

Columbus, Ohio is an academic light year away from my farm and half a world away from lonely night vigils along Korea's thirty-eighth parallel. My introduction to The Ohio State University life sure began on the wrong foot. I came in bright eyed and bushy tailed. Didn't take long for those who thought they were my betters to take me down a peg or two. Might have been the bright red and white checkered sport coat I wore to fraternity rushing parties. Looked like a slick table cloth from a pizza parlor, but I thought it was hot stuff. Or, it could have been my stories about chasin' after sheep, or my tendency to voice an opinion when I should have kept my mouth shut. I was invited to come in by more than a few fraternities, but was never asked to join. Kind of enjoyed my new celebrity until I learned my pizza parlor sport coat and loose lips were the entertainment. So, I suffered through some loneliness as an after affect of my instant celebrity and the finality of mistaken first impressions. However, like rain draining off the wool on my sheep's backs, snubs didn't get under my skin.

Got lucky, I was saved from becoming a total outsider by Air Force ROTC, those folks who wear a post office blue uniform. ROTC was called by those not keen on a North Korean vacation, the "Registered Order Of Terrified Civilians." However, it actually stands for Reserve Officers Training Corps. ROTC was more than just a haven for those of us with mediocre academics huddlin' in fear of bein' called up for the draft. For a sod bustin' sheepherder like me, ROTC meant a job, friends and an occasional pay check. The Ohio State University had three, Army, Navy, or Air Force. I could walk, float or fly a no brainer. I had enough walkin' behind my sheep, and bein' on the skinny side I couldn't float worth a damn. I still had to march around in circles on The Ohio State University's parade grounds. Wasn't long before I traded my sheep for a sheepskin, graduated in the middle of my class and was on my way to flight training at Ellington Field, Texas, halfway between Houston and Galveston. My eyes were myopic, not good enough to be a pilot. But it didn't matter, pay was the same. Pilots move sticks around in circles and tap dance on rudders. Navigators? We get to ride free, sleep a lot and look studious because most navigators have read more 'n one book.

• • •

God it was a cold and windy Midwestern winter day when I packed my gear into the back of my undertaker black Buick sedan. My four-door 1949 Buick had portholes, four on each side of the hood, and a well preserved paint job, shiny as a copper penny. I bade farewell to my family and sheep dog Ralph. He was at sixes and sevens since our sheep weren't around anymore. Soon as I trundled off to college, Father sold the whole lot. I gave one last wave at the end of the driveway and drove across the Scioto River to Bellpoint. Wasn't just crossin' over a river today, I was crossin' over from a life familiar, to one unknown. I turned southwest on U.S. 42, driving through Amish country to Plain City. Stayed on 42 to the national road, U.S. 40. Spent most of the first day on U.S. 40 to St. Louis. Scenery wasn't much to talk about, so I won't. St. Louis to

Joplin was more of the same dead grass and trees. I turned south at McAlester, Oklahoma and drove through Indian territory toward Dallas. Saw more dead grass and damn few trees. When I entered Dallas the temperature had climbed up to comfortable, but the grass was still dead. The thermometer kept on climbing to warm and humid all the way to Houston. Weather turned hot, humid, no wind at all drivin' south from Houston to the main gate of Ellington Air Field. I was in shirtsleeves while most Texans were wearin' jackets. Southeastern Texas humidity felt like early swamp to my skin, but seventy degree weather was a Blue Norther to Texicans.

## Ellington Air Field, Texas

I stopped at the main gate and asked for directions to base housing. It wasn't more than a block away. Looked like all the other buildings, another run-down temporary World War II barrack.

A fat, short tempered sergeant circled my new home in red on a base map. Not knowing what I was getting in to I asked, "Do you have a key?"

"Key? Lieu-ten-nant, you're going to live in temporary barracks. Key? Your room doesn't have locks."

"Does it have air-conditioning?"

"Your air-conditioning consists of windows, open or closed."

He was still laughing as I walked out the door. Chagrined, I paused by my car to get a better attitude. I looked around—grass was still dead, palm tree branches were green and I was in the Air Force. Couldn't figure out which was the most unusual. Wasn't the grass. It was of the Bermuda variety. Goes dormant when nighttime temperatures drop below sixty. Had to be the Air Force, it took some getting used to. I followed my map to the barracks number circled in red. It wasn't better than a run-down shack. "Sergeant was right. My new home is more suited to sheep than people," I thought.

Inside my new home was a cubicle open at top and bottom with a desk, metal storage cabinet, dresser and very small bed, a cross between a cot and a crib. And as advertised—no door and air-conditioning? Open windows. Having no door was a good idea, as having one would block air flow. I began to stow away what little gear I had when my first visitor arrived through a large hole in the middle of my window screen. A female mosquito large enough to carry passengers. She buzzed to a three point landing on the middle of my desk and began to eye me like I was dinner, so I left her alone.

As I closed the dresser drawer on the last item from my suitcase, another visitor stuck his head through my cubicle opening. I looked up at a gapped tooth smile in the middle of a round head, sorta' like Charlie Brown's. A life sized version of that oversized cherub who graces the cover of *Mad* magazine. I sat there with my mouth open, staring at him and he leaned against the cubicle opening, smiling. His smile grew and kept on growing until it disappeared around the corners of his cheeks. He stuck out his hand, breaking the spell and said, "I'm Tucker Tubbs from upstate New York. I live in the next cubicle, if you can call this living. Call me Tuck. Where are you from?"

"I'm Johnny Ropp from a place you've never heard of, a small village named Bellpoint on the Scioto River north of Columbus, Ohio."

Tucker stood there smilin', leanin' on a stick with a small net on the end.

I asked, "What is it?"

He held it out so I could see, and said, "You mean this? It's a lacrosse stick. I was captain of my team at Syracuse."

"Thought only Indians played it."

"They do and we do. Lacrosse is big time back east."

"I'll take your word for it."

"Interested in dinner?"

"Sure am."

"Best place is the cadet mess hall. Food's about the same as dorm food. We can eat as much as we can hold and it's a whole lot cheaper than the Officer's Club."

"Wait until I finish here, find the head and wash up."

"Are you building a model airplane or is that a mosquito?" he asked.

"She's a big one isn't she? Thought I'd keep her as a pet. Might call her Moe."

Tucker brought his lacrosse stick down on top of her with a flick of his wrist, "There ain't no Moe." He walked out, "Stop by when you're ready."

I finished hanging the few uniforms I had inside my metal cabinet, placed my empty suitcase on the bottom and walked to the latrine to wash up. I noticed a healthy growth of green around the base of the appliances, but it was better than an outhouse back home. When I returned, Tucker was sitting amid a stack of clothes, desperately in need of laundering, scattered around his room. His clothing was on top of the dresser, desk, arm chair and cabinet.

I shook my head, "Damn, Tuck, looks like a cyclone whistled through your room. How long have you been here?"

"This is my third day. Notice, I cleaned my cubicle today. Missin' a sock and baseball cap. Let me know if you find them."

"Where did you get your arm chair?"

"Out of your cubicle. Pays to arrive early. Ready to head over to the cadet mess hall? My stomach clock went off an hour ago."

"Lead the way, I'll follow," I replied, famished, as well.

"Do you know when we have to report in?"

"Base theater tomorrow morning at eight A.M. for greetings and orientation."

"Know what it's about?"

"Not certain. Should be what we can expect from them and what they will expect from us."

"Johnny, before I forget, I'm having one of those newfangled things called a hi-fi delivered tomorrow evening. Hope you like to listen to bag pipes, penny whistles and drums."

"As long as you keep the volume down. We'll have to burn the midnight oil if we're goin' to earn navigator wings."

"You may burn away, but not me. Nothing to flying if you follow the book and know what you're doing—which I do."

"What did you major in?"

"Journalism, going to be a high paid editor one of these days. The first prerequisite for an editor is, don't do more than needs to be done. Cadet mess hall is dead ahead."

This cadet mess hall gave new meaning to bland. The chicken the cook plopped down on my tray was flat as road kill and nowhere near as tender. The mashed potatoes were slick with butter and rancid with cooking oil grease. The green beans were overcooked, tasted like silage fermentin' over wintertime in the bottom of our farm silo. Topping this gourmet feast was a cherry on top chocolate cake, so burnt on the bottom that charcoal overpowered the chocolate icing. I ate a little off the top of my chicken, stayin' away from the tire tracks and loaded up with ice cream. Knew the mess hall cooks couldn't burn vanilla, though they might have tried. There were oven directions on the outside of the ice cream barrel. Tucker? He ate everything that didn't move and went back for more. I knew one thing for sure, there wasn't a gourmet restaurant anywhere near upstate New York. Tucker pointed his fork at my cake, "You gonna eat that?"

"You can have it." I handed it to him and watched as the crumbs disappeared. I noticed that the cadets were separated from us by a wooden planter full of artificial flowers. I waited for Tucker to wipe away the crumbs before asking, "Why aren't we sitting with the cadets?"

"Commandant doesn't want us anywhere near them. We're the first all officer class in his Nav school. He's afraid one will contaminate the other, but he's not sure which. I'm stuffed. Want to see a movie this evening?"

"Not tonight, I'm in the middle of another Michener novel and I'm tired. Think I'll read awhile and hit the sack early. Been on the road to Houston for three days—it's catchin' up with me."

"I'm rested. There's a Luigi cowboy flick at the base theater. Gonna' take it in. If you're asleep when I come back, wake me up in the morning—so I don't miss breakfast."

"Six-thirty early enough for you?"

Tucker didn't answer, just grimaced.

• • •

Next morning, I tried to wake Tucker up before going to the latrine to brush my teeth, but his only response was a moan. When I returned, he wouldn't budge. I gave one more try, but he wasn't about to get up and I wasn't about to waste time. "I'll save you a seat at the mess hall," I said as I left.

Outside, this early winter morning was sunny, pleasant. Today's cool humid air was a whole lot better than yesterday's heat. I was beginning to adjust. The mess hall breakfast wasn't bad, not bad at all. Cooking eggs over easy with pancakes fit the skill levels of the morning chef. Syrup was hot, but not maple. Couldn't figure out what it was. Didn't run off like our syrup at home, soaked right through to the pancakes' core. Bacon can be overcooked or undercooked. My strips were neither. Tucker arrived late, knocking chairs out of his way to get to the breakfast line. He filled his tray to the brim with everything in sight, including grits.

Between bites, he gave me a running review of last nights movie, "You should have gone. It was great, a real cowboy classic. Lips moved in Italian, words came out, out of synch, in English with no emotion and the translation made no sense at all. All-in-all, a memory worth sharing. What do you think they'll do to us at orientation?"

I glanced at my watch, "They'll try to scare us into toeing the party line."

Tucker looked puzzled, so I added, "That's the Air Force way of making us work and obey orders."

"Fine with me, since they sign my paycheck," he replied.

"Every day in the Air Force is like Sunday on the farm."

"How so?"

"No heavy lifting and there's the aroma of bullshit in the air."

With Tucker demolishing mess hall food, we arrived late and had to sit down front, four rows back from the podium. Our class filled all, but a few seats in the front. After we were seated, doors closed, lights dimmed and a spot shined on stage left. A tall, thickset, graying at the temples, lieutenant colonel strode to the center of the stage with the spot trailing behind. When he spat out, "Attention," we all snapped to. He looked left, then right, then center, "I'm the base commander." Words came out like The Ohio State University, making no sense at all, as if there were two more base commanders around.

He let us absorb that pearl of wisdom before saying, "I'm a py-lut and none of you myopic bastards will ever, ever be one of us, God's chosen few. You got problems, take it to your instructor. If he can't handle it, the commandant, but never, and I mean never, visit me. I don't ever want to see one of you four-eyed bastards outside my door."

Tucker gave me dig and whispered with a grin, "He likes us."

The base commander scratched his ass then his nose with the same finger and frowned at us, "I won't take any questions. I pray to God I never see one of you weak-eyed bastards again."

Our base commander left as he came in, walking fast—exiting stage left with the spot trailing behind. We were still standing at attention two minutes later, when another lieutenant colonel walked in from stage right. The house lights came up. He was younger, closer to my height and didn't seem as uptight.

He motioned for us to sit down, "At ease, gentlemen. I'm your commandant. I want everyone of you to know that even though I'm a command fighter pilot and consider you potential funny wings nothin' more than excess baggage, I'll give you a fair shake. Follow the chain of command, keep your noses clean, stay out of jail, work hard and graduate. You're our first class of officers and, to be honest, we haven't changed our curriculum from the one we use for aviation cadets. So, you'll march to retreat and attend orientation lectures just like our cadets. Stay away from them. We have several classes yet to graduate and I'll stand for no interference with their training and discipline. Welcome aboard, gentlemen. If you want to earn funny wings, you play ball with me and I'll play ball with you. Does anyone have a question?"

I sensed that Tucker was about to move. I looked over at my cherub friend with a gapped tooth grin and whispered, "Don't do it."

But, his eyes were glazed over. Tucker was on his feet before I could pull him back down, "Sir!"

The commandant looked down into the middle of a mass of sweating gold bars, searchin' for the wise-ass who called out. No one had ever spoken up before. He said, "We have a question from a brown bar in the fourth row. Go ahead, lieutenant."

Tuck began to grin, a smile almost as large as when I first met him. He spoke up for all to hear, "Sir, don't you mean, you play ball with me and I'll shove the bat up your ass?"

The base theater grew silent, silent as a vacuum bottle when its air is sucked out. The commandant frowned and then began to smile. A rustle of anticipation stirred in each theater seat, waiting for the wrath of the Air Force to descend on Tucker.

The commandant spoke softly, "That will be all gentlemen, except for you. Yes, you, lieutenant, with the silly-looking grin on your face. See me after formation. The rest of you are dismissed."

A voice from down front shouted, "Ten-Hut!"

We all stood up at once, our theater seats banging against the backs. Tucker, with his ever present "what-me-worry" grin, strolled to the podium. It's not in my nature to watch as another human being is tortured or humiliated, so it was not a difficult decision to go forward with a condemned man. Believing our commandant would tear a new opening in Tucker's posterior, I went outside and waited at the front entrance, certain Tucker was going to get his for being such a smart-ass. I was so nervous, I bummed a cigarette and a light.

I puffed and waited, and puffed and waited before Tucker strolled out through the exit with a wink and a nod, frowning at my cigarette smoke, "Didn't know you were a smoker."

"Only when I'm nervous. How did it go?"

"Guess who is a hi-fi nut?"

"The commandant?"

"You betchum, Red Rider. You know, for an illiterate pilot, he's not all that bad."

"You sure like to live on the edge," I marveled.

"I'm a cat with nine lives."

"Tucker, that's a nautical phrase, a reference to the cat-o-nine tails."

"You mean the one bos'ns flailed sailors' backs with?"

"Yes, but if we use your meaning, you'll only have eight lives remaining at Nav school. You just used your first one with the commandant this morning. His first impression of you couldn't have been a good one. I'd use your remaining lives sparingly."

Tucker took the cigarette out of my fingers and stomped it out, "Eight lives are enough to get me through this school. Commandant said the base commander doesn't hate us, he's just upset at being turned down to return to fly single engine jets. He's taking it out on us."

"Now that shows a lot of maturity on his part. With us as an outlet for his hostility, he won't have to kick his dog."

• • •

We whiled away the rest of the morning standing in line, waiting for our navigation equipment and flying gear. Our flight suits looked like farm bib overalls, with zippers instead of a row of buttons. My wool lined leather flying jacket smelled of sheep, a bit to close to a sheep-farm for my liking. After lunch, we reported to our first class. We were taught in small groups called Flights of twelve or so men each. Besides Tucker and me, there was Roger the lodger, Mart the smart, Red the temperamental, Oscar D. and others who were just as crazy. We began navigation training at the beginning, studying how to fly from point A to point B—without getting lost. Right off, Tucker proceeded to follow a path that would lead him into a land of the hopelessly lost. Tucker spent most of his time staring off into space—at the ceiling, or out the window. His mind was either in neutral, out of gear or in another world. With Tucker it was hard to tell which.

When we returned to our barrack, Tucker had two large crates waiting inside his cubicle. He let out a whoop, "My new hi-fi has arrived!" He tried to open it, "Damn, it's sealed with metal bands and I don't have a single tool. Do you have a hammer and screwdriver?"

"In the trunk of my car. I'm hungry now. Let's go to the cadet mess hall, then we'll go to my car and get those tools."

"Nah, I want to put my hi-fi system together. I'll walk with you out to your car."

I loaned him a hammer and screwdriver from my tool kit and walked to the cadet mess hall on my own. Tonight's meal was a carbon copy of last night's. Another gourmet feast of road kill and burnt cake. I returned to find Tucker sitting on his bed, watching the commandant hook up his hi-fi system. He looked up with a more than usual wide eyed smile and said, "Come on in. Almost have it ready to go."

"No thanks. My weakest subject is math and we have a test scheduled at the end of the week. With an analog mind in a digital world, I'll need all the help I can get."

Thirty minutes later the screeching of bagpipes and thumping of drums from Tuck's cubicle jolted me out of my chair. Either the British had invaded, or Tucker and the commandant had connected all of the right wires.

Tuck stuck his head inside my cubicle, "The commandant and I are going to the O' Club for dinner to celebrate. Want to join us?"

"No thank you. Mess hall fried chicken is swelling up inside my stomach like a chunk of marinated mutton. Need to get a leg up on my studies or I'll fall behind. Didn't expect this much math."

I looked over my notes from our afternoon class. I had a ton of technical stuff to learn before I would be allowed to fly our first training mission. Basic navigation covered dead reckoning, which is a Nav's way of saying, "I compute, therefore I am." We had to learn to compute and know the difference between airspeed, ground speed, drift, true heading and true course. All of which were used to discover where an airplane was, where it's going, the direction it should take and how soon it will arrive. Basic navigation isn't all that complicated, except there are no highways to follow or road signs in the sky. I was getting the hang of it when my thoughts were interrupted by Burl Ives, singin' folk music from Tucker's room.

I called over, "What did you do with the commandant?"

"His wife tracked him to the O' Club bar and hauled him home."

"Are you ready for the math they're throwing at us?"

"Math? No one told me I'd be studying math."

"Navigation is all math. Keep your music down. I'm going to burn midnight oil."

"Roger that. Math? I'm in big trouble."

• • •

Tucker may not know an algebraic sign, but he did know his limitations, and he was in trouble. Navigation math wasn't easy for a literal literary mind and the school made it more complicated than it should be. At the beginning of each morning class, our instructor rolled in a blackboard on which was painted a version of a basic navigation log. At the top of each vertical column he would chalk in titles—like TRUE HEADING, DRIFT, TRUE COURSE, AIRSPEED, WIND AND VELOCITY, GROUND SPEED, LOCATION, et cetera and each morning he would move these columns about. Plus became minus and minus became plus. By the end of the second week we were all confused, and Tucker? He was confused beyond redemption. He sat there, staring at the columns without comprehension—his eyes glazed over.

Before our first examination, I asked him, "Are you still having trouble with math?"

"Sure am—didn't know it would be this confusing. Just when I think I've got it, our instructor moves another column."

"You just lost another one of your lives."

"How many do I have left?"

"Seven, Tucker, seven."

"Can you help?"

"No, I'm hanging on by my fingernails. But I know who can."

"Who?"

"Mart the smart. If you'll listen to him, you'll pass."

When the test scores were posted for basic navigation, I couldn't believe my eyes. Not only did Tucker pass, he was right below Mart the smart, near the top of our Flight. I thought I saw his eyes wandering toward every answer sheet within his field of view, but I couldn't be sure. Before the first training flight, we all took turns drilling Tucker on how to use his equipment. This turned into an exercise in futility. Although he tried very hard, Tucker was unable to comprehend abstract concepts of time, distance and motion. Now, Tucker isn't what you would call a dunce. He possessed a well honed literary mind, with a firm grip on synonyms, semantics and the Pentateuch. Unfortunately, none of this knowledge was useful for navigation. In spite of Tucker's shortcomings, we were ready for our first training flight—in the twin engine T-29.

Now, the T-29 is a training aircraft. Took two days for Tucker to understand what the T stood for. United still had a few of these Convair birds flying short haul passenger routes. It was safe, durable and slow. So slow geese would fly by, wondering why it wasn't catching up and flying formation. You won't find the T-29 listed in aviation books because it was used to train navigators, not pilots. It had two propellers, a round stubby body and enough desks to train a flock of students. Our T-29s were configured for beginning or advanced training. The beginning ones had a limited amount of equipment not more than twenty student positions. Each position had a table, intercom, compass and airspeed indicator. Toward the aft were five drift meters. Tucker had no problem using his table. He laid his head down on it and slept. However, drift meters were beyond his comprehension. Our drift meters had a periscope looking down, not up, magnifying an object on the ground. When we viewed a stationary object, like a building, and measured the amount of time it took to pass across the drift meter's grid, we derived ground speed. To do this, we had to turn a knob on the side of the drift meter to synchronize the grid with aircraft heading. The reading on this knob provided drift. With heading, drift and ground speed, we could determine airspeed, true course and all that stuff we used to navigate. This was straightforward. Tucker's problem was there were two switches on the side of the drift meter, one labeled "gyro" and the other "heat." One was used to stabilize the gyro, the other was for heat in cold weather. We didn't need the second switch in Houston. If you turned it on and left it on, sure as Texas moonshine, heat would burn out the gyro. And along came Tucker, who was unable to differentiate between the switches.

• • •

At the end of our first training flight, Tucker left a trail of burnt-out drift meters. And he would have destroyed the last remaining one if Roger the lodger hadn't tripped him.

Roger was pissed, "Tuck, I've been elected by our Flight to tell you that we're going to give you your own personal drift meter. That's the good news. The bad news is, if you touch one of the others, we're gonna toss you overboard."

Tucker brushed himself off, "That's not fair."

I spoke up, "Okay, if you burn out yours, I'll give you access to mine, but I control the switches. So you won't get screwed up, your drift meter is the one farthest aft."

"Is that to the back?"

I had to laugh, "You don't know what 'aft' means?"

"Is it the pointy end or the blunt one?"

"The blunt end. You just lost another life."

"No problem, I have plenty, six more to go."

As sure as spring follows winter, Tucker burned out his personal drift meter on each training flight. If that wasn't enough, he didn't have the foggiest idea of where we were, where our airplane was going or when it would arrive. He did have one small chunk of luck. He was never selected as Lead navigator. As Lead provides directions to the pilot, no telling where we would have wound up. Tucker was at sixes and sevens. The more he failed to understand the basic tenants of navigation, the more hyperactive he became. He overcame his lack of comprehension with a flurry of activity, runnin' the aircraft aisle, scatterin' maps, papers and pencils in his wake.

I tried to calm him down, "Tuck, slow down, don't confuse motion for work. If you do, you just lost another one of your cat lives."

"Not a problem, four down, with five more to go."

• • •

It was a warm, almost a spring-like day when we boarded our T-29 before daylight for our basic navigation air exam. The odds against Tucker passing had risen so high, even Las Vegas wouldn't post them. None of this bothered Tucker. He sat aft in his private, blunt end section seat with a paper back novel in hand. As the sun rose over the left wing of our T-29, we climbed upward in a slow turn to the north toward Dallas. After level off, I finished my first drift meter reading and looked aft, to check on Tucker. His head was in his arms on the table, fast asleep. I returned to my seat, filled out my log and forgot all about Tucker. As the sun rose, our March day turned hot and clear, typical in Texas. Even at eight thousand feet, sweat rolled down our backs and into our eyes. We slaved away, working at warp speed, attempting to keep up with a slow moving airplane. I forgot all about Sleeping Beauty. When we were halfway to Dallas,

I glanced back. Tucker was leaning back in his chair, feet up on the table, a novel in his hand, dust cover still on his personal drift meter. After we turned, heading back to Houston from Dallas, I took time to walk aft and talk to Tucker. I spoke over the noise of our two prop engines, "Tuck, how are you doing?"

"Great, I'm halfway through."

"Our flight exam?"

"No, my novel."

"Think you'll pass?"

"No problem. This flight is a piece of cake."

"You haven't taken that dust cover off of your drift meter."

"Don't need to, navigation is a piece of cake."

I left him with his novel, shaking my head and thinking, "No way Tucker is going to pass."

I had barely enough time to finish a set of computations before it was time to begin another and Tucker was reading a novel. As we turned on final approach to land at Ellington Field, I finished my last computation, checked over my log for errors, walked forward and turned my log and map in to our instructor. Tucker shuffled down the aisle nonchalant-like, carryin' his test like it was a manuscript. I glanced over at his log, wondering what he had accomplished. His log was completed in ink, a flawless masterpiece with flourishes and scrolls, enough to make a Benedictine monk jealous. I questioned him as we walked down the steps, "Did your drift meter work?"

"Don't know. Didn't take the dust cover off."

"How in the world were you able to complete your log? Every time I looked back you were asleep or reading a novel."

"It's easy with cunning, patience and a quill pen. Beginning navigation is a piece of cake."

The next morning before class began, we checked the bulletin board outside the administration building to see if we had passed. I scored ninety points out of a hundred and stood just above the middle of our flight. And Tucker? His score was posted at the top of the page, separated from the rest of us, a perfect one hundred, three points higher than the next grade.

I turned to Tucker in disbelief, "How in the world did you pass with a perfect score?"

"Beginning Nav is a piece of cake, if you follow the textbook. Discovered we were flying to Dallas just like the sample log in our text. So, I copied it the night before, all but the times. I filled them in as we flew. As luck would have it, our winds were identical. Nice piece of work if I do say so myself. Most times it's better to look good at what you're doing than to be good at it. Notice how perfect my log was, and in ink, too."

I had to laugh, "Looked like a monastic scribe copied it. Sorry, I'm going to take away another one of your cat lives. According to my calculations, you only have four left."

"More than enough to graduate."

As we entered the classroom, everyone in our Flight stood up and we all gave Tucker three cheers. His face turned red as a beet as he walked toward his desk. He whispered over to Roger the lodger, "Will map reading be this easy?"

"Should be, that's what pilots use when they lose their electronic aids. If a pilot can do it, anyone can."

Tucker nudged me with his elbow and whispered, "Sure hope the roads are marked."

"What do you mean?"

"How can we tell them apart without signs?"

I didn't have the heart to tell him signs would be impossible to read from several miles away and ten thousand feet up, "Don't worry about road signs. You won't need 'em. Map reading isn't that hard. We're not talking rocket science. Use the dead reckoning techniques we learned in beginning navigation to find approximate aircraft location and compare that position with what you see on the ground. Place a triangular fix on your map when you make a match. With two fixes you can compute distance, ground speed, and true course. We derive drift and true heading using that information."

Tucker looked puzzled, "Fix? What's a fix?"

"You're airplane has arrived at a fixed point, or location."

"Sure there aren't any needles involved?"

"Different kind of fix."

Tucker had that blank look on his face, "Okay, but where are the road signs?"

"There are no highways in the sky. You won't find road signs up there, either. Do you remember what an ETA is?"

"No."

"We used it in the course you just aced. It means estimated time of arrival to the next navigation position or destination. Tucker, if you can't understand simple terminology, you're not long for Nav school."

He moaned, "I know, I know. I've only got three cat lives left."

• • •

Our electronics class almost washed both of us out. Not much call for this type of training in college, when our majors were American literature and journalism. We both passed by the skin of our teeth after retaking the tests. After squeaking by the final exam, our instructor took us aside, "Lieutenant Ropp and you too, Lieutenant Tubbs — listen up. I want both of you to promise me that you will never apply for an advanced course that begins with an E or an R."

Tucker wouldn't let a straight line like that pass without a smart-ass remark.

With a wide cherubic grin he asked, "Do you mean euthenics and religion?"

Our instructor wasn't buying his humor, "No, you dingbat. I mean electronic countermeasures or radar. Ropp, what did you do for a living before you graced our Air Force with your presence?"

"I was a farm boy before I went off to college."

"Not the kind of background we expect flyin' the line. But, you've probably spread more than one load of manure. If you don't buy the farm, you'll probably wind up at the Pentagon."

He was laughing at his own sense of humor when he turned toward Tucker, "Don't say a word. I know what you were, the male model for the muppet on the cover of *Mad* magazine. Remember what I told you both of you." He walked away chuckling to himself, "E and R."

As we walked to the cadet mess hall, Tucker was jumping up and down barely able to contain himself, "A sod buster—Johnny you're a sod buster and probably a sheepherder, too."

Having learned my lesson at Ohio State, I had not discussed my sheep with any of my classmates. Tucker must have sensed the truth, so I attempted a diversion, "That's why I round up strays like you."

"Roger that, you're more like a sheep dog than a farm boy."

Knowing I couldn't win, I changed the subject, "We both escaped electronics by the skin of our teeth. How many lives do you have left?"

Tucker looked skyward, "I used up another one. Looks like I have only two cat lives left in my pocket. Doesn't look good."

Tucker had a mental blackout every time he looked at a map. He couldn't relate what he saw on the ground to towns on his map. He had a blank look when our instructor asked, "Lieutenant Tubbs. Please tell the rest of your Flight what color the Red River is on your map?" Now, this is fairly standard stuff. Even on a road map, terrain is shaded brown to green depending on elevation. Small towns are black dots and larger cities are yellow. Highways are black for local and red for interstate. Rivers, lakes, lagoons and oceans are blue.

Tucker, as proud as a peacock, thought he was asked a question he knew, answered, "Why that would be red, sir."

Laughter bubbled up from our Flight and grew until even our instructor joined in. Tucker didn't have to give up another life for this elementary error, but his reprieve was short lived. Map reading was to be his Waterloo, though it was a snap course for the rest of our Flight. And it would have been a breeze for Tucker if it hadn't been for the lieutenant in charge of mess halls.

Tucker lacked basic navigation skills. To compound his problems, almost all log entries were made directly on the map. His textbook sample was now useless. After a brief ground school and three weeks of flight training, we were ready for our flight exam. As usual, Tucker, with the wandering eyes, was near the top of the Flight on our ground exam. With a lot of help, it looked like he might pass our flight check. And he would have if one of our training flights had not been scrubbed due to maintenance problems. To make up this flight, two missions were scheduled on the same day, a training flight to Dayton and our flight exam on the way back to Houston. Our morning flight to Ohio was error free for everyone, including Tucker. Towns stuck out like zits on a teenagers forehead. On our flight back to Houston, everyone was on the same sheet of music except our evaluator. As luck would have it we drew one who had passed Nav training, but failed the instructor course. Deemed too incompetent to fly the line, he was placed in charge of mess halls where he again demonstrated his incompetence. To prevent a revolt among our enlisted troops, he became the manager of the cadet mess hall.

We walked to the admin. porch after breakfast and checked the bulletin board for our grades, but they were not posted. When we gathered inside the classroom, our Flight was still buzzing, wonderin' why our grades weren't up. Shortly after eight o'clock, the commandant walked in. As we stood up and snapped to attention, he raised his hand, "At ease. You're probably wondering why I'm here and why your grades weren't posted this morning. According to your evaluator, all of you failed. Our wing navigator checked the pilot's map and log. Looks like our cadet mess hall manager was in error. We know you were in the right, but we have an unwritten rule here. Right or wrong, your instructor is always right. There is no remedy for an incompetent evaluator."

Tucker stood up, "Is this where the bat comes in?"

The commandant couldn't help himself, he doubled up in laughter. With tears forming in his eyes he asked, "Is there a second question? Look guys, I know this doesn't sit right with you. When it comes to navigation, our wing navigator has the final say and he won't allow a pilot's map to be used to grade your mission. It's a matter of pride. The best I can do for you is let you retake your map reading check ride without prejudice."

• • •

When we stepped outside for coffee during the morning break, Tucker was livid, "Damn it Johnny, I had it made. No tellin' where they'll send us tomorrow."

"You're right. Bet the powers that be send us west to desolation. At least we won't draw the same evaluator."

"What happened?"

"He's been removed from flight status. I guess this mistake was the last straw. And they ran a preliminary inspection of his accounts at the cadet mess hall. Looks like he screwed those up, too."

Mart the smart walked over, "Guess where we're flying?"

I answered, "West to nowhere."

"Right you are—San Angelo, Texas and back."

Tucker looked down at his shoe tops, "There's nothing out there 'cept mesquite trees, water tanks and rattlesnakes."

Mart the smart laughed, "What did you expect? The powers that be are going to extract their pound of flesh."

Tucker's eyes opened wide, "Even though they were wrong?"

Mart nodded, "Especially since they were wrong. No institution likes to admit they made a mistake."

"Who's our evaluator?"

"The wing navigator."

Tucker looked crestfallen, "I'm a dead man!"

Except for a glimpse of Austin on the horizon, towns along the way were as scarce as hens' teeth. Identifying terrain features was not easy. A seven-year drought had left dry creek beds and brown vegetation. Hoping that motion would save him, Tucker ran the aisle, scattering a paper storm in his wake. Without a sound basic navigation background, Tucker was in way over his head. He was fifty miles off course when we turned over nowhere, west Texas and headed back to Houston. The wing navigator kept a close eye on all of us. Wandering eyes were not going to help Tucker today. After we landed, Tucker questioned all of us to see if we had all seen the same landmarks from the air. With a sigh, Tucker seemed resigned to his fate. The good news was, we all ate a hearty meal at the cadet mess hall. With new management, dinner was better than ever. It even brought Tucker's spirits up.

• • •

When we checked our grades in the morning, Tucker was the only failure, with a grade so low it was on a separate page. He was pulled out of our class, to mission plan for his recheck. I looked for him after class let out for lunch and found him in the next classroom, all by himself. I tried to cheer him up, "Look Tuck, we'll all pitch in and help you get ready for your check ride."

"Won't do any good. The wing navigator is my evaluator and I have to fly it by myself."

"You'll be lead?"

"Roger that. I'll have to give directions to the pilots. Johnny, I'm a dead man. If I fail, will they give me another chance?"

"As you said to the commandant, bend over, here comes the bat. You remember the sign over Purgatory in Dante's *Inferno*?"

"Give up all hope, ye who enter here?"

"Tucker, you only have one life to give to your country."

We did all we could do to help Tucker that evening. He flew his recheck early the next day. His flight plan called for a trip to Laredo, Texas and back. Another flight over desolation to nowhere, a disaster from start to finish—which occurred near the halfway point. The wing navigator took control when Tucker tried to steer their T-29 over parts of Mexico that had never seen an airplane. I waited for Tucker at base operations. He hopped off the back end of the crew truck all smiles. I was surprised. He was up, not down in the dumps.

"Did you pass?" I asked him.

"Not likely, but even our pilots said they had never been to Del Rio, Texas before. When we almost flew over Acuna, Mexico, the wing navigator took control. Sure is a nervous fellow. He jumped up and down and yelled a lot at me for being lost. I calmed him down when I told him I wasn't. Hell, I knew where we were. We were over the southwestern half of the United States. Any fool would have known that."

"Looks like you've used up cat life number nine."

"Yeah, but it was fun while it lasted. I'm just not cut out to be a navigator. Better to wash out before I kill someone. Where do you think they'll send me?"

"Your background is journalism. Should be something that involves writing or editing."

"Commandant was one of our pilots. Offered to buy me a beer at happy hour. Want to come along?"

"Roger that."

"I need a shower and we should change into civvies. Doesn't want his pilot buddies to know he has navigator friends."

The commandant was waiting in the bar when we walked in. He greeted Tucker like a long lost friend, "You know, Tuck, I'm going to miss you. Won't be the same here without your wit and wisdom."

I left Tucker and the commandant in their cups at the O' Club bar. One beer was my limit and it isn't much fun watching two grown men get wobbly legged. With a new mess officer, cadet mess hall food was looking up. The mess sergeant found a surplus of funds after his boss was fired and rewarded us by cooking steak. Tucker didn't show up in our barracks that night, or the next, or the next. We looked everywhere, but couldn't find a sign of him. His clothes were still scattered about his cubicle, as well as his sports equipment. And his new hi-fi was gathering dust in the corner. I checked with administration and all they would say was, "Lieutenant Tucker has been reassigned." Nav school policy was to remove failures immediately. Three weeks went by before we received a letter postmarked Cheyenne, Wyoming. It was from Tucker. Our mystery was solved:

*Johnny,*

*How the hell are you? I'm fine. At supply school in Cheyenne. My household goods should have been her by now. Check with base transportation and see if you can find out were they're at. I'm at the top of my class in this school. Forms are so complicated, no one understands them. Remember the cadet mess hall troop? He's in my class and am I ever getting even. Don't forget to check on my gear. Don't want to lose my new hi-fi. Keep in touch,*

*Tucker*

I couldn't believe Tucker. He certainly marched to the beat of a different drummer. I could follow his thinking and that worried me a bit. U.S. Air Force sent him to Wyoming, so they must have enough sense to send his gear. An idea that might look right to anyone unfamiliar with the military. And there was no one alive more unfamiliar than Tucker. I checked with base transportation and discovered it would take a ton of paperwork and months to ship Tucker's gear north. I would have to jump through more hoops than I cared to, or had time for. It took a bit of doing, but I was able to convince our Flight to chip in and send Tucker's gear the quick way, by civilian air freight. I Scotch taped a note inside the top of Tucker's hi-fi.

*Tucker,*
*You, like your allegorical cat, have lost all nine of your lives, but now you're the cat that's out of the bag. Remember what the Cheshire Cat told Alice when she said, "But I don't want to go out among mad people."*
*"Oh you can't help that," said the Cat, "We're all mad here."*
*We'll meet again and when we do, you owe us all a beer for bailing you out, again. Keep on keepin' on,*
*Johnny*

Tucker's place was taken by Charles M. Line, liked to be called Main Line. A dyed-in-the-wool rebel from South Carolina, a proud graduate of The Citadel and crazy as a March hare. And as the Cheshire-Cat reminded Alice when she wanted to know,

*"How do you know I'm mad?"*
*"You must be," said the Cat, "or you wouldn't have come here."*

# Chapter 2

Main Line is 180°, a direct opposite, of Tucker Tubbs. Military life and Tuck were like oil and water. A proud graduate of the premier military school of the south, Main Line was a conivin' student of the military mind. He came from a spit and polish bastion, The Citadel and was drilled in military thought by some of the best, ramrod up the ass military minds ever to wear uniforms. Main Line was able to develop a certain familiarity that lets one slide around sharp, uniformed military corners without scrapping a knee. Now, he wasn't a stuffy stiff neck tin soldier. Main Line suffered through his share of disciplinary hell. Marching the quad alone, he was the proud holder of a Citadel record for punishment tours. Main Line had one glaring fault. He was always looking for short cuts where there weren't any. And that's why he washed back into our Flight. Too late — Main Line discovered there were no short cuts in daylight celestial navigation.

Our celestial navigation training class was mostly about my dreaded nemesis, mathematics, necessary to track the movements of our closest star, the sun. We were taught to use a hand held aeronautical sextant that measured elevation, or altitude of stars and planets. We aimed our sextant at the sun, turned a black collimation knob to center a small bubble and captured the sun inside. This procedure measured altitude. Converting this observation with dreaded math, we derived a sun line to draw on our maps. When we combined sun line with basic navigation data, we arrived at our aircraft position. Transferring a sun line to the map was technically called drawing a line of position, or LOP. I wasn't able to understand the mathematical mechanics of celestial, so learned how to do it by rote. And it worked, as long as there were no glitches. Main Line understood the mechanics, but didn't care for the rote, which is why he washed back to our class. If he paid as much attention to math as he did to his quest, we would never have met. He and Oscar D. were on a quest, to follow Telephone Road from Ellington Field to the last Texas roadhouse, north of Houston, seeking two more beers in each stop along the way. They began their quest in late winter, moving along at a two roadhouses a night clip, when Oscar D. convinced Main Line to return to their first stop, a roadhouse called Trails End.

• • •

Any Texas city worth its salt, considerin' itself civilized, has either a Telephone or Telegraph Road. Roads dug out of Texas dust and mud at the turn of the century were used as paths to assist in stringing wires. As a result, many a roadhouse cowboy bar popped up along these byways — like mushrooms in a swamp. And on occasion, maybe one or two real cowboys, but mostly a pack of wannabes. Trouble began one late holiday afternoon. Main Line and Oscar D. returned to their favorite waterin' hole, Trails End. It was the first, or last, dependin' on your direction, bar on Telephone Road and first among equals in barroom brawls. Oscar D., a west Texas graduate of Texas A&M, that premier military college of the southwest, was a smooth talking long drink of water, but mostly he chose to remain quiet. One of the few real cowboys in these parts, Oscar D., had an underlying meanness kept in check. You'd never know when he might go out of control. Mostly he'd agitate Main Line into poppin' off for sport, or something to do when he was tired of reading, or bored, lookin' for action.

Oscar D., well over six feet tall, had sandy blonde hair with bushy eyebrows of the same hue. Now, Main Line wasn't a tall one. He was two inches taller than me, wiry like a terrier dog in a fight. His hair was always slicked back, sort of reddish, muddled brown. Bushy eyebrows were mostly the same. What Main Line lacked in speed, he made up in quickness. Never could figure out how direct opposites were such fast friends. And Main Line would need a friend today, April 21, that most sacred of all Texas holidays—San Jacinto Day.

San Jacinto Day commemorates Sam Houston's Texican Army's victory over Antonio Lopez de Santa Anna's Mexican Army. The victory was not won because of Santa Anna's dalliance with Yellow Rose, as some lead us believe in song and tale. It was, as Main Line insisted, because this battle was fought alongside the San Jacinto River.

After a few too many beers in Trails End, Main Line asked the nearest Texan, "Do you know why all the stores closed today?"

As luck would have it, Main Line had discovered one of the few real cowboys in Trails End. He glanced over at Main Line and frowned, "You don't know what day it is? Damn, you must be a damnyankee. Son, it's Texas Independence day, San Jacinto Day. And it's time for a Yankee jackass like you to stand up and toast the great state of Texas."

Main Line just sat there with a silly grin on his face. The cowboy's voice got real low and mean as he said, "Get on your feet or I'll knock that silly smile off your face."

Not bein' too smart, Main Line stood up with his own stupid smile, displaying that he was not afraid of anyone or anything after two beers. He climbed up on his bar stool and raised his long neck bottle of Lone Star beer, turned toward the cowboy, pointed his beer bottle, raising his voice, so all could hear, "Here's to the great state of Texas and to the dirtiest bunch of scoundrels ever fought a river battle. And here's to our great Yankee friend and Union sympathizer, Sam Houston. And here's to Houston's victorious Army. Santa Anna had Sam Houston's boys backed up against the San Jacinto River. Our brave Texans had only one choice, fight or take a bath and we all know Texans would rather fight than take a bath."

Main Line downed his beer and sat back down. Oscar D., sensing trouble, began to rise. Dumbfounded by Main Line's sacrilege, the cowboy rose slowly from his stool and turned toward Main Line, "Friend, no one and no damnyankee will ever say nasty things about Sam Houston and Texans and live."

Main Line slipped the first punch and ducked under the table. Trails End erupted with a whole lot of arm waving, shoving and threatening words. Before things got too far out of hand and a real melee began, Oscar D. stepped in and saved the day.

Using his best west Texas drawl, he spoke softly, "First, Main Line here is no damnyankee. Second, he's a proud South Carolina Johnny Reb and a might hot tempered. Third, Main Line's not familiar with Texas manners and the reverence we hold for Sam Houston and his victory at San Jacinto. If you'll accept his apology, Main Line will buy you all a beer."

As Texas bar fights go, this one was over before it began. Didn't last long and no real damage was done. Now, Oscar D. wouldn't normally stop such a promising fight, but he felt obligated to, since he was the one who insisted on going to Trails End. Besides, he was familiar with the rough and tumble ways of Texas roadhouses. It was still early in the afternoon and no one was really drunk enough to brawl. However, in an hour or two, after a few more beers, no one could've stopped this one.

On their way out, Oscar D. whispered to Main Line, "You better not rile up any more Texas natives if you want to complete your quest. We have thirty miles of bars to go and damned little time. If you're not careful, we'll be out of Nav school before we can finish."

"Damn, didn't know it was that far. We're only half way. I promise to keep my warped sense of humor under control. Anyway, at twenty-five cents a beer, I'll be broke if I have to buy a round of beer at each roadhouse. If we increase to three roadhouses a night, we just might make it."

• • •

One hot muggy Friday night in late April, Oscar D. and Main Line talked me into coming along. Oscar D. sat there with a sly smile as Main Line worked on me, "Come along with us, Johnny. You've never been inside a Texas roadhouse. Got to be a national treasure. All they sell is beer and wine. If you want hard stuff, you'll have to bring your own bottle. Not worth it. They charge an arm and a leg for water and ice. Why do that when we can buy Lone Star beer for a quarter? No one in their right mind would pay fifty cents for water. Put your books away and come along."

I wasn't all that eager. I was trying to save money to buy a new car and after listening to Oscar D. spin tales about their nightly trips, joining them didn't look like a good idea.

However, I finally gave in, "It's against my better judgment, but if you two promise to bring me back and not abandon me, I'll go along."

I knew I wasn't much of a drinker. Couldn't afford to be one at Ohio State, so I didn't have much opportunity to practice. I soon discovered my past brushes with a beer or two weren't enough to prepare me for a Friday night out with two unpredictable friends.

Our first stop was at Sam's Shack for barbecue and beer. From the outside it looked like our smokehouse on the farm—just before it fell down. Now, the inside was a different story. Only thing that wasn't solid mahogany was sawdust on the floor. At the top of Sam's menu was a proclamation:

*Best Damn Barbecue in Texas and Texas Barbecue is the Best in the World.*

Main Line, weaned on South Carolina barbecue in a state with borders represented by barbecue sauce instead of counties, begged to differ. He climbed all over Oscar D.: "Beef barbecue? Best in the world? Bull shit! And mesquite wood for smoke and flavor? You've got to be kiddin' me—mesquite? Some kind of west Texas weed? Only real barbecue is South Carolina pork, smoked over a hickory and oak fire, pulled apart by hand. Any fool off the street can cook beef over a mesquite weed."

I could see smoke comin' out of Oscar D.'s ears. Main Line had stepped way over the line. Bad mouthin' San Jacinto was bad enough, but Texas barbecue? There are three taboos in Texas. One, you don't steal another man's horse. Two, you don't mess around with a woman who's been spoken for. And three, you don't bad mouth Texas barbecue, and live.

Oscar D. was up on his feet with as mean a-lookin' scowl I'd ever seen. He got right in Main Line's face, eyes narrowin', "Line, one more word out of your mouth and you won't have any teeth left to enjoy the best damn barbecue in the world. You better keep your opinions about Texas and our barbecue to yourself. Folks down here don't take kindly to an eastern poppycock puttin' down the world's best damn beef barbecue. Criticize Texas barbecue? Why, you might as well kick my dog and make nasty comments about my mother."

Main Line didn't say a word, just sat there with a silly grin on his face. He'd done his damage, now it was time for him to stay quiet.

I chewed at a beef barbecue sandwich so hot and spicy smoke came out of my nose and water from my eyes. Downed half a schooner of beer just to put the fire out. I started to say I liked it, but before one word came out, Oscar D.'s eyes began to get narrow again. He set his schooner of beer down.

He said, "Better not say anything bad. Can't abide with a poisonous nut bad mouthin' Texas barbecue."

I knew when to back off. I replied, "Never had South Carolina barbecue, but if Main Line's is half as good as this, I'll be more than happy to give it a try."

"Main Line, listen to Johnny. He knows. You came close to needin' a plastic surgeon after those criticisms. You owe Johnny and me a beer."

No sooner said than three twenty-two ounce schooners of beer slid the length of the bar. Mine stopped in front of my two bulging eyes.

Oscar D. got the bartender's attention, "Another barbecue sandwich for my Buckeye friend and don't spare the hot sauce."

So, I needed one more beer to quench a Texas barbecue stomach fire. Sixty-six ounces of beer and I was feeling no pain. By the time Oscar D. pulled into the Tiger Cat Bar's parking lot I was sound asleep in his back seat.

Later, I'm sure Main Line asked, "Should we wake him up?"

In a west Texas drawl, Oscar D. replied, "Let him sleep. Better lock the doors so no one can roll him."

• • •

My eyes were half open as a Saturday morning sun crawled inch by inch on a slow journey across the back seat of Oscar D.'s car. I had met my match, sixty-six ounces of beer and two barbecue sandwiches. I checked my watch. The big hand was on thirty and the little hand was on six. I lifted my head and looked out the back window. I was alone, in an empty parking lot, in back of the Tiger Cat Bar. As I sat up, the pounding at my temples began. I reached over the front seat, unlocked the drivers side door and located Oscar D.'s car keys under the floor mat, "At least I won't have to walk back to the air base. No use waiting, my friends must have found Texas true love last night."

Oscar D.'s car made more than a few trips south on Telephone Road to Ellington Field, so I aimed it down the highway and prayed, desperately in need of aspirin. When I walked into our barracks, didn't bother looking for two lost sheep, knew they wouldn't be there. Found two aspirin and headed toward the latrine for a shower, shave and relief. Stood in the shower for a good twenty minutes, water cascading on my head. Wasn't long before the pounding diminished. I dressed and walked to the cadet mess. Aspirin needed company. Took one look at scrambled eggs and almost upchucked the aspirin. Good news, I discovered what grits were good for.

Walked out our barracks's front door on my way to Monday morning breakfast at the cadet mess hall and a red convertible braked to a halt. Main Line and Oscar D. hopped out the right side rear door like Lazarus from his grave. I took a second look, Lazarus would have looked a lot younger than these two. As the convertible sped away, Oscar D. asked, "Still have my car keys?"

"Of course. They're on top your dresser. Where did you spend the last three nights?"

"Got lucky."

"I almost phoned the sheriff."

Main Line came back from the dead, "Guess who we ran into?"

"I'm a stranger in these parts. I haven't the foggiest, but let me guess—Tucker?"

"Close, we met two of his ladies at Tiger's. A couple of his old girlfriends."

Oscar D. spoke up, "With an extra emphasis on, old. Had to be in their late thirties, but we didn't know that until the sun came up in Galveston. They're both past winners of the Miss Congeniality award."

"What do they do for a living, bar girls?"

"Nah, TTA stewardesses."

"TTA?"

"Trans Texas Airlines. The way they worshipped old Tucker, he must have been a wonder horse. No wonder he washed out. He not only burnt the candle at both ends, he lit the middle."

My stomach clock went off, "I'm starved. Meet you at the cadet mess hall. I have one more question to ask."

Oscar D. and Main Line brought their trays over to my table thirty minutes later. I checked to see what they were carrying, "Only grits, toast and tomato juice? And four glasses each?"

Oscar D. grunted as he sat down, "If you could see the inside of my stomach, you'd understand."

"The way you look on the outside, well, I'll pass. Why didn't you wake me. Talk about waking up in a strange country."

"Only had two dates and they had their own car. A herd of wild elephants could have stampeded through the back seat and you'd still be asleep. Looked like Rip Van Winkle without the beard."

"Were you in Galveston?"

"Roger that. Tucker's ladies stopped by the barracks so we could pick up our bathing suits for a midnight swim in the gulf."

"You two had quite a California style weekend."

Main Line wiped his chin after his second glass, and said, "More like a lost weekend."

"And you lost a day of your quest," I replied jokingly.

Oscar D. laughed, "Line has decided to call it quits."

"How come?"

"When we woke up late Saturday morning, his lady friend circled three times before she got back in bed."

Main Line propped his head up with his left hand, "You should talk. I had to cover my watch every time your lady walked by."

They suffered through the rest of their breakfast in silence, except for one or two barely audible groans.

• • •

Turned out that Oscar D. was correct in his assessment of Main Line. He was certainly a reformed bar hopper, but as a team they still ran fast and loose. On one of their forays they discovered the swimming pool at Houston's Shamrock Hilton hotel. Even for Texas it was giant sized. So large, when the Shamrock's private bottle club— The Cork Club—held their yearly bash on the first of May, they celebrated by floating a good-sized yacht on the deep end. Main Line had a deal we couldn't refuse. Officers from Ellington Field were allowed the use of the pool at a deep discount.

I asked, "What's the catch?"

"None that I know of," Main Line said.

Oscar D. cleared his throat, "Houston's elite wants their daughters to meet up with officers and gentlemen. But it's a win-win situation. Can't be a better place in town to meet wealthy young ladies and Houston has more than its fair share."

Main Line was ready to go, "We can hoist a few beers, enjoy the sun, cool off in a world class pool and enjoy the view. Grab your suits and let's go."

I was more than game. I'd hit the books so hard my eyes were crossed. And the Shamrock ladies had to be a cut above the ones we'd met in Texas roadhouses. The size of the pool took my breath away. It was olympic size, but the diving boards and platforms were something else. Hadn't seen anything like this set of boards since I tried the ones in Ohio State's natatorium, two high boards, two low ones and a high and middle platform. On my first trip up the ladder to the high platform I chickened out. Came down the ladder backwards to the middle platform and looked out over the edge. It was still too high for my liking, but I was committed. Couldn't back out twice. I backed off and took a short run, sailed through the air for what seemed to me to be an eternity. Got lucky when I parted the water with my hands, a clean entry, but it almost knocked me out. Getting turned around, well that took a lot more time than I expected. When I reached bottom, I crouched down near the center drain and pushed off, clawing my way back to the surface. Swam over to the far side of the pool away from the hotel and sputtered to Main Line, "Worst part is comin' back up. Want to give it a try?"

"Not now. I've got my eye on that young lovely sunnin' over there on the grass."

Oscar D. shook his head, "No, I've broke horses to saddle, ridden bulls and done a lot of crazy things, but jumping off a tower isn't one of them. You go ahead and kill yourself. I'll pull you out after you knock yourself silly. My objective is to dunk myself in this pool once or twice, drink a few beers and meet a nice young Texas lady, not jump around like a monkey on a string."

Main Line jumped in and swam under water until he was even with the target of his attention. Conversation didn't last long. He dove back in and surfaced next to us.

Oscar D. was impatient, "Not many ladies at the pool today, Line. How did you do with yours?"

He shook the water out of his hair, "Almost a waste of time. She attends the University of Texas Nursing school in Galveston. Bad news is I spent all that time hustlin' her only to find out she's engaged. The good news is she gave me her phone number at school. She'll introduce us to a few of her friends this evening. What do you think?"

I said "It's a long drive. Should we give it a go?"

Oscar D. perked up, "I'll go, but not Johnny. If we get lucky, six in a car is a crowd."

"We'll drive down after dinner. She'll have everything arranged by seven."

"Line, one word of caution. Most of those little ladies have big, mean Texas brothers who'd just as soon kick your teeth in as look at you. So, we better not get caught messin' around. Need to be on our best behavior. Johnny, you don't mind not comin' along, do you?"

I wasn't about to say so if I did, and after spending one night in a parking lot, I wasn't about to be a two-time loser. Didn't take much to convince me. Main Line's idea of a good time was to rile up bar flies and cowboys. Oscar D. went along for entertainment.

"I promised Roger the lodger I'd go with him to a church social in Houston. You two go on ahead. If you find a lady that doesn't circle three times before she sits down, fix me up. Roger the lodger and I can double date next time if need be," I replied.

Oscar D. smiled, "So, you're going to that church social with Roger. Be careful. Besides the Shamrock, our Texas churches and universities are where classy young ladies hang out."

When I walked in the barracks a little after midnight, Oscar D. and Main Line were still up, "How was the Texas School of Nursing? You two look mighty sober for a Sunday morning."

Main Line answered, "Not exactly what I expected. Didn't even go out on a date."

Oscar D. added, "Turned out to be a real proper Texas parlor introduction visit."

"Yeah—we got introduced and that was all there was to it. I played the piano and they served tea. Talk about Victorian. They wouldn't walk out the door with us, not until we finished our social obligation."

"Line means they won't go out the front door until after formal introductions. We're all set for next Saturday night. We fixed you and Roger up, too, but we have to telephone first. School is running a check on all of us."

"What does my date look like? Is she like Tucker's TTA girl friends?"

Oscar D. took me aside, "Take a look at Line's watch. It's still ticking. Rest assured, we met four good looking Texas ladies. They're all winners. How did your church social go?"

"We met quite a few nice Texas girls," I said.

"Was there any spark?"

"Most of them were a bit young. What's the age of consent in Texas?"

Oscar D. raised an eyebrow, "If you have to ask, they're too young."

• • •

Our days at Nav school were flying by like a T-29 at full throttle. Unlike west Texas landmarks, the sun was easy to find, though Main Line made a few false sightings. The sun's reflection in our sextant mirrors would at times produce a false image. When we took a false reading, our Line of Position would be two counties over on the map. Dead reckoning, using basic navigation techniques, would resolve the problem. If you had confidence in your work, which Main Line didn't. Like Tucker, Main Line believed motion was work. He ran the aircraft's aisle, leaving a trail of papers in his wake. Must have worked. We all passed with better than average grades.

Oscar D. let the air out of our balloons, "If you can't find the sun, you're looking in the sextant from the wrong end. We all have dates in Galveston Saturday. I called and we passed the nursing school's security check. We can kill two birds with one stone. An afternoon picnic on Galveston Beach will make a great first date and we'll hold our Flight picnic at the same time. We need some diversion before we tackle night celestial. I nominate Line to take charge of our picnic."

Main Line demonstrated he had the right stuff to be a flag officer, "Great idea. Since I'm in charge I'm going to delegate all the work. Sam's Shack will prepare the main course. Oscar D. will pick up a keg, Johnny will get the ice, Roger the lodger will get chips and pretzels and those that have wives can make potato salad, coleslaw and dessert."

• • •

Roger the lodger rode with me as we trailed behind Oscar D.'s car on our way to the nursing school. As usual we were running late. Main Line and Oscar D. had hung a doozy on at Sam's when they stopped by to pick up the barbecue beef Friday night. If Sam hadn't packed it in dry ice, most of the bacteria in Texas would have been feasting on the world's best barbecue. Roger was fidgeting in my front passenger seat. "What's the matter, is my driving making you nervous? You're as jumpy as my sheep were when they follow a Judas goat into the meat packing house."

"Sorry, didn't think it would show. I'm not at all keen about going out on a blind date."

"Oscar D. gave his word. These Texas ladies are winners."

I thought a bit and then a light came on, "Don't tell me. Tucker fixed you up, too."

"How did you guess?"

"I've been down the same path."

"We had a small picnic with two TTA stewardesses at Galveston Beach before he left."

"Were they older, around thirty-five or so?"

"No, they were in their early twenties. Everything went well, at first, though they did seem a bit standoffish. We built a fire, cooked steaks, poured a little wine. A pleasant time, watching the evening sun go down. Tucker and I went behind a dune to take a whiz and when we returned our dates were walking away, hand in hand into the evening twilight. We waited for over an hour, but they never came back."

"Did Tucker explain why?"

"No, just gave me one of his *Mad* comic book smiles and asked if I wanted to meet a girl over at the Houston Country Club."

"So that's how I got roped into my blind date. You turned him down."

"Once is enough. Just out of curiosity, how did it go?"

"Unbelievable! Begged me to go along since he didn't have a car. His was in the shop getting an engine overhaul. Seems he drove it with the oil a mite too low and you know Tucker."

"Probably didn't know where the dip stick was."

"You got it. I drove north of the Shamrock on streets lined with the biggest houses I'd ever seen. Turned on a tree lined road that looked like it was right out of *Gone With the Wind*. Must have been half-a-mile long. Pulled up in front of a huge mansion. Must have had forty rooms and pillars, larger than the ones at Monticello.

I was awestruck. A doorman opened our car doors and a butler from behind the screen greeted us at the top of the steps. He ushered us into the foyer. Tucker's date descended a circular staircase to a polished marble floor. That lady was gorgeous, a knockout. Couldn't help thinking, this was going to be a great night. She gave me a million dollar smile and said, "How 'wah woo?" It was right out of Elmer Fudd in Loony Tunes. Took all my control to hold back my laughter, it was so out of place. Good thing I didn't. She is the nicest most considerate lady I've ever met."

"You'd go for her?"

"In a New York minute and not for the money, but she wasn't interested."

"Tucker would do well to stay in touch."

"Our free spirit?" I chuckled in reply.

"I forgot. Go on. That can't be all of it."

"Wish it was. We left her place and drove east to pick up my date."

"Big house?"

"A long, long way from that. We turned on a dirt road behind a drive-in movie into a trailer park and picked her up."

"How was she?"

"Good looking, smart and articulate with raging hormones."

"Sounds like a winner to me."

"The first words out of her mouth were, 'I shouldn't be going out with you.' I asked her what the problem was. She said, 'I was married yesterday.' I asked, 'Where is your husband?' She said, 'Up in Texarkana bringing back furniture for our new house.'"

"Did you take her out anyway?"

"I was stuck, had no choice. That damn Tucker was rollin' around on my back seat floor, laughin' so hard he almost wet his pants. We took in a Luigi flick and stopped by the Shamrock afterwards for a drink. She was all over me, but all I could think of was Oscar D.'s warning."

"What was that?"

"It's legal to shoot anyone in Texas caught messin' around with your wife or girl. I dropped her off when she asked me to sleep over. Tucker's date stayed with her. She gave him a proper peck on the cheek and sent us on our way."

"In spite of what Tucker did to you and me, we're going to miss that rascal."

"He sure kept things stirred up. I never did hear from that trailer lady again."

"Give her your phone number?"

"Are you kiddin'?"

I pulled up to the front of the entrance of the Texas School of Nursing, but couldn't find a parking place. While I drove around, looking on a side street, Roger went inside the dorm with Oscar D. and Main Line. When I sauntered into the lobby, Main Line was entertaining a crowd of pretty young ladies with a short Beethoven classical selection. Damn, he was good. He played a flawless rendition of Fur Elise. The room was so quiet I could hear water running from the toilets above. I was impressed, "Main Line you have a hidden talent."

Always hard for him to take a compliment, he whispered, "Great way to pick up ladies. I prefer Scott Joplin, but these ladies like the classics. Ragtime can really get down after a few beers in the bar."

"Impressed me and the ladies coming down the stairs. Are those our dates?"

"Roger that. Not bad, eh?"

Roger the lodger whistled under his breath, "Things are looking up."

After introductions, I asked my date, "Did you bring along a swim suit?"

"Wearing it under my dress."

I breathed a sigh of relief. Back home in Ohio, we had to wait until summer to find out what our girls really looked like. Texas had its good points.

Oscar D. purchased a keg of what San Antonio called ladies beer, Pearl Light. Supposed to be less fattening, but it tasted like Ohio three-two beer to me, watered down. We built a fire on the beach before splashing in the gulf. No one stayed in long. Gulf water was still too cold from winter. We drank and ate and drank some more. We talked of college days and flying. Our dates talked of nursing, medicine and doctors. They were great fun to be with, but we had nothing in common. I didn't feel a spark, nor did Roger. With nothing in common, I knew how an alien must feel after being stranded on a strange planet. I didn't even talk Texan. We all promised to see each other soon, but none of us did. The nurses were looking for commitment and we were just looking around.

On our way back to Ellington, Roger asked, "Going out with her again?"

I shrugged, "Had fun, but I didn't get that jolt of electricity. You know, the one that makes you tingle all over and sparks fly. I don't want to waste her time or mine. How about you?"

"I don't know. At least they didn't walk off into the sunset holdin' hands."

"And they weren't married the night before."

We were still laughing next morning at breakfast.

• • •

Thoughts about ladies took a back seat to Nav school. Night celestial arrived on our classroom scene like heavy, hazy Houston shipping channel fog in early spring. In day celestial we had to contend with one star, our Sun. Now, we had to locate three stars, sight them separately through our sextant, determine their average altitudes over two minutes of sighting, resolve the time difference of our sightings and compute three Lines Of Position. When we drew these LOPs on our maps the intersection would, hopefully, show our aircraft position inside a small triangle. That is, if everything goes right, which seldom ever happens. Our T-29 bounced through the night sky like a pickup truck on a dirt road and the bubble in our sextants danced around performing a nighttime version of Saint Vitus' dance. As a result, our LOP triangles were large enough to place a fist inside them. Night celestial was the harbinger of tough times ahead, but life does have its ups, too. Sometimes the fox eats the chicken. Sometimes all he gets is feathers. We finally got a taste of chicken, our air base orientation classes were canceled.

The demise began when Roger the lodger embarrassed the folks at the base legal office. A pre-law student, he discovered the forms they were using were either out of date or in error. And last week, Mart the smart mortified the entire base engineering office. On a smelly field trip to the new sewage plant, he noticed the rocks they installed as filters, were the wrong size. When the base commander decided that we didn't know enough about how an air field operates, he failed to take into account our wide variety of civilian career backgrounds. We had electrical engineers, civil engineers, a chef, law students, bartender and one sod buster, me, among others. Visiting the sewage plant had to be the last straw.

I was still kicking stones about it being a waste of time when Mart the smart took exception, "For the rest of you it's a waste of time, but for me it's a labor of love."

Oscar D. got that sly west Texas grin on his face, "You got to be kiddin' me. A sewage plant? Come on, Mart. Why in the world would you want to visit one?"

"Might seem strange to you, but this is right up my alley. It's a brand new plant. State of the art. I can't wait to take a look at it."

The sewage engineer in charge was proud as a peacock as he walked us around his brand spanking new plant, "This is the latest in sewage systems and we have it right here at Ellington Field. We are way ahead of any other community in Texas."

I was able to see the humor of it, but I couldn't see its relevance to Nav training, "By the smell of it, looks like the base commander wanted us to visit here so we could better understand where he's coming from."

Main Line jumped right in, "From the crap he's been giving us, he sure knows how to spread this stuff around."

Mart the smart's eyes grew large as saucers when we toured the sludge storage area and filter system. I could tell he was getting pretty excited. He pulled the base engineer aside, "Excuse me, sir. Did you know that the rocks in your filter system are the wrong size?"

"How the hell would you know?"

"I have a degree in sanitary engineering from Manhattan College."

It was the engineers turn to get wide eyed, "Are you sure they're wrong?"

"Sorry, I have to inform you, they're too large."

"What should we do?"

"How long have you been operating?"

"Let's see, about three months."

"Are you at full capacity?"

"About sixty percent."

"Divert your flow to Houston and replace them as soon as possible or you'll have a real mess on your hands."

The engineer took Mart aside and dismissed the rest of us. Mart stayed on until late in the evening. He was a no show at the cadet mess hall.

The next morning, posted on the administration bulletin board:

*Air Base Orientation Is Canceled By Order of the Base Commander*

Replacing the sewage plant rocks cost the Air Force over one hundred thousand dollars. This wasn't pocket change when funds weren't wasted on personnel, quarters or comfort. Not when it took every nickel to buy gas, weapons and airplanes. The notice stood alone. No explanation was given or offered. Oscar D. was upset. Our next scheduled visit was to the base contracts office, which was his specialty. Our chef wanted to go over the mess hall books and Main Line was looking forward to checking liquor purchases at the Officer's Club. Seems he had a wholesale liquor license. The base commander had ruined their fun. I wasn't a bit sorry. There wasn't one damn sheep on this base.

I chided Main Line, "It looks like your chance to be an auditor is not in the stars, but Deneb, Dubbe and Dallas are."

These two stars and a Texas city are a student Nav's mantra. I knew what Tucker would have said when he heard this alliteration, "Dubbe? Isn't that a Sinatra refrain— dooby dooby do?" Dallas is the city that almost did Main Line in on his check-ride. Main Line had a habit of looking out our T-29's windows for a map reading fix on whatever town was handy. He worked his celestial computations backwards from that fix.

Oscar D. got all over his case, "Line. You're the one stupidest Johnny Reb I've ever known. It's twice as difficult to back a three star fix in as to do it the right way."

"I know, but I can find Dallas. That's easy, but when I look through my sextant and try to find a star, I can't. They all look alike in that small field of view."

I offered to help, "Star identification is easy once you learn a crutch or two."

"For a night loving sheep herder like you maybe, but not for me. I've tried everything I know and nothing works. I'll have the star pattern identified when I look out the dome. When I return to sight the star in my sextant, I lose it."

"There might be a way. Let me think about it."

I was at home under the stars. When you're out all night tending sheep there's not much else to do. I'd lean back in the meadow, making sure I didn't lay on any sheep stuff and map the stars in the sky. Weren't any city lights to block out the sky, so I was able to memorize most of the northern constellations. My weakness was math. Learning how to do it by the book saved me, but any deviation from my routine would grind my mental gears to a halt. Deviation always came in distraction, and distraction was Main Line's middle name.

He would run the aisle, scattering papers in his wake, screaming, "Where the hell is Dubbe?"

And Oscar D. would always answer, "Up in the sky, you dingbat!"

To make sure we would all pass, without Main Line dragging us down I taught him how to identify Orion's Belt, the North Star [Polaris] and how to shoot the moon. He found Deneb, Dubbe and Dallas all by himself. We all sneaked through by the skin of our teeth after Oscar D. convinced us to give Main Line, like Tucker, his very own astrodome and stay out of his way. It worked, too, but staying out of the Harris County sheriff's posse's line of fire wasn't as easy as staying away from a wild bull, Main Line.

• • •

Our T-29 had just taxied into its parking spot after we completed our night celestial flight exam. Most of our Flight was gathered out front of the aircraft, so those who chose to smoke could, without igniting the fuel vapors. We were waiting on Main Line to finish backing in his last fix with one eye open for the canvas backed six-by to transport us to base ops. Out of nowhere, a beat up 1953 Caddie whistled by on four flat tires with a juke box sticking out of its trunk. A minute later, a flock of new Cadillacs flew by with deputies hanging out the windows firing whatever weapon they had in the general direction of the '53 Caddie. It screeched to a halt and two scared men jumped out with their hands in the air. The Cadillac posse stopped in a semicircle, facing the two felons. Car doors opened and we heard, "Stop or I'll shoot!" in unison by a dozen or so deputies, followed by gunfire. Both felons hit the ground as bullets whistled over where they were standing.

Oscar D. lit a cigarette and took a drag, "Johnny, you have just witnessed justice, Texas style."

I was so nervous I bummed a cigarette from him, "Who are those guys and where did they come from?"

"Texas citizen volunteers. That's the Harris County Sheriff's posse. They're all deputized and have police radios in their cars. The two they were chasing must have stolen that juke box. Shouldn't have. Not much entertainment around here. Has to be right up there with stealing another man's wife or kickin' his dog."

"That's a bit of overkill isn't it? A dozen or so Cadillacs chasin' after one car with a stolen jukebox."

"Not much to do around here after football and huntin' season. Keeps our good old boys from pointing their guns at each other. Those two picked the wrong place and the wrong time to do their thieving. They did have a little luck though. This posse shot high and we got lucky, too. Weren't none of our T-29s in their line of fire."

About that time, Main Line climbed down out of the airplane, "What the hell is going on out here. Whatever it was it sure helped me. Diverted our evaluator's attention. I was able to finish backing in my last fix."

Oscar laughed, "Line, why don't you just flunk and get it over with."

"What and give up flight pay? What happened out here? Sounded like a war going on."

"Nothing more than a bit of justice, Texas style."

A canvas backed six-by pulled up to take us to base ops and drowned out all conversation. On our way to base ops I asked Main Line, "How did it go?"

"Until the gunfire erupted, our evaluator kept grabbing at my map and logs, trying to get them away from me. He said I was cheatin' and he'll probably be up all night trying to prove it."

We had two things to buzz about after breakfast, our grades weren't posted and last night's shoot-out.

Oscar D. asked, "Guess where they stole the jukebox from?"

"I don't know, Trails End?"

"Not even close. The base roller-skating rink. They couldn't pry the coin box open, so they loaded it into their trunk. If they had driven out the main gate at normal speed the Air Police wouldn't have noticed. APs estimated their Caddie was doing a hundred when it flew by their shack. They called the sheriff and his posse caught up with them before they were out of the county. Pretty hard to hide with a jukebox sticking out of your trunk. Thieves hightailed it back to Ellington with the posse in pursuit, a real western shoot-out. Came back the way they left, except for the four flat tires. They were motivated. Didn't want to wind up in the sheriff's lockup."

"What happens to them now?"

"They're both in the Air Force and the crime occurred on federal property. Probably wind up in a military prison."

"Leavenworth, that's pretty stiff."

"True, but doin' time there is a whole lot easier than being black and doin' time in a Texas jail."

Our grades were posted after lunch. Oscar D. read them to us as we were walking up. He turned and said, "Line, yours is on the bottom, incomplete with a note. You're supposed to go over to admin. and visit the commandant." Main Line turned white as a sheet and disappeared through the administration building's front door, like a cat caught with a canary in its mouth.

He walked into our afternoon class with a droopy hound dog look on his face. Oscar D. whispered, "Line, tell us what happened."

Our instructor looked up, "Welcome back, Lieutenant Line. What did the commandant have to say?"

"I have to fly another check-ride."

During break, Oscar D. said, "Fess up, Line. What really happened?"

"My three star fixes were too perfect. Couldn't prove I cheated, so they couldn't fail me, but they wouldn't pass me either."

"You're caught right between the rock and the hard place, but you're better at math than any of us. It's time for Johnny to give you a refresher course on star identification. We'll get you through."

"You better, they're sending me out to Tuckerville, west by God Texas. Not a town in sight and you can't find water tanks after dark."

"When do you fly it?"

"Tonight."

"Better learn to pray."

I helped Main Line pick out the stars he was going to use and he pre-comped as much as he was able to. But he was still a negative and reluctant student. Like Tucker, he was going to fly alone and in the dark. When Main Line returned from his flight, he crashed through our barracks like a wounded deer, trying to wake us up, but we would have none of his chatter tonight. He was the last one in the sack and the first one up. He banged on my cubicle an hour before I normally rise, "Wake up sod buster. It's my big day."

"It's yours, not mine. Go on ahead. I'll catch up."

"Wake up Oscar D. on your way. I couldn't get anything but moans out of him."

I didn't have any more luck with Oscar D. than Main Line. He wouldn't move, just pulled a pillow over his head. Main Line was on his fourth cup of coffee when I pulled a chair up to his table. "Damn it Johnny, I'm too nervous to eat a thing but grits and butter. I stopped by the administration building and my grades weren't posted."

"It's dark out. Maybe by noon. How did your flight go?"

"I found every last one of those stars you coached me on. Flying lead cut into my time, but you know, by not backing my fixes in, I had time on my hands. Only problem was, when I resolved the fixes on my map, both my hands fit in one, my fist in the other and the smallest one was still bigger than a silver dollar."

"Did the evaluator take control of your airplane?"

"No."

"You did all right."

"I'm going to the administration building to see if my grade is posted."

"The sun's just now on the horizon. Relax, eat some solid food."

"Nah, can't sit still until I find out how I did. See you in class."

Oscar D. came in as Main Line went out the door, "Line looks nervous as an alley cat in a room full of rocking chairs. How do you think he did?"

"He passed."

As we walked into our classroom, Oscar D. called to Main Line, "How did you do?"

"Don't know, wasn't posted."

About that time our instructor walked in, "Lieutenant Line, our commandant wants to see you on the double."

Main Line broke into a visible nervous sweat as he hurried out the door. He came back an hour later grinning from ear to ear. At the break, everyone crowded around.

Oscar D. asked, "You look like a Cheshire cat. Did you pass?"

"Commandant asked me how I could max the course on my first flight test and come up average on the second one. I told him I avoided being perfect because I didn't want to be accused of cheating again. He let the first grade stand. I've danced around the flag pole and I'm not washed out. There's free shrimp at the O' Club happy hour this evening. The first round of beer is on me."

I shook my head, "If that happened to one of us, we'd be on our way to supply school. I hope you know that beer is half price at the O' Club this evening."

"That's why I offered."

"Is that all the commandant had to say?"

"No. He told me, 'Lieutenant, anyone who can back a fix in as good as you can is going to make one hell of a navigator. Next time around, use the periscopic sextant. It has a limited field of view, fewer stars to confuse you.'"

Main Line bought the first round as we made short work of several good sized bowls of peel and eat shrimp. Oscar D. looked around the bar, "Not a single eligible woman in the whole damn place. Pool doesn't close at the Shamrock until ten. We've got four hours. Let's grab our suits and make tracks."

I looked over at Roger the lodger, "Better take two cars. I'll drive."

"I'm game."

"Don't want to be stuck out in the country when the wild bunch decides to take off."

"Line, I'll follow Oscar D.'s car. You buying at the Shamrock?"

"The O' Club was my one time good deal and that offer is over." I thought a bit before saying:

*"The rule is, jam tomorrow and jam yesterday but never jam today."*

Roger the lodger smiled, "Quoting Alice again, aren't you. The way Line does his computations, remember what the queen told Alice,

*"It's a poor memory that only works backwards."*

# Chapter 3

Couldn't be a better place in Houston for an early evening swim than the Shamrock Hotel pool, but not tonight. Except for the four of us, it was empty. Oscar D. picked up his towel and pointed toward the men's locker, "Don't mind us being the only swimmers, but beer's fifty cents. A little steep for my pocketbook. Now don't get me wrong. I enjoy the company of friends, but I was hopin' to meet a pretty young lady here. And seein' there are none, my vote is for the Tiger Cat."

Main Line picked up his towel, "Most Friday nights this place is packed with lovelies. Wonder what's happening?"

I took a calculated guess, "We had to park over by the apartments. Cork Club must be having one of their seasonal parties."

Oscar D. snapped his fingers, "Damn—you're right. If Houston's elite is inside, their daughters will be somewhere else. Should have thought of that when we parked two blocks away."

We walked past an eight foot high stucco wall listenin' to the sound of water splashing and laughter floatin' over the top.

Oscar D. agitated Main Line, "Hop up to the top of the wall and take a peek."

Main Line wasn't one to back away from a challenge. He clawed his way up and dropped back down, his shirt white with traces of stucco. "You should have warned me. That stuff scratches."

Oscar D. was about to give him a full ration, when two large men in bathing suits came around the wall through the pool side door. The older one asked, "You make a habit out of peeking over fences?"

Oscar D. wasn't about to back away and I could see the hair rising on Main Line's neck. I tried to establish peace, "Nothing sinister, just nosy. We're on our way back from a swim at the Shamrock and heard the splashing. Party going on at the Cork Club. Couldn't park over there."

The older one asked, "Where are you from?"

Roger answered, "Ellington Field. I'm Roger and this is Johnny. We're Nav students."

"Cadets?"

"No. School's changing to all officers."

While we were talking, I noticed Oscar D. and Main Line slipping away. Our interrogator grinned, "I'm the senior OSI agent here. Not a good idea for you to be looking over walls in Houston. Too many folks with nervous fingers around here own guns. I'm Captain Attaboy and this is Lieutenant Gaylord. I'm from Detroit and Gaylord is from Fire Island, New York. Tell you what I'm going to do. You two buy a couple of six-packs and we'll introduce you to a few of our neighbor ladies. Bring your suits. Where did your friends go?"

I answered, "The Tiger Cat."

"Their loss, our ladies are lookers. Make sure it's cans. Don't want any broken glass near the pool."

As we got into my car, I asked Roger, "What's an OSI?"

"Air Force Office Of Special Investigations. Sort of like our own FBI."

"How do you know about them?"

"When I get out, I'm going to finish law school and apply to be a member of Hoover's gang."

"Are we in trouble?"

"No. If we had really stepped in it, the sheriff would be pulling up."

"Where's the closest carryout?"

"Around the corner."

We entered the pool side door with our bathing suits and two six-packs of beer. Attaboy and Gaylord were sitting by the pool with four really good looking young ladies. Attaboy looked up, "That was quick. Thought you might take off. Introduce yourselves and then go change. First apartment behind the diving board."

Turned out to be a great evening of fun. They were all stewardesses and not affiliated with TTA. When it was time to leave, I left alone. Roger and a stew were into it hot and heavy and she offered to bring him home. I thanked Attaboy and Gaylord, "Turned out to be a great evening. Don't know when I've ever been so clean—dunkin' in two pools on the same day."

• • •

When I returned to the barracks, our two turncoats were busy tossing empty beer cans at the waste basket, "Where did you go? Roger and I met four of Texas' finest. You missed a great pool party."

Oscar D. apologized, "When I heard the older one say OSI, we slipped away in the night. Did they bring you up on charges?"

"Never happened. We got along fine. All we had to do was bring along our suits and a few six-packs. They have more feminine company than they can handle. Roger broke the code. He said they came outside looking for help."

Main Line handed me a can of Lone Star, "Johnny, you've been training. You're way past your two beer limit. Tell us more about the pool party."

"Roger and I had a ball. Best party I've been too in Texas. Those OSI guys know how to live. Even have air-conditioning in their apartments, a swimming pool and a flock of single ladies. Look at us, we have windows, each other and a latrine with green stuff growing in it. Looks like we chose the wrong profession. Roger told me OSI is the Air Force's FBI. Any idea what that means?"

Oscar D. spoke softly, "Undercover work. Chase after deserters and stuff like that. Tell us about the ladies."

"Like to do a bit of undercover work with them. You two really blew it. Roger is still with his girl. He's going out again tomorrow. She's bringing him home."

As if on cue, Roger walked in with a hop in his step and a smile from ear to ear. He opened a can of Lone Star and sighed, "I think I'm in love, head over heels. Johnny, you talk about sparks, I've been struck by lightning. I set up Main Line and Oscar D. with dates tomorrow morning."

Main Line stood up, "Whoa there big fella. Where are we going?"

"Church. You get a chance to meet some honest Texas ladies for a change. I'll let you in on a secret, both of your ladies are knockouts. Hope you two don't mind attending a Methodist church."

Main Line smiled, "I'm Christian. That's close enough."

I asked, "Hey, what about me?"

"Sorry, you weren't up to their standards. They thought you were cute, but a bit too young."

"Hell, I'm older than any of them."

"You might know sheep, but you've a lot to learn about the fair sex."

Roger's offer was all it took to get a coat and tie on Main Line.

Oscar D. was reluctant, "Only because it's something to do until the Shamrock pool opens."

Roger asked, "Johnny, tag along. I'll need a ride to church. Nancy will bring me home."

I nodded, "Yes. Wish it was Presbyterian, though."

"Why?"

"I feel predestined to meet someone."

"You will. Square becomes round with a little aging."

• • •

Nancy waved to get Roger's attention as we walked up the steps outside Houston's Methodist church. Oscar D. and Main Line weren't more than two minutes behind. Nancy's friends were even better looking than advertised. Oscar D. and Main Line? It was love at first sight. I was elbowed politely out of the way as they escorted their new found loves into church. Not easy being odd man out, but when the spark isn't there on either part, it's best to not make a fuss. Using my best farm boy instinct which, if you know sod busters, isn't all that complex, I begged off when they asked me to join them for lunch. I drove over to the Shamrock and spent the afternoon in the shade by the pool reading about our next class, LORAN.

LORAN is an acronym for long range navigation. Using a special map and a simple radio wave receiver, it can provide rough, electronic location for airplanes and ships. After an hour of reading about it and being unable to concentrate, I looked up into the eyes of the prettiest stew I'd ever seen. I'd met Sally at Attaboy's pool party last night, but at the time she seemed preoccupied. She sat down beside me on the grass, "Hope I'm not bothering your studies, Johnny. When you didn't come along with your friends after church, I decided to come after you."

"Glad you did. I've had my fill of technical jargon. Missed you in church."

"I was at mine, Presbyterian, near our apartments. Are you a Methodist."

"We used to kid around back home, a Methodist is a Baptist who can read, but no, I'm United Brethren."

"Be careful about your religious humor down here in Texas. Texans take religion very, very seriously."

"I'll try to remember that. Where were our lost ones when you left the apartment."

"They were going for a swim in our pool when I decided to hunt you down. Looks like they all hit it off."

"Roger acts like he was struck between the eyes with a two-by-four. Are the wild ones tamed? Oscar D. and Main Line are as serious as I've ever seen them. Want to take a dip?"

Sally grabbed my hand and pulled me up, ran toward the pool and dove in. Didn't expect to get a kiss underwater.

As Sally towel dried her hair, I wondered, "Do you mind if I ask you a question?"

"As long as it isn't personal."

"It isn't. Attaboy is an enigma to me. He seemed friendly enough, but distant. Could you tell me anything about his background?"

"Said he was a fighter pilot during World War II. When the war was over, the only job he could get was inspecting beer bottles in Detroit."

"What does a beer bottle inspector do?"

"Sit on a high stool watching bottles go by, checking for impurities."

"Not a very challenging job, but I bet it has its rewards," I said.

"All the beer he could drink. Said he was looped by the time he arrived home almost every evening. When the Korean War popped up, he was called back in. He decided to stay. You should know, we were an item a few months back, but that's over. Since we're away flying most of the time, Attaboy and Gaylord keep an eye on our place and protect us from over amorous admirers."

"Who do you fly for?"

"I fly for TWA on their domestic routes. Tell me a little about you."

"Not a very exciting life. Grew up on a farm in Ohio and graduated from Ohio State. Entered the Air Force through ROTC. Eyes weren't good enough to be a pilot, so I'm here at Nav school. Ready for another swim? I've grown to admire your underwater talents."

Sally pulled me up off the grass and led me to the edge of the pool, pushed me in, again demonstrating her talents.

When we came up for air I asked, "Do you want to try a little Italian this evening?"

She laughed, "I know of a restaurant close by where the waiter is very short."

"But is he Italian?"

Sally pushed me under and our lips met again. Back on the surface I admitted my ignorance, "You never told me your last name."

"After."

"After what?"

She pushed me under again. When I came back up she said, "No silly, my last name is After, Sally After."

• • •

Sally was off on a series of flights, which was just as well. Our LORAN class had begun. Since LORAN didn't begin with an E or R, I thought I was safe, and I was. I didn't have to design or build a LORAN set. All I had to do was learn how to use one. Our problems began with the arrival of our new instructor, Lieutenant Stonehands, who knew as little about LORAN as we did, but wouldn't admit it. Mart the smart stepped in to fill that gap, "LORAN isn't all that difficult. Pretty simple stuff, even for a sewage engineer. LORAN uses long wave radio signals sent from a transmitter to a slave and retransmitted back. The time difference between the two radio waves gives us location."

"How?" I asked.

"Like I almost said, our set measures the time difference between both signals."

"Is that all? Sounds fairly simple."

"It is except for one thing. Our Nav school sets are worn out. Part of our training is to learn how to adjust the set with a screwdriver. And that's where the problem comes in. Instructors and students have adjusted our sets to where most no longer work and can no longer be repaired."

"Isn't there a better system?"

"Oh, yes, the new LORAN C system fixes all of those problems and more, but we don't have it at Ellington. We might see it when we fly the line."

The single most important lesson I learned from this phase of Nav training was never to use our LORAN sets unless all else failed. Mart the smart was right. Even our classroom sets were broken. Knobs had been twisted off and screw threads worn to the point that even a screwdriver wouldn't turn them.

After one more equipment failure than we needed, Oscar D. hit the nail on the head when he opined, "A navigator with a screwdriver is the equivalent of a serial killer with an ax!"

As he walked out of the classroom mumbling, I said to Main Line, "I don't know what else we should expect. These systems were built under government contract by the lowest bidder."

The sets were worthless. That was a given, but my problem was how to differentiate a true signal from a false one. Mart attempted to explain the ether layer to us non engineer types without much success, "Okay, one more time. Ether is a layer of particles above the earth's atmosphere. Long wave radio signals, like LORAN, bounce off it and return to earth. A one hop E is the first harmonic of the LORAN radio wave. If we try to synchronize it with a true signal, we'll get a false reading. Pretty simple stuff, isn't it?"

I looked over at Roger and smiled a Tucker like smile and we both said, "Right."

• • •

I was having second thoughts about waiting for lightning to strike. The embers were getting hotter between Sally and me. The flame wasn't there yet, but I could feel it coming on. I was beginning to see why an arranged courtship lasted longer than ones where you had to find love on your own. She was on a Friday through Monday flight schedule, so we were together only two days a week. My three buddies were in over their heads. Wedding bells were going ring-a-ling-ling for them, but not for me. Our flights grew as frequent as our LORAN equipment failures. Most of the ones we used were not even suitable for artificial reefs. And competition replaced cooperation in our classroom. Until LORAN, we worked on a level playing field. With our equipment being unequal and none of us trusting each other when we approached a set with a screwdriver, our training was rapidly becoming every man for himself. To pass, we had to demonstrate a screwdriver adjust in the classroom and on our check-ride. Trouble was, the damn things wouldn't adjust. And worse, Stonehands was the reincarnation of Tucker. He could walk by a LORAN set and it would wilt. If I found a working LORAN set, the only way to keep it operating was not to adjust it. So we were caught in a real catch twenty-two. We adjust and we won't pass. If we don't adjust we won't pass. A perfect no win—no win conundrum. And Main Line used his screwdriver like a sledge hammer, leaving a broken trail of LORAN sets in his wake. Stonehands stood in awe as Main Line adjusted every single LORAN set past the stops. Of course, Main Line received top marks on our ground examination.

• • •

Mart the smart was the bearer of bad tidings, "You talk about a hosing. We have to fly three training flights and a check-ride on the same T-29. No way that sucker's LORAN sets are going to hold up."

I asked, "Where to and how long?"

"West Palm Beach, Bermuda, West Palm Beach and back to Ellington, four days with our check-ride on the last leg."

"What's wrong with Florida and Bermuda? I've never been to either one. Sounds more like a vacation than training flights to me."

"Not if we don't get any down time between flights. And you know what happens when our LORAN equipment performs like it usually does."

"You're right, we'll be lucky to have two sets operating by the time we fly our check-ride."

"Better hope for a miracle. Our equipment is so old, no base outside of Ellington has mechanics that can repair them."

"Or spare parts. Whose the lucky one that's going to be our evaluator?"

"Stonehands."

• • •

Our training flight from Ellington Field to West Palm Beach Air Station confirmed Mart the smart's worst fears. When we took off, we had ten working LORAN sets, which was a miracle in itself. We landed at West Palm with only four working sets. Didn't have anytime for sightseeing. We landed two hours before sunset. By the time we checked into the BOQ, showered and dressed for dinner, it was well past seven. The O' Club wasn't bad. Ground steak was tasty and the price was right. After one beer, Roger and me walked back to the BOQ, ready to hit the sack. Oscar D. and Main Line followed one beer later.

I asked Main line, "You lived on the Atlantic. What does Palm Beach look like?"

"From New Jersey south it all looks the same, 'cept it gets warmer down here. It's a lot like South Carolina without a decent barbecue, hot, flat and sandy. Inland there's swamp, swamp and more swamp. What time is takeoff?"

Oscar D. answered, "Oh seven thirty. Better hit the rack."

Oscar D. stood up and stretched, "Sure hope we have more than four LORAN sets working."

Main Line wasn't worried, "Don't see what the problem is. I'll use your set or Johnny's. Mine went out when I touched it with my screwdriver."

Oscar D. and I both said, "Over my dead body!"

"How can I pass if I don't have a set?"

Oscar D. thought a bit, "Tell you what, Line—I'll set mine up and you can take readings. Johnny will do the same, but if we see a screwdriver in your hand, I'm gonna' put it where the sun don't shine."

I added, "And I'll pound it up. My set's a beauty. I turned it on and it works perfectly, haven't made one adjustment. Anyone that comes near it with a screwdriver is going away with more than a sore behind."

Main Line wasn't buying our terms, "That's why Stonehands read the riot act to you two. You've got to demonstrate that you know how to adjust a LORAN set or he won't pass you."

I didn't care, "No way, not with my set. It isn't broken and he isn't messin' with it."

## Bermuda

Two more LORAN sets bit the dust on the over water training flight to Bermuda. Would have had four good ones but Stonehands insisted that Main Line adjust one of them with his screwdriver. And when that didn't work, Stonehands tried to demonstrate adjustment on the other set.

Oscar D.'s and my set were the only two working sets left. As we unloaded the airplane, Stonehands informed us, "Won't be taking off on our scheduled time in the morning. Our T-29 has some kind of engine problem that needs fixing."

I noticed both pilots off loading golf clubs and guessed the real reason for our layover. Told Roger, "We may be here for a day or two, depending on how much money the pilots have. Golf here can be expensive."

Mart the smart wasn't happy, "Just as I figured. They can repair LORAN C, but not our sets. One of the maintenance types is going to see if he can cannibalize a couple of our sets and get another two up, but he doesn't hold out much hope."

I asked, "What can we do to kill time?"

Oscar D. shook his head, "You really are a sod buster. This is Bermuda, with beaches, hotels and those will attract a bevy of young ladies, like a bee to clover."

I looked at my watch, "Almost five. After we get to the BOQ, I'm going to shower and go to the O' Club for dinner. Too late to go exploring and I didn't plan on being gone longer than three nights. Don't want to run out of cash and I only brought one check."

Main Line laughed, "That should be enough."

"Not when they have a $25 limit."

• • •

Our two pilots, dressed in golfing attire met us at the O' Club for breakfast. The senior one gave us a crocodile smile, "Sorry guys. Not going anyplace today. We'll be here another night. Have an engine part being flown in today. Can't do anything for your LORAN sets. The electronic folks say they're beyond redemption. No one has parts for museum pieces and they all failed the same way. I'll leave notice this evening at the BOQ if we can fly out of here tomorrow. If any of you potential funny wings brought your golf clubs, we have room for two in our foursome. They have some great courses here in Bermuda."

None of us answered, so he smiled again and walked out the door, followed by his copilot. Stonehands stopped us, "Since we only have two sets left, Johnny and Oscar D. will share theirs. Check with me before you go out to dinner this evening. I should have our flight status by then."

Main Line waited until Stonehands left, "I vacationed here with my family a few years back."

Oscar D. laughed, "Line, how can you remember what's worthwhile. You were only nine years old."

"I was too young to remember what you're interested in. Taxis cost an arm and a leg, but we can walk to St. George, rent motor bikes and ride around the island."

Roger the lodger asked, "How about the four of us splitting costs of a rental car?"

"Won't let you rent one. Pretty heavy restriction on autos. They limit them to one per household. We can walk, ride a motor bike or stay put.

I asked, "How far is it to St. George?"

"Not more than two miles and the view is great. Right along the ocean."

• • •

It was a bit longer than two miles, the view was spectacular and motor bikes were economical. That was the good news. The bad, they looked like World War II British paratrooper cycles with a motor attached as an afterthought. They were sturdy enough to carry a trooper with a full pack, but so under powered I had to peddle mine uphill.

Oscar D. took one look and decided against renting, "Line and I are going sight-seeing around St. George. We'll meet you at the O' Club for happy hour." I led and Roger followed out of Saint George, riding our motor bikes on the right side of the road which was the wrong side for Bermuda. A lorry met us on a roundabout, its horn blowing like a wounded banshee and almost did us both in.

Roger drove on ahead shouting, "I'll lead. You're not fit for anything technical— like a wedge, wheelbarrow or left hand traffic." He almost met his maker on another British style traffic circle, going around the right side.

The Bermuda countryside is beautiful, but I couldn't prove it. I couldn't see over the flowering hedge rows that lined both sides of the road. Halfway to Hamilton my engine gave out. Darn thing only worked goin' downhill. Wasn't much fun peddling a sixty pound bike uphill. I got Roger's attention and pointed to the nearest seaside hotel.

He stopped and I caught up, "Damn thing's not running right. Only works when we're pointed downhill or on the flat. Let's stop here and rest. I need a beer."

Roger scanned the hotel and its surroundings, "Looks a bit snooty to me."

"Nothing else near by and I'm starved. Sign mentions a world famous black sand beach."

We stacked our bikes on the rack outside of the lobby and walked in. The maitre d' took one look at us and took us outdoors to a table overlooking the beach.

He smiled, "Coat and tie only in the dining room, gentlemen." We ordered fish and chips and an imported Dutch beer. It was really good. However, when the bill came, we both groaned. It was six dollars, each beer was a dollar.

Roger shook his head, "That very same beer was twenty-five cents last night at the O' Club. I'm ready to leave. Can't stand a steady diet at these prices. And we're separated by at least ten tables from the others. Must be worried that folks who ride motor bikes will contaminate their guests."

I looked over the side, "Want to walk down to the world famous black sand beach?"

"Looks like a postage stamp to me and stairs look like they'll break if we go down together. This place has a nose up in the air as high as its prices. Did you take a look at tonight's menu?"

"Yes, black tie formal and nothin' less than ten dollars."

"Don't you wonder how troops stationed here can afford to go out?"

"Probably don't. Better head back to St. George. Don't want to push my bike uphill after dark."

Wild flowers and trimmed hedges dotted the landscape on the wandering road to St. George. It was as if the road builders had followed a herd of dairy cows on their way back to the barn. Roger was getting ahead of me, 'cause pushin' my bike uphill was easier than peddlin' it.

I shouted, "Slow down! I'd enjoy this view if I wasn't pushing this damn bike uphill. Want to trade for a spell?"

Roger either didn't hear or didn't care, "Try to keep up or we won't make it back in time for happy hour."

I wasn't getting any sympathy from him. Three miles out of St. George my engine quit for good. Roger motored back as I tried one restart after another with what appeared to be a makeshift lawnmower cord. His only encouragement was, "Keep pushing. I'll motor on ahead and send the owner back to pick you up."

"Roger that, but hurry. At least walking this contraption is faster than peddling."

When I looked up, I noticed I was talking to myself.

Roger disappeared over the crest of the hill and I followed, pushing my bike up the incline. After an hour of walking and pushing I finally arrived at the motor bike shop. The owner took the bike off my hands and placed it back on the rental rack. He wiped his hands, "You brought it in two minutes after five. Looks like you owe me for another day."

"Not likely. You owe me a refund for a bike that won't run. You're lucky I pushed this piece of junk back and didn't leave it on the road."

"We'll call it even. Couldn't come out to pick you up. Didn't have anyone to watch the shop."

"Where's my friend, Roger?"

"He walked back to the Air Force base with two of your friends."

"Don't know if any of them are my friends. Friends don't leave friends stranded alone out on the road."

The colors of Bermuda's forever spring-like flowers, a spectacular ocean view and the setting sun turned my lonely walk back to the air base into a pleasant stroll. I was soon over my irritation with former friends. My anger had evaporated by the time I reached the BOQ. Roger posted a note on my door.

*Meet me at the O' Club. Airplane is fixed. We take off at six A.M.*

*Roger*

My salt water shower was mercifully short and equally unpleasant. Fresh water was in short supply. Bermuda received most of it's water by catching rainfall and storing it in cisterns. It was used sparingly. I toweled off the salt water and checked my suitcase to see if any clothes remained suitable to wear. After three days on the road, I was running short. I wandered outside into an evening sky turning from burnt orange to deep purple. I wondered what mischief Oscar D. and Main Line were into.

Roger the lodger waved for me to come on over and join him at the bar, "What kept you? I sent the owner out to find you."

"Never left his shop. Said you walked back with our two wild ones."

"Promised to phone Nancy at five, Bermuda time, or I would have made sure he picked you up. Did he give you a refund?"

"Refund? He wanted to charge me for an extra day because I didn't bring his bike back on time."

"Did you pay?"

"No, but he sure has a weird sense of humor. We agreed that I'd paid half his rental fee."

"Did he bring you back to base?"

"No and he didn't offer. I walked. That's why I'm late."

"How are your finances holding out?"

"With half a rental fee back, I won't need to cash a check."

"You're better off than Oscar D. and Main Line. They were in here earlier looking for a loan."

"What for?"

"They met two ladies from the hotel we stopped at. They have dinner dates."

"Didn't you tell them about black tie and the price?"

Roger had a canary-cat smile on his face, "Didn't ask and I didn't offer. And you know Main Line. He's been here before and knows it all."

"I'd like to see his face when he sees the prices on the menu."

"And when they find out dinner is black tie and tux."

"I'm hungry enough to eat British food. Let's go to dinner. I want to hit the sack early. Have to get up at four to eat breakfast."

On our way to the dining room, Roger stopped. "Almost forgot. Nancy says Sally wants to go out when we return. Said she'd like a little Italian."

I laughed, "Private joke."

• • •

When Main Line and Oscar D. dragged their bodies into base ops the next morning they looked like they had been rode hard and put away wet.

I asked, "Where did you two run off to yesterday evening."

Oscar D. gave Main Line a dirty look, "Line here talked me into taking a couple of ladies to dinner. Of course he didn't check to see how much it would cost or that we'd have to wear formal dress."

Main Line shook his head, "Worked out, though. Had room service deliver dinner to their room and they put it on their bill. Only cost us the tip. Ever try to get a taxi to bring you back here after midnight? Bermuda closes up at ten. We had to walk back."

Oscar D. added, "If it wasn't for Roger's note, I'd still be in the sack. What do we have planned for today."

Stonehands came over and our conversation stopped, "You will take your LORAN check-ride on our flight back to West Palm."

Oscar D.'s face turned beet red, "What the hell for!"

"Relax Lieutenant, we have two working LORAN sets. If we lose either one, your check-ride from West Palm to Ellington will have to be scrubbed. If we have to add on a flight, it will cost Uncle Sugar gas and money."

The sun was barely on the horizon when we met our pilots at the airplane. As the senior pilot loaded his golf clubs on board, Roger asked, "Why are we flying back so early."

"Bermuda is way too expensive for our pocketbooks. We're broke. We'll gas up at West Palm and keep on chugging to Houston."

Right there and then I knew we wouldn't see much of Florida on this trip. After we loaded our gear, I came back outside and sat down on the coral outcrop. My mind was working overtime trying to figure out a way to keep our LORAN sets running and still pass the flight exam.

After we finished preflighting our equipment, I waited for Stonehands to go outside for a smoke before motioning to our Flight to put their headsets on. I had each one check in over intercom. After I was certain they were all on and listening, I offered my solution to our dilemma, "If we want to complete our check-ride with working LORAN sets, we need to establish a few ground rules. Oscar D. and me have the only two working sets. Mine will give pure LORAN fixes. It is sacrosanct. No one, not even me is going to approach it with a screwdriver or even twist a knob after I set it up. Get your reading and get out of the way for the next guy. If Stonehands insists that we demonstrate how-to adjust a set, we'll use Oscar D.'s. And Main Line will go last. Don't do any adjusts until we're at least three quarters of the way to West Palm. Any questions?"

Main Line called, "Johnny, did you check this out with Stonehands?"

"No and I don't intend to. Do we have an agreement?"

A chorus of "Roger that," resounded over intercom.

I added, "After we level off we can evaluate our situation again. If we need to do something else, we'll discuss it then and take another vote."

• • •

My plan worked like a charm for everyone, but me. We were able to keep Stonehands occupied until we were an hour out of West Palm. Oscar D. held Main Line back until everyone but me had demonstrated a LORAN adjust. Main Line approached Oscar D.'s LORAN set like a gandy dancer carrying a crowbar. Using his screwdriver like a sledge hammer with Stonehands twisting synchronization knobs so tightly the knobs snapped off, they demolished Oscar D.'s set. LORAN signals were left to dance wildly across the scope like green worms on a dead body. Oscar D. got up in disgust, came over to my position and obtained a reading from my set. He shook his head and whispered, "Whatever you do, don't let those two near this set until we're getting ready to land."

As Oscar D. walked away, Stonehands came charging down the aisle, screwdriver held aloft, waving it around like a pirate's sword, shouting, "Get out of my way. I want to use your set to evaluate Lieutenant Line's adjustment techniques."

I stood my ground and blocked his path, "You lay one hand on my set and I'll break both your arms. This is our last workin' LORAN set. If we lose it, we're out over this ocean with nothing more than a wet finger to navigate with. It isn't broke and it won't be if you stay away from it with that sledgehammer you call a screwdriver."

Stonehands stopped in his tracks, dumbfounded. No student had ever talked back to him before. Slowly, the realization that we were out over open ocean and he was about to throw our last remaining oar overboard came home. I could see wooden spoked wheels in his mind crank slowly in ever increasing circles. His eyes grew narrow. I could feel the wrath of a Nav school instructor comin' down on me. I was beginning to wonder what supply school would be like in early summer when Stonehands backed off.

He put his screwdriver away, "Lieutenant Ropp, would you mind if I use your set for a reading?"

"Only if you don't turn a knob or attempt to adjust it."

Oscar D. came by after Stonehands walked back to his instructor station, "He hasn't given up. You and Main Line are going to demonstrate adjustment when we're within sight of West Palm. Only reason he backed off was he would face a severe ass chewing if we made landfall somewhere near South Carolina."

"You're right. I've embarrassed our instructor." I had that sinking feeling, like the one I used to get when I discovered one of my sheep was missing, "I've broken the unwritten rule."

Oscar D. laughed, "The instructor is always right."

"And even if he is wrong, he's still right. What do you recommend?"

"Simple, place your head between your legs."

"Is that all?"

"And kiss your ass good-by."

When the pilots announced they had intercepted West Palm TACAN and were taking control of the airplane, we closed out our logs. Stonehands took his screwdriver out of his pocket quicker than a gunfighter at the OK Corral and stormed down the aisle toward my LORAN set, "Out of the way Lieutenant. I'm going to throw your LORAN set out of adjustment and you're going to demonstrate how to bring it back on line." I watched Stonehands's screwdriver move like a bludgeon toward the top adjustment screw on the right side of my LORAN set. Too late for Stonehands to back off, an electric discharge wide as a jagged bolt of lightning flew out of my LORAN set to his screwdriver. Stonehands fell to his knees and rolled over on the floor. He tried to get up, fell over again and laid there unconscious. Smoke bellowed out of my set's cooling vents. I turned it off and popped the circuit breaker to prevent an electrical fire. We carried Stonehands back to his seat with a charred screwdriver and hair sticking straight out frazzled. He looked like a convict after a bout with an electric chair.

Oscar D. opined, "Damnedest thing I've ever seen. If I didn't know better, I'd say your LORAN set sacrificed it's electronic life to get even with the guy who destroyed all of his brothers."

"Great show wasn't it, but I'm a dead man—I'm never going to pass this course." I walked over to see how Stonehands was doing. He was trying to write. His pencil was making circles, but the lead wasn't touching the paper. When the senior pilot called back over intercom, Stonehands came out of it.

The pilot yelled, "Is that an electrical fire I smell back there? What's going on? Do you need help?"

Stonehands clicked on his intercom mike saying, "No problem I have everything under control. What are your plans at West Palm?"

"After we land, your students can grab a bite to eat at the base ops snack bar while the airplane is being gassed up. We're going to have a fast turnaround and continue on to Ellington. Are you sure there isn't anything wrong? Smells pretty bad up here."

Stonehands didn't answer. His pencil was still making circles above the grade sheets.

The senior pilot walked back to Stonehands's position, "Damn it, when I call you I want a response. Is everything all right back here?"

Stonehands was on his feet, "Yes, sir—just a small electrical fire. It's out and everything is under control. One of our LORAN sets smoked a bit, but I pulled the circuit breaker. Everything is all right now."

"You're a mess. Looks like you were hit by lightning. Have your students button up their equipment. We're going to land in less than ten minutes and make sure this doesn't happen again."

"Won't, all of our equipment is out. We'll have to use your TACAN on our next flight."

As the pilot walked forward, Stonehands slumped over, passed out again as our airplane flew through puffy white cumulus clouds with another instructor in la-la land.

• • •

Stonehands avoided our Flight at the snack bar. Mart the smart carried his tray to the table, "Don't worry Johnny, that asshole will have to pass you. He's telling the pilots he saved their airplane when it was him who started the fire. You're home free. A liar has to cover his tracks so he won't get caught. Bet Stonehands tries to buy you off."

I had to laugh, "The electrical shock knocked Stonehands senseless."

Oscar D. said, "Well, he didn't have far to go. Mart, tell us all about this TACAN thing pilots navigate with."

"Piece of cake. TACAN is the acronym for ultra high frequency tactical air navigation. It's a line of sight navigation system, more accurate than any system we're allowed to use. Unfortunately it's for pilots, not for us funny wings."

Oscar D. said, "Stonehands told the pilots we were going to use it on our way back to Houston."

• • •

After level off, we took turns using the pilots TACAN. Roger the lodger was ecstatic, "It's almost like cheating, it's so easy to use. If the evaluator on our first map reading check-ride used it, Tucker would still be with our Flight."

I gave Roger one of those you've got to be kiddin' me looks and added, "You forgot about celestial."

Oscar D. spoke up, "Ain't no TACAN over the Arctic or ocean. That's why we're here in school and their ain't no Tuckers wearin funny wings."

Mart the smart stepped up, "Not true. If Tucker had twenty-twenty eyesight he'd be a damn fine fighter pilot."

I added, "He's crazy enough."

Stonehands stayed away from us. He hobnobbed with the pilots, moving out of our way. He sat by himself on our ride to base ops and turned away from me when I attempted to talk with him in the parking lot. Roger called for me to come back inside, "Nancy says they're waiting for us. We need to get a move on. They're cooking, we're bringing the steaks, wine and beer."

"You and me?"

"Yes, and they both want to know what we brought back from Bermuda for them."

"Tell Sally I'm bringing a little Italian."

## Ellington Air Field, Texas

We had a wing-ding of a return party. My head was still hurting when we checked the bulletin board for our grades after breakfast. They weren't posted. Main Line pulled us aside at midmorning break, "Words out that the commandant is having a heart-to-heart talk with Stonehands. After we landed, Oscar D. pulled the pilots aside and told them what really happened coming into West Palm. When they confronted Stonehands he stonewalled them. Not smart. Pilots have a union. They stick together and Stonehands lied. You can lead your men into a trap and get them all killed, but you never ever lie."

"You think I failed?"

"You shouldn't have passed. Incomplete is the best you can hope for. You didn't adjust."

"You better be glad I didn't. We'd all be flying another check-ride."

Oscar D. walked over, "Hell isn't it?"

I asked, "What?"

"Bein' right when it pays to be wrong."

Our marks were posted late in the afternoon. As usual, Main Line had top marks, even though he didn't adjust and I was buried in the middle. When I offered to buy us all a beer, Main Line shook his head, "No. Don't you remember—we're supposed to take our girlfriends to the Shamrock for a swim after dinner."

"Got wrapped up in our grades. How soon are you going to ask for their hands in marriage."

All three turned red and I had my answer. The wedding bells were gonna' ring-a-ling-ling for them, but not for me. And our instructor, Stonehands, should have never gotten crossways with the pilot's union. He was on his way to supply school in Cheyenne, Wyoming.

*"How are you getting on?" said the Cheshire Cat.*

*"I don't think they play at all fairly," Alice began, "and they all quarrel so dreadfully, one can't hear one's self speak and they don't seem to have any rules in particular: at least if there are, nobody attends to them."*

# Chapter 4

Fall and an R class, Radar, arrived at the same time—on the twenty-first of September. A glorious season, fall is heralded by the dying leaves falling from tree after tree. Radar training was heralded by radar sets failing in airplane after airplane. I set forth into the dreaded world of E and R, knowing that I would soon be up to my eyeballs in sheep dip. Main Line didn't help me when he reminded me, "Same government contractor that built our LORAN sets."

"I know, from the lowest bidder. We don't have to design one, so I should be okay."

"You'll have to adjust it."

"You would have to remind me."

"Did you call Sally about our get together this weekend?"

"She's out of town until Thursday."

"Are you getting serious?"

"We could, but we've decided to stay friends. Never can tell, though. Gets pretty hot and heavy at times. How about you and Oscar D.?"

"Nervous time. We both are learning how a gazelle feels when he sees a lioness circling him."

"Understand the prey goes numb just before the kill."

"And that's how we both feel."

• • •

Unmatched components hooked together in an electronics device are called a kludge. That aptly described what I saw when I looked at my first radar scope. Our sets were not only old and worn out, they were designed to operate above fifteen thousand feet. Our T-29s were lucky to get up to twelve. Now this wasn't all bad since our airplanes were not pressurized. Cities the size of Houston and Dallas looked like blurs on our scopes. We were told to use ground and water contrast. That was fine along the coast, but the rest of Texas was in a deep drought.

Oscar D. opined, "Our equipment is older than dirt."

Trouble was, I couldn't tell dirt from brick when I looked into my Radar scope. I battled it out for two weeks to no avail. When I was in scientific trouble, I knew who to go to, Mart the smart. I said, "James Thurber saw a blur when he looked into his microscope in Botany class at Ohio State. I see the same blur when I look into my radar scope."

Mart looked at me as if I was a dufus, "What you really see is a Rorschach test. A Thurber blur? You must learn to use scientific terms if you want help. A Thurber blur indeed."

"Okay, I know we live in parallel universes, but I need a boost. Radar reminds me of the Wizard's smoke and mirrors."

"You're right about smoke and mirrors."

Mart proceeded to give me the whole shovel full, "Radar is an acronym for Radio Detection and Ranging when it should be called Midar, Microwave Detection and Ranging."

"You lost me on midar. What's the difference?"

"Radio is in the medium to high frequency spectrum and radar is in the microwave spectrum."

"And a spectrum?"

"Like a scale from one to one hundred with long waves at one end and short waves at the other. Don't confuse short wave radio signals with my scale. They would be down at the low end and ultra violet at the high."

"You lost me again with your scale. Explain the nuts and bolts of radar range and resolution."

Mart's eyes lit up, "That's the fun part! The radar range equation is:

*Distance equals the speed of light times the time to travel that distance divided by two for the round trip.*

"Say What? Round trip? To where and why?"

"Simple, the transmitted Radar pulse is sent out to an object, bounces off and returns."

"What about unambiguous range?"

"A little more complicated. It's:

*Distance between radar pulses R equals the speed of light times the pulse interval, divided by two.*

Do you understand the concept?"

"I hope they have multiple choice. It's my only hope."

"You have a fine literary mind, but one not suited for modern science."

"Hate to say it, but our electronics instructor was right. I'll have to stay away from anything that begins with E or R."

"Tell you what I'll do. I know how they construct our multiple guess tests. Did some mathematical computations on the probability of certain questions. I'll coach you."

"I'll need it."

• • •

I resorted to the same technique I used in celestial—do it by rote. Master how to operate a system using the data without comprehending the concept, design, or mechanics of it. I called it my I and S equation. *Ignorance and superstition will always win out over science and fact!* I wasn't the only one with problems. Main Line was desperate for help, too. I gave him my insight on how to pass by the rote system.

He tried, "And it works!" We all passed the ground examination with Mart the smart's help. His insight into the construction of Multiple Test questions helped everyone but him. As usual, Main Line came out at the top and Mart, the only one of us who understood radar theory, came out just below which really wasn't very far from the top. Knowing how questions are made up and using the data—well, let's just say he didn't. Mart got wrapped up in the individual trees and missed the forest. With our ground phase out of the way and flying training underway, we now had time to celebrate passing radar. And we had only two more classes to go, grid and combined navigation. Oscar D. came up with a way to celebrate agreed too by all.

• • •

He called a meetin' on the morning we were planning our first radar training flight, "Listen up troops. I can get half priced tickets for the Texas A & M, University of Houston football game next Saturday night. It's gonna' be at Rice Stadium. We can celebrate our passage and give you Yankees and Main Line an opportunity to see what real football is like, Texas style. A& M has a brand new coach, Bear Bryant and a better than even chance of beating Texas University this year."

Roger the lodger asked, "How are your Aggies doing?"

"Won our first two games and we've been selected by the press to win the national championship. I'd say we're doing pretty well. Have an All American candidate at fullback by the name of John David Crow."

Main Line opined, "How come all of you Texans have two first names?"

Oscar D. stared him down, "Line, how can you be so stupid? Everyone should have two first names. Gives you a choice if you get tired of the first one. Besides having two first names has a poetic ring."

Main Line jumped right back in, "A cowboy poet? That's like a marching symphony band. Is John David Crow an Indian?"

"Could be, but I think he's mostly Cajun from Louisiana Bayou Country."

Oscar D. returned to his topic, "Bring your wives and girl friends. A & M will impress them all. Tickets are five dollars each, a real bargain."

Main Line needled, "We'll all go, even if it is just a bunch of marching farmers."

I asked, "Is Houston any good? Didn't know they had a school."

Oscar D. got serious, "I didn't either. Someone up at the State College Athletic Department screwed up. They violated the number one rule of scheduling. Never schedule a team named after a city. Bound to be full of mercenaries instead of students. I bet most of Houston's football players major in travel agent, communication or gym."

Roger the lodger didn't agree, "How can you be sure. Do you have any proof?"

"Yes, remember Tucker. He went to Syracuse, was captain of his lacrosse team and could barely count past two."

I had to stick up for Tucker, "But he majored in journalism."

Oscar D. smiled, "Proves my point. Another name for a Communications major. Everybody going?"

We all nodded, "Yes."

"We'll meet at the apartment where my girl friend lives, out near the Shamrock Hotel. We'll carpool from there. Johnny, you can cook burgers on the barbecue grill by the pool. The rest of us will bring hot dogs, chips and beer. Game is at eight. We'll meet at five."

Turned out to be a great feast and a wonderful game. Sally prepared the burgers and I did the cooking. She laced them with ground pepper and soy sauce, something she had learned in San Francisco. After Oscar D. devoured three dogs two burgers and several beers, he called for us to gather around, "Now about my school, Texas A & M. It is an all male university and those that can walk wear a uniform—and proud of it. Hubris is part of our motto. So you'll be in the middle of a lot of Sam Brown uniforms."

Sally asked, "Sam Brown?"

"Uniform our Army wore before World War II. Brown and tan with a belt and strap on the outside of the coat. Our tickets are in the middle of the A & M student section. You'll have to stand the entire game."

Main Line asked, "What for?"

"The twelfth man, you idiot. Years back, one of our coaches asked for a player to come out of the stands. He did, we won and now we all stand ready. If you are in the A&M section, you stand or else."

I asked, "Do you have alumni support?"

Oscar D.'s eyes narrowed, "You must be from another planet, Johnny. Do we have alumni support? Let me tell you a story. Happened right here in Houston. One of our old alumnus was visiting with a friend that had to attend a funeral, so he tagged along to be sociable. When they were planting the body, the minister asked everyone to say a few kind words about the deceased. When it came time for our alumnus, he obliged, 'I do not know anything about your dear departed. I am here with an old friend, but while we are all here together, let me say a few words about Texas A & M.' And you ask if we have alumni support. We have the best alumni, greatest band in the world, all military and precision drill and the best school anywhere. You'll have a great time."

Main Line asked, "Is that an order?" And we all laughed.

Roger and Nancy rode with us to the stadium, oblivious to our presence in the front seat. Sally sat closer than usual, stroking the inside of my right thigh.

I whispered, "Looks like they're heading to the alter."

Sally nodded, "Yes."

I placed my right arm around her shoulders, "Are we still friends?"

She drew closer and whispered, "More than that, but . . ."

"No commitment?"

"Right," she said as she moved closer.

"I get mixed signals."

"Matches your personality. You're my kind of mixed up guy."

"Is there someone else?"

"I'm still reluctant after my break-up with Attaboy. I hope you understand. Follow my directions." She placed a special car pass on the dash that allowed us into the faculty section.

"Another old flame?" I asked her.

"How did you guess?"

There is something about a college football game that gets the hormones buzzing. After I turned the engine off, Sally came into my arms and I really wasn't interested in leaving the car. Roger broke the spell, "Are those Texas Rangers?"

Sally separated from my arms, "They're A & M seniors, silly."

"But they're wearing knee-high boots."

"Tradition—only the seniors are allowed to wear them." Sally gave me a gentle dig to the ribs and whispered, "We better go outside, or we'll embarrass our friends."

I nodded, "Yes."

• • •

Oscar D. had good seats, right in the middle of the A & M student section. There is something about the odor of wool uniforms that sticks in the back of my mind, like manure to a shoe. Neither comes off, or can be forgotten. The band was even better than advertised, even though they carried a bunch of sissy reed instruments, like the Michigan band. I knew better than to make a comparison with the best damn band in the land, The Ohio State Band. The A & M Band was the best military band I'd ever seen or heard and I let it go at that. Besides, Aggies weren't too happy. Houston played them to a tie with a fourth quarter touchdown.

I wanted to ask Sally why the A & M students kept singing, "Good-bye to Texas University" when they weren't even here, but thought better of it. I enjoyed myself and Sally seemed like she did, too. We hadn't been close for quite awhile and the warmth of her body next to mine felt good. I was beginning to hear a faint ring-a-ling-ling in my ears. I Wondered if she heard bells, too. Sally knew her football and asked all the right questions. She was even interested in the outcome. This was a woman worth waiting for. We were separated from the others when a phalanx of A & M students rushed by, streaming through the stadium portals.

Sally drew closer as we walked, "Doesn't it make you want to go back to school?"

"Sort of, but when my memory kicks in, I remember how anxious I was to get out."

"Don't you like academics?"

"College is like priming a pump. Once you learn how to draw water it's time to get pumping on your own. One of my literature professors said, 'We teach you how to use the library. Once you've learned that, it's time for you to leave school and go to the library'."

"I still miss it. Maybe it's because I left after two years."

My three compadres were leaning up against the portholes of my Buick, while their dates chatted away. Oscar D. insisted, "Let's take our young ladies to Trails End for some good old cowboy music." I looked over at Sally.

She said, "No" with her lips, not making a sound.

I replied, "Sorry—Sally and I haven't had much time alone. We'll take a rain check."

Roger and Nancy decided to go. "We'll ride with Oscar D. to Ellington and pick up my car. Sure you don't want to go?"

Sally said, "No" and they understood.

We drove back to her apartment in silence. Inside, she turned off the light.

• • •

When Sally was off on a flight, I was on the ground and when I was in the air, she wasn't. We didn't see much of each other during October, but I saw my fair share of busted radar sets. Our radar training flights should have been a piece of cake, but they weren't. Radar was supposed to be very accurate. Our systems were far from that, but that wasn't the school solution. Tolerances on our fixes became stringent, decreasing from twenty miles to five. However, when I looked at my scope, everything toward the center, the most accurate area, looked like a fluorescent blob. No matter how many adjustments I made to my radar picture, I couldn't get rid of ground clutter.

Mart the smart couldn't help. He'd look at his own scope and moan, "Just like our LORAN sets, knobs are too loose. They've been adjusted too many times."

I agreed, "The clutter at the center of my scope looks like the aftermath of a nuclear explosion."

Mart got a Cheshire-Cat grin on his face, "Don't try to identify anything near the center."

"I'll lose accuracy."

"But you'll pass."

On our first training flight, over half the radar sets were busted before wheels were in the well. By the time we touched down, all but one set bit the dust. Main Line was a whirling dervish, a cyclone of motion. Scattering papers everywhere. He charged aft toward me and kneeled down beside my desk, "You got us through LORAN. Get us outa' this mess."

"Simple, find a set that works, share it and don't adjust it out of focus. Don't forget to cross-check aircraft location with a look out the window, use map reading."

"I get it, we demonstrate adjustment on one of the sets that's fogged."

"Right and we listen to Mart the smart, don't use an object too close to the center of the sweep."

Radar, which began as scientific enigma, resurrected as an art form. Oscar D. found words to describe our Jackson Pollock abstract scopes, "With map reading, the law is:

*I see therefore I believe.*

With radar, the law is:

*I believe therefore I see.*

All we had to do was believe the blobs that blossom on our radar scopes."

Oscar D. was right as always. "A positive frame of mind, not the scientific method, is the key to our success."

• • •

We sailed through training, ready and waiting for our flight examination on election day.

It was Main Line's turn to sponsor our Flight outing and he had a doozy, "Listen up. I have tickets to a political rally tomorrow night. If it's like the ones we have in South Carolina, there'll be a pile of barbecue and plenty of free beer."

Oscar D. stood up, "Line, what kind of political shindig are you getting us into? We're supposed to be neutral."

"Couldn't be more neutral than a Democrat for Eisenhower gathering at Herman Park, eight o'clock Friday night."

Oscar D. smiled, "Line looks like you may have a winner. Might get a chance to see if Republicans have horns, like my Daddy told me. I've never seen a live Republican, not from my part of Texas anyway. Least ways, none that would admit to it. Don't count on any food or beer, though. This isn't a local election. Now if it was for sheriff or some important office like that, there'd be more than we could eat or drink. A politician won't make much money running for president."

Called Sally and she was game, but she wanted to talk to me alone, "We have things to discuss, Johnny. You're getting way to serious."

"I was under the impression you were too."

"Pick me up at six thirty at the TWA gate. I'll shower and change there."

"Wear something comfortable. Main Line says it's an outdoor rally, not a tea party. Are you flying out this evening?"

"Yes, I won't be able to see you until I return."

It was twilight when I picked Sally up at the airport. She bubbled over, teasing me unmercifully on our drive to Herman Park. I couldn't remember seeing her so up, so happy. And she was driving me crazy, stroking my inner right thigh, cuddling closer than the law allows. It took a Herculean effort on my part to get out of my car and walk to the rally. When we joined our friends, my face was flushed, but Sally was as cool as a cucumber.

Oscar D. took one look at me and laughed, "You sure look hot and bothered, Johnny. Not much of a crowd here. Can't be more than fifty or so."

Roger quipped, "They look like Republicans to me."

Oscar D. was puzzled, "Don't see no horns, so I'm not sure, but it doesn't matter. Eisenhower is a hero around these parts. If he's a Republican, they must be okay."

Main Line said, "Pay attention. You're going to get a lesson in politics—TV style. They're going to make fifty of us look like a throng of thousands".

One of the managers placed us in a section of a very small bleacher. Sally linked her arm in mine, "They must have expected a small crowd. This won't seat more than fifty." We were Galveston, or at least our sign said so. Roger and Nancy were Houston, Oscar D. and his lady, Pasadena and Main Line and Mart the smart were given torches. When the TV lights came on, we waved our signs and cheered while Main Line and Mart came out from behind the bushes carryin' two torches. The MC identified them as the tail end of a mile long parade of supporters and us as an enthusiastic group numbering in the thousands. The Texas governor, a Democrat, spoke of his support for the general while the cameras took tight crowd shots. We cheered and waved our signs on cue, like monkeys on a string.

After it was all over, we shook hands with the governor and wandered off to our cars. Main Line was sufferin' much disappointment, "Oscar D. was right, no beer or barbecue. Sorry I drug you out for this."

"Not a problem, Line. I enjoyed every minute of it. Won't believe all that I see on TV the next time, so it wasn't a waste of time. Let's head out to Sam's Shack for a late dinner."

Oscar D.'s fiancé gave him a dig to the ribs, "Now Oscar, we're closer to the Shamrock Hotel. Let's take all of your friends there. We'll use my Daddy's membership card. He won't mind. He just struck oil again out near San Angelo. They have the nicest jumbo shrimp and the sauce is to die for." First time I'd ever seen Oscar D. blush. Knew he was a gonner.

• • •

I didn't get back to my room at the barracks until late Sunday night and even then I had to pry myself out of Sally's bed. For someone who didn't want commitment, well it sure felt like she did. Main Line's comments about me having a lot to learn about women popped into my head. He was right, but I had a suspicion we all had a lot to learn. At mission planning the next morning, I discovered that when we voted absentee, we canceled each other out. Oscar D. liked Eisenhower, but was afraid lightning would strike him dead if he ever pulled the lever for a Republican. Don't know how Sally voted. She was on another flight to San Francisco. I felt the same way as Oscar D. Don't remember anyone in my family ever voting Republican. But, unlike Oscar D.'s part of the country, my county was all Republican except for my relatives.

Next day, we flew north to Dallas and south to Houston. A combination of a few good sets and good luck carried us through our flight exam with passing marks. As usual, Main Line stood alone at the top of our class. Oscar D. surmised, "Either the rules of engagement have been changed or the Air Force needs warm bodies to fill vacant slots. Can't believe all of our motley crew passed. Mart? How about the next phase, Grid?"

"No flight test. All we have to do is demonstrate proficiency. Maps are weird though, grid lines on them. We use a gyro instead of a compass. Navigators use it in the Arctic where the Magnetic Pole is unreliable. Should be an interesting couple of weeks. After that we fly two training flights using all we've learned and then a final end of course check-ride. Pass that and they pass out our funny wings."

Roger the lodger smiled, "And we're out of here!"

Oscar D. waved for quiet, "Time to celebrate. Why don't we all go to that little Italian place Johnny and Sally are always talking about."

I telephoned Sally. She had not returned, or if she had, wasn't home. I drove alone to our little Italian restaurant and left the party early.

• • •

Our days at Nav school were dwindling down to a precious few. We had only three or four more weeks before we received our funny wings and moved on to advanced training, or flying the line. My three friends were attempting the Texas side step without training and without success. They didn't know this dance and if they did, wouldn't have helped. Their fiancés were on a full court press to get commitment before we packed our bags and left Texas.

Main Line was as skittish as a cat in a room full of rocking chairs, "Don't know if I want to make a commitment. Not sure if I want to settle down, but I'm certain I don't want to spend another lonely year in barracks."

Oscar D. was more philosophical, "Don't fret, Line. You can't control your life. If someone is gonna' tell you what to do, might as well be the one you sleep with. Johnny how about you and Sally? Sure looked like you were hot and heavy there for awhile."

"Acts like I'm the only one for her, but won't commit. If she doesn't, I'll sure miss her. She's a good sport. Wouldn't be all bad going through life with her. Besides, what's love got to do with commitment?"

Roger looked up, "Doesn't sound romantic to me. Love is everything."

"My grandfather said, 'What's love got to do with it?' What he really meant was, friendship and caring are more important than a brief episode of red hot romantic love," I explained.

Oscar D. nodded, "Your grandfather is right. With today's high divorce rate, friendship seems to last longer than love. Say, I thought you said Sally was out of town. When I came back to the apartment from your Italian restaurant I saw her dangling her feet in the pool, talking to Attaboy."

I gulped, but said nothing. I had one of those deep down sinking feelings and a knot in the pit of my stomach. Like when you open the barn door and the sheep and your sheep dog are gone.

It was hard for me to concentrate. My thoughts weren't on navigating. When we flew our last two practice flights, combining all of our skills, I barely passed. I was still seeing Sally, but I knew something was wrong. Usually I'm an optimist, but having been down the bumpy road of love before, I was reluctant to let it all hang out. Experience taught me that a small hurt to my psyche was a lot better than a broken heart. Maybe that was our problem. Neither of us wanted to be wounded, so we didn't give our relationship a chance. So it looked like we were both going to wind up losers, at least I was.

• • •

After our next training flight, we were scheduled to choose our new assignment, a ritual of passage that we trained for all year long. I sensed it would be one of those few remaining times we would be able to choose a path to determine our future. We were approaching a time where we had to shoulder personal responsibility or wind up in a home.

It took Oscar D. to snap me out of my funk, "Don't worry Johnny, you'll find the right girl much sooner than you expect. I've watched and you're learnin' what it's all about. Get your mind on our mission. When we're done, and choose where we'll go, then you can mope. When we get to choose, remember what your electronics instructor said, don't choose anything that begins with an E or an R. Said he'd shoot you and Tucker on sight if you did."

"Me maybe, but Tucker escaped from this asylum to supply school. You're right, there's nothing I can do about a love affair gone sour. It's probably all for the best."

Turned out our last training flight was a piece of cake. And it didn't seem to me that they were trying to get rid of us. But Oscar D. knew what he was talking about. Air Force had to be short of navigators. We flew leisurely from Houston to Dallas and back combining map reading with night celestial and radar for a flawless flight. This simplicity came to a screeching halt when we flew our check-ride. Instead of flying overland, we flew south from Galveston over open ocean, the Gulf of Mexico. There were no towns, water tanks or rivers. Radar and map reading were out of the question.

After departing Galveston, my Flight members performed like trained circus elephants, except this time the big top was on fire. Main Line topped us all, running amok. Shear terror gave him the solution to our dilemma, "Listen up—we're saved, TACAN. We can use TACAN! And it's legal! Mix it in with one night celestial fix, a radar fix at the end and we qualify!"

Oscar D. was laconic, "Line, we'll have to. You just destroyed our only working LORAN set."

TACAN worked, but I could smell the odor of flight suits loaded down with nervous sweat as we battled each other to use the few astrodomes available. After it was all over, we drove directly to Trails End without changing out of our flight suits and closed the bar at midnight.

Our grades were posted after breakfast, early in the morning. Main Line was on top, Mart the smart next, and we all passed. As I headed for our class room, I bumped into our electronics class instructor. He pulled me aside, "Didn't think you'd make it this far. How about Tucker?"

"Tucker washed out. He was banished to supply school."

"Remember your promise?"

"Yes, sir."

"Keep it. Don't choose an assignment with an E or R. Where do you stand in your class?"

"Top quarter."

"Shouldn't be a problem."

"If there's a choice, I'll keep my promise."

I was happy and mad. It was almost mid-December and no more Nav training, but we still had to attend class—gym class. And we didn't receive our funny wings. Classes were over, but the time allotted wasn't. Not knowing what to do with us, the commandant decided we needed to exercise. And we did—four hours in the morning and four hours in the afternoon. We played touch football, swam laps, volleyball, capture the flag, basketball, baseball and every other team sport known to man, except field hockey. And we were getting in shape, as if lean mean second lieutenants needed it. We were so thin, couldn't see us if we turned sideways. Even with this athletic diversion, choosing our assignment was still an all encompassing obsession. Rumor and fact flew in tandem and separately.

• • •

We knew that Strategic Air Command was a tough place to work, long hours and more testing than most schools. B-36 and B-47 bombers were the backbone of SAC and the B-52 was just entering the inventory. SAC needed fresh blood and we were prime candidates. The main drawback was location. SAC bases were isolated from modern civilization. If the town didn't have a TV station or department store, Air Force built a SAC base near it. North and South Dakota might have the friendliest folks on earth, but San Francisco had ocean and ladies.

Roger the lodger didn't want any part of SAC, "Too many planes fallin' out of the sky and most of the bases are a hundred miles from a good cup of coffee."

Air Defense Command had its share of problems, too. navigators were in the back seat of fighters, with a teen-age killer up front. As a GIB, Guy In Back, Navs operated radar, guiding the airplane on an intercept toward enemy bombers. Rumors had filtered back to Nav school and were spreading like a wild prairie fire. Up in Alaska, when a teen-age killer bailed out, his GIB was left behind, pinned in by his equipment 'cause radar had to be stowed before a GIB could eject.

Mart the smart wasn't worried, "Better than flying a twelve hour round trip mission from the middle of nowhere and back in BUF [Big Ugly F]."

Oscar D. got that sly smile he gets when he's been given the mother of all straight lines. "You mean SAC crew members have to fly around naked? Gives new meaning to moon shot."

We broke up, but engineers don't have much of a sense of humor. Mart was serious, "BUF is what they call a B-52."

We couldn't help it, we were rolling around on the ground, holding our sides.

A week before Christmas, when we reported in for another round of physical training we received the news we had been waiting for, Nav school was finished. We were to receive our wings in the morning and would choose assignments at one o'clock. I decided that I wanted to fly the line in Big Shaky, The Crowd Killer, an under powered propeller driven C124 transport. It was a no brainer considering SAC air fields were in clean air places like Minot, North Dakota, upper peninsula Michigan and Roswell, New Mexico. Military Air Transport Command's bases were on the coast. Big Shaky flew to every exotic location in the world from hardship bases like San Francisco or New York. Someone had to take the tough assignments and it might as well be me. With top quarter standing in my Flight, I had as good a chance as any of my contemporaries. Main Line and Oscar D. decided to stay in Texas. They had been caught in mid-step by their ladies. Roger the lodger wanted to stay on at Ellington, as an instructor. The wedding bells went ring-a-ling-ling for them, but not for me.

• • •

In the morning, we marched up as our names were called and received our funny wings. Piped-in music over the sound system of the base movie theater seemed appropriate for the occasion. The notice was so short, wives and girl friends were not in attendance. We had as much ceremony as a tree falling in a forest when no one was around, sound and fury over nothing. That afternoon, assignment selection began on schedule. I was nervous enough to smoke another one of Oscar D.'s cigarettes. We were back where it all began—minus Tucker. After we were seated, our commandant strode in from stage left to the sound of, "Attention!"

"At ease, gentlemen. Don't we all look fine in our shiny new funny wings." He stood silent, waiting for us to settle in.

He cleared his throat, "I believe we all have a clear memory of our first meeting. Our base commander is no longer with us. He transferred to Alaska and took command of a squadron of our newest radar interceptors. While flying a familiarization ride in the back seat, his plane lost its engine. He was pinned under the equipment and did not make it out. I'm certain we all feel a great sense of loss. Now where was I? Oh, Student Officers were new to us then. We flew uncharted skies with your class, so to speak. We've had a few air bumps along the way, but all-in-all its been a good learning experience for students and staff alike. I'm certain you remember the question I was asked by Lieutenant Tucker who, by the way, has just graduated at the top of his class at supply school and he still doesn't know how to ship his own household goods. When I said, 'You play ball with me and I'll play ball with you,' Tucker said, 'Don't you really mean you play ball with me and I'll shove the bat up your ass.' To your great misfortune, gentlemen, Tucker was right. Here comes the bat.

"In the past we allowed you to select your assignments by academic standing alone. Not any longer. Air Training Command has decreed that those with the longest service commitments will select first. Those of you scheduled to return to civilian life will select last. Therefore, regular officers will pick first, reserve officers with an indefinite term of service will pick second and reserve officers with a date of separation will pick last. Within those categories you will choose by academic rank. In case there is another wise-ass like Tucker lurking among you funny wings, I won't take any questions. I want you to always remember this—you may be pure of heart and have the strength of ten.

You may be smarter and have the wisdom of Solomon. You may be a charismatic, like Patton. But gentlemen, in this man's Air Force, you can rest assured, as far as navigators are concerned, there will always be a pilot in charge."

My stomach went looking for its pit. I couldn't believe it. My date of separation was less than four years away. I had dropped from the top quarter of my class to lower than whale shit. I was devastated, while Oscar D. and Main Line were jumping up and down with joy.

Oscar D. tapped me on my shoulder, "Line and me are regulars. If you want a better assignment you can change your DOS status to indefinite. Personnel has a guy ready to sign you up in the back of the room."

Roger the lodger signed up. Mart the smart and I didn't.

Mart shook his head, "Not much call for a sanitary engineer in the Air Force. I'll do my hitch and return to designing sewage plants. Why aren't you signing up."

"Not much call for someone with an American Literature B.A. degree. Air Force is moving toward the electronic age and I've been warned to stay away. Might change my mind later, but for now four more years seems enough. Don't want to lock myself in to sixteen more."

I looked up at the movie screen, where our commandant was last seen standing. Assignments were projected and names were called, regulars first. Assignments to Big Shaky were the first to go, instructor assignments next, overseas assignments to Japan and Germany followed. When my turn came, all that was left were assignments beginning with E or R. I certainly wasn't excited about being a GIB. That left Electronic Warfare training in Biloxi, Mississippi, but it began with a dreaded E and way out of my knowledge banks.

EW training along the Gulf met my criteria of coastal living. I marched to the podium and chose Biloxi. I walked outside and asked around, but no one knew what an EW was.

Main Line speculated, "Not sure, but it might be a ground job runnin' a radar site along the coast."

Oscar D. shrugged, "Doesn't matter what it is as long as you don't have to fly behind a teenage killer who'd just as soon die as live."

Oscar D. and Main Line chose to become instructors and Roger the lodger chose to be a GIB. He discovered that the school was in College Station and he'd be near his intended. Mart the smart didn't get to choose, Pentagon needed a sanitary engineer and he was the only one around. Didn't make sense to me, they all ready had experts who knew how to turn manure into regulations. Posted outside the administration building was a notice.

> *Orders will be picked up tomorrow!*
> *All new navigators will clear off base by December 20. Merry Christmas!*
> *By Order of the Commandant*

It was a fitting ending to our sojourn at Nav school. Before we scattered, there was one more farewell party at the apartment pool. This time I didn't cook and was without a lady friend. Sally and Attaboy had again become an item. I was odd man out. Wasn't much of a party. It began as a celebration and ended as a wake. Sally treated me like a merry widow treats a dearly departed after he is planted under the sod. With a single tear, she kissed me on the cheek and said she'd miss me. Might have been true, but Attaboy made sure we didn't get too close. I smiled through the whole ordeal and told her I'd write, but knew I wouldn't. I left early, stopping at the O' Club for one more farewell drink. With not much to pack and carrying it all in my car, I was almost ready to leave.

• • •

I slept in spurts, but by morning I was ready to pack my car and move out. Sally's treatment aside, I was beginning to enjoy military life. It was a lot more entertaining than herding sheep, though I was beginning to feel more like a sheep than a shepherd. However, Air Force sheep could talk and outside of the pilots' union, there didn't seem to be a herd mentality. Most of the crazies I had been associated with might be regimented on the outside, but inside they were still unique. I would miss the friendship, but it was time to move on. I packed my car, drove to the base gas station and immediately ran into my electronics instructor. I tried to gas and run, but couldn't get away before he said, "Johnny, hold up."

"Tried to sneak out. They changed the rules. All that was left was E & R."

"Understand. What did you choose?"

"Electronic Warfare. Leaving for Biloxi as soon as I crank her up."

"When you find out what an EW is, write me so I can warn the others."

"It's on the coast, so it can't be all bad."

"So is Nome, Alaska. All I know is it's a spook operation and knowledge of it is hard to come by. Don't forget, write."

"I will if I survive."

I paid for my gas and hopped in behind the wheel, wonderin' if I'd ever see my Nav school friends again and stopped, "Haven't seen one soul from high school or Ohio State."

*"In another moment down went Alice after it, never once considering how in the world she was to get out again."*

# Chapter 5

## Arkansas to Ohio

Outside it was pitch black, cold, damp and rain comin' down like a cow pissin' on a flat rock. I drove northeast away from Houston, out of the familiar, into the unknown. With nothing to do except fight the hypnotism of synchronized windshield wipers and out of range of all but country music radio stations, my mind wandered, "Just what is a spook operation? Is it an operation connected with graveyards, ghosts and haunted houses? No, couldn't be that. Had to be something Top Secret or rumor of it would have reached Nav school. When the Air Force wants to hide something, the whole world finds out about it, except the troops. We're always the last to know. Better not to worry. EW can't require good hand and eye coordination. If it did, Air Force would have pilots doin' it." I smiled to myself, "Hope I'm not on the graveyard shift."

Sally kept creeping back into the recesses of my mind. We were close friends and sometime lovers, but neither of us allowed our spark to ignite into flame. Still, I really did miss her. Attaboy was getting quite a woman. Wondered if I had made a full court press, would she would be beside me now, traveling to Biloxi? Then again, probably not. I caught Sally on the rebound from Attaboy and when I wasn't paying attention, she bounced back. It was lonely driving off to a new adventure alone. I asked myself, "Are we having fun yet?" And the answer came back, "No."

• • •

I stopped in a small east Texas town called Texarkana for gas before crossing over the border into Arkansas. The gas station attendant warned me about going on, "Better stay overnight here. Next town of any size is in the middle of Arkansas. Sidewalks don't roll up early or late in Little Rock."

"When do they roll up?"

I had just provided another mother of all straight lines. "Never, 'cause they don't have sidewalks in Arkansas."

I drove east with his laughter still ringing in my ears. In spite of this warning, I drove on through the night in a steady downpour. Couldn't see any of Arkansas in the dark and there were darn few lights visible through a heavy rain. When I reached Little Rock, I pulled into the driveway of a brand new motel near downtown.

• • •

The desk clerk was quite proud, "Only motel in town and it took quite a bit of political maneuvering just to get it built."

I was too tired to ask why so I nodded, trying to stay friendly.

"Do you want a wake-up call?"

"Not in any hurry," I said. I fell asleep as soon as I turned down my bed.

I never thought of Arkansas as part of the deep south. As a mater of fact, I never thought of Arkansas at all. It was hard to spell, hard to pronounce and out of sight of anyone growing up in the midwest. Grits, a foul tastin' inedible concoction made from corn, proved me wrong. Grits can only be eaten when smothered in butter and covered with syrup. Grits filled half my breakfast plate. I tasted it—plowed around it like a farmer trying to avoid rocks, "Only good for a whiskey stomach." I wondered if folks down here knew they were making Yankee farmers rich buying corn for grits. I finished eggs and bacon and sipped away on several cups of excellent restaurant coffee. I couldn't help but overhear the conversation at the next table. Two suits with open neck white shirts were discussing local politics. The large red-faced one was upset, "We got trouble in our new state legislature."

The short, thick set man across from him answered, "Should never have let them outsiders build a motel here. Now they want to sell whiskey by the glass. Gonna' cut into our moonshine operation if we ever let 'em sell it over the counter."

"I'm against it."

"We can get the religious folks to oppose it."

"Might cost us an arm and a leg. How about cornering the distribution?"

"Now your talking sense. We'll have to cross a lot of palms at the State House."

"So, what else is new."

"We're changin' an institution when we make mixed drinks legal."

"Want me to explore?"

"Might as well. Won't be long before our roads are paved and our folks will find out what's across the border."

"We'll have a revolution on our hands."

I paid my bill at the cash register and returned to leave a tip.

My waitress was cleaning up, "Don't mind those two. They fought this place going in tooth and nail and now they spend all there time here. Best grits in town. You stayin' on?"

"On my way home for Christmas."

"Stay on the main road, only one paved road between here and St. Louis. That red mud on our side roads sticks to a car like glue. We have too many folks, like those two, lining their pockets and not enough money going into pavement. We're not change friendly in this state."

The way she frowned when she picked up the change, didn't take a CPA to figure out those two weren't big tippers.

• • •

I topped off my gas tank before leaving Little Rock. After listening to her warning, I didn't want to get stuck in the mud trying to buy gas along the way. Drove northwest toward the border of Missouri on what she said was the only paved highway in the state. Last night's heavy rain had turned the side roads into seas of bright red mud. I shook my head. Little Rock was a paved island surrounded by rural poverty and red dirt. I looked for and couldn't find a single paved side road or paved road leading to a service station. Autos traveling my way were the color of red dust. Those folks in Little Rock had really done a number on their rural cousins. My car was almost out of gas by the time I found a service station with pavement in southeast Missouri, just before crossing the river into Illinois. I discovered grits were still a favorite morning food. Passed through St. Louis and drove fifty miles across southern Illinois before finding a suitable motel. I might be back in Lincoln's home state, but the flavor was definitely deep southern, grits and all the pork trimmin' for the evening meal.

• • •

The morning weather forecast was ominous. A fast moving cold front had moved out of the Rockies, into the plains of Kansas and was bearing down on the upper midwest. Folks in Houston called these storms blue northers. I decided to try to make it to Cincinnati on U.S. 50 before the snows came. Passing through Illinois farmland was like being back home again. I traveled out of southern poverty into the rich rolling, black bottom farm land of Illinois. Prosperous farms stretched out before me as far as the eye could see. All the way towards a slate gray horizon, barns and silos dotted the countryside like pimples on a teenager with overactive oil glands. I stopped only for coffee, candy and gas in middle Illinois, attempting to stay ahead of the fast moving cold front. By early evening, I crossed southern Indiana into Ohio Territory. Traveling away from the unreconstructed south into the known civilized world, a city like Rome, Cincinnati, Ohio.

Southern ways and southern women come loaded with charismatic charm. One can be lulled into a deep sense of euphoria when the scent of magnolias drift in on a warm summer night's breeze. Southern folks had to be who Kipling had in mind when he wrote: *"Many religious people are deeply suspicious. They seem, for purely religious purposes, of course, to know more about iniquity than the unregenerate."* The south is a land full of ambiguities, where one can be run down by a car full of God fearing Christians speeding away from Bible study on a weekday night. But there is only one civilized city in America, Cincinnati. Like Rome, it has seven hills and a coliseum (called Crosley Field) with thick stone walls protecting a diamond of green grass. Like Munich, it was dotted with world class breweries and like the Rhine, had more than one outstanding winery on its river banks.

• • •

I stopped at the first beer garden I saw and bought a case of pure ambrosia, Golden Hudapole's Royal Amber beer before driving northeast to the tree lined suburb of Norwood. I passed by twenty or so beer gardens along the way. I found a motel to my liking and checked in. The storm had reached southern Indiana and would be here soon. I had one more pilgrimage to make before returning to our family farm. Like the gateway to Rome's Coliseum, Caruso's Italian restaurant is chiseled out of stone, but, unlike the coliseum, it is in Cincinnati.

My pilgrimage was rewarded. Caruso's cuisine provided great pleasure to every single one of my senses. I lingered over the last drop of Chianti before venturing outside. The wind had switched from mild southwest to numbing northeast. Large flaky lumps of snow flew sideways past the tip of my nose. I had been in the south, too long. I turned up my jacket collar and walked backwards into the wind, turning my head every dozen steps or so looking for my car. The chill wind of this early Christmas storm blew up my pant legs and whistled through my shorts on its way through my jacket into a snowy Cincinnati night.

While I slept, this whirling cyclone weather system spilled more than a foot of snow on top of Cincinnati's seven hills. If my father still had sheep and they were outside roaming the Scioto River hills, he'd lose more than a few to last night's storm. I stayed on for another day, unable to travel on snow blocked highways. The outdoor beer gardens were closed, but not the inside. The debate over who was a better hitter, Cincinnati's Ted Kluzuski or Chicago Cub's Ernie Banks, would go on for many a cold winter night. After a night's rest, I was ready to move on. The forecast was for clearing skies and ice covered roads. Sally was in the past, slipping slowly out of my mind as I drove northeast toward Columbus on Route 3.

• • •

I turned north on River Road, driving past the Columbus Zoo, toward Concord Township and Father's farm. My heart quickened as I passed Uncle John's great white barn a mile up the road. As I drove uphill over Grandfather's old stone creek bridge, a small flock of sheep sheltering in our farmyard came into view. Their thick wool coats protected them from all but the worst of this early winter storm. My trip north from Cincinnati had taken forever—two slides forward, one slide back until I was anxious to be done with it. I could see a Christmas tree through the front window of our farmhouse. The lights were on, it was Christmas Eve on the farm.

I carried the case of Royal Amber into the kitchen and gave Mother a kiss. Father shook my hand and gave me a hug, "Figured you'd be flying home every weekend now that your in the Air Force. Been almost a year."

"Don't own a plane and they frown on that these days. Noticed the sheep."

"Just to keep my hand in. Not more than twenty, though we do have an ambitious ram."

Mother poured coffee and asked, "What happened to that young lady you wrote to us about, Sally. Airline stewardess, wasn't she?"

"We parted friends." I didn't feel obliged to unload all my troubles on my folks, so I didn't, "Don't worry. As Parson says, 'It's marryin' time.' Won't be long before I take that step."

"Make sure we get to meet her early on," she said as she refilled my cup.

Father added a touch of brandy, "Doctor says it's good for my heart."

"And he's had two fingers every night since. Dad, tell Johnny about the new houses going up."

"Some foolish city folks want to build down by the river."

"In the hundred year flood zone? Where the water can rise twenty feet during a severe spring flood?"

"Said they were foolish. We sold fifty two-acre lots to those folks."

"Are you going to continue to farm?"

"Land can stand a rest. I'll put it in the soil bank and let it return to good healthy sod."

"Are you moving to Florida?"

"No. I've been asked to coach football full time and teach a little on the side at the new consolidated high school."

"How much land will remain?"

"'Bout two square miles or so—not really sure. Been in the family since your ancestors received it in lieu of soldiers pay from Washington's Army. When you want to return, land is yours to farm."

"Not sure I want to farm."

"I said the same thing when I was your age. When I'm gone, I want you to promise you won't sell the main farm. Your grandparents are resting on the hilltop. Mother loved that view of the river. Be a shame to move them to town and a cemetery full of strangers."

"I'll pass this farm on to your grandchildren."

"Where is the Air Force sending you this time?"

"Biloxi, Mississippi for Electronic Warfare training."

"What the dickens is that?"

"Don't know, but I'll soon find out. You still smoking those sugar cured hams?"

"Mom has some sliced in the pantry, waiting for you. Thanks for remembering the Royal Amber beer. Don't have any for sale around here. Cincinnati's the only place anyone can find good beer."

• • •

As anxious as I was to leave the farm, go on to college and enter the Air Force, I was reluctant this time to leave hearth and home and drive south. But as shepherds say, it was time to get the flock out of there. The road from Kentucky to Tennessee ran clear and dry. Grits on Nashville's breakfast menu reminded me, I was in the south. Drove south to Tupelo, Mississippi after breakfast. From there, through Meridian, Laural and Hattiesburg. Mississippi looked almost as poor as Arkansas, but roads were paved and farms had rich black bottom land.

While Arkansas is hard scrabble and mean, Mississippi looked fat and sassy, like it was waiting for the good times to roll in. Arkansas roads were flattened red mud. The road south from Hattiesburg to Gulfport was a paved modern miracle, with limited access through forests and wetlands. Wetlands is nothing more than an environmental euphemism for swamp. Driving through southern Mississippi, I saw that most of folks were sittin' on the front porch, rocking, watching me. When the good times finally begin to roll in, Mississippi's minions were as ready as her highways.

Gulfport is a sleepy resort town, five miles wide and two miles deep, the lynch pin of Mississippi Gulf villages. To the west, Bay St. Louis, Pass Christian and Long Beach. To the east, Mississippi City, Biloxi, Edgewater, Ocean Springs and Pascagoula. All sounding like a refrain from the train station announcer on Jack Benny's radio show. Strung like an open necklace of pearls, offshore are a string of barrier islands. Beginning with Lake Borgne in Louisiana and ending at Dauphin Island south of Mobile, Alabama are Cat, Horn and Petit Islands, marking the southern boundary of Mississippi Sound and the beginning of the Gulf of Mexico.

## Biloxi, Mississippi

I continued driving south until I almost ran into the gulf and then turned east on East Beach Road. As I drove by the Friendship House my eyes focused on the loveliest lady I had ever seen, walking the beach in the evening breeze. In an instance, all thoughts of Sally vanished. I thought about stopping and chasing after her, but knew that wouldn't be a good idea. I sighed, deeply and drove on to Keesler Air Force Base. The Air Policeman at the main gate was polite and helpful, gave me directions to base housing that I could follow. I parked my car outside another World War II administration building, got out and stretched. This air patch looked a lot like Ellington Field, condemned barracks and all. I slapped my arm. Mosquitoes were small, but feisty. I waited for the desk sergeant to hang up the phone. He reminded me of Bilko when he smiled and said, "Sorry, lieutenant. There's no room at the Inn. You'll have to stay downtown. Keesler is the new electronics training center for the Air Force and we're packed with students. You wouldn't want to stay here anyway. Our buildings aren't fit for hogs. Plenty of room at the local hotels. Try the Broadwater Beach. They'll give you military rates. A friend of mine runs the bar there, Herbie. Tell him Welko says hello. He'll treat you right. Oh, you can't afford to stay there full time."

He handed me a list of apartments and underlined one of them in red, "Right behind Gus Steven's place. They rent to salesmen, strippers and military there."

I smiled, "At last, I'm out of the ordinary and into the exotic. Thanks for the help. I'll look at the Broadwater and I'll give Herbie your regards."

I wasn't the only one distracted when I drove along East Beach Road. The object of my distraction had also noticed me, but I didn't know it at the time. The lovely lady was Bobbie Jean Langtry, the one who was about to change my style of living. She strolled on sand packed firm from last night's rain. The warm winter gulf breeze blew sand across her toes and straw blonde hair into her eyes. She brushed it away from the tip of her nose and turned toward home, across the road from the beach and next door to a southern shrine, Jefferson Davis's winter home. For some reason she noticed my old four door black Buick as I drove by. She returned my wave, wondering who I was and probably answered it with, "Must be another young lieutenant reporting into Keesler by the looks of the boxes stacked in the back seat."

It had been a year to the day since Bobbie Jean's husband, Ralph, passed away from a boating accident. He was a fond memory, but she knew it was time to move on. When she crossed East Beach Road to her house, I was nothing more than an electron lingering in the recesses of her thoughts, but she was a bolt of lightning in mine.

• • •

I drove into the Broadwater's driveway, forced to chuckle to myself. The Broadwater Beach Hotel was big enough, white and well kept, but it looked like a giant dumpy white elephant sitting on a mound across the road from the beach. One glance at the rates, even reduced for me and I knew I'd have to begin an apartment search. Welko was right, "Maybe Welko's friend Herbie can give me a leg up." I stowed my luggage in the room and wandered downstairs to the bar. Two days on the road had taken their toll. My body still felt like it was in a moving car.

The Broadwater's bar adjoined the dining room. There were several patrons on stools and a dozen or so at the tables. Pretty standard, except it was a reminder of an ornate turn of the century bar, decorated in early Queen Victorian. I introduced myself to the bartender, "You must be the famous Herbie that Welko mentioned. He said to give you his best." Herbie leaned over the bar and stuck out his hand, "Glad to meet you, Johnny did you say? Are you new to the Gulf Coast?"

"Newly assigned to Keesler and looking for an apartment."

"Might be able to help you. Did Welko give you a base list?"

I handed it to him. He scanned it, "Hmm, the one underlined in red isn't for you. Unless you want strippers and their boyfriends keeping you up all night. What would you like to drink? The first one's on me."

"Might as well have a Jax. Better get familiar with the local brew. New Orleans?"

"On the river. What school are you attending at Keesler?"

"EW, Electronic Warfare. Do you know anything about it?"

"Not the school, but you must be a lieutenant."

"You guessed right. Tell me something. I'm sitting in an ornate bar, drinking beer, looking at liquor bottles with black state tax stamps on them in a dry state."

"Hope you noticed we have several carry outs, too. Our state legislature got tired of losing taxes on bootleg whiskey and decided to issue a black market stamp. Now we have a ton of money at the capitol we can't spend because it's illegal. The state is dry."

"Is it all right to ask why?"

"Too many well connected citizens here in Harrison County. Our Gulf Coast is a cash cow for the state treasury. Money is in the bank drawing interest, waiting for Mississippi to go wet. Where are you from?"

"Ohio—don't think I want another Jax."

"How about a Bud."

"One more and after that, think I'll eat dinner. How's your dining room?"

"Not bad. Pepper steak is wonderful and our fish is too."

Herbie refilled a room full of drinks and returned, turning Welko's apartment list over in his hands. He scanned it again, "None of these are for you. I have a friend who owns the best vacation apartments on the gulf. She converted her mansion's bedroom house into four one bedroom furnished apartments and refurbished the apartment over what used to be the stables. They're usually spoken for a year in advance, but she might have one open. How long will you be staying at Keesler?"

"Less than a year, probably seven months."

"When I have some free time, I'll give her a call." Herbie wrote down her name and address on a cocktail napkin, "Lady's name is Mrs. Langtry. Her husband owned this hotel. Passed away last year. She didn't need the money and the kids did, so she sold it. Watch your manners around her. She's quite a lady and a good friend."

"Langtry? That's the name of a famous singer. If she has room, I'll stop by tomorrow morning. Think I'll give that famous pepper steak you recommended a try."

• • •

The maitre d' handed me Herbie's note at breakfast. I opened it. Mrs. Langtry had an apartment open, but wanted to talk to me before making a commitment. Herbie added, "Stuck my neck out for you. Mind your manners." Knew I was in the deep south and thought, "Mrs. Langtry must be a grand southern dame, celebrating her sunset years." I ordered bacon, eggs and toast. Filling half the Broadwater's ornate plate were grits and more grits, whipped high, like a pile of mashed potatoes. Looked good, tasted neutral, which means they were the best I've ever had. I didn't check out of the hotel, but at thirty dollars a day, I could only spend another night on lieutenant's pay.

When I stopped at Keesler's Main gate to ask directions, the Air Policeman manning the gate was as good as the one who helped yesterday. I found the EW school admin. building on my first try. The only one around was the clerk typist, "Your training isn't scheduled to begin until January 9, but don't worry. You won't be idle. Our commandant has farmed you out to the Technical Training Wing. Report over there at eight in the morning, day after New Year's Day."

"What are they going to do with us?"

"You'll assist them with their military training."

"Can you tell me what an EW is?"

"Not supposed to, but you train on the ground and in the air. Everything around here is secret."

"Are there any officers running the school?"

"Yes, but you won't find them here."

"Where are they?"

"Not allowed to tell you where or what they're doing, but they're not working for Uncle Sam."

I walked out the door, hoping that someone at Technical Training Wing could tell me what EWs do.

So far so good, didn't know what an EW was, but no one seemed concerned. I returned the air policeman's salute as I drove out through the main gate, "Everyone seems friendly here. The assignment shouldn't be too bad, even if I don't know what I'm doing." I drove west on East Beach Road with one eye out for the apartments Herbie touted. I passed two carryout liquor stores, several bars and Gus Steven's strip joint. The marquee advertised:

*Bonnie the Body Beautiful*

This strip joint looked clean. As a matter of fact the entire Gulf Coast was well groomed, "Sheriff must keep tight control here. Can't believe the prices. Have to be twenty-five percent lower than Texas. Gus Steven's, that's the place Welko mentioned and Herbie said not to rent an apartment. I slowed down when I saw the Friendship House restaurant and turned right, into the driveway of Mrs. Langtry's apartments. I scanned the area, "This is close to where I saw that good looking lady yesterday. Wonder if she rents here?" Mrs. Langtry's home was in front of the apartments. Wasn't a mansion with pillars. Looked like a brand new modern ranch style home.

I rang the bell and the vision I saw on the beach opened the door, "Herbie didn't tell me that you were so young."

Bobbie Jean laughed, "You were expecting a mature southern lady."

Our eyes locked and that spark I had been waiting for all of these years flew into my brain and short circuited my thought process. I was speechless, but Bobbie Jean motioned for me to come inside and my tongue untied, halfway, "Herbie didn't tell me you were so beautiful. And young, why you're younger than I am. I'm sorry. I don't think that came out right."

Bobbie Jean laughed and her eyes lit up, "You must be the lieutenant Herbie called about."

"I'm Johnny Ropp and I'm standing here like a fool with my mouth open when I came to buy your apartment. There I go again, I mean rent."

She stared deep, deep into my eyes and smiled, "I'm sorry, what did you say your first name is?"

"Johnny, Johnny Ropp."

"Well, Johnny, I don't normally rent to strangers or military, but I rented to a military couple recently. Newlyweds live in the bedroom house, turned out quite well. Most of my winter guest are from up north and the summer ones are from New Orleans. However, you are in luck. One of my winter tenants was in an auto accident in Iowa during the Christmas storm. They won't be able to come this year. I have a large one bedroom apartment over the garage that you might find suitable. Are you interested?"

I breathed a sigh of relief. I had passed the first test, "Yes ma'am."

"Follow me." Bobbie Jean led me around a large ante-bellum building at the rear of her home, "This bedroom house was built at least twenty years before the War of Northern Aggression. It originally had eight bedrooms. My mother converted it into four apartments after the hurricane took down the mansion out front. She lost interest after Daddy died. I added a fifth apartment over the livery stable. It's now a five car garage with storage and laundry room."

"Did you build the house out front?"

"Yes. I lived in it when I met Ralph. Rather proud of it. Designed it when I was sixteen. I had to have a place to get away from Mother. Our family home is outside of Jackson. My great great grandfather built this place to winter in before the War of Northern Aggression."

I didn't rise to her bait. I didn't want to lose a beginning friendship and an apartment at the same time. I asked, "How much land do you have?"

"I really don't know. My family has several large plantations and I have my own holdings." She blushed, "You meant around here. Six hundred or so acres out back, but it's mostly swamp and trees. Don't go tramping around back there. We do have snakes."

We climbed the outside stairs of the livery stable and Bobbie Jean unlocked the door, "Completely furnished with dishes, silverware and cooking utensils. There is a sitting room, one bedroom, dining area and kitchen. You won't need linen. I'll have my maid stock the place."

I looked around. It was better than most of the homes I'd visited. Herbie was right. This was the best place to live on the Gulf Coast. I turned and bumped into Bobbie Jean, "Sorry, I should watch where I'm going. Do the ceiling fans work?"

"Best ones ever made. They were in the Broadwater before I installed air conditioning there."

"I'll take it. Do you mind if I move in today?"

"Rent is eighty dollars a month and that includes electricity, water and gas."

"Who do I make the check out to?"

"Langtry Enterprises. Remember, this is a quiet place. When you have guests, make sure they mind their manners."

"Yes ma'am. I've said more yes ma'ams than I've said since grade school. I want to apologize up front. You can't help it if you're drop dead gorgeous. I shouldn't be standing around with my tongue tied in knots. It's impolite."

Bobbie Jean had that southern flair. She just smiled at my awkwardness, "I've had enough ma'ams, too. I'm not a grand dame, why I'm barely twenty-one years old. You may call me Bobbie Jean, and is Johnny all right for you?"

All right? She could have called me a dirt bag, anything and I could have cared less. With foot in mouth I said, "Yes ma'am. There I go again."

"Do you have a household shipment on the way?"

"Everything I own is in the back of my Buick or at your hotel. Do you mind if I move in this morning?"

I handed her the check, careful not to hold her hand, which was foremost on my mind. Bobbie Jean smiled, "An Ohio bank. My great grandfather had his leg saved by a Yankee surgeon from your state, outside of Atlanta, when that butcher Sherman burned his way to the sea. I wonder? Move in when you want. Stop by for the key when you return."

I smiled, "My great grandfather was a surgeon with Sherman on his march through Georgia. Claimed the confederate medal he had was given to him by a Reb officer for saving his leg. Didn't saw it off. We may have more in common than you think."

Bobbie Jean gave me a hug, "Why I believe there may be such a thing as a good Yankee. Wait till I tell Mother." She kissed me on the cheek and walked quickly back toward her house. I stood there, like your average sod buster, with my mouth open.

• • •

I looked around my new home and then out the window. Pine forest to the rear, crushed stone driveway to the front. Hurricane must have taken all the big trees down in the front yard, along with the mansion. There were only two left between my place and the bedroom house. I sighed as Bobbie Jean disappeared around the corner of her apartment building. Then laughed at myself. I hadn't been this tongue tied since my first date in junior high. I wanted to ask her if every lady in the south had two names and remembered Oscar D.'s response to the same question and thought better of it. Bobbie Jean had raised more than a few questions for me to ponder over. When our eyes met, an electrical spark was created that almost dropped me to my knees.

I sat down in the easy chair and placed my feet up on the ottoman. Sally was different. Four inches shorter than me and more than ample on top. I'll have to flat out say it, Sally was well stacked. Not that I was all that concerned with ladies' breasts. When you grow up on a farm, if a cow's udder is overly large, you have to worry about them stepping on their teats. Bobbie Jean was my height. Maybe that was the reason our eyes met and locked. What knocks me out is a lady with a complete package, well proportioned, thin enough, but not so bones stuck out. And that describes Bobbie Jean. Face and eyes made the difference, body was well toned, a smile, and those eyes. That had to be it. Sally and Bobbie Jean both had it. And Bobbie Jean had an aura about her. Twenty-one and already a widow? Rich—so she couldn't have time to attend college. Intelligent, good looking, a sense of humor and the sparks flew. My brain had turned to mush. All my defenses were down. I wondered, "Does this happen to everybody. Am I the only romantic in the world? But more important, does Bobbie Jean feel the same way I do? Can't find out sittin' here. Better get a move on to the Broadwater and pick up my stuff. The keys? Bobbie Jean could have handed them to me earlier. I wonder?"

• • •

I shouldn't have worried. Found out later that Bobbie Jean's heart was pounding, too. Back in her kitchen, she made a pot of tea and scolded herself, "Bobbie Jean! Under normal circumstances you'd never rent to a bachelor, or military, and a Damn-Yankee?"

"I didn't check his credit. I will, but not for money. I want to know more about him. Many a married man runs around pretending he's single. Now I remember, his car, he's the young man I waved to yesterday as I returned from my walk. But why am I renting to an unmarried man and one so close to my age? Is it because most of the young men around here are in love with themselves or all ready married? I wonder if he felt the electricity I felt when our eyes met? Bobbie Jean stop that. You are acting like a school girl. You haven't had one date since Ralph passed away and the passes started at his funeral. Men! Bobbie Jean, you are a mess."

"Johnny will have to stop by for his keys. I should have given them to him. I better change out of these jeans. He'll be back soon. Oh fuss and feathers, I'll invite him to dinner. Come on girl, get back in the swing. Don't let this one get away."

• • •

I pulled up to the outside stairway and opened the trunk of my car. As I reached over to pull out the first box, a presence of a warm fragrant breeze enveloped me. I turned around and saw a pair of well shaped feet in summer sandals. Then up into Bobbie Jean's eyes and it happened again. She looked flustered, "You forgot to stop by for your key."

"Not really. I wanted to clean up first. I left the door open—unlocked."

"We were so busy talking about ancestors, I forgot to tell you about the deposit. A month's rent in advance."

"I'll write the check out as soon as I carry this box upstairs."

"Oh, you won't need to. Why don't you bring it over this evening. We'll have dinner together, if you don't have plans."

"If I did, I'd cancel them. I was about to ask you out, but my brain is tied up in knots. What time?"

"We'll have cocktails on the verandah at five. Don't bring a thing."

I felt color rise in my cheeks and noticed that it was happening to her, too, "Seems very warm outside today." She gave me her best southern smile.

An ethereal vision in winter white opened Bobbie Jean's front door, escorted me in and linked her arm in mine. I brought forward a bouquet of flowers I had hidden behind my back with a bow and flourish. Bobbie Jean giggled, "Your mother trained you well."

"Mother's a midwestern school teacher and doesn't have much time for romantic foolishness. You may credit it to too many lonely nights at Saturday movies."

"Rhett would be proud. While I put these in a vase," and she pointed at the verandah, "you can pour us a glass of wine."

"White?"

"My favorite."

"I'll have red. It's not Chianti. What is it?"

"French, an exquisite little Medoc."

I knew when I was overmatched. I opened both bottles and filled two glasses as Bobbie Jean set my flowers on her table and said, "Do you mind if we dine out on the verandah. Most of the year it's so warm here. Tonight it is perfect."

"And it's not just the weather."

"Why Rhett dear, you do carry on so. Makes my little heart flutter?"

"I hope so. It would be a perfect match for mine. Did I use the wrong wine glasses?"

"Yes, dear. You need training. I'll take care of that."

Bobbie Jean looked me over, up and down, a lioness licking its lips at prey, ascertaining if she had selected the right antelope for dinner. I hoped so, I had on my best midwestern serious dating clothes, khaki pants, dark blue sport coat and regimental tie.

I raised my glass, "To the prettiest lady on the Gulf Coast."

She blushed and changed the subject, "Before you ask. I really am twenty-one and a widow. Ralph, my late husband died in a boating accident last year. It was unexpected and tragic, but life must go on. You're the first boy I've been out with in over a year."

"I wouldn't count a quiet dinner at home as going out on a date."

"You really don't know anything about the south, do you? This is more serious than going out. Dinner at home is the final step in courtship."

It took all of my strength not to mention eating dessert first, but it wasn't proper.

Bobbie Jean gave me a dig to the ribs and smiled. We were on the same wavelength. She asked softly, "Would you care for another glass of wine?"

I nodded, "Yes."

She motioned for me to sit in the swing. As I toasted her beauty with my eyes, Bobbie Jean sat down beside me and linked her arm in mine. We both shivered and laughed, as we looked out on a glorious winter gulf sunset. I couldn't remember ever being this excited and happy. She leaned her head on my shoulder, I could resist no longer. I turned and kissed her lightly on the lips. She pulled my head closer and our kiss turned into passion. Bobbie Jean slowly moved her lips away, reached down and held my hands, "Johnny, if I don't put dinner in the oven, we'll never eat tonight."

"What did you prepare?"

"A little Italian . . ." She stopped, "Johnny, why are you smiling like a Cheshire-Cat?"

"Nothing important—I was thinking of an old flame when you mentioned a little Italian."

"Are you engaged?" she asked me.

"Don't worry, it's over. We parted friends. One look at you and her memory has been erased from my mind forever."

"I just knew you would have a lady friend."

"No longer, it's in the past. What is our main course?"

"Veal Marsala."

She stood up and I followed at her side. I took her hands in mine. We kissed lightly and I felt her body relax—passion began. She looked deep into my eyes, "I know, it's too soon, but . . ."

She put her finger to my lips, "I feel the same way, but it is too soon." She turned away and walked to the kitchen. I stood in front of the verandah window, looking out over surf lit by sunset's afterglow, beads of sweat dripping down from my temples. Bobbie Jean called out, "Bring our wine glasses to the kitchen. You can keep me company while I cook. I want to know all about your family."

"Don't you want to know about me?"

"If I know your family, I'll know you."

"We have a family farm, several thousand acres along the Scioto River north of Columbus, Ohio. Been in our family since the Revolutionary War. Mother and Father are teachers. We're United Brethren by faith and liberal by practice. I graduated with a degree in American Literature from Ohio State. All in all, we're pretty ordinary. You've packed a lot of living into twenty-one years."

"I was married at twenty. Two years at our local finishing school in Gulfport. I have been running either my family's business or my husband's hotel since I was fourteen. My college of hard knocks leaves very little time for books."

"A real live Miss Scarlet."

She nudged me with her elbow, "Help me carry dinner to the verandah."

After dinner, we lingered outdoors sipping coffee and wine at the table. Bobbie Jean asked, "Do you know that damn senator from Tennessee?"

"Gore?"

"No, Kefaufer. Don't ever try to say a kind word about Estes on the Gulf Coast. Most of our hotels are still recovering after he closed gambling down here. Took a few years, but the Broadwater was finally showing a nice profit when I sold it last summer. Ralph had children from his first marriage, but they weren't interested in the hotel business and I certainly wasn't. Let's take our coffee to the swing. I'm sorry, I get upset just thinking about that damn Tennessee senator."

We spent the rest of the evening searching for a common ground to cement a budding relationship, but a search wasn't necessary. The electric spark had all ready ignited a flame far beyond our control. When the clock struck ten I knew it was time to go, or I might never. It was as if we had been matched by fate. We embraced and agreed to be together to celebrate New Year's. Bobbie Jean took control, "You'll be my guest at the Broadwater. Will you join me for breakfast? Is nine to early?"

"Do I have to leave?"

"An old southern custom and good manners says yes."

• • •

I walked back to my apartment on air. My feet barely touching the ground. I turned to see if Bobbie Jean was watching. She was, from her back porch. I waved and she smiled. I hoped her inner self knew that I was her future. Mine did. I was tempted to call when I climbed the stairs. And I would have, but my phone was not installed. She pulled strings and had a phone installed after our first breakfast and she made sure my apartment met with her approval. After I was settled in, Bobbie Jean took me on a cook's tour of all of the geographical highlights along the Gulf Coast from the shrimp fleet at Biloxi to her fishing cottage along the river, inland. An octagon one room affair, it was built on a boardwalk out over the water with windows that hinged upward for fishing. Though only one room, her little cottage could hold as many people as a good sized parlor. After the first of the year, when I had to return to Air Force life, I didn't want too. Talk about finding true love in strange places. The Broadwater bartender, Herbie, was going to be my friend for life.

• • •

I was a reluctant soldier when the second of January came around. I made my own breakfast and was away before dawn. I met my new partner in military discipline and training, a fellow EW classmate. Oliver T., an unreformed surfer from southern California loved to march, unlike his web footed friends, and wallowed in military life. After our first meeting, I knew why. One too many wipeouts over a rocky shore under erratic surf had left an imprint on his skull. A newly minted gold bar lieutenant from Aviation Cadets, Oliver T. reported in early. Unlike me, he followed Welko's advice and rented an apartment behind Gus Steven's. T. was chomping at the bit to give his new found authority a baptism. However, Oliver T. was in the rear of our marching formation. I was out front, leading one of the many massed electronic squadrons on parade. I was not a happy camper, "Marching at electronics school is like diving into an empty pool—unnecessary and downright foolish."

Being off center helped T., "We got two types of folks in charge here, pilots and ground-pounders. Neither of which knows an electron from a goat. Pilots think electronics is for fools and our ground pounders think with their feet. Neither group can compete on a technical playing field. So in order to take control, they resort to a military mind set. Therefore, *we march because we are.*"

"When training begins, that'll be the end of this nonsense for us, but not for the enlisted trainees. There ought to be a better way."

*"Would you tell me please, which way I ought to go from here?" said Alice.*
*"That depends a good deal on where you want to get to," said the Cheshire Cat.*

# Chapter 6

Oliver T.'s enthusiasm for marching didn't carry over to inspecting barracks. He wasn't alone, I considered these inspections beyond the pale. Bein' clean I could understand, but Keesler's training folks took it one step beyond, with Saturday night scrubbing parties. As a result, barracks floors were reduced to splinters with the middle of the floors two inches lower than at the walls. "T., I have never seen a more destructive, make work punishment."

"Looks like they'll have to install new floors."

"Right, we better call the inspection off and talk to the Commandant."

Oliver T. stopped at the door, "Wouldn't do that if I were you."

"T., they better install new floors or someone will stick a leg right through one of these upper floors."

"Its been goin' on since 1941."

"The officers in charge of this school can't be too bright. No one in their right mind would scrub a floor to splinters. Can't put me on report for telling the truth."

After I had my say, I was immediately relieved of military duties with the Tech Training Wing. Oliver T. stayed on. We met again outside of EW school admin., two days before class began. T pulled me aside, "Where have you been' hiding? Did you see the new flooring stacked by the barracks?"

"Haven't been around. While you were marching, I helped Bobbie Jean paint her apartments."

"After you left, the Commandant fell right through the second floor of the barracks we inspected and broke both his legs."

• • •

Electronic Warfare school began without the fanfare we enjoyed at Nav training. We were ready, but no one gave us the opportunity to acquaint the powers that be on the proper use of a baseball bat. Split into two Flights, morning and afternoon, Oliver T. and me drew the morning class. Other than the clerk, the administration building was still empty. Someone had to ask the remaining sergeant and this time it was Oliver T.'s turn, "We have civilian instructors and you. Isn't anyone in charge here?"

The school sergeant replied, "I am."

"Where is the commander?"

"Don't ask."

"I just did."

"I just answered." The mystery remained, but our mystery about what an EW is, was answered.

"T, we're being trained to operate electronic equipment in the bomb bay of a B-47 or upper deck of a B-52. I thought we were going to be in charge of radar sites."

Oliver T. was not happy, "And a waste of time if you ask me. Have to go through another beginning electronics class and we're stuck in classes that begin at six in the morning. God is getting even with me for living in an apartment in paradise. Parties don't end until two in the morning. We can't switch classes, there's no one around to talk too except the school sergeant, and he won't give us the time of day. I bet you a beer you can't find a single officer in our admin. section and if there are any, you can't find out where they're hiding."

I couldn't duck a challenge. Bobbie Jean was visiting her mother in Jackson, so I had time for a beer.

I collared Oliver T. before class the next morning, "That was a sucker bet. I still couldn't find anyone, but our school sergeant in admin. However, I did find out where the officers are, so you owe me a beer."

"Not until you tell me where they're hidin'."

"See that smoke in the trees out past the end of the runway?"

"Don't tell me. Our bosses are running a moonshine still on federal property?"

"Don't order anything stiffer than wine downtown. If you do, there is a good chance you might go blind."

"How about Gus Steven's and the resort hotels?"

"Bobbie Jean is coming back from Jackson this afternoon. She knows who's buying what on the strip. I'll ask her."

• • •

It was a better dream than usual during my early afternoon nap after class. Getting up at five had taken a toll. Then, I felt the warm breath of someone near and dear. And then I felt two soft lips kiss me on my cheek. This was too good to be a dream. My eyes opened, Bobbie Jean was leaning over the edge of my bed, "Are you playing Rip Van Winkle?"

"I've been trying to get you in bed for over a month and you decide to come on your own."

"Just got back. When you didn't answer your phone, I decided to check on you. I was worried that you were either dead or someone had taken my place."

"Will never happen. How is your mother?"

"Feisty as ever. Still attempting to run my life."

"Did you tell her about me?"

"Yes."

"What did she say?"

"After she recovered, something like, 'A Yankee! A damn Yankee! Bobbie Jean, how could you? A Yankee? Over my dead body!'"

"I take it she's not keen on me coming up for a visit."

"Not now, but she'll come around sooner or later."

"Sounds like later."

"Anything happen while I was away?"

"As far as I'm concerned, nothing will ever happen when you're away. Say, what do you know about a moonshine still operating at the end of Keesler's runaway?"

"Nothing. Is it on federal property?"

"Certain it is, looks like it's in swamp and trees. Our school commanders are running it."

"Don't think our local cartel will appreciate that. First bad batch and they're history."

I reached over and took Bobbie Jean's hands, "I like the appetizer. Let's skip the main course and go right to dessert."

"You may be a Yankee, but you do have southern ways."

"There's an old saying, 'Life is short. Eat dessert first.'"

"Not now my Yankee soldier, you're still in the deep south and we have rules about courting."

• • •

My worst fears came to pass during the third week of basic electronics. I passed the electronics theory test and was faced with hands-on training in a lab. "T, this doesn't bode well for me."

"Not to worry, I'm your lab partner—I'll pull you through. We'll do just fine."

"Like I said, I'm in trouble."

Now I had two worries—electronics lab and Oliver T. Drawing Oliver T. out of a hat meant never being able to train on our lab equipment. Oliver T. wasn't a complete flake. As a matter of fact he was on the borderline of electronic genius. However, this expertise turned out to be our downfall. He dismantled our lab equipment and began to build an FM radio.

He did his best to reassure me, "Any fool can do a simple experiment. If you really want to learn electronics, watch while I build another modern electronic miracle."

"I'd feel better if we had an FM station."

And watch was all I could do. T. reduced our equipment to wires and tubes scattered around the work bench. While the rest of the Flight adjusted vacuum tube, plates and grids, I watched as Oliver T. assembled his FM radio from the parts he dismantled. Turned out to be a better show than a three ring circus. Wires were wrapped around magnets, crossing over and under a sheet metal base. Tubes were catty-wampus, tying resistors, capacitors, switches, in parallel and in-line. Two days before we were to take our laboratory exam, Oliver T. asked our Flight to gather around his experiment.

As he pulled the cover off of his electronic miracle, T began, "Listen up my fellow funny wings. What we have here is the latest miracle in hi-fi FM radio. You'll hear sounds you've never heard before. Watch and learn as I dazzle you with the finest receiver ever found in this part of the great state of Mississippi."

We watched as Oliver T. turned knobs, threw switches and fluttered about like a wounded butterfly. But all we heard was the sound of silence. T.'s smile turned to a frown. He kicked the corner of the work bench and then it began, first as a low moan— he tweaked his knobs and a low moan became a loud whistle. It grew in volume, until its squeal sounded like a thousand pigs being run over by a semi trailer truck. Oliver T.'s FM radio's output became unbearable. We covered our ears, but should have covered our eyes from the blinding white flash, followed by a cloud of black acrid smoke. Oliver T., covered with soot from head to foot, stood dazed next to his experiment, a pile of smoldering melted metal, while we bolted for the door. In the distance the sound of sirens drew closer and closer.

T came outside, brushing soot out of his eyes and hair, "How about that? Something else wasn't it?"

I had to laugh, "You were right about one thing."

"What?"

"I've never heard a sound like that before in my life."

As we waited for the fire engines to leave, the school sergeant walked up. "You guys stepped in it. Commandant wants to see both of you in his office, pronto."

As he walked away Oscar T smiled, "Hey, there's always a bright side. We'll finally meet a live officer in the admin. building."

Oliver T. had delivered the mother of straight lines. I couldn't resist, "That's another fine mess you've gotten me into, Ollie."

T looked at me with a laconic smile, "Funny, damned funny. We better get it over with. What do you think he'll do to us."

"At worst, we're on our way to supply school. Which may be a blessing, seeing were facing an assignment in the belly of a B-47. And at best, a tongue lashing."

• • •

The desk sergeant motioned with his head for us to go in. The commandant stood behind his desk, a mousy major wearing radiator wings. Our Nav school commandant was right, pilots were in charge of everything in the Air Force. We saluted and stood before him at attention. He looked us up and down, obviously bothered by being here and not at his business, "I don't know which one of you two is at fault, so I'm going to assume it's both of you."

He looked closely at Oliver T., "Lieutenant Tugwattle, haven't I met you on the strip. Outside of Gus Steven's wasn't it?"

"Yes, sir. You had a load of clear liquid jugs on the back of your truck."

The major turned bleach white and his left eye began to twitch. He collapsed into his chair and rummaged in his desk drawer for a pencil. After placing it on the front edge, to separate us from him, the color returned, but the twitch was worse, "You are washed back to the following afternoon class. You'll DIA your lab and Tugwattle?"

"Yes, sir."

"Stay out of trouble downtown."

I had to hand it to Oliver T., "You saved us with that moonshine bit. Is it true?"

"Don't know. Just guessed and got lucky. Some kind of punishment. We get afternoon class from noon to six and another three weeks of living on the beach. What the hell is DIA?"

"I thought it might be Defense Inertia Agency, "Think it's pilot talk for do it again. Time to break our team up if we want to pass. Why don't you work on your radios at home?"

"Don't have time—what with my engagement and all."

"Engagement? Who to?"

"Bonnie The Body Beautiful. You and Bobbie Jean have got to meet her. She's quite a lady."

• • •

I confided to Bobbie Jean, telling her of my new circumstance, "I'm really embarrassed. We're the first two to ever wash back before taking an exam. Won't happen again. Oliver T. won't have time. He's engaged."

"Who to?"

"A stripper, Bonnie The Body Beautiful. T. spends all of his free time warding off her suitors."

"I have to meet this Oliver T., he sounds interesting. He must be a real flake."

"Not sure I want you to meet the friends I attract. Remember, he is a surfer from LA."

"I know Bonnie. She has a good head on her shoulders. Everyone needs a flake or two in their life or this world would be very dull indeed."

I let it drop, but wondered how Bobbie Jean knew Bonnie.

• • •

Met up with Oliver T. at our new lab class the following afternoon. He had forgotten about our falling out over not being lab partners. T was not one to look back, "You and Bobbie Jean have got to meet Bonnie. She is wonderful. We can surprise her tonight at Gus Steven's."

"Is Bonnie still the headliner at Gus's?"

"She is and does she ever live up to her billing! I won't take no for an answer. The table will be in my name."

"Bobbie Jean wants to meet you and she knows Bonnie. What time?"

"How about seven?"

"Unless Bobbie Jean has a commitment, we'll be there." When we entered our afternoon class, our new Flight treated us like heroes returning from a distant war. I phoned Bobbie Jean at first break and told her of T.'s invitation. Again, I was surprised by her response, "I'm delighted, Johnny. Seven will be fine. Gus is an old friend. I haven't seen him in a long time."

I decided it was better to ask my twenty-four dollar question over the phone, "Where did you meet Bonnie?"

"I was wondering when you would ask. She performed at our hotel when Gus managed the showroom. This is a very small town. I'm an investor in Gus's Club."

"You are full of surprises. We'll meet at the dock after my last class. I'll be there by five-thirty."

"Thought your class wasn't out until six."

"Our instructor cuts the afternoon class short."

"We'll go to the dock for shrimp, but pick me up at home."

"Southern manners?"

"Why, of course."

• • •

Shrimp was out of this world, cooked right off the boat. Two dollars bought three pounds. Bobbie Jean made our own shrimp sauce at the stand.

I whispered, "Does the owner mind?"

She whispered back, "No, he's been trying to steal it from me for three years. I bring my own premixed spices. He'll never be able to duplicate it."

Later when Bobbie Jean entered Gus Steven's, it was like Moses parting the Red Sea. Oliver T.'s table was not good enough. Gus escorted us to a ringside seat, "Bobbie Jean! Its been a long time. You haven't been here since Ralph passed away."

"No need to. You run an honest place and give an honest count."

"You remember Bonnie from the Broadwater Showroom. She is packing customers in."

Bobbie Jean took my arm, "Gus, meet my new beau, Lieutenant Johnny Ropp."

Gus's eyes popped wide open. He stood there speechless and then offered his hand, "Never thought I'd see the day when Bobbie Jean would be out with a new beau. How long has it been?"

"Over a year?"

"It's time, a year is long enough. Son, you should feel honored."

Gus rushed away, beet red. Bobbie Jean squeezed my arm, "Gus and Ralph were very close. He still blames himself for Ralph's death. Gus believes if he had been driving the boat, Ralph would still be here. Gus had an emergency at home. It will take my friends quite awhile to adjust to us as a pair."

"Longer than your mother?"

"Hush now. What is—is that your friend Oliver T. coming this way?"

"That's him."

Oliver T. pulled up a chair, "Hey Johnny, this must be Bobbie Jean. You're just in time. Bonnie will be on in five minutes. How do you like my table? Right up front."

Bobbie Jean was a sea of tranquillity in the midst of T's turbulent storm, "I'm so pleased to meet you, Lieutenant Tugwattle. Do you mind if I call you by your first name?"

"Please do. There's the drum roll, Bonnie's on."

Bobbie Jean squeezed my hand, "Your mouth is hanging open, soldier."

"I haven't seen anything like this since I went to a burlesque theater in Kansas City. And none of those ladies looked anywhere near as good as Bonnie. She does have a beautiful body."

Oliver T. was all smiles, "Isn't she somethin'. We're getting married a week from Saturday at the Roosevelt Hotel in New Orleans. We want you to stand up for us."

I looked over at Bobbie Jean and back to Oliver T., "Isn't this too soon. You're barely a brown bar lieutenant, fresh out of Aviation Cadets."

"You're right, I have a lost year to make up."

Bobbie Jean smiled, "If you will excuse me for a moment, I need to powder my nose. When I return we'll give you our answer."

I watched Bobbie Jean out of the corner of my eye. She stopped on her way to the ladies room and spoke with Gus. When she returned, Bonnie had arrived a our table. Bobbie Jean hugged Bonnie, "Your beau, Oliver, asked us to stand up for you at your wedding in New Orleans. Johnny and I will be honored to be there."

On the dance floor she whispered into my ear, "Gus speaks highly of Bonnie. She doesn't mess around and she's never been married before. But, and this is a big but, Gus is not sure about your friend, Lieutenant Tugwattle. He thinks Oliver is a flake. I've seen matches made in heaven that wind up on the rocks and ones made on the spur of the moment that last a life time. One never knows."

I nodded, "Yes, but three weeks of dating is shorter than most state's waiting periods. Are you ready to leave?"

"Let's stop by the Broadwater and visit with Herbie. He makes a great cup of Irish coffee."

"And he's a great matchmaker."

• • •

On our drive to the Broadwater, Bobbie Jean sat quietly, withdrawn. I knew enough about ladies to keep my mouth shut. As we entered the hotel, she broke her silence, "My first night out on the town since Ralph passed away and I agree to go to Gus Steven's."

"Can't be a problem, you own a piece of it."

"My minister was sitting at the table behind us. He doesn't know I'm a part owner. You and I are going to church this Sunday."

"I wouldn't worry if I were you. He'll have more to explain than you—why he was there."

She looked into my eyes and smiled, "I didn't think of his being at a strip bar, I was only thinking of myself."

We strolled into the Broadwater bar, arm in arm, back on track. We stood at the bar, "Herbie, remember Lieutenant Johnny Ropp?"

Herbie's grin grew wider, "Of course and it looks like you two are beginning to know each other. Two Irish coffees on the house?"

Bobbie Jean blushed, "Cajun style?"

"Of course. Gus called. He wants you to give him a ring."

She squeezed my hand, "I'll be right back."

Herbie carried our drinks to a window table overlooking the moonlit gulf, "Be a full moon next week. You certainly are a fast worker. After Ralph died, Bobbie Jean would have nothing to do with our local boys. You're a lucky man."

Bobbie Jean returned with a wider than normal smile, "Gus rarely calls. He forgot to mention Lieutenant Tugwattle is carrying."

"Carrying what?"

"A standard police 38. Better hope Tugwattle isn't the jealous type. Bonnie has more than a few admirers. Gus is afraid there'll be fireworks."

"With Oliver T. that's not a probability, it's a guarantee. You do love to call Oliver T., Lieutenant Tugwattle, don't you?"

Bobbie Jean laughed, "I do, it has a certain ring to it. Doesn't Herbie make the best Irish coffee in the world?"

"What's the unusual taste?"

"Herbie's own secret blend of chicory. Let's take a walk on the beach before we turn in. Mustn't waste this southern moon."

• • •

An almost full, wolf moon, cast our elongated shadows across white Gulf Coast sands as we walked hand in hand, arm in arm and then closer than the law should allow. The warmth of our bodies, pressed together almost as one, spoke more than words would ever do. Neither of us would break apart alone, but together we did. As we turned to walk across the sand to Bobbie Jean's house, our lips met gently, lingered, then our bodies touched briefly and parted. Bobbie Jean took my hand in hers and held it tightly until we were at her front door. Bobbie Jean looked into my eyes and drew my head toward hers. Our lips again met with rising passion. She pushed me away gently, "I feel like a school girl. Touch my cheek."

"You're burning up. Do you feel all right?"

"Yes, I feel wonderful, wonderful. But I must have time, time to think. We'll talk tomorrow. Wake me, it's your turn to cook breakfast for me."

"Here?"

"No, silly. I'll come over to your place. Now give your best girl a kiss and hurry on home."

The phone was ringing, "It must be Bobbie Jean." I ran up the stairs, but I was too late. It stopped as I opened the door. I wondered, "Should I call?" and thought better of it. I must respect her wishes if I was to play her game.

Bobbie Jean controlled the playing field, but I still wanted to call. I sat by my window, watching the moon rise over her giant magnolia. My cheeks were warm, too. My thoughts only of Bobbie Jean with her soft caresses and winning smile, "If I want to win at her game, I better play by the rules." I turned down my bed, but sleep did not come. I tossed and turned, and tried to remember Sally, but she was only a lingering vision in my memory. I wondered what she looked like, but could not remember the details of her face. Like all things past, my memory of her was gone. Bobbie Jean had erased all lingering thoughts of her.

• • •

I woke with a winter sun in my eyes, still remembering Bobbie Jean's last embrace. Mississippi's early February sky, swept clear of clouds, glittered brightly as a crystal prism. I tried to shut off the alarm, but the ringing continued. I picked up the phone and was disappointed. It was Oliver T., not Bobbie Jean, "Where were you last night when I needed you?"

"I was climbing the stairs when the phone stopped ringing."

"Get your butt out of bed and put the coffee on—I'm comin' over. Need your advice about something personal."

"Give me time to take a shower. I just woke up." I filled a deep pan half way with water, brought it to a boil and dumped in course coffee grounds, turned the temperature down to a slow boil and headed to the shower. When I returned, my shepherd's coffee was done. I poured it through a strainer into my large thresher pot. The one my grandmother willed to me with a note, "You always sneaked coffee from this pot at threshing. Remember to always use fresh grounds." And I thought she hadn't noticed. I phoned Bobbie Jean. Her line was busy. I checked the clock. I had time to start a load of wash before Oliver T. arrived.

T. drove up as I was closing the lid and turning on the water. I took one look at his car and covered my eyes, "What the hell is that?"

"Like it? Not many Packard Caribbean convertibles left."

"And darn few painted bright psychedelic pink with a matching top. I can see why there aren't any around. Had to cover my eyes so I wouldn't go blind. When did you purchase your rolling representation of abstract art."

"Didn't. Belongs to Bonnie. Can only stay for a few minutes. Bonnie wants to drive to New Orleans and make arrangements for our wedding."

"I made coffee like you asked. Come on upstairs and we'll talk."

"Just one cup—Bonnie is dressing." Oliver T. followed me up the stairs, pissing and moaning with each step, "One of Bonnie's admirers followed Bonnie home. Got overly excited when I told him to leave. Tried to grab her, so I pulled my gun. One shot at a drunks feet sure sobers 'im up. Law took me in for firing a weapon. I had one phone call, you're the only one I could trust. Turned out okay, though."

"What happened? Who saved you?"

"Dead luck and a forgiving sheriff. He took one look at the guy who pressed charges, locked him up and set me free."

"What do you need from me this morning?"

"Coffee first, need something to mix with all the beer I drank last night. Do you have any aspirin?"

Oliver T. gulped two aspirin down with his first swallow of coffee, "Not bad. Mighty fine cup of coffee. Anything special?"

"Learned to make it over an open fire tending sheep. Boil it in an open pan and filter out the grounds."

"Bonnie wants to know if you and Bobble Jean both meant it when you said you'd stand up for us at our wedding."

"I haven't known Bobbie Jean for very long, but when she says she'll do something, she does. Of course we'll stand up for you. How did you meet Bonnie?"

"She lives in the next apartment."

"A lot of that going around lately."

"Thanks for your help and that really is a good cup of coffee. Got to get going. Our appointment is at noon, sharp."

• • •

As I watched Oliver T. drive off, all I could think of was Uncle Remus and his fable about a tar baby. Seemed like everything Oliver T. touched turned sticky. I phoned Bobbie Jean, "You up?" Which of course she was. "Coffee's ready."

"Give me ten more minutes and I'll be over." I carried a second load of laundry down the steps and almost dropped the whole thing. Bobbie Jean came around the corner of her apartment building in short, short denim cut offs. She kissed me on the cheek, "I don't wash clothes or windows but I'll watch you. Have you learned to separate whites from colors?"

"By trial and error." I loaded the first batch into the dryer and turned on water for the second load, "Did you see the psychedelic cloud in your driveway?"

"Wasn't that a brightest pink? Was Lieutenant Tugwattle driving or floating?"

"Bonnie wanted to make sure you meant it when you said we'll stand up for them. I said yes."

"How about your coffee?"

"I'll follow you up the stairs. You sure put new meaning to short shorts."

"Do you think they're too short? I'll change."

"I'm admiring the view."

I poured coffee and Bobbie Jean took a sip, "Not bad for a Yankee. Could use just a touch of chicory."

"That's an art form I'm not familiar with."

"I'll be your teacher."

"I certainly hope so."

"Where is Lieutenant Tugwattle off to?"

"Roosevelt Hotel to set up the wedding."

"I might be able to help out. Hotel owners have a union that lasts, even when we're out of the business. Now, what's for breakfast?"

"You?"

"Not yet, though I'm weakening." Bobbie Jean looked inside my refrigerator, "It looks like beer and baloney sandwiches if we stay here."

She took my hands and pulled me up, "Carry our coffee. We're going to my kitchen."

• • •

Oliver T. was all smiles as he walked into our Monday afternoon class, "Your lady has quite a bit of influence. When Bonnie mentioned that Bobbie Jean is her maid of honor, all of the Roosevelt doors opened. Wedding is set for their courtyard. Want me to switch and be your lab partner? I owe you."

"No way. Exam is this Friday and I'm beginning to like Biloxi. And I certainly don't want to wind up in supply school."

"Stop by my car after class. I've got something special to show you."

"As long as it isn't a live snake or a dead skunk."

"No, it's much better."

"Long as it doesn't bite."

"It will do that."

Oliver T. was grinnin' like a proud papa as he opened the trunk of his car, "What do you think?" He lifted up the biggest pistol I'd ever seen. "T, you've gone off the deep end. The love bug must have sucked all the blood from your brains."

"Okay, but what do you think?"

"Is it a cannon or a howitzer?"

"Traded my 38 in for a Magnum."

"How do you hold it?"

"With both hands. One shot will bring down a buffalo."

"Not many buffaloes this side of the Rockies. Why did you really buy it?"

"Scare off the crazies Bonnie seems to attract."

"Has she ever thought of a new line of work?"

Oscar T. grinned. It was my turn. I gave him an atomic bomb straight line. "What? And leave show business?"

He was still giggling at his effort when I asked, "What's the dress for the wedding."

"White dinner jacket. Bonnie will let Bobbie Jean know."

• • •

New Orleans is a special place when you get away from the French Quarter and not too bad when you're there. Known as the Big Easy to shady folks, it was sixty miles west of Biloxi. As we drove toward the city, Bobbie Jean bubbled over, like a freshly popped bottle of uncorked champagne, "You've never been to the French Quarter?"

"Never been in the city."

"We'll go there after the wedding and when we call it an evening, we'll stop at the Coffee Stand for real coffee, New Orleans style."

"I can hardly wait."

"For coffee?"

"No, afterwards."

"Hush and pay attention to your driving. It's too early in the day for foolishness. We must look proper at Bonnie's wedding. Did Lieutenant Tugwattle behave this week?"

"Has a new pistol. Big enough to bring down an elephant."

"He's too hot-headed to carry."

"I Agree. He thinks everyone is after Bonnie. Can we park close to the Roosevelt Hotel?"

"Shouldn't be a problem. Shrove Tuesday is several weeks away."

"Never heard of it."

"Oh, you Yankees call it Fat Tuesday. It's the end of Mardi Gras—the day before Lent."

"Lent? My grandfather always said, 'Ne'r a borrower or a lender be.'"

I felt Bobbie Jean's elbow gently nudge my side, "Very funny. Over there. See— I've found you a parking spot next to the hotel."

As Bobbie Jean took my hand to exit the passenger side of my old Buick, I swept her into my arms, but she escaped. "Johnny, no. Don't rumple me or smear my make-up. Not until we give the couple away. For ladies, weddings are serious business."

## New Orleans

Oliver T. had done another number on me. I show up in summer white dinner jacket and he's wearing a blue blazer, khaki trousers, sandals and a white French silk shirt, open at the neck. Bonnie, and her body is certainly beautiful, was clothed in white wedding lace. She waved for Bobbie Jean to come to her side.

I had to smile, "Looks like they're in a hurry."

Oliver T. led me to the beer keg, "They have Jax on tap. This is going to be a first class wedding."

"T., you said wear a white dinner jacket and you're dressed in a blazer."

"Why in the world should we dress alike? Besides, you look good in white."

Bobbie Jean took me aside, "I refuse to drink beer at a wedding. There is only one beverage suitable." She whispered a few words to the Roosevelt wedding coordinator and buckets of champagne appeared a few minutes later, followed by half the hotel staff to bear witness. The preacher was as surprised as Oliver T., when he arrived. He had expected an intimate little wedding.

Oliver T. smiled, "I didn't know Bonnie and I were this popular. Let's get on with it." Ten minutes later, Bonnie and Oliver T. exchanged vows in front of over two hundred waiters, maids, busboys, bellhops, managers and assorted Roosevelt Hotel employees. I whispered to Bobbie Jean, "Is that it? I've stood in line at the market longer."

"Me too. Better toast our newlyweds before they run off to their room."

I raised my champagne flute, "To Bonnie, who is certainly beautiful and to Lieutenant Oliver T. Tugwattle, who is certainly lucky—may you live long and happy lives and, we hope, together."

Bonnie and Oliver T. drained their glasses. She handed her corsage to Bobbie Jean and our two newlyweds walked away, arm in arm, toward the hotel and their room, all to the applause of the hotel staff.

It was Bobbie Jean's turn to be amused, "Not only is this the fastest outdoor wedding I've ever been too, this may be the fastest consummation on record." Bobbie Jean made sure the staff had another glass of champagne and offered the keg to whomever would carry it. We toasted each other with another flute of champagne and our eyes. As we lounged in the hotel courtyard's early afternoon sun, Bobbie Jean noticed, "The preacher is still here. Our groom forgot to pay. Make sure he's taken care of while I wrap things up with the wedding coordinator."

When I returned, a hundred dollars lighter, my best girl was her cheerful self and ready to go, "Let's walk the French Quarter. We have a complimentary room here and the manager reserved seats for us in the show room tonight. And pray tell me, why are you smiling like the cat who caught the canary?"

"Not a canary, but you my love. I'm the lucky one."

• • •

The French Quarter is Coney Island with bars, the Left Bank of Paris in Cajun, with barely a lingering memory of why it was named. Artists sold prints instead of originals—quaint antique shops sold copies instead of antiques and carnival barkers stood in front of every bar and strip joint. All of this noise and commotion were a great strain on a once gracious lady. I enjoyed the walk and I enjoyed the company more. Bobbie Jean brought New Orleans to life with intimate details only a partisan would know. We walked and talked and walked and talked like lovers do when they cannot get enough of each other. When we could walk no more, she whispered in my ear, "Only a carriage ride to the Roosevelt will do, a perfect end to a marvelous afternoon."

As I helped Bobbie Jean up into our open carriage, I asked, "Is this all there is?"

She squeezed my hand, "No silly. We're going to have New Orleans-style coffee and blueberry muffins in the Roosevelt's courtyard."

I followed a bite of muffin with a sip of rich creamy coffee, "How can chicory coffee taste this wonderful? It should be bitter."

"Good roast and lots of rich cream. Your friend, Lieutenant Tugwattle and Bonnie are the talk of the hotel. Our waiter whispered to me that he knew Bonnie from somewhere, but wasn't sure."

"Whoops, how so?"

"She was wearing clothes."

"Talk about the mother of all straight lines. I fell in love with a comedienne. What does the manager have planned for us this evening?"

"I know of only one thing that can top today's wedding, our walk and coffee under the magnolias in the Roosevelt's courtyard. We're guests of the hotel for dinner and a show in the Blue Room."

"That wasn't it. Any idea who is headlining?"

"The Glen Miller Orchestra and a comedy team. The concierge says they are quite good, Rowan and Martin."

"If they're as good as Martin and Lewis it ought to be a night to remember."

"We can rest and freshen up in our suite before dinner."

"Right out of *Gone With The Wind*."

"Afternoon naps are a southern custom. That's why we live longer than you Yankees."

"I see you dropped the damn."

"Only because I'm in love with one."

"I can't remember a better afternoon, anywhere," I said.

"This time of year, but never in summer. The concierge has our key."

• • •

I laid on my stomach, head propped up in my hands watching Bobbie Jean dress for dinner. I pinched myself. She knew, "I can see you in the mirror, why did you pinch yourself?"

"Trying to find out if this is a dream, or if I'm alive."

"If you want to know, I'm the expert, you're very much alive, and lively. If anyone needs further proof, I'll vouch for you."

"What made you decide . . ."

"That's my secret. Never ask a lady why. Her answer is too complex, a lady might read about it, but never ever will a lady explain why. Get dressed. I don't want to miss the show—I'm famished."

"Will a white dinner jacket be out of place?"

"The concierge had our clothes cleaned and pressed while we . . ."

"This is first class. I don't know about you, but I didn't get very much sleep."

"An hour nap is proper and more than enough. Now hush and hurry."

When we entered the Blue Room, I noticed Bonnie and Oliver T., "Look over to your left. Our newlyweds are trying to eat dinner and cuddle at the same time."

"Cute, aren't they. We don't dare interrupt."

Bobbie Jean whispered to the maitre d'. He seated us on the other side of the room. She whispered to me, "True love?"

"Us or them?"

"I won't ever question ours. Will you?"

"Only if you leave me for someone else."

"The staff is taking care of our newlyweds."

"Oliver T. thinks it's because of his influence. I hope he doesn't suffer a letdown when you're not around to grease skids."

"Oh, I didn't think of that. Do you think he will?"

"I'll be surprised if he doesn't."

Bobbie Jean stood up, "Order while I powder my nose."

"What do you want."

"The fish here are excellent. You choose."

"Wine or champagne."

"White, my favorite."

She squeezed my hand, "After you, of course" and smiled, "I'll be right back."

She spoke to the maitre d' on her way back to our table. "Did you order?"

"Pompano. Caught under torch light at night and baked inside a paper bag."

"My favorite and Rhine wine, you have paid attention."

"You talked with the maitre d'?"

"He is very upset over some of the demands made on his staff by Lieutenant Tugwattle. Your friend is not staff friendly."

"He marches to his own tune."

"And it's off-key."

"I can't be dishonest about the wine. I chose Rhine because I couldn't decipher your French names. I didn't pay attention to your preference. When we're alone together, my eyes are only for you."

"Now that has the ring of a song to it, soldier. What did you order, as if I had to ask. Pepper steak?"

"You didn't have to ask. I hope you like Blue Cheese."

"You didn't pay attention did you? I'll have the waiter change it. They serve the salad dressing separate here."

"What do you prefer?"

"Anything but Blue Cheese and I'll give you a wine lesson the next time we dine out. What in the world were you thinking?"

"The blood rushes out of my brain when I'm with you."

Bobbie Jean seemed satisfied with our dinners and the hotel service. I asked, gingerly, "Was everything to your liking?"

"Pedestrian, but excellent for a showroom. The wine was average. I prefer one from Chile."

"Rhine wine from Chile?"

"Of course, they purchased cuttings. The climate there must be perfect. How was your steak?"

"A steak is either wonderful or it is not. Mine was wonderful."

"And the pepper sauce?"

"You're asking someone who doesn't know wine about sauce."

"Touché, order coffee. Do you want an after dinner drink?"

"Not if I have to drive back to Biloxi after the show."

"I'd like to stay on, but . . ."

"Coffee it is. We'll keep your reputation intact."

Bobbie Jean moved her chair close to mine and took my hand in hers. I wondered, would I wake up and would all of this be gone? She nudged me, "You've left me again and with such a silly smile."

"The band is wonderful and so are you. Do I have to tell you, I love you?"

"Yes and often." I kissed her neck. The show was about to begin, lights dimmed, the spotlight appeared at stage left.

• • •

Dan Rowan walked in briskly to our applause and stopped at the microphone, adjusting it. Dick Martin stumbled into the showroom through the band, bumping into the drum set, to a series of rim shots. Dan Rowan looked skyward:

*"You always enter a room like that?"*

*"No sometimes the drummer drops his sticks."*

*"Why don't you come in like a normal person."*

*"And miss the music?"*

*"That's about all you missed. I understand we have a newlywed couple in our midst."*

*"Did the bed break?"*

*"Of course not. Why would you say a thing like that?"*

*"I couldn't find my midst. Their bed is on the floor above mine. With all that bouncing it was bound to happen."*

*"Now cut that out. Shine the spot on our newlyweds. Bonnie is an old friend of ours. She just married Lieutenant Tugwattle this afternoon."*

*"She doesn't look old to me."*

*"She isn't old. That was just a figure of speech. Don't you remember her? We're in the same business."*

*"She doesn't look like a bar fly to me. And with a figure like that, she doesn't have to speak."*

*"Now cut that out. Can't you say anything nice?"*

*She has a beautiful bippy."*

*"Don't you mean that Bonnie has a beautiful body?"*

*"You look at your part and I'll look at mine."*

*"All right, Dick. That's enough. Your mother didn't wash your mouth out often enough, did she?"*

*"My other mother?"*

*"Whatever."*

*"She washed part of me last night and it's my best part."*

*"How can you go from description to debauchery so quickly?"*

*"It's easy when you have a fast car."*

*"Say goodnight, Dick."*

*"Goodnight Dick."*

*"I give up."*

*"That's what she said, too."*

*"Say goodnight, Dick."*

*"Goodnight Mrs. Tugwattle, whoever you are."*

*"That's Callabash and it belongs to Jimmy Durante."*

*"He can get his own girl."*

*"Goodnight, Dick."*

*"Goodnight, Dan and you too, Bonnie You can tug my wattle anytime you want to."*

*"Now cut that out."*

*"That's what her husband tried to do."*

• • •

The laughter lingered long after they left the stage. I was impressed, "They were really funny. I hope Oliver T. and Bonnie took it like good sports."

"I know Bonnie did, but Oliver T. dragged her out as soon as the lights came up."

"That will be the story-line for the second show." Bobbie Jean frowned, "It's my fault. I gave the showroom manager the information. I didn't realize Lieutenant Tugwattle was so sensitive."

"Don't blame yourself for other's faults."

"Your right, what is, is. Let's dance." We waltzed across the floor to each and every set until the band played Moonlight Serenade, announcing the break for the second show. Overcome by the Glen Miller melody, I held Bobbie Jean in a warm embrace. A romantic glow enveloped us like the heat from a thousand fireflies.

She looked into my eyes and I melted.

## Biloxi, Mississippi

The moon over Mississippi City made a magical pathway from my car to Bobbie Jean's front door. Her arm linked tightly in mine, we were like sheets blowing in the breeze brushing lightly together. I could sense our passion in the balmy salt air. She opened the front door and drew me to her bosom. I lifted her from the floor and kicked the door shut with my foot. Her spell was as magic as the Mississippi moonlight, until I heard that soft giggle and, "Just like Rhett." I carried my laughing lady into the bedroom knowing laughter and passion were emotional twins.

• • •

I reached over to touch Bobbie Jean's hair, but she wasn't there. I opened my eyes and looked at the clock. It was after ten. We were in bed by one, but I had no idea when we fell asleep from sweet exhaustion. I sat up, then stood up and walked to the bathroom. Bobbie Jean handed me a towel and pointed to her shower, "Hurry. Breakfast will be ready when you're finished. Are you awake or sleepwalking?"

"Ask me if I'm in love. Did I ask you to marry me?"

"Yes to both questions. We'll see about marriage. My mother is a very formidable obstacle."

"I forgot, I'm dealing with southern women. They must teach teasing in your home economics classes."

"And we're taught how to fire a man up, then keep him at bay. Now hurry or I'll pop in and scrub you myself."

"Is that a promise?" She pushed me into the shower and turned on the cold water. I grabbed for her hand, but missed, "Foiled again by a fair maiden."

"Your toothbrush is the blue one and your razor is on the sink. Use it. Your cheeks feel like wire brushes."

"Say face, quick."

I needed cold water to cool my passion. I toweled off and entered the kitchen. I stopped in my tracks, mouth open. I was speechless. Bobbie Jean was dressed in the skimpiest shorts and top I'd ever seen. I turned into a yo-yo, springing back into her arms. She pushed me away, "I have steak and eggs ready for the condemned man."

"Is that a yes to my proposal?"

"Of course it is. After yesterday and last night, all my doubts have taken wing. Now you'll have to make an honest woman out of me."

"So this is how courting is done in the deep south." Bobbie Jean sat on my lap and held me tight, "Only if a woman has brains, it is."

"You know, somehow I pictured this as more formal, with me down on my knees."

"Isn't it better this way?"

"My God, yes. I feel like I've been rode hard and put away wet."

"We do have one formality, our announcement. After breakfast we'll visit the Broadwater and tell Herbie."

"Is that formal?"

"One word to Herbie and everyone but my mother will know. It doesn't get more formal than that."

"You left one problem unsolved, your mother."

"She's not well, but is getting along."

"What's the problem?"

"Heart trouble. She's had it for ten years, ever since Daddy died. If she knows we're getting married it might finish her off. But that's only minor. Daddy knew how independent and strong-willed I would grow up to be. He made me promise on his death bed that I would only marry someone Mother approved of."

"We've got trouble."

"How about your family?"

"Not a problem. Mother wants to meet you before we tie the knot. Wants to see if you're good breeding stock and if you have horns. You'll do just fine."

"Your mother isn't like that."

"She's more like your mother than you'd expect. She's as sweet as can be, but she wasn't born yesterday."

"That describes Mother to a T. Speaking of T., I wonder how the newlyweds are doing?"

"I haven't had one thought of them."

"For some strange reason, I thought this was our wedding night."

"It is for now."

Oliver T. failed to show up in class Monday afternoon. When he failed to show on Tuesday, I checked at the admin. office. The school sergeant was aware of his absence, "Lieutenant Tugwattle is in a heap of trouble. Absent without leave for two days. I sent the OSI looking for him this morning."

"Holy cow! He was just married Saturday in New Orleans. They honeymooned at the Roosevelt Hotel. Didn't he have enough sense to ask for leave or a three day pass?"

"Wouldn't get a pass or leave. Against school regs. He could have called in sick or just called and there'd be no problem, but he's nowhere to be found."

"Hell of a way to begin married life."

*"Oh you foolish Alice!" she answered herself. "How can you learn lessons in here. Why, there's hardly room for you, and no room at all for any lesson books!"*

# Chapter 7

We found out later that Oliver T. spent the second night after his wedding in jail and the next night, too. Seemed he waved his pistol in the face of one of Bonnie's fans. Had it been anyone else it would have been okay, but it was the sheriff's son. When he returned to Keesler, Oliver T. was given two options, court-martial or immediate release. The charge was conduct unbecoming of an officer. He took the later and was gone. Even Gus didn't know where they were and Bonnie was his dear friend. I told Bobbie Jean, "I'm worried, Oliver T. and Bonnie have puled up stakes and disappeared from the face of the earth. Admin. won't tell me and Gus doesn't know. Can't believe they took off without giving us a call."

"When hormones go wild, you men lose all control of your senses."

"Maybe sheep have the better of it. They only go crazy when they're in season."

Bobbie Jean shrugged her shoulders, "Don't worry, I can find Bonnie through the night club circuit. Why did they kick Lieutenant Tugwattle out of the service without a hearing?"

"Air Force is a bit old fashioned about wives. Don't think they took kindly to T. marrying a stripper and used the charge as an excuse."

"You moved in with me and we're not married."

"Neither are you, so they don't look upon it as adultery."

"Will I cause you any trouble with our arrangement?"

"Only if we go public or stick our rear ends in the powers-that-be faces."

"I'll work on Mother, but it doesn't look good. I know it will take time before she will mellow."

"Maybe if she becomes a grandmother."

"Do you want to put Mother in an early grave?"

• • •

Time really does fly when you're happy. The second half of training arrived and it was time for us to learn how to become Electronic Warfare Operators, EWOs, sometimes called Electronic Countermeasure crew members, or ECM. Pilots, not thrilled with haulin' us around, redefined ECM to extra crew member.

Bobbie Jean asked, "What do they make you do in flying training?"

"We get to put into practice all the theory we've absorbed. Outside of that, it's a mystery to me."

"Is all your work Top Secret?"

"That's what I've been led to believe."

"What will you be called?"

"Blackbirds—Ravens or Crows."

I had just delivered another straight line to Bobbie Jean, "Edgar Allen Poe is alive and well."

• • •

A Raven is an EWO who does sneaky things, such as electronic eavesdropping. He intercepts and records radar, telemetry and such. A Crow is an EWO who uses electronic emissions to confuse, deceive, or jam radios, radars and things like that. It was as if their names came from above—my two flight instructors were Captain Raven and Lieutenant Crow. Raven was obsessed with the terrible condition of our planes. We flew in four prop, converted cargo aircraft, C-54s. They had never been able to get all the coal dust out of them. These were the famous planes that flew the Berlin Airlift. Dirty as they were, we were proud to fly in planes with such an honorable past. Like the T-29 our C-54s flew slower than the fastest duck. Lieutenant Crow wasn't worried about dirt, he was concerned about the equipment we used for training.

His concern, "Air Corps sold all of our equipment to salvage folks after World War II. When the Korean War came along, we had to buy it back for more than it cost new. You're going to train on equipment older than dirt and not as useful. All the new stuff is going to SAC B-52s. Captain Raven and me will be unable to fully train you. You will leave here ill prepared to do your job."

I was impressed with his honesty, but as an optimist, I knew we'd handle whatever came along. Hi-fi equipment was in its infancy. Air Force equipment was hooked together with cannon plugs, so called because of its shape. Quick disconnect plugs were in the experimental stage and transistors had not replaced vacuum tubes. Semiconductors? The minds that were to develop them were in the future. Silicon Valley was a stuffy school in California called a farm.

• • •

After a dozen flights staring at empty equipment racks, I complained to Bobbie Jean, "If it wasn't for the flight pay, I'd just as soon not fly. Racks are mostly empty and when we do have equipment, it's broken. If we do find a working receiver, there aren't that many radio stations or radars in this part of the country to listen, or record."

"Why don't you fly where there are such things."

"Our pilots would rather fly around our air patch and practice takeoffs and landings."

"At least you can check on the still at the end of the runway."

"It's still cooking."

Although EW flight training was a waste of time, my new life with Bobbie Jean was fulfilling, "We need to celebrate our engagement."

"I've celebrated it every single night since we've been together. I can't ever remember being this celebrated."

"How about New Orleans?"

"Look what it did for Oliver T. and Bonnie. You don't own a pistol and I'll never take my clothes off in public."

"You'd put Bonnie to shame."

"And me, too. I'll make arrangements at the Broadwater."

"I'm so happy I could burst, we must celebrate."

Bobbie Jean asked, "How did your parents take our good news?"

"They still want to meet you, but when they saw your photos and listened to my rave reviews, they both said, 'Go for it! Don't let this one get away.' They thought I would procrastinate my life away until you came along to jump-start my heart."

"Jump-start, what foolishness."

I whispered into her ear, "And what about your mother?"

"Not talking to me. She had to take an extra heart pill when she found out I was engaged to a Yankee. We'll go up to Jackson this weekend, if you don't mind. Maybe, just maybe, if she meets you in person and will listen, we'll get her blessing."

"What if she doesn't?"

"You fell into my trap, so you're mine. I've measured you up and down and you're a keeper. If we have to, we'll live together and tell everyone we're married. I won't go back on my promise to Daddy and I won't break my promise to you."

"Wow, talk about being caught between the rock and the hard place. Look, do your best to convince your mother. I prefer marriage, but I'll happily take the alternative if it's the only way we can be together. Have you found Bonnie?"

"Not a word. And when she starts working again, it's a tight little world she lives in. I'll know where she is."

"Bonnie may wish to drop the nightclub scene, put her career behind."

"Behind?"

"Now cut that out." We both laughed.

• • •

Friday night and we opted to stay at home, preparing for our trip to Jackson. Life in our world did not come with a warranty. I knew we might not get the life we expected. We all die, but when, that's the mystery. All we could hope was for more pleasure than pain, along the way. Would my introduction to Bobbie Jean's mother be pleasure or pain? Bobbie Jean nudged me out of my thoughts, "What are you thinking about?"

"Will our trip to Jackson be pleasure or pain."

"What is, is."

"Definition time again."

"Don't worry yourself into a self-fulfilling prophecy."

"Dress?"

"For you, blue sport coat, regimental tie and khaki pants. For me, southern and flowery."

"I'm as nervous as a suitor in a room full of maiden aunts."

"You will be and you should be. Let's go out for a late dinner."

"Shrimp, or steak?"

"Or fish."

"Decisions, decisions."

"I know."

"What?"

"A little Italian."

• • •

Bobbie Jean's mother would not meet us at the door, but her butler did. I whispered, "You didn't tell me your family owned a mansion. Your entry hall is so large it echoes."

"And Mother can hear every word. Pretend you've been here all your life."

"Not easy to do. Your butler checked my suitcase to see if it was made out of carpet."

"Mother will be in the sun room. It's your turn to follow."

Her mother turned as we entered the room, "Why, Bobbie Jean. You didn't tell me your Yankee boyfriend was so nice looking. I'm Mrs. Langtry and you must be Lieutenant Johnny Ropp. Sit down and tell me all about your family. Where they live and where they come from."

"Mother, Johnny will need a little whiskey and branch water before you give him the third degree."

"I apologize, it has been such a long time since I was a hostess to my only child's new male friend. Johnny, help yourself to the decanter of whiskey on the table by the wall. We distill it right here on our plantation. Water is in the pitcher. Ice is in the silver bucket. Would you pour a glass of white wine for me and put one cube of ice in it? Bobbie Jean, your room is ready. I have Johnny staying in our guest wing."

"You do want to keep us apart, don't you."

"Of course, we don't bundle in our family."

Sitting next to Bobbie Jean's mother, I felt like a schoolboy at a tea dance. When she smiled I knew she was an older version of Bobbie Jean, "I expected someone much . . ."

"Older and infirm, if you listen to Bobbie Jean. Now tell me all about your family."

"Not much to say. Family moved to Ohio out of Virginia after the Revolutionary War on one of Washington's land grants. My father's family moved north from Alabama before the Civil War on a territorial land grant and we've been there ever since."

"What does your father do?"

"My father and mother were teachers. Most of the family were teachers, as far back as I can remember. We have a two-thousand acre farm along the Scioto River north of Columbus. Father has it in the land bank to help restore the soil."

Bobbie Jean strolled into the room and saved me from further questioning. Her mother fired one more shot, "Bobbie Jean tells me that your great grandfather may have saved my grandfather's leg outside of Atlanta."

"Yes ma'am. I think we have several of your grandfather's medals at home. And as I mentioned to Bobbie Jean, he probably killed more Yankees with his surgeon's knife than Johnny Reb did on Sherman's March to the sea."

Her mother frowned at my humor. I realized I had stepped in it.

The rest of the visit was cordial, but I did not win her mother's unconditional approval. On our return trip, even Bobbie Jean could see the humor of the trap I fell into, "You would have to mention Sherman. You pushed Mother's 'forget, hell' button."

"Is she opposed to our marriage?"

"You scratched out half a victory. She has accepted our engagement, but has not signaled her approval of marriage. She asked that I wait a year. She is hoping you'll go away."

"Damn, I stepped in it. It's my fault."

"If you had been dishonest, it would have been much worse. We got all we could really expect from Mother. Now it's a waiting game to see who can wear the other one down."

"Southern women! You are a strange, but wonderful lot."

"And I love you."

"Enough to love, honor and obey?"

"Common law, yes."

"I won't press. You made a promise and our word is our bond."

• • •

Our life together made time fly by like a fast rabbit, but my EW training crawled along like a slow turtle. I was ready to move on, but couldn't until training was finished. The only item that peaked my interest was the still at the end of the runway. When I mentioned our unusual landing aids, Bobbie Jean gave a knowing smile, one up on me and the rest of this world, "You still have a lot to learn about southern ways and Mississippi politics. Two of our stills have operated for so long we joke about them being historical landmarks. Wasn't honest work for our boys returning home from the War of Northern Aggression, so they took up whiskey making."

"Your mother's is smoother than any I've ever tasted."

"As long as they pay our sheriff's tax, he warns them when the feds are on the way. Besides, it's a family operation with all the tradition of Mr. Daniels. Whiskey—good whiskey is an art form. Let amateurs get into the business and a lot of people will be poisoned or go blind. Most of our folks have chemistry degrees from our state university."

Bobbie Jean took my hand, "Time to show you the rest of my cellar." She pressed a button on the wall and the wine rack swung open.

I looked inside, "You must have fifty cases of whiskey stored down here. Why so many?"

"Several years back, Ralph discovered a particularly good batch. It was so fine he aged it in barrels. When we were married, he had it bottled and labeled with my name on it." I poured two fingers into a mason jar and took a sip, before passing it to Bobbie Jean. She took a sip and smiled, "I forgot how good this really is."

"It is pure ambrosia."

"And bottled like a fine wine. I'll never part with these. It's one of the few things Ralph did right."

"He had problems?"

"Most southern men do. He would rather hunt, fish and gamble."

"You ran the hotel?"

"After we were married. Took a year to get it solvent again and then he died."

"What about our Air Force amateurs?"

"We'll shut them down soon."

"I'm the luckiest man alive."

"How so?"

"We have an old saying. If you must marry, marry a rich madam with a liquor store. Two out of three isn't bad!" Her elbow dug into my ribs, a bit sharper than normal.

• • •

It was bound to happen, sooner or later. One of our students interfered with the radars at Pensacola Naval Air Station. Air training was disrupted and several students almost ran out of gas. Naval aviators were forever making mock attacks against our C-54s, which wasn't much of a challenge unless you consider the skill level of your average Navy pilot. Somehow, one of us funny wings got even. Now that wasn't all bad. He didn't disrupt anything but federal activity and it was fun listening to the Navy guys panic as they chatted away like a bunch of magpies on emergency guard, UHF radio, known by the entire civilized world as Navy common. But, we really got in hot water when one of our boys snapped and took the Jackson TV station off the air. Most of the time, it was the only TV station we received in Biloxi. And about the only thing it carried were faith healers and self-appointed preachers.

Now, Bobbie Jean has a sense of humor equal to anyone I know, but she didn't smile when I told her about the TV episode, "Johnny, shame on you boys. Half the Mississippi television audience believed God had struck their preacher dead."

"For that, I'm sorry. But, you have to admit it's a little weird to encourage a TV congregation to lift its backsides up to a TV screen to cure hemorrhoids."

"Now Johnny, you must remember, our favorite Oklahoma evangelist is the only entertainment we get on TV."

"Even if we have to cover our ears when he shouts, 'Heal!'"

"We're not all that technical down here in the deep south, Love. Has the Air Force decided where it wants to send you or do you get to choose?"

"Not yet. Rumor has it we'll be told next week. I was thinking about Japan or Germany, but . . ."

"I know. I wouldn't be allowed to tag along, unless we are married."

"It won't happen. If we select by class rank and time remaining in service, I'll be the last to choose. All that will be left will be good hunting and fishing assignments."

"And where would that be?"

"Far, far away from civilization."

"As long as it isn't in the middle of a desert, I'll be happy. There really isn't an Air Force base in the middle of nowhere, is there?"

"Of course, more than just' a few. I was hoping for something on the beach, near the sea."

"You have your wish. You're here with me on the Gulf Coast."

"And Houston is a port. It may be time for me to pay the piper."

• • •

My premonition of impending doom was a self fulfilling prophecy. Our flight instructor called us together for the choosing, on a late August day. "Gentlemen, you select by your academic rank and date of service. Before we begin—are there any questions?"

In Tucker's memory, I had to raise my hand, "Is this where the Air Force shoves the bat up our ass?"

"Only if you don't like good hunting and fishing. As I said, we'll select in the prescribed order."

I asked, "What are our choices?"

"B-52s at Walker Air Force Base, Roswell, New Mexico."

So we all stood up and chose, in order, the same unit at the same location in the middle of a New Mexico desert.

• • •

Bobbie Jean asked, "Did you pick your assignment?"

"Yes and we all picked the same place."

"Is it all they offered?"

"Yes, but we were allowed to choose and rest assured there will be plenty of good hunting and fishing in Roswell, New Mexico."

"Did you say Roswell, New Mexico? Don't you really mean Roswell, Georgia?"

"No, New Mexico. We'll live on the beach in Roswell, by the sea, New Mexico."

"Isn't it in the middle of a desert, a thousand miles from any ocean?"

"Horizontally, yes, but a mile below is an old sea bed."

"Funny, very funny. I'll go, but I'll scream and kick all the way."

"I hope it's in bed," and I received another dig to my ribs.

"Tell me about this desert oasis."

"High, hot and dry. A place folks see mirages."

"Mirages?"

"Something you believe you see, but really doesn't exist."

"That happens here all the time."

"It does?"

"When the good old boys go fishing with too much moonshine in their bait bucket, we get reports on flying saucers."

"Well, the Pecos River is there and I know you've read tall tales about Pecos Bill."

"Can't say I have, but there was a judge out there who worshipped Lilly Langtry."

"Not as much as I do you."

"I'm going with you in spite of your sweet talk. What type of Blackbird will you be, a Raven or a Crow."

"I drew SAC's new bomber, the B-52." Bobbie Jean smiled, "I know which one, you'll be an Old Crow."

"And wiser."

• • •

Our last month in Biloxi flew by so fast we lived two-step time in a three-quarter world. And our living arrangement had more than one bonus for me. I saved enough cash to trade in my undertaker black, four porthole, inline eight Buick for a more substantial auto. And it was fortuitous. My Buick had developed a mysterious clank emanating from its rear end that I was unable to diagnose. A new Ford station wagon was a much better choice for a trip across country. With Bobbie Jean along, I needed all the extra space the luggage rack on top provided.

Bobbie Jean worked all week boxing the things she knew we may need. When she finished, I was escorted into her den, "What do you think?"

"I'll need two more wagons and a truck."

"We will mail them to Roswell?"

"No, to Merced, California."

"We're moving to California?"

"I was just informed today, I have to report there first, to attend B-52 crew training."

"How long?"

"Two to three months and then we return to New Mexico."

"I want to drive up to Jackson on the way."

"If your mother sees you driving west with me, she'll have a heart attack."

"Or it might move her in our direction. And I want to meet your folks."

"And they want to meet you. I almost forgot, we need to prepare your cars for storage."

"Not going to store them."

"You're selling your Jaguar and Bentley?"

"Of course not. Herbie promised to take them out for a spin at least twice a month and I have our family mechanic. He's the only person outside of New Orleans that understands English motor cars. I've asked Herbie to manage my investments including these apartments. I want to see how he does."

"You must all ready have faith in him."

"I do, but it is prudent to make sure."

## Mississippi to Ohio

Last minute packing filled the rear of our station wagon to where I had to use side mirrors to see out back. As we drove north to Jackson, the good times were rolling north with me. When we drove up the magnolia-lined drive to Mrs. Langtry's mansion, I had that feeling, Bobbie Jean had returned home with a share cropper traveling to their new farm. We stayed for only an hour or so. Her mother avoided any and all conversation with me. She tried, but her tears didn't work on Bobbie Jean. She did have her butler place a case of plantation whiskey under our luggage in back and admonished Bobbie Jean, "That's for your Yankee boyfriend's father. Make sure he knows where it comes from and the history behind it."

After we were on the road to Nashville, Bobbie Jean gave me the bad news, "Mother would not give her approval. I don't know what has gotten into her. If you will put up with me, I'm ready to live like this forever."

"I have an idea. Why don't we get married in Reno on our way to California."

"I made Daddy a death bed promise."

"What, to wait?"

"That I would not take a on new name without Mother's approval."

"You followed that with Ralph?"

"And I took my name back when he passed on."

"We'll get married and you can keep your maiden name."

"Is that legal?"

"Of course it is."

"I can't let Mother know. She would die on the spot."

"Do we have an agreement?"

"When she changes her mind, will you promise that we'll have a second, formal garden wedding."

"Of course. I'll have to explain it to my folks, but we've had mixed marriages before in our family, with similar problems."

"North and south?"

"Catholic and Protestant."

That comment got another gentle poke in the ribs, "We need to make a legal commitment, too."

"Are you worried about my properties going bankrupt?"

"No, what you bring into our marriage should remain yours."

"And you?"

"This car and the family farm when my folks pass away."

"Agreed, we must not lose our heritage to lawyers. Mother despises them more than you Damn-Yankees."

"Now that we've committed, let's stop in Nashville."

"Early in the afternoon? Shouldn't we wait until we're married." It was my turn for a gentle dig and we laughed, together.

Nashville had grown a bit, one or two new motels since my last visit. We ate an early dinner and hopped into bed, exhausted and relieved. I knew we were in the deep south when grits appeared on our breakfast plates. Bobbie Jean smiled, "I know how you love them so."

"Can't replace good home fries for breakfast with a white cloud of grease. Are you nervous. You woke me up a dozen times, tossing and turning."

"I'm meeting your folks for the first time, we've decided to marry without Mother's blessing and you ask me why I couldn't sleep. I'm as excited as a teenage bride marrying a southern music star."

"I'm country music?"

"Well, no, but you're as close as I want to be to one. Did you remember to phone your parents?"

"I didn't call. I think it's better to surprise them. We can only stay a day or two at the most. I want to have several extra days on our trip across country, in case we have a breakdown."

• • •

Since the marriage question had been resolved, Bobbie Jean covered a multitude of living arrangement what ifs on our drive through Kentucky. By the time we drove into Cincinnati, she was exhausted. And by the time I filled the tank with gas and purchased a case of Royal Amber, she was fast asleep. It was well after dark when I turned on River Road, driving north from Columbus along the Scioto. As we pulled into our farm lane, Bobbie Jean woke up, "Are we there?"

"Yes, the farm house is up ahead. The lights are on so my folks are awake."

"Are you certain they will approve of me?"

"Yes, but even if they don't, I do and that's all that counts."

"I love your qualifier, but I'm more nervous than ever."

She shouldn't have been. Bobbie Jean got more of a hug from Father than I ever did and Mother bubbled over, visions of grandchildren dancing in her eyes. Bobbie Jean won their rousing approval. We stayed an extra day. Mother insisted. She had to show all of her friends and all of our relatives my prize catch. The evening before we departed, I unveiled our marriage plans and explained why. Mother made us promise to have a formal wedding when Bobbie Jean's mother finally approved, "The wheel turns, yet everything remains the same. Your father and I ran away to get married. Your grandfather Mac didn't approve, but he came around."

"How long did it take?"

"Quite awhile."

"What happened?"

"Grandchildren—your older sisters came along."

## Heading West

We followed the national road west to Saint Louis, Oklahoma City and jogged south of Denver to Colorado Springs. Bobbie Jean picked a hotel high up on Pike's Peak. Now that was a mistake. Not being used to the altitude, we turned in early and slept long. Romance took a back seat to getting well. We had to stay overnight in Denver, still groggy. By then we had acclimated to the altitude and were ready to cross over the Rockies. On the drive over the mountains to Steamboat Springs, Bobbie Jean sat dead center in the middle of our station wagon, "You're on the inside of these curves. My part of the car is hanging out over the edge of a thousand foot drop. Who built these roads?"

"Don't know, but this time of year the southern route is too hot."

"And that's where we're going to live?"

"Roswell is up on a high plain, so it'll be cooler than Arizona."

"I hope so, I've been to Phoenix and it cooks this time of the year."

• • •

Steamboat Springs wasn't more than two wide streets crossing in the middle of nowhere, on the bottom of a mountain valley. We stopped at a diner for lunch. Mountain oysters were the special. Bobbie Jean was about to order them when a diner cowboy, two stools down, whispered, "I wouldn't if I were you, ma'am. They come from the wrong end of a bull."

She thanked him and we both ordered hamburgers and fries.

She whispered in my ear, "Always order something fully cooked on the road. Don't want to end up with cramps or worse."

Our lunch was hot and quick. And we survived another meal, heading west.

Salt Lake City is an oasis surrounded on three sides by salt flats and one side by the Wasatch Mountain Range. I couldn't believe what I saw, "There are more bars here than in Biloxi. What's going on? I was lead to believe Mormons don't drink."

"They don't, but Jack Mormons do."

"Have you been to Salt Lake?"

"Ralph took me on a honeymoon trip across the west. He stopped here to trace his ancestors. They have the worlds best archives up in the mountains."

"A Jack Mormon must be someone overly familiar with Mr. Daniels. Want to visit the sights tomorrow?"

"I thought we were in a hurry to get to California?"

"Car is running good. We won't need those extra days. And we're a day ahead of schedule."

"Remember our wedding in Reno?"

"Right, we'll move on. Our honeymoon will be short enough as it is."

• • •

Our drive west to Elko, Nevada was hot, dusty and dull. Bobbie Jean kept me company in the morning, but the bright white salt flats wore her down. She fell asleep halfway to Nevada, waking up only to comment, "How much more desolation do we have to drive through?"

"Looks like it goes all the way to Reno. Didn't you spend your honeymoon out here?"

"We flew over the desert part. Funny thing about driving out west, it looks like it's all the same from the Rockies to the Sierras, a brindle desert kaleidoscope."

Bobbie Jean took off her sunglasses and looked around, "I'm tired of desert brown and tans, I want to see green."

"We'll have to climb a mountain. According to the map, this desert stretches from the jungles of Mexico to the Arctic Ocean."

"And the only difference is the temperature. Now I know why our government encourages air travel. The next time we decide to go across country, let's take a plane."

Bobbie Jean spotted it first, "Look to your left. I see green."

"That's Elko, Nevada and it's time for lunch." Elko is your average western town. One main drag with curbs so high you can rip out the bottom of your car doors when opening them, and gutters doubled as storm sewers. We parked two feet away, but Bobbie Jean still had to get out on my side of the car. I took her hand, helping her up from the street to the sidewalk, "Looks like they're expecting a flood of Biblical proportions."

"Is that what they call a gully washer?"

"Yes, town looks clean. They must care here." Wasn't a bad restaurant. Looked a lot like all the others we had eaten in along the way. The only difference was the rack of slot machines up near the cash register. Meal was the same as Salt Lake, but tasty, hot and quick.

Bobbie Jean tried the dime machine while I paid our check. She was all smiles, "You know, I could live in a place like this. Clean air, why we can see a hundred miles."

"And lots of good hunting and fishing. Maybe you're being influenced because you hit the jackpot on the dime machine on your first pull."

"Well, I'm glad we stopped for lunch. The emptiness of the west must have driven the early settlers' wives mad."

• • •

Back on the national road, Bobbie Jean settled in for the long drive across Nevada to Reno, "Are you excited?"

"About the trip or flying in a jet bomber? Our life will never be dull."

"No, silly, getting married in Reno."

"I am nervous. I can see how some folks bolt at the church door. It's a big step when two people make a lifetime commitment to stay together. Makes me wonder why arranged marriages work as well as they do."

"That was off the wall. Your mind does wander. The west's wide open spaces must be getting to you. We haven't seen much civilization between Salt Lake and here, except Elko."

"The big winner always gloats. Lots out here for a geologist to love. Mountain gullies are full of alluvial fans. Really shows up when there isn't much vegetation."

"Only a fellow with a jackass and a pick could love it."

Bobbie Jean curled up, "Wake me when you see the lights of Reno. I want to make sure the condemned man eats a hearty last meal."

## Reno, Nevada

The western Nevada landscape changed from light sand to brindle-brown hard pan. And then to dry moss, with patches of green, as we approached Long Valley Creek outside of Sparks. I jiggled Bobbie Jean's shoulder, "Time to wake up. We're almost there. The open country between Sparks and Reno looks like wild grass over hardpan, a pretty good place to raise sheep."

Bobbie Jean was wide awake and feisty as ever, "Or a good place to shear a reluctant bachelor." The lights of Reno looked like Times Square to two desert rats rolling in, out of the Nevada waste lands. She was full of surprises, "Ralph and I stopped here and in Las Vegas on our honeymoon. It's a fun town with a block full of casinos that decree, 'Come as you are and bring money.'"

"That eliminates the unwashed Californians."

"Don't worry. Mountains are too high for them to walk over. The Beat Generation stays on the coast, Monterey to San Francisco. Reno is cowboy country."

"You mean the Frederick Remington working kind?"

"You'll see. Boots and jeans are formal here."

We selected a new motel a block from downtown, without a pool, dining room or bar. Reno was Spartan, but clean. I showered and Bobbie Jean unpacked. As I toweled off, she warned me, "Don't gamble at any game except blackjack. We have a line of credit at Harold's and Harrah's under my maiden name."

"You've got casino connections in Nevada?"

"I was in the business."

"Hurry up, I'm eager to lose my hard earned cash."

"With that kind of an attitude, the Reno casinos will oblige. Go on ahead. I want to shower, change and make a few calls."

"Your mother?" I asked.

"Yes and we need to line up a chapel."

"I should be doing that."

"Your job is to show up and bring the ring," she smiled

"Ring, you didn't mention ring."

"Very funny, I helped you pick them out. I'll meet you at Harold's."

"Any last minute advice?"

"Don't put money in any machine."

"You did in Elko," I reminded her.

"One thin dime and I know when to quit. Don't bet one nickel over two dollars, don't double up and never bet on anything that talks, walks or runs. Set your limit and stick with it. The Dealers are honest here and the owners are like family. But remember, no matter how lucky you are, eventually the house will always win."

"I'm off."

"Be careful."

• • •

"If I had only listened to you I would have walked away a winner."

Bobbie Jean sat down beside me in Harold's bar, "Never, if you do it's only temporary. The house has the odds, money and patience. Tell me the bad news."

"A hot streak at blackjack was my undoing."

"Don't tell me, you doubled up."

"And redoubled. Went from five hundred ahead to one hundred behind."

"Your limit?"

"Yes."

She kissed me. "I'm the lucky one, Ralph never knew when to quit. I have a chapel reserved for tonight at nine."

"So soon?"

"We're not going to live one more night in sin."

"My lady is proper, too."

"You do have a lot to learn about women. Though my nesting urge is ferocious, my moral fiber is tough."

"Do I need to dress proper?"

"Reception is at the best restaurant in town. I made reservations for nine thirty."

"Talk about Oliver T.'s wedding being quick."

"Does my condemned bachelor have a last request?" I was beginning to get those before wedding, nervous sort of clanks, "Coat and tie?"

"Coat, but no tie, this is Reno. Your last request?"

"You, you're my last request."

• • •

I wouldn't recommend a Nevada wedding to anyone who wants a formal one. Our preacher was ordained and the papers were legal, but it didn't seem proper. And he was surprised when we insisted Bobbie Jean keep her maiden name. It was a first for him. Now, it might have been quick and more than a little plastic, but to tell the truth, my knees buckled as we took our vows. I couldn't have been happier when we walked out of that chapel as man and wife. I really did look like the cat that caught his canary. Bobbie Jean was more than a little misty eyed, too, "Are those tears of joy?"

"No, I'm crying for Mother and Daddy. I do wish they could have been with us. I have no tears for us. We're the lucky ones. I'm loved and love you in return. I don't remember ever having so much fun."

I was going to say something about Ralph, but knew better. "And now for the reception. Lead the way." There was no limo and no need for one. We were within walking distance, less than a block away.

Bobbie Jean was wide eyed, "You didn't order pepper steak? My, my, we are full of surprises."

"Never had scallops before. Do you mind that I ordered the same dinner as you?"

"No, but seafood?"

"Man does not live by steak alone." I was too far away for her to dig my ribs.

Dinner was delicious, but we played with most of our food, except the scallops. They were bigger than silver dollars and about as good as any food I've ever had. We ordered after dinner drinks, brandy for me and Irish coffee for Bobbie Jean. She moved close, "You've been awfully quiet this evening."

"Not often one gets married. And it was almost too quick. It took fifteen minutes to seal our fate for sixty years. My mind hasn't caught up with my body. I chased you, caught you and we're now one. My thoughts have turned to providing a warm cave and protection from animals that are about. I'll cherish this moment and maybe look back."

"Must be a male thing. All I want to do is curl up on a bear skin next to my cave man."

"Now you have my attention."

"Do you want to try our luck?"

"At the tables."

Bobbie Jean gave me one of those looks. One given to immigrants just stepping off the boat. She smiled and linked her arm in mine, "Do you mind if we wake up early and leave for California?"

"Nesting urge?"

"Yes, it's overwhelming."

• • •

And curl up we did, until the wee hours. I was up at the crack of dawn, tiptoeing around our motel room like a bull elephant in heat. I turned on the shower, to wash the cobwebs away. When I stepped in, two soft hands caressed my back and shoulders. "Mind if I join you, soldier?" We fell together, in a tight embrace, catching ourselves with one hand free, stopping the slide, squeezing together at the same time. We both laughed, stepped back locked in an embrace. Our laughter soon turned into passion. All thoughts of leaving early vanished in the morning mist.

An accident had traffic on the National Road slowed to a crawl from Truckee to the Donner Summit. Forewarned, we sped south toward Carson City. I looked over at Bobbie Jean, she had that glow, a blush new brides always have on the morning after. Always romantic, she said it was, "Whisker burn," but I didn't believe it. She cuddled near and stroked my leg, "For such a talker, you're a quiet one this morning. What's on your mind?"

"You're my gambling expert. I really had a high at the blackjack table. Winning wasn't it and losing wasn't either. And afterwards I felt like a well-spent buck."

"On a Spring-made sheet. It's the thrill one has in looking for the unknown. When you turn over a card, matching your hand to the dealer's, not knowing whether you'll win or lose until the dealer turns over his hole card. It's a rush that can bring ruin if you lose control."

"It could take me down, hard. It's difficult to back away," I agreed.

"Knowing about it is the cure."

"Reno is a friendly town. Everyone treated us like long lost friends."

"We were. We are their industry. Without us, it's back to digging in a mine. And when the money runs out, we'll be strangers again."

"I not only get a bride, I get a watcher, philosopher and a psychologist all in one pretty package. We'll skirt Lake Tahoe. Good place to take a few wedding pictures."

"And I have my wish."

"What's that?"

"We've driven out of the desert and into tall trees."

Our drive west, downhill from South Lake Tahoe to Placerville was twist, turn and turn some more. Bobbie Jean motioned for me to stop, "Whoa, Big Felluh." I stopped at a pullout, "I've trained you well, but not my stomach. If we hadn't stopped, you'd have my breakfast in your lap."

"Stretch, take in some oxygen and get your land legs again. I'll snap a few more pictures. When you're ready to go, I'll drive a bit slower." The cool mountain air did its trick. She held my hands and pulled me towards her. We kissed and she said, "California or bust." I smiled and she gave me a little dig, "California first, bust later."

*"Who are you?" said the Caterpillar.*

*Alice replied, rather shyly, "I-I hardly know, Sir, just at present—at least I know who I was when I got up this morning, but I think I must have changed several times since then."*

# Chapter 8

## California

"It's all so, so brown. Golden California must be a press agent's release." I looked out from the center line of the winding mountain road, "Yup, miles and miles of dead grass," and focused again on a very narrow roadway.

Bobbie Jean was disappointed, "I expected a land of milk and honey. And the valley below, there must be a million miles of dry parched grass land."

"If you were trying to sell this place, what slogan would you use?"

"Touché, you got me again, soldier. If California isn't gold, I'll bet the Golden Gate Bridge isn't either."

"Never seen it, but we will," I promised.

Bobbie Jean sat up and pointed at a town below, "Sacramento?"

"Maybe, but probably a mining town. Hungry?"

"Famished. I'm ready for red meat. Are we going to drive through town?"

"Let's skirt the southern edge and turn south to Merced. It's not too far. Keep your eyes open."

"There. See the sign: STEAK DINNER $1.99."

I whistled, "We've got to try that. It may give our stomachs something to talk about."

And it certainly did. We were served a baked potato, tossed salad and a good sized steak. That was the good news. The bad? Salad greens were bitter. Bobbie Jean thought it might be endive, but wasn't sure. The baked potato? Was it ever overcooked. I tried to bounce it off the floor, but Bobbie Jean grabbed my hand. Our steaks were wonders. Couldn't cut them with a knife and we'd still be chewing our first bite if we hadn't taken it out of our mouths. We didn't leave a tip.

• • •

Bobbie Jean was still giggling as we continued our trip south, "We'll remember that meal for the rest of our lives. Have you ever had a piece of meat that tough?"

"We raised our own and aged it proper. No, I never have, not even at YMCA camp."

"I'm still hungry, but not enough to eat shoe leather."

"We'll stop in Modesto."

"Is that a town or an attitude?"

"Probably both. Keep an eye out for a restaurant sign. I'll give you a second chance."

"You watch, I'm going to take a nap" and she curled up by my side.

I nudged Bobbie Jean, "Wake up. You've got to read this sign."

She sat up and looked out, "My goodness! Haven't our California press agents been busy little beavers. I like it. Has a certain rhythm to it."

"Read it to me."

"Modesto, California, Water Wealth Contentment Health."

"It is catchy. Sort of like a Burma Shave jingle. What valley are we driving through?"

"Almost goes the whole length of the state, from Fresno to Sacramento, the San Joaquin Valley. Sierra Nevada Mountains on the east side and the Coastal Range to the west. Have you seen a restaurant sign?"

"Minnies."

"Mouse?"

"No Minnies of Modesto" and we both laughed, "We follow the road to Dodge Ridge."

"What's that?"

"Must be a ski area. There it is, Minnies is on the left."

"Chinese, should be good."

Not knowing Chinese food, I mentioned, "Chow Mein?"

"Time to give my farm boy a lesson in oriental food. Do you mind? I'll order."

"Go ahead. All my experience comes out of a can."

She ordered Lemon Chicken, Kung Po Shrimp and Wonton Soup. It was more than just a culinary delight to someone who grew up on steak and potatoes.

I asked, "Why is the rice sticky?"

"So you can pick it up in your chopsticks and eat your food over the rice bowl. If anything drops, the bowl catches it. The Chinese are very practical."

Minnie's meal wiped out our memory of the Sacramento steak. Back in the wagon, I asked, "You've been reading our tour book. Tell me about Merced."

Bobbie Jean opened it to the M's and said, "It's called the Gateway to Yosemite. If it is, the road to the mountains from the valley has to be over fifty miles. It is renowned for figs, tomatoes, grapes, almonds, cotton and potatoes. The San Joaquin was a desert until irrigation came along. They trap snow runoff in the mountains. Other than Castle Air Force base and agriculture, there is no other industry. Summers are hot and dry. Winters are cool with lots of valley fog. Kind of like Elko with humidity and wine grapes. Can't see more than ten miles. We could see forever in Elko."

"Not many grapes growing in Elko. I'm stuffed. Ready to look for a new home, Mrs. Langtry?"

"That doesn't sound right. I looked around to see if Mother is here."

"Best we can do until she comes around."

"Call me Mrs. Ropp."

I smiled, "We are married. Have to stop at base housing."

"I'd rather live in town."

"Have to see if they have quarters for us. Might have a list of apartments. Like the one Oliver T. found behind Gus Steven's."

"Oh no you don't. I'll not have you anywhere near strippers," she warned.

"Can't have strippers without a strip."

"Near an air base? If there aren't any around we are in the wilderness."

• • •

We followed the signs to Castle Air Force Base. Castle, like all the others I'd been on, hadn't seen a new building since World War II. We saw barracks type buildings as far as our eyes could see. However, the hangers were new, but only because jet bombers were many times larger than B-17s and B-29s. We followed the signs to base housing. Inside I was greeted by a desk sergeant, an identical triplet to the ones I had met at Ellington and Keesler. He was, at the least, friendly, "You're going to have to find your own place in Atwater or Merced."

"Which one do you recommend?"

"Merced, Atwater isn't much more than a vineyard with a couple of stores and some new tract houses."

"Do you have a list of apartments?"

Took awhile before he stopped laughing and composed himself, "Castle is our only B-52 and KC-135 training base. We're packed with students. You may have to live in a motel."

"Do you have a list," and he began to laugh again. "Ours is so out of date it's useless."

I opened the door to our wagon, "No room at the Inn and Atwater isn't. Merced wins by default. We'll have to look for a place to live on our own."

"Good, drive south until we see green."

• • •

The first motel we stopped at had a swimming pool so small, if we attempted a dive we'd hit the opposite wall and water so brown, no one would find you. First time I ever heard Bobbie Jean swear, other than at Yankees. "I'm not staying in a damn dump. It's barely one step away from a migrant worker's camp. We're right across the street from a giant Orange Julius stand. Let's move on. I just stepped on a bug larger than a Mississippi mouse."

"Sheets look clean enough."

"Only on one side."

• • •

We stopped next to a series of bungalows nestled in grove of Sugar Pines with an appropriate name—*Pine Cone Inn*.

Bobbie Jean tugged at my arm and giggled at the next sign, *The Branding Iron*. "Do you think they serve seafood?"

"Only if you can rope it from a horse. We'll find out after we check in. Put a dime in the slot and get a copy of the local newspaper."

"There's one left. I'll look for apartments at dinner."

Our motel room was Yosemite-rustic, but clean. You have to like ranch oak to really get the flavor. Dinner was at, where else, the restaurant next door. And they did have seafood and it was branded by the top of the grill. I finished a superbly thick and juicy sirloin, while Bobbie Jean had a delicious trout. She scanned the classifieds while we sipped two mugs of excellent coffee. She folded the newspaper, "Do you want dessert? Our waitress said they have their own bakery downtown."

"Cherry pie?"

"Can she bake a cherry pie," charming Johnny.

Why did I answer, "Of course I want cherry pie for dessert. And your the young one that cannot leave her mother, but I know my duty. I'll be your permanent straight man. Did you find a lead?"

"Yes and I'll find a place for us tomorrow, even if I have to buy a house. We've spent too much time in motels on this trip. I want to begin nesting."

"Are you serious about buying?"

"Yes, it's obviously a good rental market. We can turn a profit in three months if we rent to people like us."

• • •

After I turned off the light and climbed into bed, Bobbie Jean curled up like a spoon to my backside and pulled my pillow down to share, "Did you hear what the waitress said about the entertainment here?"

"No, must have been when I was using the little boy's room."

"The main entertainment is watching bears eat garbage at the dump in Yosemite."

"Not my cup of tea."

"Their second favorite is squashing tarantulas under their car tires on the way back."

"Are you sure she wasn't kidding?"

"Yes and the TV reception is so bad here we only get two channels, intermittently."

"I can do nothing for three months, with you at my side. Learned how to do that tending sheep."

"Well, if you expect nothing, that's what you'll get. Not us, we're going to see the Golden Gate, Yosemite, Cannery Row, the Pacific Ocean and tramp through the Redwoods. I'm going to make my Yankee farm boy into a man of the world."

"That will take some doing. We still have a lot to learn about each other and now we have time."

"Hate to admit it, but you're right."

"Let's make this our extended honeymoon."

• • •

After breakfast, Bobbie Jean dragged me all over town looking at resales, new homes and apartments. Late in the afternoon, we found what she wanted. She asked, "What do you think?"

"It's walled in and the only place to park is on the street. It's Cool enough. We may not have to use the swamp cooler."

"I noticed the vents. How does it work?"

"Water flows over felt pads and a blower vents air through. Works in a dry climate, not Biloxi."

"I like it. Hardwood floors and it's furnished right out of 1930, almost Art Deco. Clean and comfortable."

"I thought you wanted to buy?"

"I did until I saw the construction. The new places are being finished with packing crate wood. We'll rent."

"We'll have to convince the owner."

"No problem. When I retrieved the keys we hit it off quite well."

"But it said no short-term rentals."

"I remember a young lieutenant in Biloxi who solved that problem. You'll convince her."

"And we'll offer a large deposit and pay three months up front."

Bobbie Jean did all the talking. When she finished the apartment was ours at the long term rate. I asked, "How did you convince her?"

"Remember, hotel owners have a union and apartment owners have the same bond. And she thought you looked cute."

"Right, did you tell her we were newlyweds?"

"Of course. She looked as straight laced as any lady I know in the south. You and I both have incomes, so I'll pay my share and we'll split all costs."

"I can afford . . ."

"Not the way I like to live, not on lieutenant's wages."

"Where were you when I was scratching my way through Ohio State?"

"Cursing you Yankee carpetbaggers."

"In your Biloxi finishing school?"

"No, silly, in high school Confederate history class."

"Did I transport a minor across a state line?"

"Almost, my lucky one."

• • •

We spent the next three days picking up packages from the post office and buying household items to make our new (to us) two bedroom apartment livable. She had picked well. Although the furnishings had age, they were well preserved and sparkling clean. After watching Bobbie Jean in action, I gained a large share of respect for homemakers. Our waitress was right about poor TV reception. And we drove up to Yosemite to look at the bears. Talk about big browns. We didn't stay long at the dump. Wasn't appetizing. And the tarantulas were swarming all over the road on our way back. I avoided what I could and squashed the rest. Must have been a fall mating procession or something like that. We found two excellent restaurants, the Lodge at Yosemite and a little Italian place, on the road back.

• • •

All good things had to come to an end and so did our short honeymoon. I reported into B-52 ground school early on a Monday morning. Our instructor's welcome was short and to the point, "Welcome to B-52 Combat Crew Training. You'll have a month and a half of book training before you get to fly. Your crew consists of two pilots, a radar operator, a navigator, a gunner and you, an EW. All of the crews you'll join up with were together in B-36s, so they'll treat you as odd man out. The B-36 used gunners to protect the airplane. In the B-52 we use electronics and that's you. You have an important job to do, but your crew may not recognize it as such. From the feedback we're getting, most look at EWs as dead weight. The B-52 counts on high altitude, speed and deception to survive. You provide the deception. Can't see it, feel it or hear it, so EW will be a hard sell. Ground School begins tomorrow morning at eight sharp. In the back of the classroom you'll find B-52 Tech Order books under your name. They cover the airplane from nose to tail, inside and out. And there is an emergency procedures book, also. I want you to spend the rest of the morning memorizing the applicable parts for your position. This afternoon, I want you to draw your brain buckets and flight gear from supply. We won't be flying above fifty-thousand feet, so you won't need pressure suits. Walker's wing operations officer wants to see you at the base theater at noon. Any questions?"

It was time for Tucker to be served, "Is it, you play ball with me and I'll play ball with you—or you play ball with me and I'll shove the bat up your ass?"

"No, Lieutenant Ropp, isn't it? Rest assured, the Tooth Fairy won't leave a quarter under your pillow, and SAC will play fair, but if that's your attitude I just might leave it where the sun don't shine. That's all I have to say. Now get to work."

I not only learned emergency procedures, I discovered the B-52 pecking order before I wandered over to the base theater. First came the senior pilot, or aircraft commander, followed by radar operator, navigator, copilot and I fell in behind the gunner. It was the same as joining a fraternity at Ohio State. The new guys were always on the bottom.

The bomb wing director of operations was a full eagle colonel. The first of that rare bird that I had ever seen. And he didn't waste any time. He strode to the podium with the authority of a Texas Ranger at a riot. As a result, our packed base theater grew suddenly silent. He tapped the microphone, "Gentlemen, and I say that loosely, I'm for having a good time as much as anyone, but World War II is over. Getting drunk, driving down a California railroad track at midnight with your headlights on high and playing chicken with an oncoming freight train is not my idea of good clean fun. If you have too much to drink, pick a sober guy to drive home. I don't want any more early morning phone calls from California's Highway Patrol. Let's do our job, learn what we need to know about our new airplane and return to Roswell without any more trouble. The next officer who winds up in a drunk tank will be dismissed from the service. For you new guys, we work hard and play hard. And remember, keep your play reasonable."

• • •

When I returned to our apartment that evening, I told Bobbie Jean about our lecture, "This assignment is looking up. Looks like I'm joining a group that really knows how to party."

"I'm party enough for you, soldier."

"I'll watch my step. Most of them are here without their wives."

"Like sailors on leave. Let's go to San Francisco while we can."

"Drive over Friday night?"

"I'll make reservations at that downtown hotel with the rooftop bar, Top of the Mark."

"We'll have to return Sunday evening."

"It'll be fun. We can see if the Golden Gate Bridge is really painted gold."

"And if there are any forty-niners left."

• • •

By the time Friday morning arrived, I was certain B-52 ground school was going to be a piece of cake. SAC trained like it flew, with realism. No trick questions and the airplane exams were called, practical, straight and to the point. Our trip to San Francisco turned out to be great fun. We visited the Fleishecker Zoo out near Cliff House and rode an enclosed carousel shrouded in coastal fog, right out of a California movie scene. Did all the tourist things—rode a cable car, had drinks at the Top of the Mark and dinner at Trader Vic's. It wasn't as good as Minnies in Modesto, very few Chinese restaurants were. The Golden Gate Bridge wasn't gold, not at all. It was a disappointment, painted in bright international orange. Cold, with fog and wind off the Pacific, I've never been as cold anywhere. We were dressed for San Joaquin Valley warm, not California coastal cold. If I had one thing I'd do again it was ride that carousel at the zoo. In the dense fog, with it's barrel organ playin' Paddlin' Madelin Home, it was the land of enchantment. Bobbie Jean was starry-eyed as we strolled through Golden Gate Park, arm in arm. Like most things in life, the best memories are free.

• • •

The next weekend we drove to Monterey. Cannery Row was a ramshackle pile of wharf and warehouses with seals and sea lions all over the docks. John Steinbeck would still feel at home there. We were dressed for the cold breeze of Seventeen Mile Drive, but not well enough. It was two in the afternoon before the sun poked through. We stopped at Pebble Beach and several pullouts to take photos, but didn't stay outside the wagon very long. The wind was winter sharp. We stopped at several tea houses in Carmel, but gave up trying to get in without reservations. All in all we came away with a memory that said, pack a lunch next time you come this way and wear another layer of clothes. I had to needle Bobbie Jean on our return trip via San Luis Obispo, "You weren't able to crack that cutesy quaintly town without reservations."

"And I thought Old Mississippi was a closed society. I like this mission town better. If California is the land of fruits and nuts, Carmel has the fruits and San Luis Obispo really does have nuts."

"Say English walnut, quick. That's a harsh judgment, Bobbie Jean."

"What do they say about a woman scorned? I don't take turndowns lightly."

• • •

B-52 Ground training, like Gaul, was split into three parts. First, emergency procedures. Second, EW equipment knowledge and third, equipment operation. I aced the course, which was a first for me. But of course, most everyone else did, too. Flight training was a horse of another color, with more than a few airplanes falling out of the sky. Took the pilots awhile to learn the B-52 flew better with its tip tanks attached than without. And then, an instructor toggled off a tip tank by mistake. Landed point down in an orchard. The newspaper photo of the smiling farmer standing next to it, looked like a fisherman who'd caught a prize salmon. Wasn't long before the same instructor backed over the fire hydrant in front of our ground training building where he had just been reassigned. He was on his way to supply school in Cheyenne before water was restored to the west side of base.

I wasn't scared, just cautious. You see, my ejection seat centered on the tail, or as smart ass fliers call it, the vertical stabilizer. And that B-52 tail section stood almost two stories high. I was certain if I had to punch out, I wouldn't clear it. I kept thinking, "This is where the bat comes in." Our instructor tried to assure us in a strange way, "At least you won't have to use a can opener to get out like EWs riding the capsule in the bomb bay do." I asked, "Can opener? What do you mean?"

"When you activate that ejection seat, knives come out of the bottom. And when the seat rocket fires, the knives cut a path for your seat to follow." Tucker would have an answer, but all I could say was, "Right."

"Works fine, we think, at high altitude, but it isn't worth a hill of beans down low. Doesn't pay to have a rocket tied to your ass when your seat is pointing down and you're flying close to the ground. But don't worry, we lost the first B-52 carrying a capsule on takeoff, so it looks like SAC is going to cancel the project. Besides, EWs were in short supply after the accident."

I needed reassurance, "Has an EW ejected from a B-52 and survived?"

"Roger that. Even cleared the tail. Really funny, that one, now that you ask. Entire crew bailed out over the base. All except the instructor EW. After the crew left, the plane corrected whatever problem it had and circled the high cone. The instructor wandered around, then called the command post on UHF radio for instructions. Told him to bail out. Couldn't steer the thing without a seat. Just be happy you're not in Royal Air Force Bomber Command. They only give ejection seats to the pilots, everyone else has to fend for themselves."

• • •

Even Bobbie Jean had to laugh when I told her the story about the lone EW, "Isn't that just like the Air Force, dear. One of you is in position to fly the airplane and they tell him to jump. At least you know you'll clear that tail thing."

"Only if they let me know when it's time to go."

"Have you met your crew?"

"No, they're not due in for another month. I'm flying with an experienced crew, though. This pilot is right up front about what he wants from me."

"How so?"

"He said that not failing is the only reward I can expect. SAC expects and gets professional results."

"Is he safe?"

"Yes, he refuses to push the envelope."

"Envelope?"

"Take it past the stops."

"Speak English."

"When you were in kindergarten, didn't they teach you to draw within the lines with your crayon?"

"Yes."

"That's what I mean. Know your limits and stay within them." I watched her smile grow and I knew another zinger was coming, "You've been around one too many pilots when you speak of crayons. How many more weeks do you have to train before we journey on to Roswell by the sea?"

"Depends. If the weather remains good, I'd say at least five more weeks."

• • •

Our last five weeks flew by, pun like. Flying in a B52 raised my heart rate more than a little bit. To some it might be uneventful, but not to me. Like EW school in Biloxi, we were short of equipment, so I was able to look through an empty equipment rack and watch two pilots practice bounce, bounce, bounce and go landings. Bringing a B-52 down was akin to landing a glider. It preferred to stay in the air once it got there. We had an equal number of takeoffs and landings, so I received SAC's highest mark, not failing. My reward was being allowed to work eighty hour weeks—like every other crew member in SAC.

## Las Vegas, Nevada

Bobbie Jean began packing a week before we were scheduled to leave. She still didn't trust the Air Force and we had too many things to mail. So, she scheduled a moving van. Leaving Merced was much easier than coming. All we had to do was point our car south towards Fresno and step on the gas pedal. The trip was uneventful until we drove through a late fall cold front outside of Fresno. One that extended all the way into old Mexico. Bobbie Jean had a word for it, "West has two climates, too hot or too cold."

"And miles and miles of emptiness. Did you make reservations for any particular hotel in Las Vegas?"

"A new resort on the way into town called the Desert Inn."

"From what I've seen so far, it's aptly named. This desert is too firm to plow and too dry to pasture sheep."

"And too far away from a radio station for music."

• • •

We could see the lights of town through the evening twilight way out on the distant horizon. The sign announcing the entrance to the Desert Inn glowed clearly a half a mile away, "This is out on the edge of nowhere. Why did they build this far out?"

Bobbie Jean knew, "To be the first major stop on the road to LA. You can find a bellhop while I check in. We're supposed to have the first ground floor room on the right front of the casino."

Bobbie Jean's name worked its usual magic. I expected a hotel, not a two story motel, but the accommodations were first class. Our room was directly across from the west entrance to the casino and showroom.

Bobbie Jean led the bellhop to our car, "I'll go ahead with the luggage. You can park the car next to the walk outside our room."

She was arranging our clothes when I entered the room, "With a location like this, it must cost a pretty penny."

"For us it's free. We're comped, wouldn't accept our money."

"Takes more than us walking in from the street for that."

"I wired ahead for a line of credit—casino owner's courtesy."

"You've been here before?"

"Yes, before it opened. I have a very small piece of this resort. Start up money."

"You never cease to amaze me. Is there a show tonight?"

"Someone by the name of Ernie Kovacs, a very funny guy."

"Do you want to go?"

"We have reservations for the dinner show. It's the only place serving this evening. Not enough customers to keep the regular dining room open. So if we want to eat dinner here, we don't have a choice."

"I'm going to shower and dress. Coat and tie?"

"Sport coat, shirt open at the neck. Las Vegas is still a cowboy town. Don't lose more than your limit."

When Bobbie Jean entered the casino in her drop-dead evening gown, even the gamblers turned their heads away from the tables. I whistled, "I thought you said this was a cowboy town?"

"Cowboy not cowgirl. How did you do at the tables while I was making myself beautiful."

"Glass of white wine?"

"Yes, you're sitting at a table in the casino bar. Like Reno, did you lose your limit?"

"No, but I screwed up. Sat down to play a couple of hands of blackjack and guess who relieved my dealer?"

"I wouldn't know."

"Dean Martin. I sat there betting and not paying attention, star struck. When he left the table I was seven hundred dollars ahead."

"That's the one rule I didn't tell you about. Blind luck will always win out over knowledge and skill."

"Think I've heard that another way. Ready for dinner? Show begins in thirty minutes."

The maitre d' recognized Bobbie Jean as we walked into the show room. He opened the ropes and provided his own personal escort to a front row owner's table. Dinner was served almost as soon as he placed napkins on our laps. As the lights dimmed, I whispered, "You have more influence than even I expected. How did they know I liked pepper steak and you, grilled salmon?"

"While you were playing blackjack, the maitre d' called our room and asked. If it wasn't for this lamp on our table, I couldn't see my plate."

"Is it polite to dine while the show is on?"

"Yes, delicious isn't it?"

"You are, and the food is, too."

Kovacs put on quite a show with his classic Nairobi Trio pantomime. As the house lights came up, Bobbie Jean whispered, "Did you notice the group behind us, to the left?"

"Between the show and the way you look in your gown, no."

"It's the Marks Brothers."

I glanced back, "I wouldn't have picked them out. How did you?"

"Maitre d' asked if we'd like to be introduced and I declined. It's Harpo's birthday. They're having a private party."

"Looks just like average grandfathers with trophy wives." Bobbie Jean took my arm, "If you want to gamble, count me out. Packing all week and the drive have caught up with my body."

"Mine, too. Let's call it a night."

• • •

It was a miracle, Bobbie Jean was up before daylight. She tapped me on my shoulder, "Rise and shine, soldier. You wanted to be on the road by eight. Breakfast is on the way—so hop to it and make yourself presentable."

"Do you want to stop at the Grand Canyon on the way?"

"El Tovar hotel? Why not. Do we have time?"

"Our airplanes haven't arrived at Walker, no one is pressuring me."

"I want to stop in Prescott to look at property. Is it out of our way?"

"Out of the way but doable. Should we call ahead to the Grand Canyon?"

"I will while you're dressing."

Breakfast arrived while I was shaving. Bobbie Jean called out, "Hurry, your eggs will get cold."

"Not if you leave them covered. What else did you order?"

"Bacon and toast."

"I'm dining with the loveliest lady on the Las Vegas Strip.

She smiled, "At least I've trained you to wear a robe at breakfast."

"It's cold, but I remember. Did you make reservations at the El Tovar?"

"Tried, but they're full up. One of the few places where my union card doesn't work."

"Prescott it is. Should we call ahead?"

"Not more than a wide spot in the road and late fall shouldn't be a problem."

"Is it a resort town?"

"No, but that's why I want to take a look, it may become one."

## Nevada to New Mexico

We stopped at Boulder Dam so this farm boy could look down, which I did. I said something quotable like, "Damn, it's a long way down."

Bobbie Jean held on tight to my arm, "It won't bother you if you look straight ahead."

"If I do that, it looks like the rest of Nevada. That's enough of looking down for me. Strange, I don't get a queasy feeling looking out of an airplane. Poured a lot of concrete here."

"And ruined a good canyon. In an airplane your surrounded by metal." We did the tourist photo bit and got back into our wagon, "Better gas up. It's a long haul to Kingman, Arizona. Bobbie Jean solved the problem of desert driving. She curled up at my side and fell fast asleep.

• • •

We traveled through high desert and big sky, on our drive south of Lake Meade. Dull, I had to talk to myself to stay awake, "It's so dry here, there aren't any bones laying about. A vulture would have to pack a lunch if it was flying over this desolation."

Bobbie Jean lifted her head, "Did you say lunch?"

"Talking to myself to stay awake."

I said "We'll eat lunch in Kingman," and she went back to sleep. She woke up as we slowed to a crawl behind an ancient truck on the outskirts of Kingman. "You're awake, so you have the restaurant-finding detail."

"That's easy. There's only one decent place in town." Bobbie checked out the bathroom and peeked into the kitchen, "The bathroom is clean, kitchen looks okay. Play it safe, we'll stick with cooked food." The hot roast beef sandwiches were tasty, because the gravy had some age to it. Coffee had a burnt acid taste, strong, almost borderline terrible.

• • •

As we drove outside of Kingman, scrub trees announced this part of the desert had seen some rain, but not much. When we turned southeast toward Prescott, red canyons and pine began to fill the landscape. Bobbie Jean sat up and took it all in. I had to ask, "Well, what do you think of Arizona?"

"I like this area, coming into Prescott. Still high and dry, but it has trees and some water in the bottom of the canyons. Don't think this area will ever become a resort."

"Didn't they say the same thing about Las Vegas."

"But Las Vegas has gambling. All this place has is red dirt that blows when it's dry and sticks when it's wet. No, I don't think this will ever be a resort real estate market. I'm going to pass."

"They have a good press agent. Arizona deserts are described as painted and rocks as petrified. Must have hired the same press agent that coined the phrase, 'Golden California.' I take it you want to drive straight through to Roswell in the morning."

"You've got that right, soldier. I've seen enough of desert desolation to last me a lifetime. Let's stop at the first decent motel."

Wasn't much of a choice, only one motel in Prescott. The owners made ends meet by selling Indian Jewelry form their office. Good quality, too. Our Mexican dinner at the motel was excellent and breakfast was even better. Bobbie Jean purchased a map of the area and inquired about an honest real estate broker. Surprise! There was one and only one. She made contact and promised to call after we arrived in Roswell. I asked, "What changed your mind?"

"The motel owners. They're very happy here. Cooler than Phoenix in the summer and winters are mild. And they're sinking their profits back into land. I'm ready to travel, are you?"

"I packed the car while you were on the phone."

• • •

Phoenix? A series of ranch houses growing into a city. Bobbie Jean took mental note, "Notice the high gutters? Lots of adobe and it's above one-hundred degrees in November. Not my cup of tea." She held her nose, "What is that smell?"

I had to laugh, "Horse country. Beef cattle, too."

"Phoenix smells like a feeder lot."

"Let's drive on. I'd rather stop in Tucson for lunch." Giant cactus dotted the hillsides along the highway. Farms appeared, looked like folks were barely scratching out a living on rock hard soil. Water had to be pumped out of the ground for irrigation. The rivers had run dry. Tucson had its own rough style of beauty—forests of giant cactus and mountains. Lunch was almost civilized and coffee? An improvement over the acid taste found in Kingman. East of Tucson we entered more of the same desert desolation we found south of Lake Meade.

• • •

Bobbie Jean checked the map, "Next stop is the middle of nowhere, New Mexico. Looks like more hot sandwiches and acid coffee."

"I take it you don't care for the desert."

"I thought I might grow to like it, but I don't ever think I will. The air is so dry here, I'll wrinkle up. No, give me the salt air ocean breeze along the gulf, anytime. I've slept so long on this trip, I'm wide awake and there is nothing to see. I would hate to have traveled across this desert in a wagon train. Where do you want to stop for a snack?"

"If you see something decent, let me know. We could starve out here."

"Now that's a confidence builder."

"Find a place with hot sandwiches."

"I hope you like Mexican food. That's all I've seen along this road."

"That's what we had for dinner in Prescott."

We crossed over the Rio Grande River at Las Cruces, New Mexico and turned north toward Almagordo, the mother of the Atomic age.

"Rio Pequeno," Bobbie Jean said.

"What's that mean in English?"

"Little River."

"Right, not much more than a wide drainage ditch. We'll have to drive through the Sacramento mountains after dark. Any towns where we can gas up?"

"Mescalaro, Ruidoso and Hondo."

"Sounds like titles for a John Wayne Western."

"Or a Jack Benny radio program train announcer. Stop for a snack in Almagordo."

• • •

With a sunset on our left and moonrise on our right, driving past White Sands made me feel like we were in the middle of an ocean on a honeymoon cruise. Bobbie Jean wasn't impressed. She curled up at my side and drifted off. I smiled, she was a world champion napper.

She woke as we entered Almagordo, "What was that?"

"The crunching sound?"

"Yes, are we driving over gravel?"

"No locusts."

"Locusts!" and she sat straight up. "My God—they're a foot deep in the road. I've lost my appetite. I won't step out of the car here."

"Don't worry, just big grasshoppers. Must be attracted by the lights."

"Now I know what a locust plague is. I didn't know they swarmed in the United States."

"Remember the stories about Salt Lake? We need gas."

"Not here. Don't stop. They may attack."

"Only if it's plant food, but they might get into your clothes and hair."

"Drive on."

• • •

Mescalaro was another without town: without a gas pump, or sidewalk, or general store. Ruidoso was a one town: one gas pump, one sidewalk and one general store. But, the gas pump was closed, as was the store behind it and the sidewalks rolled up when the sun went down. Hondo? It's gas pump closed down during World War II and never reopened. Our last hope was Tini.

Tini turned out to be a ghost town. Bobbie Jean looked worried, "Looks like we should have crunched a few more locusts. What are we going to do now?"

"Coast down hill, save gas and pray."

She leaned closer, "We're coming into our new home town, coasting in on a wing and a prayer."

## Roswell, New Mexico

We coasted downhill into the outskirts of Roswell on fumes. Bobbie Jean perked up, "Reminds me of entering the outskirts of Las Vegas. The lights of town have been visible for the last twenty miles." She breathed a sigh of relief when I pulled up to an open, working gas pump. The gas station attendant filled our tank with gas and our minds with information, "Roswell has two main roads—east and west, north and south. Your on the east-west one. Best bet for a motel is north of town. Out past the New Mexico Military Institute. You've come a long way traveling east with Mississippi license plates. Are you bein' assigned to Walker Air Force Base?"

I answered, "Yes. How do I get there?"

"Drive to the center of town and turn south. Can't miss it. Road dead ends at the main gate."

"You said the best motel is north?"

"Yup, out near the Institute."

• • •

Bobbie Jean checked out the only two motels north of town and decided on one across the street from the New Mexico Military Institute Golf Course.

She frowned, "Lesser of two evils."

The night clerk advised, "Plenty of rooms. Take your pick. Restaurant closed at nine. If you're hungry, bar down the road serves a great hot sandwich. Breakfast is six to nine. Oh, don't wander around in the grass."

Bobbie Jean asked, "Why?"

"Rattlesnakes. Sometimes they get ornery when you step on 'em."

I asked, "Is the Pecos River nearby?"

"More like a stream. It's a mile to the east. Not much good to us since we sold the water rights to Texas. When we do get a gully washer, it can spread out. No one around here is foolish enough to build near it. Better hurry if you want to get a bite to eat. Bar closes at eleven."

• • •

I unloaded while Bobbie Jean unpacked, "Why don't you get two hot sandwiches while I shower away my road grime."

"Any particular choice?"

"Cheeseburger with everything on it and a beer."

"Beer? You never drink beer."

"Can't carry out a glass of wine and it's too late for coffee."

I returned with two giant cheeseburgers, French fries and a cold six-pack. "Wasn't expensive and cooking looked good," I told her.

"Burger is wonderful!" she said with a mouth full.

"They must have a meat packer in town who knows how to age a side of beef. Finish your burger and shower, soldier. I'll wait up for you."

Bobbie Jean opened a second beer for me as I toweled off. Before I could pick it up, she opened my towel and pressed close, "It's time."

"Didn't we do that in Reno."

"Doesn't count until we're home and this might be as close as we'll get."

I picked her up in my arms, "Almost stepped on a rattler when I was outside." It worked, she held on for dear life.

• • •

I rolled over, woken by a dawn sunbeam crawling slowly across my pillow through a crack in the drapes. Bobbie Jean stirred and propped her head in her hands, "I'm awake. How long have you been up?"

"Just woke up. I'm happy just being here with you."

"One beer and a rattler and we turn to lust."

"I'll fill our refrigerator if that's what it takes. What do you think of New Mexico?"

"Not a place I'd choose to honeymoon. It's different. Looks like we've discovered the real west." She draped the sheet over her shoulders and cracked open the drapes, "Wow! Look east—the air is so clear I can see forever. And the sun is so bright it hurts my eyes. Roswell looks a little worn around the edges. I'm not happy about rattlers, but we'll make the best of it. How long do we have to stay?"

"I get out of the Air Force in three years."

"That long? After we're settled in, I have to fly to Mississippi."

"Business or Mother?"

"Both."

"Do we look for a place for one or two?"

"For two, silly. I won't stay long. Did you check the menu?"

"Tex-Mex all day long."

"Join me in a shower?"

"We may miss breakfast."

"Who cares."

Breakfast was, Tex-Mex, a Mexican omelet, tortilla wrapped around cheese, shredded beef, salsa and grits instead of potatoes. The coffee tasted as if it was brought to a boil over a campfire. Bobbie Jean ate around the edges, "Salsa's too hot, but the grits are wonderful. Can we look for a place to live before you report in for work?"

"Yes, but I have to stop by base housing, first. They may want us to move on base."

"I hope not. I found a new home with a pool for sale or lease in the want ads."

"Expensive?"

"For here, yes, but I don't like second best."

"Better eat your omelet. You'll need sustenance if your nesting urge is taking over."

She pulled apart her omelet, brushed away the salsa and ate the egg, cheese and shredded beef, "I don't need salsa when I'm around you."

*Alice was just beginning to think to herself, "Now what am I to do with this creature when I get it home?"*

# Chapter 9

"Are you sure you want to go out to the base with me? I might get hung up on administrative matters."

Bobbie Jean moved closer, "I'm still on our honeymoon. Point this car toward your Air Force base. If you get hung up, I'll go to the Officers Club and make a few phone calls. We have furniture arriving and I want to check on the house I found in the paper."

• • •

I followed the directions given to us by the gas station attendant last night. He was right. The road dead ended at the main gate. The Air Policeman wore a pearl handle revolver, I knew I was in SAC, "Which way to the 666th bomb squadron orderly room, Sergeant?"

"Turn right at base headquarters, left at the first intersection and drive toward the flight line. It's a temporary building left over from World War II, out in an open field all by itself. Can't miss it. Can I give you a word of warning? Be careful around Sergeant Bidup Bidwell."

"Why?"

"He'll hustle you out of your socks. Welcome to Walker Air Force Base." He punctuated his welcome with a snappy salute.

Bobbie Jean got the giggles, "I think I know Bidwell."

"Really?"

"If he's handy with a deck of cards, Ralph lost a few poker hands to him. I'll stay in the car. He might remember me."

• • •

I opened the orderly room door and a stocky, yet handsome, technical sergeant greeted me, "Fill out our sign-in sheet, lieutenant. You might as well save leave time. You have plenty of time to get settled in. It'll be a month before we get organized. Oh, I'm Sergeant Bidup Bidwell. My friends call me Bidwell."

"I'm Johnny Ropp. What do I do next?"

"Nothing until Monday. Report at eight to roll call and our ops officer will tell you what to do."

"More school?"

"Some, but our airplanes aren't here. They're still building them up in Wichita, Kansas. You'll have plenty of free time to get settled in. Is that your wife out in the car?"

"Yes, why?"

"You look like you can use a second car. I'll make you a deal you can't refuse. Got forty of them parked outside the gate."

"Forty cars?"

"Won a used car lot in a poker game last night. Have a beautiful pink and white Packard Caribbean convertible. Your wife would love it and I'll sell it to you for half of list, if you'll pay cash."

"Maybe later, after we get settled in. Where is base housing?"

"Back the way you came in. Right next to the Officer's Club. You'll have to live off base. No room at the inn, here."

"Good, my wife was looking at a new place with a pool for sale or lease."

"Just put it in the paper. Here are the keys. Address is on the holder."

"Poker game?"

"No, the builder had a run of bad luck with dice. I'll be here all day. Give me a call if you want it. If not, leave the keys under the door mat."

• • •

"You know the house you saw in the paper this morning? Here are the keys. It's brand new. Never been lived in."

"Bidwell?"

"How did you guess? And he has forty used cars outside the gate for us to look at."

"We'll need a second car. I don't want to drive one of mine back. That's not one of the things I want to do when I go back for a visit."

The sergeant at base housing was blunt, "You don't want to live in our temporary quarters. Sand stacks up a foot deep on the inside wall when the wind blows. Dust storms are New Mexico's middle name. Stay downtown."

"How about if I move in on a temporary basis?"

"Wouldn't recommend it. Once you're in, it'll take an act of congress to move out."

I hopped back in the car and told Bobbie Jean, "We can live off base."

"I want to make a few phone calls at the Officer's Club."

• • •

Looked in the bar. It was open early. Sat down next to two silver bar lieutenants and introduced myself, "I'm Johnny Ropp, just arrived in town."

The heavy set one stuck out his hand, "I'm Joe Carry and this is Dick Hoar. Where are you going to be assigned?"

"666th."

"We're in the 333rd. Are you a pilot?"

"No, EW."

"Roger that—we are too. Do you need a place to stay? We have a room open in a four bedroom, downtown. Dick rented it and is subletting rooms. You can have a room for a hundred a month, includes maid service."

"Wife's on the phone in the lobby. We'll need a place of our own, but thanks for the offer. Who's your third?"

"Copilot in our squadron by the name of Chris Cherry. Don't see much of him. Sticks to himself. Have a beer. Cheap here."

"What's that red stuff in your beer?"

"Called a Red Dog, beer and tomato juice. Settles a stomach after a late night binge."

I ordered one. Dick Hoar wrote down their address, "Don't have a phone yet. Supposed to hook one up tomorrow. When you call information, ask for Hoar's house," and they both laughed.

I took a sip of red beer. Wasn't bad, a nice change of pace. I asked Joe, "Anyplace good to eat in town?"

"You're sitting in it."

"What do we do until our airplanes arrive?"

"Go to morning roll call and training, when they have some. That's about it. The roll call is to make sure we don't take off for civilization. We're inside the O' Club playing poker most every afternoon."

"When do we pick up our crew."

"When they get here. When did you leave Keesler?"

"Late August. Sent me straight to Castle."

"That's new. We came here first. Have you gone to Survival training?"

"No, what's that?"

"Send us to Reno, Nevada and throw us out into the snow. Teach us how to live off the land, so we can survive if we get shot down. Rumor has it we go there in January."

"How long?"

"Think it's thirty days. Did you run into Bidwell in the 666th Orderly Room."

"Yes, he signed me in and tried to sell me a car. Seems nice enough."

"You'll se a lot of Bidwell. We do. He owns our house. Won it in a poker game."

"I'm looking at another one this afternoon, he won with magic dice."

"That's our Bidwell. Has his own federal gambling stamp. Pays his taxes."

"Is he honest?"

"Squeaky clean. He doesn't need to cheat. As he always says, 'Odds over emotion.'"

I asked Dick, "Anything I should know about Walker Air Force Base."

"Almost like that sign over Purgatory, 'All hope abandon, ye who enter here.' Walker is in the midst of major changes. The B-47s are moving north to New Hampshire and the only thing left of the B-36s is the giant hanger on the west end of the Flight Line."

"Why did the B-47s move?"

"This time it's practical, not political. They'll save a refueling or two if we have to go to war. Rumor has it that Walker will get an Atlas Missile Squadron one of these days. Talk about foolishness, New Mexico is eighty percent desert hardpan and the Army Air Corps built this place on the only swamp. The runway keeps cracking, so they're repairing it now, before our airplanes come in."

Joe added, "Someone in base engineering said they only know how to build a runway on top of underground springs. Have another beer."

"May take you up on it. Let me see if Bobbie Jean is finished making her phone calls."

I sat back down and ordered another beer, "On the phone with her mother in Jackson, Mississippi. I'll have time. Tell me what you know about the B-52. All I got was the school solution at Castle."

Dick deferred to Joe, "Boeing engineers designed it out of a cigar box and strings in a hotel room in Dayton, after Wright-Pat turned down their first design. It's designed for high altitude and speed. Like the B-47, the wings flex upwards in flight. Problem is Russians aren't stupid. They're building high altitude high speed fighters to counter the B-52."

"Sounds like a billion dollar chess game."

"You got it. That's where we come in. We were an add-on, to counter their fighters by blinding radars directing them to our airplane. If they can't find us, they can't shoot us down."

"And we don't have any equipment."

"Designed, just isn't manufactured."

"Do we have any fighters protecting Walker?" Joe laughed, "What for? We only have one TV station and it shuts down at six P.M."

Dick added, "And the only movie theater in town is chilled by a swamp cooler."

Joe quipped, "But we do have good hunting and fishing."

• • •

When she had finished her phone calls, Bobbie Jean asked, "What did you learn about our new home and your job."

"Both are going to be like flying a B-52 during a nuclear exchange. Many hours of boredom followed by a microsecond of chaos. Did you finish your phone calls?"

"Yes, did you finish your beer?"

"Only had two."

"Before lunch?"

"Touché! Show me the way to Bidwell's pool home."

"I want to look at his used cars first."

Bonnie's Packard Caribbean looked in good shape, but Bobbie Jean would have none of it. "It reminds me of your crazy friend. I wonder why they sold it?"

"And where they are."

"There is nothing here I care for. I'll drive the Bentley back."

"What changed your mind?"

"You won't believe the airline connections from here to New Orleans."

"Show me the way to our new home."

Bidwell's house was more than either one of us expected. It had all of the modern conveniences and built-ins. Bobbie Jean smiled, "We'll lease."

"Looks like a great place. Why not buy?"

"We're north of the institute and country club—all by ourselves out in the country. It's a lot more than double the price of the median home here. You'll have a very long commute to the base. Resale may be a problem and if the base closes down, a disaster. I called around, they have a salt water intrusion problem here. I want to freshen up. Let's head back to our motel."

"Lunch at that little bar with the hamburgers we had last night?"

"You're on."

• • •

Now, like I said, preparing to fly a B-52 and living where civilization ends isn't all that exciting. Bobbie Jean and I settled down in Bidwell's pool home. His lease terms were more than fair. He offered Bobbie Jean an escape clause in case she changed her mind and wanted to move. Her being an ex-owner of a casino didn't hurt. She decided to stay on until I went to Survival training, though her mother applied all the pressure she could, without totally alienating her. Bobbie Jean wouldn't budge. She was having too much fun satisfying her nesting urge. I played a bit of poker at the O' Club and attended every type of training possible, from judo to altitude chamber. New Mexico's hunting season was almost over and that gave us something to talk about.

Texas hunters travel west to New Mexico's Sacramento Mountains to hunt turkey, deer and bear. They do a lot of drinking, which might explain two accidents that happened up in the mountains. One of the hunters came around a mountain trail near Carlsbad and met up with a bear comin' the other way. Scared the hell out of both of 'em. So much so, both the bear and hunter tumbled down the mountain. Bear came out all right, but the hunter lost his rifle, broke both his legs and collarbone. Said the last thing he saw before he passed out was the bear running away with his rifle. But our Mayor's son took the cake. One of those silly Texans climbed a tree and gobbled, tryin' to attract a turkey. Our boy from Roswell heard all that gobbling and shot the Texan right out of the tree. Claimed he thought the Texan was a big turkey, which come to think of it, he had to be if he was sitting in a tree. Now, the local folks weren't sure about his tale, very few turkeys are six feet tall and dress in international orange. But nothing was done because it was the Mayor's son. Most of our big game hunters got their ammunition and fortification from the same store. Didn't pay to go on a hike in the mountains during hunting season. Too drunk to walk, most hunters parked their trucks on the side of the road and fired away at any movement or sound up, down and across canyons. After the snow melts, New Mexico rangers would find a dozen or so, if the coyotes left anything but bones. And you know how canines love to chew on bones.

As dull as it was for Bobbie Jean and me, Roswell was worse for bachelors like Joe Carry and Dick Hoar. Though a couple of telephone operators did stop by their place to see what Hoar's house was all about. Joe and Dick had tickets for the local Junior College football team, New Mexico Military Institute. West Point and Annapolis hid more than a few players here, to work on bringing up their grades so they'd pass admission tests. Roger Staubach was this years prize catch. And there were four golf courses, but the one at the base was overrun by jackrabbits. Had to brush turds out of the way to putt and golf balls didn't smell all that good. Joe said the lady population was so depleted, he was getting desperate enough to wait outside high school at recess. So, they had decided to make home brew to help kill time and cut down on their drinking costs. I was warned never to stand in front of their garage refrigerator door. One of their friends opened it when the temperature was 105 degrees and an entire row of home brew bottles exploded. He is at the military hospital in San Antonio, recovering.

• • •

Christmas came and passed, still without airplanes. When I received orders to attend Survival Training at Stead Air Force Base, Bobbie Jean made airline reservations for New Orleans. She flew out on TTA to Amarillo, Dallas, Little Rock, Memphis and New Orleans. She was not a happy camper, "Call me at my place in Biloxi. I have at least a month's work to catch up on while you play mountain man in the Sierra Nevadas." And I wasn't anxious to discover how the Donner party wintered over in the mountains.

## Reno, Nevada

Took us three days to drive to Reno. Caught in a snow storm outside of Albuquerque, we had to make an unscheduled stop. Joe Carry wasn't as sure about the length of survival training as he was the last time we talked, "They're going to keep us guessing. That's part of the game. But I do know we'll be hiking in the mountains above Donner Pass, up to our noses in snow."

Dick asked, "How deep?"

"Been skiing around Tahoe. We'll be tree top deep. Can't say what the first part of survival training is. Not allowed too, so I won't. But I'll never forget those mountains."

After our first day in the mountains, I figured the only survival training we'd get was how to starve, freeze, or get worn out trying to walk on snow shoes. Other than that, this training was about as exciting as watching sheep forage in winter. In this case, we were the sheep. Our rations consisted of what we could catch or pemmican. Problem was, we couldn't catch anything that wasn't there. And we had to dig through thirty feet of snow for something green to eat. So we were stuck with what Air Force tried to pass off as pemmican. Our American Indians invented this treat. The way they prepared, pemmican it was quite tasty, but not our Air Force version. Indians pounded lean deer meat flat, smoked it and mixed it with stuff to make trail food. Air Force paid the lowest bidder to mix fat, flour, molasses and suet to produce their bar. Ours smelled rancid and tasted God awful. Now that's an item you could prescribe for fat folks. Easy to lose five pounds a week on a diet of pemmican when the only way to eat it is to gag it down. We received lectures on how to catch rabbits, eat roots and other neat to know stuff. Would have worked, too, but over the years, previous trainees had scoured the country clean, like the cloud of locusts in Almagordo.

• • •

We hiked three days, straight up a series of Billy goat hills, climbin' high up in the Sierra Nevada Mountains. On the afternoon of the third day, as we reached the top, the clouds parted. The view was spectacular. Mountain peaks as far as we could see, to the four points of the compass.

Joe whistled, "Look down, over there, to our north."

It looked like any other mountain pass, tree deep in snow. "That's Donner pass. We're lookin' down at where people ate people with nothin' to eat, but pemmican."

I was so busy putting one snowshoe in front of the other, I hadn't paid attention to why I was running out of breath. We were in reasonable shape, but not for above nine-thousand feet. That solved another mystery, but didn't help with walking in mountains on snow shoes. Dick Hoar took his snow shoes off, "I can go a lot faster without . . ."

Didn't hear the rest of what he said because of the scream. Had to throw a rope down in the hole he made to pull him back up. Had to be at least thirty foot deep. He made the mistake of thinking these were little Christmas trees. We were walking through the tree tops of forty foot pines.

On the fourth day, we hiked down the western side of the mountain in bright sunlight, cheerful as children in the Alps. Didn't last long. Instead of building a teepee with a warm fire inside, we split into pairs.

Our instructor informed us, "Gentlemen, I've provided each one of you with a map. You are to rendezvous at the pickup point marked with an 'X' at nine sharp tomorrow morning. I'll send each team out at ten minute intervals. You are going to attempt to escape and evade. We have patrols in snow track vehicles. They will attempt to intercept and incarcerate you. Are there any questions?"

Tucker had to be honored, "Is this where the bat comes in?"

"Lieutenant, you've been out on this mountain too long. Stay low and keep hidden."

• • •

My partner, who will remain nameless, waited behind a tree half as wide as he was. I looked out over a wide open mountain valley meadow ten miles wide and two miles across to the opposite tree line. I looked up at a full moon and down at our green Air Force flight suits and parkas. We were going to stick out on the snow like a whore in church. There was no way we could evade anyone. I decided it had to be a game. When the instructor tapped my shoulder and pointed, we struck out on snow shoes, alternating the lead to break a path through the snow.

My partner was into the game, "Let's get as far as we can up the other side of that mountain before we catch a few winks. We can wake up at dawn and walk into the checkpoint at nine."

Turned out that meadow was closer to four miles across than two. And walking on snow shoes takes twice as long as hikin' in summer. When my partner took the lead, three quarters of the way across, we hit a particular shallow and smooth patch of snow. He was chugging along. I almost had to break into a trot to keep up.

All of a sudden, Partner disappeared from view. I looked down, "Anything broken?"

"You son of a bitch. You should have been lead."

I figured we were wearing one too many layers to duke it out, so I said, "Looks like you've found the Truckee River. Any water down there to put in our canteens?"

"Come on down and find out for yourself."

Had to cross it anyway so I slid down the bank and began to chop through the ice. When I reached gravel, I gave up. Partner, still pissed off, was plowing through the snow a hundred yards ahead. I packed my survival shovel away and followed. If it hadn't been for the full moon and deep snow, I would have lost his trail as I climbed up the mountain through the trees. And maybe I should have. When I finally caught up with him it was two in the morning. He was all ready sound asleep in a double sleeping bag on top of the snow. Remembering the Donner Party, I moved a safe distance away and pulled the sleeping bags out of my pack. I climbed in, boots, parka and all. My feet still felt like icicles. By the time the sleeping bag's outer zipper hit my chin, I was fast asleep.

• • •

I woke up with the sun in my eyes and partner gone. Now I understood why no one else wanted to work with him. I made a mental note. If I ever had to work with partner again, I would never trust him with sharp objects or money. I checked the map. My destination was over the top of the mountain, another mile down hill to a road and then two miles north. After I crossed over the crest and walked downhill for thirty minutes, I found the road and began walking north. I met two trekkers walking south. They tried to convince me to come along, but I continued walking north. Partner passed by me without saying a word. He too was walkin' south.

Joe Carry and Dick Hoar arrived at our check point early, leaning against a canvas back six-by, our transportation. Dick Hoar asked, "Where's partner?"

"Heading north, following two other lost souls."

"You mean pilot and copilot?"

"Guess so. Looks like I drew a winner with partner."

"We chuckled all the way here over that. Partner brings new meaning to loner."

"Think he'll fail?"

"No one fails unless he's dead, or lost forever."

Joe laughed, "Sending out a search party for two pilots in need of a navigator."

"Is the water okay to drink?"

"Better be, we filled our canteens from the stream."

• • •

We hopped into the back of the six-by and bounced downhill on a mountain road to Stead Air Force Base, tossin' pemmican bars out the back. Crows seemed to like them at first, but soon returned to peckin' at road kill.

I rode out of the high Sierras fifteen pounds lighter than when I went up, most of it water loss. Melting snow to drink didn't hack it. I showered, shaved and put on a clean uniform. The mess hall had a special steak dinner for us. I tried to eat it, but a shrunk stomach will only hold so much. I was lucky to down less than half. After two cups of coffee, had to run to the bathroom. It's not what you think. Lack of water had dehydrated my system. Intestines felt like a compactor. I think I now know a little about what a woman goes through when she has a baby.

• • •

Bobbie Jean listened to my reason for not calling last week and my lack of water problem and began to giggle, and then laugh. After she composed herself, I received her standard warning, "Stay away from the tables. If you must gamble, remember the rules. I didn't set up a line of credit for you, but we have an account at Harold's. You can cash a check there. I'll have to stay on a little while longer than I expected. Do you mind?"

"Yes, but if you must. Business?"

"No, it's Mother. She is either not well or doesn't want me with you."

"Did you tell her we are married?"

"That would kill her for sure. I'm sending some furniture out next week. The moving people will contact you."

"Are you going to drive back?"

"Yes, flying TTA is a mistake I'll not make again. I'll call before I leave. When will you be back in Roswell?"

"If we don't run into snow, I'll be home in two days."

After I put the phone down, Joe called for me to stop by his room, "They found Partner. He was curled up next to a tree, ten miles from the pickup point."

"And the pilots?"

"They returned an hour late."

"Will they have to take survival training over."

"No, we all passed."

## Roswell, New Mexico

Bidup Bidwell met me at the orderly room door, "Welcome back lieutenant. You look like you could use a good home cooked meal."

"Don't tell me. You've won a restaurant."

"Come to think of it, I have, a little bar with great hamburgers north of the Institute. How did survival training go?"

"The only thing I learned was how to starve. You're living in this orderly room. Who did you piss off?"

"My fault. Got carried away and cleaned out the top sergeant in a poker game. But this won't last long. You've returned just in time."

"What's happening."

"We crew up tomorrow."

"No big deal. I all ready have one."

"Not anymore. You've been moved up to the Egyptian's crew and I'm your gunner."

"The Egyptian?"

"Captain Scarcopha."

"Is he good?"

"We're the lucky ones. He's one of the best there is. Stays within the envelope!"

"If I'm so lucky, how did I get you?"

"I'm crafty and bear watching."

"When are you going to be out of the Top's dog house."

"Payday at the NCO' Club. He will have an amazing streak of luck. Understand Bobbie Jean is back in Biloxi."

"She is. How did you know that?"

"I travel in a small, elite world. Knew her husband."

"Ever been to the Broadwater?"

"I own a piece of it now. Didn't win it from Ralph. Bought in with some friends. We're betting that Mississippi will allow gambling in again. Bobbie Jean turned a handsome profit for his kids. How do you like your new home?"

"Great. Can't wait for it to warm up so I can use the pool."

• • •

Captain Scarcopha's greeting was friendly enough, but all business, "You met Sergeant Bidwell. He's given you his stamp of approval. Captain Godsend is our copilot, Major Duckshoot is our radar operator and Captain Fix is our Nav We have the makings of an award winning crew. Except for you and Sergeant Bidwell, we all served together on B-36s. We will address each other by position or rank. No first names. I want us to be professional at all times. Welcome aboard. When can we meet your wife?"

"As soon as she returns from Mississippi."

I saluted and walked to the rear of the crew briefing room and motioned to Bidwell, "Pretty formal isn't he, Gunner?"

"Call me Bidwell. The Egyptian's rules only apply to officers. Underneath all that formal stiffness is a pretty nice guy who cares about his people, but he's still a pilot. And most pilots don't relate to people, except fast women. They only relate to things, like flying machines, fast cars and boats. Air Force tests them to see if they have twenty-twenty eyesight, coordination and a death wish. They're afraid if they read anything deeper than Dr. Seuss they'll ruin their distant vision. We got lucky. Our Egyptian has all the pilot attributes except a death wish. That's why I steered you and me onto his crew."

"Knowing you won't bet on anything that's not a lead pipe cinch, we must have drawn a prize out of the pilot's Cracker Jack box."

"It'll take awhile to get used to the Egyptian's formalities. After awhile he'll loosen up."

"If he's safe, I don't care how formal we are."

I spent the rest of the day moving the furniture Bobbie Jean sent from Biloxi. She was due in three days and I knew we'd move it again, but it was something to do, for now.

• • •

After roll call the next morning, Captain Scarcopha motioned for Bidwell and me to join him and the rest of the crew at the front of the room. "EW and you, too, Gunner. We're flying to Wichita this afternoon. We'll ferry a B-52 back here. Bring your flight gear and earplugs. We're flying up in a 123 and they can be noisy."

"Will we stay overnight, sir?"

"No, but be prepared to. Do you have a brain bucket and oxygen mask?"

"Yes, sir. Got fitted for it before I went to Stead. Not very comfortable. Tight around my ears."

"That's the way they're supposed to be. We leave from base ops at ten. I want to be back at Walker tonight."

• • •

On the flight to Wichita, Bidwell took me aside and began to teach me how to spot someone dealing from the bottom of the deck. I learned one important lesson, I was a sheep ready to be shorn. His final lesson was blackjack. He let me shuffle and triple cut a deck of cards right out of the box. And then proceeded to deal to five players and himself. He won twenty straight hands before he put the cards back in the box. I had to know, "How did you do that."

"Magic cards."

"But you broke the cellophane."

"Lesson number two. I sealed the cellophane after marking the cards."

"Do you cheat when you're playing for high stakes?"

"Don't have too with a photographic memory. I know the odds and most important, the players. Most players gamble for the rush it gives them, so they take chances. I don't. Remember, it's only important to know how to cheat so you can spot the ones who do."

"How do you tell if a deck is marked?"

"Take too long to show you, have to keep some secrets."

"What do you do if you catch a person using marked cards?"

"Wait, change the marks and burn the cheater."

"Why do you stay in the Air Force? You can buy or sell almost anyone in town."

"Simple, my rush is poker at the NCO' Club on payday night."

The pilot signaled for us to buckle up. Our Little Shaky was coming in for a landing.

• • •

Our 123 taxied to the Air Force side of Boeing's Wichita factory. The Air Force rep, a colonel, met us at the ops building, "Sorry, gentlemen. The airplane you're scheduled to ferry won't be ready until tomorrow morning. I've made motel reservations for you downtown. Everything's up to date in Wichita, except our liquor laws. If you want a mixed drink, you'll have join a private bottle club."

We were driven downtown in an Air Force ten passenger van. I tried to phone Bobbie Jean in Biloxi after I unpacked my gear. She didn't answer, so I knew she was at her mother's and I didn't want to push my luck calling her there. Bidwell stuck his head in the door, "Found a poker game. Care to join in? You can practice what I taught you."

"Out of my league. I'm going to buy a steak and turn in early. Call me if you need any help."

"Won't need too. The sheriff is an old friend and he's sitting in."

• • •

Bidwell met us at breakfast, "I'm buying. Sheriff and I did better than expected last night. He had to draw his pistol on a west Texas rancher and one of the players got a little surly, but other than that it was pretty tame. Got in bed before midnight. Is our airplane ready?"

Captain Scarcopha wasn't happy, "Thank you anyway, Gunner, but we'll pay for our own breakfasts. We're due at the factory in an hour. We'll meet out front in twenty minutes. Gunner, I want to talk to you in private." They adjourned to an empty table.

Later I asked Bidwell, "What happened?"

"Nothing. Egyptian discovered it was the factory colonel's game and we had a visiting general sitting in."

• • •

I climbed up the short flight of the steps that led from the Radar/Nav compartment to the top deck of our new B-52E and looked back at my position. Two UHF receivers, an HF radio, an ejection seat and an empty electronic equipment rack. My area was directly in front of the center fuel tank. This, of course, gave me a lot of confidence in my ability to survive if the fuel tank was ever penetrated by shrapnel from flack, or an exploding hydraulic pack. My position was the only one absent of most of its gear.

I sighed, "Looks like ECM really does stand for extra crew member." I took the periscopic sextant out of its box, spun the dials and checked it out, "At least this is working." I strapped in for taxi and watched the pilots get ready for takeoff through the empty spaces in my equipment rack.

After takeoff, the Nav called me over intercom, "EW, this is Nav I want to check our compass and then shoot a day celestial leg on our way home. I'm getting rusty."

"Roger, Nav I'll give you a call when I'm in position and ready to go."

I moved forward to the stool used for operating the sextant and set up my equipment. It didn't take long for both of us to work out our kinks. We finished the celestial leg over the high cone at Walker.

The Egyptian banked right and began his approach, "Crew, this is pilot. We're going to shoot a couple of touch-and-goes before we call it a day."

I could hear the moans and groans rising up from the seats on the lower deck. After eighteen touch-and-go landings, I understood why. Bidwell crawled forward from the gunner's compartment when we were at a safe altitude. This was to become a common experience. I was going to learn how to manipulate a deck of cards.

• • •

When Bobbie Jean drove into town in her Bentley, she created quite a stir. She did her duty, meeting the other wives, but mostly we stayed to ourselves. With our airplanes arriving and training ratcheting up, ten hour weeks were in the past. We were now working twelve hour days and eighty hour weeks. SAC Headquarters sent in an Operational Readiness Inspection, ORI team to test us on everything from flying to nuclear safety. We didn't fail, accomplishing that with flying colors. We were declared operationally ready and joined others in SAC's mission of nuclear deterrence. With missiles still in the future, we were allowed to stay at home. It would take enemy bombers at least twenty hours to reach targets in the interior of America. We had plenty of time to drive to the air patch, load up and go.

• • •

The age of the intercontinental ballistic missiles changed our lives. Twenty hours warning had become twenty minutes. An Alert facility was built and our bombers were parked near the end of the runway, ready to go. We lived on the flight line, three days on and four off over weekends—four days on, three days off during the week. And the morning we came off alert we flew hours and hours of training to maintain SAC's required high standards of proficiency. Eighty-hour weeks had turned into one hundred hours.

After two years in the New Mexican desert, I was offered a regular commission. I wasn't certain if I wanted to continue a life that separated me from Bobbie Jean for at least a third of the year. But she surprised me, "When you're in business for yourself the hours are just as bad. And you might be around, but you're away. We won't stay here forever and moving on will be exciting. We might be assigned near Washington DC Mother wants to visit the Lee Mansion. Her Daughter's of the Confederacy maintain it."

"And all those dead Yankees in Arlington Cemetery."

"Johnny! It's up to you. I have properties to manage and my investments keep me busy."

I signed up knowing if push came to shove I could resign and return to reserve status. The clincher came when I was given a spot promotion to captain. Hubris swayed me.

• • •

I won't cover all the things that went on at Walker Air Force base because, outside of mind grinding work, not a whole lot happened. Bobbie Jean's mother still wouldn't give us her blessing and if it wasn't for Bidwell, life in Roswell, New Mexico would have been very dull indeed. One late fall Tuesday evening after pulling a weekend on alert, I arrived home from a flight and discovered a living room and entryway stacked high with boxes of golf clothes, clubs, bags, shoes, balls and other assorted equipment. Bobbie Jean met me at the door with a smile, "Guess what Bidwell did this time?"

"It looks like our boy won a pro shop."

"Half, he won half the country club pro shop in a dice game with the golf professional. The golf pro delivered the equipment here."

"What in the world is he going to do with it?"

"I'm going to buy clubs, bags clothes, everything for us. His half price cash offer is too good to pass up."

"We'll go from part time golfers to full time hackers?"

"Of course. We can play the Institute course whenever you have free time during the week."

"Where did you learn the game?"

"Great Southern, next to my home in Biloxi. I used to play twice a week. Where did you learn?"

"In the pasture while tending sheep. I'd hit ball after ball. Got pretty good except for sand, didn't have any. Dropped it after I went to college and never bothered to take it up again."

"Pick out shoes that fit, clubs and bag. We're going to try it tomorrow morning. You do get two days off, don't you?" We played with Bidwell's equipment whenever we had free time, but not more than two days a week. New Mexico's good hunting and fishing were not our cup of tea.

• • •

About six months after Bidwell finally sold off all of his golf merchandise, Bobbie Jean pointed out the lead story on the front page of our local newspaper, "Did you know about this? *Gambling equipment discovered in an abandoned house.*"

"No, but I know only one person who has the wherewithal to set up an operation like that."

"It says here the sheriff found a roulette wheel, blackjack tables, dice, the works. He impounded all of the equipment and is searching for the owner."

"Did our boy do something wrong?"

"Election is coming. It may be a set up, to help back the local sheriff. Isn't Bidwell coming off your crew?"

"Yes, they made him NCO in charge of the Officer's Club."

"Bet the equipment winds up there. Why is he leaving your crew?"

"Something about running football pools on base. They couldn't touch him because he has a federal gambling stamp and he is on federal property."

"Bet they close that loophole."

• • •

Two months after Bidwell set up shop in the O' Club, the club decided to purchase gambling equipment from the sheriff and sponsor monthly Monte Carlo nights. Bidwell's fingerprints were all over this operation. He had a pretty good run of luck with his new casino. Lasted almost a year before orders came through shipping him north. He was transferred to Alaska, on an Aleutian island so far out in the Bearing Sea the International Date Line was bent around it. We enjoyed the turmoil and chaos Bidwell brought into what might have been a very dull world for the better part of four years. With Bidwell gone, the only excitement left in Roswell was an occasional dust storm and sighting of Aliens by the deranged or drunk.

• • •

Six months after Bidwell departed I received a phone call from officer assignments. Orders had just come in from SAC Headquarters sending me to Alaska. I was asked to stop by in the morning for a briefing. Bobbie Jean was excited, "We can buy a four-wheel drive station wagon and drive up the Alcan Highway, or sail up the Inland Passage. It ought to be great fun!"

"Don't get too excited. We're being sent to another good hunting and fishing assignment."

"How were you picked for Alaska?"

"Bidwell, his fingerprints are all over it."

"We have a phone number for his unit. Why don't you give him a call?"

As usual, Bidwell answered the phone at the unit orderly room, "Stick with me, Johnny. We're going places."

"Don't know about that. Every time I turn around, you're doing a punishment tour in the orderly room."

"You must have gotten your assignment."

"Do you know where my air patch is located?"

"It's classified, but don't worry."

"Why not?"

"Not a place up here that doesn't have good hunting and fishing."

The sergeant in charge of officer's assignments laughed, "You're going to buy a four-wheel drive station wagon and drive up the Alcan Highway to Alaska?"

"Wife is out lookin' for one as we speak."

"Better call and tell her not to sign a contract. Captain Ropp," he rolled the R like a German umlaut, "You'll need a boat or an airplane to get to where SAC is sending you."

"SAC has a unit in Alaska?"

"Roger that, you'll be so far out in the Aleutians, it'll take Santa Clause to find your ass. And forget about your wife tagging along. Women aren't allowed where you're going. Who did you piss off?"

"No one. I thought Bidwell was doing me a favor with his connections at SAC headquarters."

"Bidwell? Bidwell did you a favor?"

"I thought he did."

"Captain Ropp, you're being sent to Shemya, Air Force's Alcatraz of the north. I warned Bidwell about screwing over folks at SAC headquarters. It's the chief master sergeant in charge of officers' assignments, Bidwell cleaned him out in one of his poker games. That's how he wound up where you're going. He could have forgiven Bidwell, but I think the pink and white Packard Caribbean convertible did you in. SAC folks hold a grudge and do they ever know how to get even. He didn't do you a favor. Not when you're assignment is to Shemya Air Force Station."

"Sounds more like it should be in Japan, north of Hokkaido"

"You're half right. It's north of Hokkaido and east of Siberia."

"How do I get from here to there."

"You report to Wright-Pat for training after the New Year. SAC arranges transportation north from there. Your new unit is detached out of Fairbanks. It'll be sixty below by the time you get there."

"Where do I send my gear?"

"You'll have to mail what you can't carry."

"What's the duration?"

"It's a remote assignments, one year."

• • •

Bobbie Jean took the bad news like a real trooper, "At least we'll spend Christmas on the Gulf. And I can go north to Ohio with you. We'll have to caravan to Biloxi."

"Do you have room to store our furniture at our Biloxi home?"

"No, but I have room to store it in Jackson. We're leaving here just in time."

"I'll bite—why?"

"The supermarket tabloid says Air Force is hiding aliens at Walker."

"Was it next to a man having a baby?"

"How did you know that?"

"When Bidwell left, the only Alien we have around here went with him. How soon will you be ready to go?"

"As soon as we pack up. What do we do about Bidwell's house?"

"Joe Carry is handling Bidwell's local enterprises. Did you know that Bidwell owns a ranch south of the base?"

"No, but nothing he does surprises me."

*That was a narrow escape!" said Alice, a good deal frightened by the sudden change, but very glad to find herself still in existence.*

# Chapter 10

## New Mexcio to Mississippi

After I squeezed the last bag into our station wagon, Bobbie Jean unfolded the map over the hood of her Bentley. She asked, "Do you want to lead or follow?"

"I'll follow—I've got a load and a-half."

"Stop in Pecos for breakfast. If we lose each other we'll meet there."

"After that we'll turn southeast at Sanderson," Bobbie Jean smiled, "and have lunch in Langtry, Texas."

"Langtry?"

"We have to stop at my namesake, don't we?"

"Are you sure your family didn't move west?"

"Maybe. We'll find out."

"The rest of the way reads like towns out of a western movie, Del Rio, Uvalde, Hondo and then San Antonio. What about the house keys?"

"Almost forgot, after we lock up, they go under the door mat. Hoar said Bidwell might have a buyer."

"He's not coming back?"

"Would you?"

"Knowing Bidwell he must have advance knowledge of something."

"Is the base going to close."

"Not as long as the head of the Senate Armed Services committee is from New Mexico."

"Chavez is his name, isn't it?"

"Believe so. They just bricked all the buildings and spent a fortune on renovation."

"Walker will never close."

• • •

I followed Bobbie Jean's Bentley east into a low winter morning sun, wondering if I would ever return this way again. I looked around at desolation and Eastern New Mexico. The terrain answered my question, "Never!" Bobbie Jean wasn't impressed with west Texas when she drove her Bentley this way three and a half years ago and was less impressed today.

I caught up with her in the town center of Pecos, Texas, "Looks like breakfast in Pecos is not breakfast at Tiffany's."

"I've had all I can do to stay awake. Next time we drive long distance, I'll bring along coffee."

"Ready to eat breakfast at the diner? You can get a cup to go from the waitress."

"Easy choice soldier, it's the only place in town." The service was fast and friendly, but Bobbie Jean was still a bit testy, "Eggs aren't bad, but these grits are terrible."

"Do you still want to stop for lunch in Langtry?"

"Okay, but let's make it quick. Let's get this part of the trip over with. Can't stand the sight of one more tumble weed. Drive until we see green." When we stopped for lunch I asked, "What do you think of your namesake, Langtry Texas?"

"Not much."

• • •

We stopped for the night at Halletsville, east of San Antonio. After breakfast, Bobbie Jean purchased two Thermos jugs, "We'll eat sandwiches and drink coffee until we reach civilization."

"Biloxi or New Orleans?"

"Either, I've had enough of the west for a lifetime."

"Not a cowgirl?"

"Or a westerner. The only thing romantic about the mountains is leaving them." We drove straight through to Biloxi, stopping only for refills of coffee and an occasional hot sandwich. As we drove east, both food and drink demonstrated a marked improvement. I followed Bobbie Jean's Bentley as she turned on East Beach Road, with a chill in the air and warmth in my heart. We had returned to our beginning.

• • •

Herbie opened up Bobbie Jean's home. All of the lights were on to welcome us. As I stepped out of my station wagon, a cold damp wind chilled me to the bone. A Blue Norther had dropped Mississippi temperatures below fifty degrees. Bobbie Jean checked over the house while I unloaded both cars, "Herbie had the house cleaned and all the dust covers removed. If you'll carry, I'll unpack."

As I hauled the last load into our bedroom, she asked, "Shrimp scampi in garlic sauce with Italian bread and salad?"

"You finally sound chipper again."

"Don't like driving alone. No one to talk to."

"You said a little Italian? Here or at the Broadwater?"

"Dinner first, dessert second. Call ahead and order while I finish unpacking."

"After I shower away this road grime. Does it feel good to be home?"

"I'd feel better if you weren't going away for a year."

After dinner, Bobbie Jean curled up by my side on the couch in front of the Broadwater's fireplace and we warmed our hands over mugs of Herbie's special Irish coffee. Herbie pulled up a chair, "Slow night. Too early in the season for northern guests and too cold for southern ones. Had one of our maids open up your place and clear away the dust. Was everything all right?"

Bobbie Jean placed her hand over his, "You're ready to go solo. Have you heard anything about Bonnie?"

"The Body Beautiful? She's back on the circuit, little older and wiser. Left her husband last year."

"Did she give a reason?"

"Oliver T. became insanely jealous. He couldn't hold a job and wouldn't let her work. She's working in New Orleans. Oliver T. moved to Palo Alto, California."

I asked, "Any idea what he's doing?"

"He's developing a new thing, computer or something foolish like that. Spends all day long working in a friend's garage."

Bobbie Jean wondered, "You said left him. Are they divorced?"

"No, she doesn't believe in it. You know Bonnie, she thinks her absence may bring him to his senses."

Bobbie Jean took a sip of Herbie's Irish, "Do you want to open your own place? I'll back you."

"I'd like to open up a large lounge with a grill. Nothing fancy. Only live entertainment would be a piano. Mostly taped light jazz, piano, you know."

"Start looking tomorrow. I'll fund your start up for half. Do you want to make a career out of it?"

"No, get it running and sell it at a profit. Did you speak with your mother?"

Bobbie Jean couldn't hide her surprise, "No, not since just before we left New Mexico. Why?"

"She found out you two are married."

"And she's still alive? That old fake. She never let on. So much for heart problems. Will I give her a piece of my mind. Was she upset when she found out?"

"Not at all, I believe she may be hiding a little pride in your Yankee husband."

"When did she know?"

"Two, maybe three years ago."

"And she never said a word."

"When do you travel north?"

Bobbie Jean looked at me and I answered, "I feel like a prize lamb at auction time. Class begins the second of January. Should try to drive there before the 29th. Snow can pile up this time of year and I want to stop and visit my folks."

Bobbie Jean added, "And I do too. Have to find out if you Yankee devils really do grow horns at night."

"I do when I'm near you."

Bobbie Jean's face turned a light pink, "Herbie, start looking. I like your idea."

"Do you have time to check out a location I found on the beach."

"I knew you were ready. First thing tomorrow."

• • •

It was as if we had never left, a relationship always magic, blossomed on the water. The early winter cold snaps soon faded away and warm nights returned. In the evening, we stuffed ourselves at all of our old haunts. Under a misty Mississippi moon, we wore out the beach sand with long romantic walks. Bobbie Jean and Herbie completed the plans for their new lounge while I repaired and replaced appliances and fixtures in her apartments.

I asked, "How did you get a liquor license on such a short notice?"

Bobbie Jean laughed, "Mississippi is a dry state. The Sheriff handles it. Herbie and I are part of Biloxi's in crowd."

"What if I tried to get a license, as an outsider?"

"You would help our sheriff demonstrate he is cleaning out a corrupt influence."

"Are all outsiders corrupt?"

"You're catching on. But since we are a dry state, it's cheaper to do business here than in Alabama or Louisiana."

"That doesn't make any sense."

"It does when you consider that we have fewer politicians on our payroll."

## Mississippi to Ohio

Although we were reluctant to depart, it was time to leave the sunny Gulf Coast and travel north to the snowbelt. We drove north to Jackson the day before Christmas and left the day after Christmas. This time her mother allowed us to stay together. Though, I had to retrieve my personal items from a room at the far end of the visitors' wing. And one evening, after cocktail hour, her mother linked her arm in mine as we entered the dining room for the evening meal. When we were alone on Christmas night, Bobbie Jean cuddled close, in front of a pecan log fire in the sitting room. "Mother is resigned to our marriage, but she has one last request."

"I couldn't deny her one. What is it?"

"You might want to. I'm an only child. My father wanted the Langtry name to continue. So, Mother wants one of our sons to carry on the family name."

"Are you pregnant?"

"No, but when you return it will be family time."

"How many?"

"At least two, then we'll talk."

"I really don't have a problem with the name thing. Tell her I agree, not because I don't care for my family, but I believe in family tradition. Not sure I want one of my sons to be a Reb, though. We have all the potential of producing another Cain and Abel." I flinched, but did not receive the expected dig to my ribs. Instead, we drew nearer, until we were one.

• • •

We arrived in Concord Township early in the afternoon on a slate gray wet Ohio winter day. The time of year when twilight in central Ohio lasts from sunup to sunset. Bobbie Jean became an immediate favorite of my family, again.

She asked to see all of my childhood secrets, "I know you Yankees must have caves and hidden places. The kind where you learn all types of wicked things."

"We're short of caves along the Scioto, but wicked things maybe." As we strolled along Mill Creek Road, I pointed, "The old mill was right over there."

"I can't see a thing."

"It's under water now. They raised the height of O'Shaughnessy Dam."

"Is that what they call the dam by the Columbus Zoo?"

"Yes, I had more than one run in with a moonshiner by the name of Old Ned Smith and his gang near that mill."

"You didn't drink whiskey when you were a boy, did you?"

"My goodness, no. Not in my family? A glass of wine was for medicinal purposes back then."

"Where was his still?"

"On a creek about a mile away from the Scioto River in a place called Dublin. He tried to kidnap me and the preacher's boy, so I turned him in."

"He wouldn't have done that in Mississippi and live."

"You have a different set of laws down there. Ours were a carry over from Prohibition."

"That explains it. You had gangsters—we have businessmen. Have you seen Mr. Smith since you had your troubles with him?"

"No, not for, let's see, at least fifteen years. Why?"

"I thought I saw an ugly scarecrow of a man watching us from behind that stand of Walnut trees." I turned around, but saw nothing.

"We'll go see the dam I told you about. Had a wild ride over the top of it when I was a boy."

"You must have been fearless."

"No, stupid is more like it."

We parked in the Roadhouse lot, across from zoo and walked across to look at the downstream side. Tons of water, two to three feet deep, cascaded over the top to the snow covered rocks on the rapids below.

I talked above the water's roar, "Can't believe this is the huge dam I rode a rowboat over when I was younger. After Hoover Dam, it looks small. Grandfather Mac's favorite fishing hole was on the other side. Caught lots of bass there."

"Was it like this when you rode over the top?"

"Didn't have the boards then so it wasn't as high. Water flow was smoother and the channel below was between the rocks. Wouldn't want to do it today."

"That's the Roadhouse across the street?"

"Yes. Want to drop in for a drink?"

"I've never been in a real Yankee bar. Do they have horns?"

"And drums."

As we entered, Bobbie Jean wrinkled her nose, "Do all your bars have the musty smell of spilled beer."

"It's a cold sharp smell, much warmer and soft where you live."

"You'll have to go to the bar for us to be served. I don't see a waitress."

The bartender recognized me, "You're the Ropp Boy from down the road. Ned Smith said you were drowned."

"He tried to drown me himself. Is ol' Ned around."

"Didn't you hear. He passed out the night the river rose, where the old mill was, a couple of days after they put boards on top the dam. Drowned in less than a foot of water. Emaciated, he looked worse than road kill. Floated down stream. Found his body near Dublin, wedged between some rocks below the dam. His last request was to be buried near the old mill and that's where they planted him. What would you like?"

I carried wine to Bobbie Jean and beer for me back to our booth. She shook her head, "You took your time. An old friend?"

"No, this is the first time I've ever been in here. He told me about the passing of my nemesis, Old Ned Smith. Buried where you thought you saw him. You must have seen his ghost. Taste your wine. It may have turned. They don't sell much of it in here."

"It's okay. Do we have plans for New Year's Eve?"

"No, do you want to go out?"

"I want to hold you close and curl up in front of a warm fire. In another month you'll be a long way from my arms."

"We'll stay at the farm. Did your mother mention a formal wedding."

"Only if we're assigned to Washington DC. And then she will reserve the Lee Mansion. That's where she wants us to renew our vows."

"She doesn't give up, does she?"

"No, she doesn't. I think she wrote the motto, 'Forget, Hell!' Let's leave for Dayton early, so we can be alone.

## Dayton, Ohio

Bobbie Jean didn't care for the hotel in downtown Dayton or most of the motels, "Too old and rundown. They'll go past break-even to bankrupt if they're not brought up-to-date."

We found a clean motel near what was Wright Field. Bobbie Jean was not impressed, "You Yankees live Spartan lives, don't you? Most of your motels are equipped like Trapist monasteries. Do you sell sack cloth at your department stores?"

"We're plain folks up here. Where would you like to eat?"

"Somewhere where the restaurant isn't rated by how good the home fries are."

"The Ratskeller at the O' Club has great hot roast beef and pastrami sandwiches."

"Don't tell me. We're back in Kingman, Arizona."

"You'll change your mind."

"I'll go if I don't have to stand around outside in the cold. It feels like twenty below. Your northern winds are colder than San Francisco in summer."

Wasn't any school to report to, or a commandant—or even a pilot—around to tell us where to go. I saw FTD on my orders and thought it meant Field Training Detachment. The civilian guard at the main gate to Patterson Field straightened me out, "You're assigned to Foreign Technology Division. It's located on Flight Line Road, on the golf course."

After several wrong turns, I found the parking lot and a red brick building with very few windows. I entered through a bullet proof door, showed my ID to the guard, signed in and was escorted to my classroom.

As I was soon to find out, there were only ten of us. We were greeted by a government scientist and a contractor physicist from Santa Monica, California. The government guy asked, "How many of you EWs have an engineering degree?" Four raised their hands.

"How many of you have a science degree?" Five raised their hands.

He looked at me, "Captain Ropp, isn't it. Can you explain what the cosine of theta means?"

I looked around, sensing I was being hung out to dry. I honored Tucker, "Don't you really mean, you play ball with me and I'll shove the bat up your ass?"

When the laughter died down, he repeated the question and I answered, "I dated a Theta in college, but she didn't need anyone to cosign. Does that count?"

"Damn those assholes at SAC headquarters personnel. They promised that every single one of you would have at least a Bachelor of Science degree." He looked at my folder, "Tell me Ropp, how in the world does one get a BS degree in American Literature?"

"I didn't. It should be a Bachelor of Arts, BA."

"Someone in SAC got even with you. It's too late to get a replacement. You'll have to do the best you can. At least you're an EW, aren't you?"

"Yes sir. What is it we're supposed to do?" He didn't answer.

Trying to explain the ins and outs of my friendship with Bidwell would take too much time, so I didn't. I hunkered down and hoped the tempest would blow over. The first two weeks of our course covered Optical Physics. Not anywhere close to any schooling or work in my experience, or for our engineers, either. I mean, why in the world would I know K, Kelvin is the equivalent of Absolute Zero or, 273.15 degrees centigrade and that spectral response over wavelength range -300K background 2 Steridian field of view formulated an optical background. None of this was covered by Mark Twain in Tom Sawyer. I had found a course that I could not overcome by rote, or sweat. With infrared, ultraviolet, reflection, refraction and angstrom floating around in my brain, I longed for the days when all I didn't understand was electronics.

Bobbie Jean drove me to class each morning and picked me up at night. By the end of the second week she could tell that my frustration level was over the top, "Can't you get out of optics?"

"As of today I'm out. Four electronic engineers and me have been relegated to ELINT and Telemetry. It's refreshing to know that American lit. and electrical engineering are equal in status. Only those with a physical science degree will be allowed to operate optical equipment."

"Can you get out of this trip north?"

"I can always go to Leavenworth."

"Leavenworth?"

"A military prison in Kansas."

"How many more weeks of training do you have."

"We're supposed to finish the first of February and no one has explained what it is we're supposed to do."

Bobbie Jean laughed, "And it's sixty degrees below zero in Fairbanks."

As we turned into our motel, Bobbie Jean asked, "You know what I like about Ohio?"

"Can't be the cold, slate gray winter days. What is it?"

"We get to dine out every night."

"Only because you turned down a room with a kitchen."

"And you know what I don't like?"

"Probably the twenty degree temperatures and twenty knot winds."

"Brr, I really don't care for that, but that's not it. I can't stand a place that judges its restaurants by the quality of their homefries."

"You'll have to admit our home fries are pretty good. Better than the slime you southerners call grits."

"Watch your tongue. Where are we going to dine tonight?"

"At a steak house that rates it's steaks by size."

"Not quality? Ohio is a very strange place indeed."

"You get to meet a childhood friend of mine."

"What does he do for a living? Roast babies?"

"Close, Slick's a lawyer."

Bobbie Jean laughed, "Slick? And a lawyer. That's an apt name."

"Slick and me played Tom and Huck when we were little tikes. We explored all the caves, quarries and rivers around here when my father taught at the local high school."

"What was its name?"

"Bath, Osborn Bath."

Bobbie Jean got the giggles and all discussion of my childhood ended.

I discovered it was easy to return home, but not easy to return to a friendship separated by too many years. Slick and I were trapped in different worlds. The evening was pleasant, but limited, with stories only of childhood. Soon, the end of January arrived and an end to our training and me none the wiser. Bobbie Jean dropped me off at base ops after she discovered today's Air Force would not allow her to wave good-bye on the tarmac. I embraced her as she needled me, "So much for June Alyson kissing Jimmy Stewart good-bye before he climbed into his SAC airplane."

"Only in the movies. I'll phone you at the farm after we touch down in Alaska."

"Dress warm. It's still sixty degrees below zero in Fairbanks."

## Fairbanks, Alaska

SAC, always frugal with the taxpayer's nickel, diverted a KC-135 Tanker to fly our newly formed, all EW aircrew to Fairbanks. We left Dayton in twenty six degree weather, landed at Eielson Air Force Base, greeted by sixty-six below temperatures and cold soaked on the tarmac for twenty minutes until transport arrived. Our escort, a local reconnaissance wing EW, apologized, "Welcome to Fairbanks. Sorry about the delay. Couldn't find where they parked you guys. We'll fly you to Elmendorf Air Patch in Anchorage tomorrow. You'll draw Arctic gear and parkas there. Until then, don't wander to far away from the O' Club or your VOQ. Without proper clothing you might become a statistic. Travel in twos and bundle up the best you can. We'll have a crew bus pick you up in front of the club at eight thirty tomorrow."

Couldn't hold it back. Tucker had to be served, "Don't you really mean, you play ball with me and I'll shove the bat up your ass."

He did not respond, so I added, "You left us out here on the tarmac without proper gear. We damned near turned into ice cubes."

"I promise—we'll not cold soak you tomorrow." But they did.

• • •

We arrived at our VOQ in the dark. My room was warm enough, but had nylon carpet. I learned not to touch metal after two electrical discharges from finger tips arced, in visible flashes, to electrical ground. From the our bus, Eielson looked just like Ellington, Keesler, Castle and Walker, all barrack buildings left over from World War II. I dressed as warm as I could and walked to the O' Club with C. Little. One of the optical guys, C. Little was wiry and intelligent, almost too smart for his own good. We looked around. From appearances this O' Club was the same as any other club, except its bar was packed with lonely men. I ordered popcorn while C. Little opined, "A clock stopper would have a field day. Do you know what the ratio of men to women is here?"

"No, I don't. And I don't see any married couples."

"I don't either, but it must be six to one. An there's an Army post nearby. It would take a strong frontier style lady to live all winter, in the dark at sixty below."

"Save me a seat at the bar and buy me a beer. Told Bobbie Jean I'd give her a call as soon as we landed. See what you can find out about our new home."

"Here, or the one on Shemya?"

"Both."

Bobbie Jean seemed happy about her stay at the farm, "I'm learning about your escapades when you were a little boy. It's a wonder you're still alive. What time is it there?"

"A little after ten."

"It's five o'clock in the evening here, but dark enough to be midnight."

"Tell me about Alaska. Have you seen any polar bears yet?"

"Too dark outside to tell. Only have an hour or so of twilight each day. It's dark, cold and no wind. Like a refrigerator, only difference is the light doesn't come on when we open the door. How soon do you plan to leave for Biloxi?"

"I'm waiting out a storm. Your Alaska sounds like Ohio, with a shorter twilight. Can you call tomorrow?"

"We fly over to Anchorage to pick up gear. By the time we get back, it'll be past midnight your time. I'll phone the day after."

My beer was still cold when I sat down on a bar stool next to C. Little. He had all the answers, "Bartender says that the only single women here are teachers and they're married before the end of the fall semester."

"That fast? Being a bachelor up here must be the pits. Why does the Army have a base up here?"

"Winter and Arctic training. Army camouflaged one of its tanks so good last winter they couldn't find it when the exercise was over."

"Did it ever show up?"

"Early summer. Sun melted the snow off and heated it up. Tank melted the tundra underneath it, until it sank forty feet down. Couldn't pull it out, so they left it."

"Wonder what an archeologist will think a million years from now when he discovers a tank under the permafrost."

"I know what I'd say. My stomach clock says it's time for dinner."

"After I finish the rest of my beer."

The King Crab legs were great, but the next time I'd order steak. Coffee was a bit watery, but didn't bite back. It was hot, which is a major criteria here. C. Little ate his fill and part of mine. He asked, "Another beer in the bar?"

"Might as well. I didn't see a TV set in my room and I didn't bring along a book. Did you find out anything about Fairbanks?"

"If you own a car, you have to plug in a heater or the oil will get so thick the engine will never turn over. They heat the base with a central steam plant."

"After I finish this beer, I'm going back to our VOQ and hit the sack. Been up five hours longer than the clock says." On our walk back, C. Little chattered on mostly about things we couldn't do like open the windows for fresh air and wander around outside on your own. We were members of a new flock who didn't know the identity of their shepherd.

• • •

Next morning we flew to Anchorage in the back end of a two engine, prop driven, C-123 transport owned by Alaskan Air Command. And we were cold soaked again, at sixty below zero before takeoff. We landed at Elmendorf Field in balmy, twenty-three degree temperatures, an eighty-three degree shift. We peeled off our topcoats and scarves to cool down. After lunch, we were driven directly to base supply and issued Arctic clothing. My issue parka had a smoky odor, like it had been to the North Pole and back. The inside of the hood was lined with something that looked like domestic cat fur. Flight crew supply issued winter flying suits, brain buckets, oxygen masks, brief cases and Nav equipment. Needed a wheelbarrow to carry our gear back to Little Shaky. We wore our parkas. And looked like Nanook of the North on our return flight. And I wondered, "Who's the idiot in supply who flies people to things instead of things to people?"

• • •

When I phoned Bobbie Jean, she commented, "From what you've described, don't slip and fall on your back, you'll be like Charlie Brown, an oversized turtle, unable to get up."

"Darn, I was beginning to think I looked like Trapper Dan."

"Do you know when you're supposed to leave for your tight little island?"

"Don't know for sure. They had a rebellion on the island."

"It must be caused by a lack of sunlight."

"Could be, all the folks I've met here act a little paranoid."

"Can I fly up and visit?"

"Don't know if it's allowed. I'll ask around."

"Check on a hotel room."

"Are you sure? You'd be standing around in sixty below weather?"

"Not as a steady diet, but we could start a family."

"I was hoping we all ready accomplish that."

"We just might have, if we're lucky. It will be a month before I know."

Evening meals at the O' Club were one lonely affair after another. Three nights of bachelor food was three too many for me. Most of the live-on at Eielson stayed home, working on cabin fever. If it wasn't for my crew and a few bachelors, the Eielson Club would have to close during the week. I ate whatever the special was. And I couldn't get a straight answer as to how long we were going to be here. Eielson's senior EW tried to be our shepherd, but we wouldn't let him use his crook to take charge of us. He wasted our time with daily lectures about his airplane and his mission when we were being assigned to an island with our airplane and our mission. I warned Bobbie Jean, "We have no idea what we're doing or when we're going. I wouldn't bother flying up, not into all this indecision."

After a week of nonsense, we finally discovered why we were being held prisoner. The Eielson folks were attempting to establish control over us. Another mutiny had occurred with the current crew on the island. This nonsense could have been unbearable, but my literature training came to good use. Mr. Christian's mental state and why he cast Captain Bligh away from H.M.S. Bounty, was alive and well. Three thousand miles of ocean, without daily communication, was an impossible span of control. No one would admit to the problem, what it was, or what caused it, so paranoia was rampant. We were drilled in the conviction that authority and control were to reside in Fairbanks. We flew with a temporary flight crew, two pilots and a navigator rotating out to our island on a weekly basis. Our senior crew EW was in charge of the mission. A situation ripe for mutiny, when temporary pilots attempt to regain control.

I did learn how to bail out of a KC-135. It consisted of falling out of the entrance hatch. But it didn't matter. Where we were flying no one could live longer than fifteen minutes in Arctic waters, not in our flight gear. Bobbie Jean was worried, "Why would SAC have you fly over areas where you will die of exposure if you crash land, or bail out?"

"Never thought of asking. Might be that our mission is more important than the safety of an individual. Might be the powers that be are convinced we have the necessary gear to insure our safety."

"Even though it won't?"

"That's called catch twenty-two."

"I read the book."

"We're living it. If you're planning on flying up to surprise me, don't."

"Why not?"

"We leave for the Rock tomorrow."

"Why so sudden?"

"No one will say for sure, but my guess is there's been another mutiny. All but three of the old crew have been shipped off island."

"It must be an awful place. Do you have to go?"

"Yes, but don't worry. They say adversity brings out character."

She finally saw the humor of it, "And mutineers. Can you phone from the island?"

"Only if you have stock in the telephone company. It is costly."

"I do, so please call. I'm anxious to know about the mutiny. It sounds so military, so exciting."

"I will, I fly away at dawn with the replacement front-end flight crew."

## Shemya Air Station

Shemya Air Force Station looked like a run down South Pacific island movie set with a Moscow apartment building smack dab in the middle. We landed after dark, which isn't unusual in the Arctic, in a snow storm driven by forty mile-an-hour winds, which is normal for Shemya. Like prisoners in a transport, we taxied directly to the SAC hanger—our new office, home and recreation area. The three remaining crew members waited at the bottom of the ladder. I immediately gave them nicknames, See-evil, Speak-evil and Hear-evil.

C. Little asked the first one he saw, "Where do we eat. I'm starved?"

Speak-evil responded, "I'm in charge here. I'm Major Cure to you, lieutenant," facial tic a-twitter, he continued, "You can forget all those lies they told you about me at Eielson. There's nothing wrong with me, I'm fine. Starting tomorrow you go on alert twenty-four hours a day as long as our airplane isn't broke and the wind is below fifty knots. I'm on my way to the O' Club on top the composite building. Does anyone want to join me?"

Wouldn't pay to use Tucker's you play ball with me response, so I asked, "Do they serve dinner?"

"Food, who eats food here? I wouldn't if I were you. Not when they're trying to poison us."

He wandered off, "Food, food indeed."

C. Little told Hear-evil, "We need to stow our gear."

And I said, "I'm getting wet and cold standing outside in the snow. You can introduce yourself to us when we're inside—out of the wind."

He had a crazy smile, but looked harmless enough. "I'm Captain Bat, but my friends call me Broke. You will pick your rooms by rank. Bring your gear inside. This is our airplane." He pointed to a clean, well maintained RC-135, modified to carry reconnaissance gear.

After we were escorted to the orderly room at the top of the stairs, Bat apologized, "Sorry you had to see Major Cure in his condition. He has been sipping from the source of all knowledge. All but Ropp and Little will live here on the second floor. Little and Ropp, your rooms are across the hanger. Stow away your gear and meet me back here in twenty minutes. I'll drive you to the NCO' Club for dinner. Our mess hall in the composite building stopped serving dinner two hours ago. Ropp and Little, follow me. We live in the quiet zone."

I knew, "Away from Speak-evil."

On our way back downstairs, I asked, "What is the source of all knowledge."

Bat laughed, "In Cure's case, Johnny Walker Black Label. When he starts sipping, he can't stop. Wanders around the hanger hanging on to anyone who will listen. Damned difficult to get away from him when he ties one on. He teaches optics. I teach telemetry, Elint and electronics."

I dropped my gear on the floor of my new home and looked around. It was long, narrow, with thirty foot ceilings reminiscent of a Russian prison cell. Bat stuck his head in the door, "Are you ready to go?"

"Yes, who was the other major? The one with his right hand inside the front of his parka like Napoleon."

"Larry Plager. He's strange. Don't startle him."

I looked up, my gymnasium style ceiling lights were swinging back and forth, "What's going on?" Bat looked up, "Earthquake. We get them all of the time." The light's arc increased, "But this is a big one. Run for your lives!"

The floor rolled in a visible wave. In the hanger, our airplane bounced up and down dancing with warped wings. Bat's eyes grew as large as two silver dollars. He ran outside to the tarmac and we followed.

I had to wonder, "You say this happens all the time?"

Bat was shaking, "Not like this one." The earthquake stopped as quickly as it began.

C. Little shook his head, "Not a bit of sound. Hardly felt it when we were standing up. I only noticed movement when I was sitting down. What a wild ride." We didn't have to wait for the rest of our crew. They were outside with us.

I asked Bat, "Who owns this island, SAC or Alaskan Air Command?"

"To your great misfortune, AAC does."

We rode past the base theater and gymnasium to the NCO' Club. So far Shemya looked a lot like every other air patch I'd seen except there were very few buildings and not a tree or bush in sight. Bat advised, "We only have two buses. One for the flight crew and one for our maintenance guys. They live on the second floor on the other side of the hanger. On the same side as Ropp and Little. We have five, six man pickup trucks. Front end crew has one, commander, chief master sergeant each have one and we share the other two with our maintenance guys. So you now know who's on the bottom of the food chain. Cure has ours tonight. NCO' Club is around the corner, other side of this hill."

• • •

The NCO' Club had seen better days. It was as windy inside as a mess tent on MASH and twice as cold. We left our parkas on. Snow inside reminded me of dust piled against the windward walls in Roswell. We were the only ones in the club. Sat at a long table left over from when it was a mess hall.

I asked, "Does the wind always blow like this?"

Bat laughed, "No, sometimes it blows harder. You'll get used to walking with your back to it. Sixty knots is normal for winter and summer. Slows down a bit in fall and spring. Low pressure cells move across Shemya at record speed. Most days the wind swings 180 degrees from all points of the compass. We lean into the wind so much that when it stops we have to remember how to walk."

We ordered a round of beer at a quarter a pop. Bat loosened up after the second round, "Beer used to be a dime. Last July, Big Shaky was carrying in our yearly supply when it lost an engine. Pilot ordered the cargo master to dump our beer to lighten his load. So they raised prices to cover the costs. Won't dent your pocketbooks. You'll be on alert most of the time and that means no alcohol twelve hours before a flight. Better order before they shut down the kitchen."

The menu said gourmet, but the meals were frozen, served in cooking containers like TV dinners. I whispered to C. Little, "Closing the kitchen must mean turning off the knob to the oven."

C. Little asked, "When do we start training?"

"Tomorrow morning. I'll give you a walk around and begin Morris code training for the Ravens. Cure and Plager will work with you optical guys."

I mentioned, "We did all our emergency procedures work at Eielson, test and all."

"Great, you can get right to work on the equipment. The quicker you check out, the sooner I get to go back to the world. Let's head back to the hanger."

On the ride back, I asked, "Is this all there is to do up here?"

Bat answered, "We're thousands of miles away from civilization. We have a small PX convenience store inside the composite building. Take you two days to memorize all the items for sale. Movies are always six months old. Cable TV is tape. Reruns of old shows. No live sports. No live anything. What we do get is in black and white and out of synch. Gym has basketball and bowling, but you'll find it's too hard to go there. Staying within twenty minutes of takeoff, twenty-four hours a day is time constraining. When the klaxon sounds, we go. We're like firemen answering the bell, except we have no relief. Takeoffs and landings in high winds might subtract a few years off your lives. And fog, you won't believe the summers here. We get sixty mile an hour winds and zero visibility."

C. Little shook his head, "Textbook says that can't happen. Winds have to be light and variable to create fog."

"The professor who wrote that book was never on Shemya. Fog here is like a cloud base on top the Bearing Sea. One word of caution—some of our RC-135 pilots think they're fighter pilots. They sometimes push the envelope on takeoffs and landings."

• • •

C. Little stopped in as I was stowing away my gear, "What do you think?"

"My gunner described our weekly issue pilots."

"How so?"

"Keen eyesight, coordinated and possessing a death wish. You're lucky if you get one without the wish."

"And we're going to push the envelope. No wonder they carried off seven basket cases before their tour of duty was up."

"Not true. You forgot the three we met today."

"Right, that makes ten. Wake me up, I want to eat breakfast at the mess hall."

"Better leave here no later than seven."

I sat down on the edge of my bunk. World War II springs bent downward with my weight. It was going to be like sleeping in a metal hammock. I looked up at caged lights, "Damn! I'm living in an Air Force version of a high school gymnasium." I grabbed my towel and toothbrush and headed for the latrine.

*"In that direction," the Cheshire Cat said, waving its right paw 'round, "lives a Hatter; and in that direction," waving the other paw, "lives a March hare. Visit either you like: they're both mad."*

# Chapter 11

Morning on Shemya is a carbon copy of morning on any other military outpost, where mandatory barracks form a basis of society. Stubble bearded men stagger out, bundled in robes, washing away sleep from lonely eyes. I woke at oh-dark-six o'clock. Arctic dawn was four hours away. C. Little didn't answer when I knocked on his door. He was up and shaving in our private latrine. It lacked the green stuff that grew in the corners of southern ones. Green spores couldn't live this far north. We dressed in flight gear, in cold rooms, ready to fly away when the klaxon called. Captain Broke Bat led us out single file in blowing snow to the detachment bus. The first of many trips to the composite building mess hall for breakfast had begun. Bat was right about Shemya's wind whirling halfway around the clock. This morning's sixty knot breeze blew one-hundred eighty degrees opposite last night's gale. A full compliment of bright eyed, almost sane, new guys motored up the only hill on Shemya, in an Air Force blue school bus.

As we shuffled up the steps to the composite building's front door each of us detoured around Major Cure. His arm was around a big bear of a dog, Boozer, an Alaskan Husky—the island mascot. Boozer and Cure were singing, or howling in disharmony, a tune neither could understand. It was a toss-up as to which one was howling and which one was singing. But it really didn't matter. They were both covered with six inches of snow and seemed quite happy in their circumstance. Speak-evil and dog had been sipping away at the source of all knowledge since the O' Club bar closed at midnight. Only Boozer's warmth kept Cure alive through another Arctic winter night. Cure's bowl of scotch and milk made for one happy husky. C. Little frowned as he sidestepped these two snow covered canines, "Brings new meaning to be kind to your web footed friends."

"One has paws."

We entered the composite building, a Moscow-style apartment building constructed of prefabricated cement. If a Russian Trawler could sail close enough, our building would remind them of home. Like our hanger, it provided offices and quarters for everyone on the island, but us. And we would live here too—if it wasn't for mission requirements to stand alert. However, if there had not been a mission, we wouldn't be here and neither would the composite building. This mess hall was much better than any I'd ever seen or ever will. We were on Arctic rations, more of everything and since our cooks had to eat their own food, it didn't take them long to learn to season food. This morning's mess hall breakfast was like a beach hotel's Sunday buffet. Like all buffets, I took more than I could eat and then ate every bit of it. When we walked out the front door, Cure and Boozer were on the steps passed out in each others paws. After the medics sobered Cure up, our commander confined him to his room. He was dispatched to the world on the next Alaskan Airlines flight. Boozer lost a drinking buddy and we lost an instructor, and the world gained another unstable outcast of Arctic isolation.

Captain Broke Bat accelerated our training. Now this wasn't difficult since our equipment was simple enough to operate. The only complex items were the tape recorders used to process mission tapes, and we had a civilian tech rep to assist us. We were ready to fly the day after we arrived, so missions were flown in spite of the fact we were still in training. However, our training came to an abrupt end. On the third live mission See-evil, Major Plager ran amok. While sitting in the instructor pilot seat during final approach See-evil grabbed the throttles. Most pilots would take exception to another pilot doing this. And they really took exception to a non-pilot. As usual, we were landing in high cross winds. Control of the airplane was critical. Plager left the island that night and Broke Bat followed a week later. Bat broke, like twelve o'clock high, refused to climb on board our airplane. When the klaxon blew, Bat assumed the prenatal position and would not come out. In two short weeks, we became the crew by default—we were the only sane ones left and certain we would be much saner than the crew we replaced. The truth is, the only one who could live here for a year and not go crazy was our island mascot, Boozer.

Boozer had been on the rock for more years than anyone could remember. He arrived as a pup under the coat of a civilian contractor, when they were building the new phased array radar at the west end of the island. He became fond of scotch and milk as a pup and addicted to it as a dog. By the time we arrived, it was estimated by some that Boozer was over ten years old in real time and one-hundred and ten in Shemya years. Boozer's addiction to scotch had resulted in partial loss of control of several important body functions. However, he retained just enough control to complete his mission as Shemya's foremost movie critic. And he had a particular distaste for romantic comedies, showing his displeasure by lifting his leg on the lower right corner of the theater's movie screen. And if he really hated a film—Boozer would amble along, marking the entire screen. No mean feat when you're a large husky with a malfunctioning bladder. After Cure's departure, Boozer developed an off and on attachment to C. Little and me, but mostly he remained independent, the leader of our pack. He had an uncontrolled dislike for authority figures such as pilots and island commanders, so our front end crews stayed their distance and island commanders should have.

Winter temperatures out on the rock were one-hundred degrees above those in Fairbanks, but sixty knot Bearing Sea winds brought a wind chill that made it colder. After we had our feet on the ground and felt comfortable with our airplane and mission, we began to explore. If the wind was below twenty knots, it was beach time. No one stuck as much as a toe into Shemya's surf. The Bearing Seawater temperature hovered a degree above or below freezing. We were warned to stay out. Hypothermia would occur in seconds and death was certain to follow. Walking the beach was good exercise, but that wasn't why C. Little and I wandered there. Boozer came along for the ride and a romp while we searched for glass fishing floats. Isolation brings forth legends and Shemya has one, too. Ours was—you would not return to the world unless you found a glass fishing float. If it still had net attached, you would leave sooner. All I ever found were World War II aluminum mess trays wedged in the rocks along the shore, still shining like silver plates and Shemya jade, Coke bottle fragments worn smooth by wind, sand and wave action.

Our trip today was for whale watching, Shemya style. Boozer rode along for a ride and a romp. Away from the beach, wedged in ocean volcanic rocks, an Arctic sperm whale met an honest death. Sea gulls walked on top and occasionally, one would disappear into whale muck. A minute or so later, a head would pop up, followed by the rest of the gull, all goo and feathers. True, this was pretty sick entertainment, but for Shemya it was standard fare. What else was there to do when this week's movies remained at Elmendorf Air Force base because the sergeant in charge wanted to view them again.

C. Little whistled for Boozer, "Time to get back in the truck."

Wind had switched and the dead whale's odor was overpowering. Didn't seem to bother Boozer. He sniffed the breeze like he was looking for his next meal. I helped boost him up to the bed and we returned to his domain.

I searched for months, but failed to find a fishing ball. I didn't believe in Shemya's legend and I wasn't the only one. Our medics had been harassed by the Air Police for over a month. More for something to do than any real offense. The APs made a game out of how many tickets they could give them, but our medics found a way to get even. One sunny day in May, two of the largest glass fishing floats ever seen were found floating off our concrete pier. Two APs jumped off the pier into freezing water and attempted to swim after them. Medics had to treat them for hypothermia. I found out about it when two more APs appeared at our hanger and asked to borrow my rowboat.

Now about my rowboat, not long after we arrived, I was appointed detachment Safety Officer by our new commander. He decided we needed to augment Air Sea Rescue. This was an extremely difficult concept, as we had none to augment. The nearest was two thousand mile away. C. Little believed our commander was correct and the rowboat might save lives, "If we slide off the end of the runway into the ocean, how do we get to shore?"

"Not in a rowboat built for two. This one isn't safe enough to float on one of our lakes. Most of the time we take off in a force six gale. If we crash off the cliff, the surf will drown anyone attempting a rescue in our boat. We'll have to take our chances with the life rafts we have on board. No use killing two more in a foolish rescue attempt."

"Orders are orders."

"Even though our commander is gathering nuts with the squirrels?"

"You have to bring the rowboat to the hanger." We carried it to our hanger in the crew's pickup and leaned it against the leeward side of the building. Later, I drilled holes in the bottom so the boat would sink before anyone would drown in it.

Without my knowledge, the APs hauled our rowboat to the end of the dock and jumped into it. As I had planned, it sank. Our medics had filled two green plastic garbage bags with air, tossed nets over and tied sea anchors on the bottom. The whole affair ended with shots being fired at the garbage bags and my Air Sea Rescue craft at the bottom of Shemya's unsheltered harbor. It wasn't a complete waste of time. As Safety Officer, the sinking of my boat helped me maintain safety. I haven't mentioned much about our new detachment commander. He became immediately frustrated. Commanding a group of EWs, whose mission he could not comprehend or control as a lieutenant colonel pilot. Two weeks after his arrival, he began to seek solace in the source of all knowledge. We didn't see much of him after that. All our guidance now came from the ops officer, another pilot, who was able to make a sane adjustment to being in charge of crazy technical guys wearing funny wings.

Now, I know I haven't said much about our mission because I signed an oath not to tell, so I won't. Some say it's to protect sources of intelligence and some say it's to protect the lack of it. But it really doesn't matter which because one's word is one's bond, unless you're a skirt chasin' president. Flying in a B-52 meant hours of boredom followed by a microsecond of ultimate chaos. Fortunately a real war never happened. Flying our reconnaissance missions from the rock was chaos, followed by more chaos, finishing in chaos. We flew at a moments notice, at all hours of the day and night to the sound of a klaxon. There is nothing in this world that vibrates your nerves like a klaxon horn, so loud it could wake up the dead Aluets who lived here long ago. We were so busy flying, four months flew by in an instant, and we were going back to the world. I phoned Bobbie Jean and gave her the good news, "We're flying back to Wright-Pat in two days. Can you meet me there?"

"I'm leaving as soon as I pack your station wagon. Any reason for your early return."

"Airplane is in for mandatory repair and modifications."

"How long can we spend together?"

"I have seventy-five days of leave in the bank. That long, maybe longer. How are things at home?"

"Looking up. Mother is all atwitter."

"Is she finally resigned to a Yankee son-in-law?"

"Finally, but there's more to it than that. I'll fill you in when you return. Are the squirrels still gathering nuts in your land without trees?"

"As we speak. Our commander has become a complete recluse. Has to stay on island with our ops officer. And our ops officer is trying to convince him to fly over to Attu and do a little fishing while we're gone."

"Why there?"

"Closest island of any size. Navy has a LORAN station and a dozen men to keep it operating. Lots of mountains and streams full of trout and salmon. A fisherman's paradise. Maybe it will bring him back to life."

"How do you get there?"

"Reeves Aleutian Airlines. They fly resupply in a modified C-54 once a week along the entire island chain. Attu's runway was split in two by an earthquake. Their plane is the only one out here that can fly long distance and still land there. And the runway is built into a box canyon. There is only one way in and one way out."

"Isn't that the place you told me about where the fog sets in and no one can get in or out for weeks at a time?"

"You remembered. If that happens, they'll have to carry our commander out in a basket. Where are you going to stay?"

"Same motel. Since you and your airplane don't exist, I'll wait for news from you there. Oh, Oliver T. has surfaced. He and his California computer friends are in the news."

"Serial killers?"

"No, silly, they invented a new memory device for computers."

"Bet it's for short term."

"Don't laugh. While you're wasting your time up north he's become a multimillionaire."

"You've got to be pulling my leg."

"No, it's true."

"Did Bonnie move back?"

"What—and leave show business!"

## Shemya to Ohio

Our return flight to the world began in cold Arctic fog and ended in fuzzy bureaucratic fog at Wright-Pat. As soon as I could get to a phone, I called Bobbie Jean at her motel, "We finally made it in."

"You're a day late."

"They made us land at Eielson and change front end crews."

"Where are you?"

"I'm at base ops."

"Don't move. I'll pick you up out front and we can have lunch at the Club."

"Are you checking out or do you want to stay over?"

"Our wagon is packed and ready to roll south."

"I need a shower and change of clothes. Don't have anything summer with me."

"And I tossed out most of your old clothes." I waited for the punch line, "But I bought new. Is there a place for you to change?"

"At the gym next to the O' Club. I'll shower and meet you there."

• • •

Bobbie Jean took one look and frowned, "You look so pale. Don't you ever get any sun up there?"

"Darned little. You're brown as a berry and you've gained a little weight."

"Not much else to do in Mississippi when your best friend is away. And I'm glad you noticed my weight. I'm almost five months pregnant."

I held her in my arms, "So that's the surprise. Why didn't you tell me before this? No wonder your mother is excited. I am, too!"

"We're lucky. We got it right on our first try. I didn't tell you because you have enough problems on your plate without worrying about me."

"Bobbie Jean, I know you can handle anything including pregnancy. But me? I would worry. Might even go AWOL from the rock."

"Hurry up and change. You did shower?"

"That's why my hair is wet." Her little dig to my ribs told me I was home again.

We parked outside the O' Club and walked in, arm-in-arm. Bobbie Jean asked, "Did you find out how long we can be together in Mississippi?"

"They're taking off some of the optical gear here and flying the bird to Dallas for new equipment. They say it will take three months, but if we follow past updates it'll take much longer."

"I'll try again. How long before you have to return to work?"

"I have forty-five days until I'm supposed to return to Wright-Pat."

"Can we be together, then?"

"As long as you can travel. Hot roast beef sandwiches in the Ratskeller?"

"Just cheese and crackers for me and a whole lot of you. Now that we're away from phones you can tell me what you're really doing on the other side of the world." I returned to our table with food and drink. Soda water for Bobbie Jean and a beer for me, "You drive while I sleep this time. I'm still wound up from our flight out of Alaska." Hard to eat and hold hands like schoolchildren, but we did.

"You were going to tell me all of your island secrets."

"I'm not allowed to tell you any of those, but I can tell you what it's like. It's a tight little island in more ways than one. Our runway begins at one end and ends at the other. Right after World War II, when it was a fuel stop for Northwest Orient, families were allowed, but that didn't work out. Wind and isolation got to the women. You can still see the remnants of a one room school."

"Are there any Aleuts left?"

"No, they moved toward the mainland. Even they don't care for it. It's too isolated, the weather is rotten and it's hard to live on shell food, grass and fish as a steady diet."

"You said there weren't any trees or bushes and you call it the Rock. Is it bare rock?"

"No, Shemya is covered by an Arctic grass we called tundra. Can't walk in it, too thick, like saw grass. Our island is perched on top the stem of an old volcano, like a giant mushroom. Are you ready to travel?"

"After I powder my nose."

• • •

I woke up when we were halfway to Cincinnati. Bobbie Jean pulled my chain, "One beer and you turn into sleeping beauty."

"Out of practice."

"Can you see any of the other islands?"

"Two, Aggatu and Attu. Aggatu is the closest."

"Sounds like they're twins."

"Not really, Aggatu is like a table top with cliffs all around. When it's halfway clear we can see it most every day. No one on it, though. When we flew over it on a training mission, I could see buildings, telephone poles, wires, roads and buildings. Really spooky, like a ghost island. It has cliffs above the ocean all the way around. Probably why the Air Force decided on Shemya. Attu is the largest island of our little group. We can see its snow capped mountains, when we have a clear calm day, which isn't often."

"Is it your Bali Hi enchanted island?"

"Not really. Snow capped mountains in the Arctic have a cold remoteness to them not found in the South Pacific."

"Your island doesn't sound remote, with theaters, clubs and a gym."

"Runway is our problem. Planes fly in and out at least three times a week. So the temptation to leave is there. Kind of like a prison without walls. And with high winds, freezing cold rain and fog, we spend most of our time indoors. Cabin fever sets in."

I read the map as we navigated our way through downtown Cincinnati and across the Ohio River. Bobbie Jean wasn't finished grilling me, "Shemya really sounds quite desolate. Has anyone run away, or as you say, gone AWOL?"

"We had a really bad example this spring. The Protestant Minister disappeared after our Catholic Priest got stuck over on Attu. Priest meant well enough, but got weathered in over there for a month. Reeves couldn't get in to fly him out."

"And the minister?"

"No one knows where he is. They're still looking for him. He must have snapped after reading one too many Dear John letters for our troops."

"That's terrible."

"It's so bad up there even God has left our island." I moved away to miss the dig coming at my ribs.

"You won't tell me what you do?" she asked again.

"Maybe when we're old and gray. Where do you want to stop tonight?"

"Nashville. We'll get in late, but I want to get back home. Are you ready to take the wheel?"

"Better keep a watch on me, I haven't driven since January."

Bobbie Jean laughed as she pulled over at the first turnoff, "That's not all you haven't done."

## Biloxi, Mississippi

Mississippi was unbelievably hot and humid after Alaska. The sea breeze off the gulf helped, but it took a while to adjust. And it took a while to adjust to Bobbie Jean's mother. With a grandchild on the way, she popped in and out like a mother hen, checking to make sure its chick was safe. Sun, swimming and walking the beaches with Bobbie Jean made the days whistle by. Biloxi was in the middle of its normal lazy southern summer, moonshine stills sending columns of smoke to the skies, only to be trapped under a high pressure dome of haze. I spent mornings scraping and painting Bobbie Jean's apartments and home. Afternoons, we escaped the heat in air conditioned comfort or lounging at the Broadwater's pool. It was hard to pack up and leave for Ohio after this vacation. Bobbie Jean's mother wasn't keen on her traveling north with me, being over six months pregnant. But Bobbie Jean would have none of it, "Women traveled west on wagon trains under worse conditions." Her only concession was to travel light for a change, "When I reach seven and a half months, I'll move to Jackson with Mother. You won't have to worry about me getting good care. My nanny is preparing to spoil our child just like she spoiled me."

• • •

As we drove into Nashville to stay at our favorite motel, Bobbie Jean sat up straight, "I forgot to ask. What ever happened to Sergeant Bidwell? You haven't mentioned him once, not even in your letters."

"Bidwell left the island before I got there."

"He was there less than six months.

"What happened?"

"He almost bankrupted the island. It was a compassionate transfer."

"For him or the island?"

"For the island. He was assigned to Bergstrom Air Force base near Austin, Texas."

"Won't be long before he pops up in your life again. Does he keep in touch."

"Phone call after I arrived, but that's about it."

Our motel represented the demarcation line between Bobbie Jean's old south and my new north. At breakfast, I continued our friendly culinary battle over homefries and grits, "You know the only thing I like about grits?"

Bobbie Jean grimaced, knowing a barb was coming her way, but she was a good sport, "What?"

"They don't serve them with dinner."

"Watch your tongue. Our soon to be new family member is listening. And my child is going to grow up on grits just like his granddaddy. You never mentioned where you'll be working in Dayton?"

"Same place—Foreign Technology Division."

"Aha! I know what you're doing."

"No way."

"Yes I do. You've been capturing little green men in Alaska. And now you're going to interrogate them."

"Where did you get that idea?"

"Our supermarket tabloid identified FTD as the place where the Air Force keeps all the little green men in a giant walk-in freezer."

"Isn't that Roswell?"

"They identified both places, you sneaky Yankee you."

"Remember the supermarket in Dayton?"

"Yes?"

"Don't buy the green mint ice cream. And don't scare our soon-to-be new family member with stories about aliens."

"But doesn't FTD dissect aliens?"

"They do what the name says—investigate foreign technology."

"Is that what you do?"

"You're digging again and you know I can't tell. I'll dance around it. FTD processes our technical stuff and sends it to Washington. Sort of like a big brother. It's all very technical and dull. Now that's about as far as I can go. Want to stop in Cincinnati for dinner? There's this little Italian restaurant downtown called Caruso's."

"Careful. I got this way after a little Italian."

"So that was the night!"

## Dayton, Ohio

We had reservations for our favorite motel outside of Dayton. But, this time Bobbie Jean reserved a suite with a kitchen. Almost seven months pregnant, she wasn't anxious to dine out. It was my turn to accept her barb, "You know what I don't like about your Yankee home fries?"

"Go ahead, I deserve a shot across the bow."

"They make me feel the same way I did when I had morning sickness."

"Touché, my love."

"We'll stay in and order Chinese tonight. I thought I would never see a place as hot as Jackson, but Dayton qualifies. It's steamier than a sauna."

"Remember last winter?"

"When this sauna turns into an ice cube?"

"What do you plan to do while I'm working."

"What the doctor ordered. Take it easy, lounge around the pool and read."

"Who's watching the store?"

"Herbie."

By the time we completed our make-work projects at FTD, Bobbie Jean was seven and a half months pregnant and ready to go home. She was swelling up faster than the Goodyear blimp, but still had her sense of humor, "We planned to be together until you returned. Looks like our new addition is going to change that. I think it's time to go home to Mother while you gallivant around. Oh, your island friend, C. Little, sent you a letter. I didn't know he had returned to your island."

"Commander wanted one of us to keep him company and he drew the short straw."

I opened the letter. C. Little had solved the mystery of our missing minister.

*Johnny,*

*Living up here on the rock in summer is worse than winter. Wind is blowing sixty knots and visibility is zero/zero. You won't believe where they found our minister. He was holed up in the basement of his house in Washington State. Threatened to shoot anyone that tried to bring him back. Crazier than a March hare. Oh before I forget. You may want to send Booser a dog biscuit with a file inside of it. He bit the base commander on the ass and is in the lock-up. The radar conract civilians are sneaking whiskey and milk to him.*

*Our commander came back from his fishing vacation with enough fish for a fry. Vacation didn't help his mental state. Still gathering nuts where there are none. Wing at Fairbanks must have noticed. They ordered him to stay at least one week there each month. Bad news for you—Ops Officer wants you up here in two weeks. SAC is sending up a replacement airplane until ours is fixed. You and I have to train the crew. You'll get word soon. They're going to divert a KC-135 to pick you up. We'll come back to the world to train at the factory and pick up the airplane. See you soon,*

*C. Little*

I was reluctant, but I had to tell Bobbie Jean the bad news, "C. Little says I have to return to the Rock. I'm supposed to receive orders in a day or two. Going to divert an airplane to pick me up. I'll drive you back to Jackson and make arrangements for a pick up."

"Is this all necessary?"

"It is if you're into playing games. I don't think it's all that important, but the powers that be must."

"If this is the way the Air Force operates in peacetime, I'm not sure it's safe to be on our side if there's another war."

"As C. Little says, 'Orders are orders.'"

My orders arrived at FTD three days later. I had time to drive Bobbie Jean home to Jackson. From there I drove on to Biloxi and stored my car. Herbie drove me to New Orleans and I flew to Dallas, stayed overnight and departed the next day with a KC-135 crew from Carswell Air Force base in Fort Worth. We flew directly to Eielson Air Force Base. I returned in August to Indian summer in Alaska and was ill prepared for the tail end of Fairbank's summer. And not at all prepared to fight off tundra mosquitoes. They were as large as my salt water friend in Houston and ten times hungrier. When the sun melted snow off the permafrost, a million miles of ice turned into instant swamp and clouds of these airborne piranhas filled the sky. Fairbanks, locked in ice in winter, is closed down by hungry mosquitoes in summer. I was lucky to arrive at the tail end of their season, but the few that nailed me were healthy enough.

All Bobbie Jean could do was giggle at my predicament, "Now will you listen to me and think about leaving the Air Force?"

"What and leave snow business?"

When she stopped laughing she had a surprise, "Know why I'm getting bigger than a house?"

I took a deep breath, "You're going to have a baby?"

"Can you say two?"

"Twins?"

"That's what the doctor said."

"How soon?"

"On schedule. Can you return in October?"

"It shouldn't be a problem. We're supposed to go through more training in Texas and bring the airplane back up. Factory is having problems. Hit a few snags, so we won't fly up until after mid-November."

"Twins solve one of our problems. We can carry on both family names."

"I'll have to explain that to my parents. How is your mother?"

"Pure ecstasy. She is so proud of you, she wants to make you an honorary son of the Confederacy."

"I'll bet you want to get out of the baby business after this."

"You've got that right, soldier. I've never been so uncomfortable in my life."

A week later, I was still feeding mosquitoes in Fairbanks and wondering why I had to hurry up here and wait. C. Little set me in motion again when he phoned from the island, "Sorry they jerked you around."

"What's up?"

"You weren't needed out here until next week. Commander took one too many sips from the source of all knowledge and brought you back early."

"How am I going to get out to the Rock—swim?"

"You'll have to fly out commercial on the next Alaskan Air Line flight."

"Isn't scheduled until next Wednesday and it leaves from Anchorage."

"Take the Alaskan Railroad to Anchorage. You might even see a moose."

"And it skirts by Mt. McKinley. Give Boozer a pat on the head for me."

## Fairbanks, Alaska

While Fairbanks enjoyed early Indian summer, winter and snow arrives on top of the Alaskan mountain range in August. Green leaves were turning from red to gold along the Alaskan Express' slow, long climb to Summit. Now, Alaskans are a practical people. Towns are named by distance from, like Twenty Mile. I looked, but could not find one moose from the train windows. As a matter of fact, outside of streams and trees with an assortment of rocks, I saw not one living thing. Found out later that moose were all in high summer pastures. When snow stacked up ten feet or better in the trees, they would use the railway tracks as an easy way to wander about. Lunch on the Alaskan Express, which barley exceeded forty miles an hour, was a feast of dry white bread, mustard and lunch meat which was almost, but not yet, turning green. Table tops of linoleum were covered with oil cloth, permeated with an odor of creosote. Ambiance and cuisine were as rugged as the country the train rolled through. As we approached Summit, clouds were clinging to McKinley's sides in ever increasing layers. I gave up my search for life and leaned back. I awoke to the squeal of railroad brakes. The Alaskan Express was chugging slowly into the city of the great white north, Alaska's Anchorage.

Got lucky, an Air Force van was waiting to pick up a courier, so I hitched a ride to Elmendorf Air Force base. As usual, I dined at the O' Club, the temporary bachelor's friend and afterwards phoned Bobbie Jean, "Remember when I said the sun never rises except for twilight last winter?"

"Yes, is it just as dark now?"

"No, just the opposite. Except for twilight, the sun barely sets in summer. How is your mother handling the blessed event?"

"I'm carrying the twins high, so she is certain they are boys. She's out buying two of everything. Your mother is coming to help when my time gets near."

"Oh my God, dueling grandmas!"

"Of course not. Your mother can charm the devil out of his den and she'll charm my mother out of her distaste for anything north of the Mason-Dixon line. What time do you leave in the morning?"

"Alaskan Airlines—seven o'clock takeoff."

## Shemya Air Station

I flew out to the rock on one of Alaskan Airlines few four engine, prop driven, Lockheed Constellations. I had always wanted to fly on one. After World War II, airline advertising promised that Connies were the wave of the future. However, as I was now accustomed to jets, this flight seemed like an eternity. When we landed at the Navy base on Adak, at least half the passengers departed. I looked around. Adak, shrouded in Arctic summer fog, looked a lot like our Rock. Our pilot, not wanting to be delayed in the middle of nowhere with fog setting in, made a quick turnaround. Our flight droned on and on from nowhere to emptiness, half loaded with happy new rock residents. Their response would be quite different on the return trip a year from now. It took six months for Rock residents to become withdrawn, another three to be hermits and the last three to become mad as hatters. We landed at the isle of the damned twenty minutes before fog closed the runway.

I was greeted as if I were a long-lost friend. C. Little and Major Birdsill, our ops officer, met me with a pickup on the tarmac. Birdsill threw my duffel and suitcase into the back of the truck, "Welcome back, Johnny. Don't complain about your lot to the commander if he happens to pop out of his room. And if he does, treat him with kid gloves. Any stress and he just might go off the deep end. Air Force shouldn't send someone up here lacking in a good sense of humor. How is the world?"

"Still there—full of people we're not familiar with, sane folks. Wife is going to have twins in October. I'd like to be back for that."

"Depends on how long the RB-47 stays up here. A long as they're here, you and C. Little are the designated stuckees."

"What are we supposed to do? Were not trained on their airplane or equipment."

"You know that and I know it, but our Commander believes you two are the secret to his promotion."

"How so?"

"He's convinced you two know all there is to know about what you're supposed to know"

"I think I feel the large end of a bat coming my way."

"I know the RB-47 troops know their stuff and don't need training, but I couldn't convince the boss. So, play along and help them mission plan and process their take. Go through the training motions. We have to humor our CO."

We dropped Birdsill and my gear off at the hanger and drove to the mess hall. C. Little broke his silence, "I didn't want to totally screw up your vacation, so I didn't tell you the rest of the story. Birdsill is right about our commander. He's out of it most of the time and when he returns to the land of the sane it's only for a short stay. He still wants to make decisions, plays the game at running things. Good news, we have a new station commander on board. Our pal Boozer is free at last. Medics are weaning him off scotch and milk, loading him up with vitamins. Damn dog gets better treatment than we do. Talk about the devil. Birdsill is following us. Wonder what's going on."

Boozer greeted me like a long lost friend from his throne on top the composite building steps. I held his huge front paws as he jumped up with a wag and a bark, "Damn, you're getting frisky for an old pup, but you're looking good—not as mangy as the last time I saw you. New diet must be doing you a world of good." I scratched him behind both ears as Birdsill ran up the steps to join us, "Boss came out of hibernation looking for me. Been on the source of all knowledge for two days. Had to get away. Mind if I join you two for dinner?" We both nodded, "Yes." I looked around—we were enveloped in fog, I had returned.

Birdsill sniffed the mess hall air, "Chicken smells good today."

C. Little filled his plate, "and it can't be road kill, too plump."

As we removed the plates from our trays, I asked Birdsill, "What have you been doing while we were back in the world?"

"Fixing myself new quarters in the other hanger and trying to stay as far away as I can from our boss."

"Hanger two? Are we finally getting the new bird?"

"Anytime now. They say her radar will fry hamburger a mile away. Sorry to eat and run. Promised to give a tour of the island to one of the Alaskan stews."

C. Little smiled, "A tour of what? For whom?"

"Met her at Anchorage when I had a little R & R last month."

For a pilot, Birdsill knew his EWs. There wasn't much we could put in a training guide that would be useful for the RB-47 troops. They did the same thing we did, but in another part of the world. I thought a bit and came up with the solution, "C. Little, listen to this. We developed a signal environment and sequence of events for the troops who replace us next winter. I recommend we copy it for the RB-47 crew."

"And we can formalize our processing procedures, packing and mailing. Kill two birds with one stone."

"Got a problem no one's thought of."

"What's that?"

"Our tape machines may not be compatible with their tapes."

"Whoops, different contractors."

"Right. Might have a problem checking results in real time."

Birdsill asked, "Can you think of anything else that may help them?" C. Little answered, "Might as well make up a newcomer's guide while we're at it. Let the new guys know where they can go and what they can do."

"Are you going to include whale watching?"

"Need a new dead whale. Carcass of the last one disappeared in our last storm. Wind got up to one-hundred and sixty knots."

"And no one knew?"

"And no one knew."

When the time came, Birdsill picked us up at the mess hall, "RB-47 is coming in." C. Little asked, "How soon?"

"Within the next thirty minutes. They just reported in over the high cone." He parked on a small knoll, overlooking the runway. The RB-47 flew around the landing pattern once, twice, three times before landing. I laughed, "Like a dog trying to get comfortable." Birdsill looked worried, "Don't know if that bird can handle our cross winds. Only thirty knots and he's all over the place." Birdsill drove our pickup to the Hanger and welcomed the new outlanders to the Rock. The RB-47 crew consisted of two pilots, a navigator and two EWs, called, Ravens. C. Little and I took charge of the Ravens, and Birdsill escorted the front end crew to the day room. Unlike our RC-135, the Ravens had ejection seats. However, their seats ejected downward from a bomb bay capsule.

Our training course for the Ravens took less than half a day. We spent the afternoon taking them on a Cook's tour of the island. When they both found a glass fishing float where we had found none, C. Little worried, "Legend has it you can leave the island, but doesn't say how. Johnny and me haven't found ours."

Raven One asked, "What do you guys do for excitement here?"

C. Little and I were laughing so hard, we couldn't answer, but didn't need too.

Raven Two offered, "If there is nothing to do here, but eat and sleep—you might as well take a look at our bird before dinner. Mess hall is it?"

I answered, "Unless you like frozen gourmet dinners at the NCO' Club."

"Isn't there an O' Club?"

"Top of the composite building if you care to dine on peanuts, popcorn and the source of all knowledge."

"Source of all knowledge?" We explained our detachment's disease on our drive back to the hanger.

After crawling around their capsule and looking at equipment, I was impressed, "Looks good to me. Do you see any problems?"

Raven One answered, "Two great big ones. The good news is that our receivers are preset to intercept and record when signals come up. The bad news is they're set on the wrong frequencies for this area."

Raven Two added, "Our antenna pattern won't work. Not wide enough and cut for the wrong frequencies."

I couldn't believe it, "Christ all Friday, didn't anyone think of this before sending you up here?"

"We tried to explain it to our folks, but sometimes pilots don't listen."

Raven One laughed, "And our commanders are frustrated fighter pilots. Kick the tires, light the fires and go mission mentality."

C. Little asked. "Anything we can do to help?"

Raven One nodded, "We're going to fly a training sortie in the morning. Pilots want to get familiar with your air patch—touch and goes that sort of thing. We'll check over our gear and see if we can come up with some kind of fix. Your maintenance guys, can they help?"

I offered, "We'll have our troops standing by after you land. Our guys are good. Your receiver frequency, maybe. Antenna patterns, I don't think we have that kind of capability."

After breakfast, we rode to the crest of the hill overlooking the runway and watched as the RB-47 attempted a takeoff in twenty-five knot cross winds. I asked Birdsill, "Can they handle it?"

"RB-47 should be safer than our RC-135, depends on how good the pilots are."

We watched as the airplane began its takeoff roll. Halfway down the runway, something went wrong. It could have been a compressor stall or an unexpected gust of wind. The RB-47 veered to the right before its initial lift off point. Too late to throttle back, all four engines made popping sounds as its wheels touched lightly over the tundra. Straining to leave earth, but without power to do so, the RB-47 dropped out of sight below our cliffs. Birdsill hopped into the pickup, drove down the hill and across the runway like a mental patient running away from a lobotomy. We expected to see parts of the RB-47 scattered across the ocean. Instead we saw the RB-47 reappear in view, straining to regain altitude over the wave tops. It flew with gear retracted, engines screaming in a full power whine, trying to climb. After a minute to us and an what seem like an eternity to the crew, it climbed slowly out over the ocean and disappeared into the bottom of low summer overcast.

• • •

C. Little whistled, "SAC almost lost an airplane and five good men. Where is your Air Sea Rescue rowboat?"

"At the bottom of our harbor where it belongs. We'd only lose two more, me and you, taking it into that surf. Swells have to be seven feet high."

Birdsill returned to the hanger driving slower, but almost sticking his pickup in the tundra. He was excited, "Made tracks right to the edge of the cliff. The jet exhaust cleaned out a wide swath of tundra grass. Johnny, you're safety officer. I'll get the manuals out when we're back at the hanger, but I don't think you'll need them."

"Why? Aren't they coming back here to land?"

"No, they're hightailing it to Fairbanks. Bet that pilot's ass is in-between his shoulder blades. Copilot requested clearance to fly direct."

C. Little asked, "Are you sure they won't return."

Birdsill laughed, "Airplane might, but not that crew."

• • •

Birdsill was half right, neither crew or airplane came back. The drop off the cliff scared them witless. They made three passes at Eielson, attempting to land in a dead calm and couldn't. On the fourth try they hit the runway so hard it caused structural damage to the RB-47. SAC sent another front end crew to fly it back to Kansas. A week later we were visited by an airplane full of safety inspectors. They were pilots and since I wasn't one, they didn't read my report. Birdsill kept them away from our detachment commander. He shrugged, "A report on one pilot gone crazy is enough. One look at our commander and they'll try to put the blame on him. You two pack your gear. I'm sending you back to the world on the KC-135 with the safety team. Just don't spill your guts."

I asked, "Aren't they sending in another RB-47?"

"Don't have one to spare and someone must have told them it wouldn't work if they did."

"Are you coming with us?"

"I don't mind it up here. Stews are arriving tonight and someone has to watch over the Boss."

*"Well!" thought Alice to herself. "After such a fall as this, I shall think nothing of tumbling downstairs! How brave they'll all think me at home!"*

# Chapter 12

## Shemya to Mississippi

Birdsill shouldn't have worried about us spilling our guts. The SAC safety team wasn't interested in talking to a lieutenant or a captain who are non-pilots about an almost airplane accident. Left alone and glad to be so, I slept or read most of the way on our flight while C. Little practiced his navigating. Our early morning landing in Omaha, Nebraska was uneventful. Leaving the Aleutians in summer is the same as traveling from England to America. The climate change is noticeable, but not drastic. I phoned Bobbie Jean from base ops at Offutt Air Force Base. Out the window, up a small hill, hovering over me was the mother hive of the defenders of the free world—SAC Headquarters, Strategic Air Command. When I told her of this vision, the terminal phase of Bobbie Jean's pregnancy had not eliminated her sense of humor, "You're as close to the source of all knowledge as you're going to get, soldier. What are you doing back so early? Thought you were stuck up on the Rock for at least another month."

"Would have been if fate, two glass fishing balls and a near accident had not intervened. I'll fill you in when I get there. I'm going to get some rest at the VOQ, catch the next flight out to New Orleans, rent a car and drive to Jackson."

• • •

As I rode from base ops to the VOQ, I had to chuckle to myself when I noticed a pink and white Packard Caribbean convertible parked in the SAC Headquarters' east parking lot. The rocker panels were beginning to show a little rust, but it looked in pretty good shape. I wondered how my boy Bidwell was doing in Texas, but for only a second. There are a lot of high rollers in the Lone Star State. As we rolled up to the VOQ office, I admired the location. SAC folks are as practical as Alaskans. The VOQ was across the street from the front entrance to SAC Headquarters. The O' Club was next door and a little used nine hole golf course surrounded it all. If anyone stormed this citadel, there would be a clear field of fire.

There was no room at the Inn, so I phoned base ops to see if I could get a military hop out of here. Didn't have any flights going my way, but they did provide several airline telephone numbers. My luck was holding better than my ability to stay awake. I booked an afternoon flight to New Orleans, connecting out of Love Field in Dallas. And base taxi had a van leaving in thirty minutes to pick up VIPs arriving at Omaha's airport, north of town. The ride north through Omaha's suburbs is a journey through time, homes of waves of immigrants who traveled west to work in the meat packing plants, or at the stockyards. South Omaha is the home of the Polish Club, feeder lots and of course, stockyards. The Bohemian Cafe announced the home of Czech immigrants followed by an area dominated by Italian restaurants. Omaha was one of the last cities in the west to retain its ethnic neighborhoods. Central Omaha was boarded up. Business and hotels had moved to the west side. North Omaha reminded me of the outskirts of Fort Worth—not farm or ranch, but not suburb or city. Several oxbow lakes explained the reason why. Missouri River must have meandered through here before Army engineers dredged a pass through channel, stabilizing its banks.

• • •

Whoever designed airport terminals must have gotten the contract for every one I'd been through. Omaha's was like all the rest, crescent shaped, like a continuous motel entrance. Convenient though, one room deep. Everything was located in one place, including the waiting rooms. I fell asleep in a chair and would have missed my flight if the ticket lady hadn't noticed me after all the others had cleared out. I woke up in time to board as the engines were cranking on the airplane. Herbie was waiting for me in New Orleans. I couldn't believe his loyalty, "You shouldn't have gone out of your way. I'm causing you too much trouble."

## Biloxi, Mississippi

"When you made Bobbie Jean an honest woman, she gave me a jump start on the path to independence and wealth. Least I can do for the best friends I have in this world. Parked right outside the front door."

"How did you do that?"

"Don't ask."

"Don't tell. How is your new lounge coming along?"

"Incredible! Paid for itself in six months. We've all ready had six offers."

"Are you going to take one?"

"Not until I can find a new opportunity. Bobbie Jean said she'd help me look after your twins are settled in."

"You ought to include a chef in your next mix."

"It'll be outside Biloxi."

"Why?"

"Getting a little seedy. With jets, folks are finding new vacation spots. I thought it would come back, in spite of the lack of gaming, but it hasn't. We're not Miami Beach. Only good waves we get is when a hurricane passes through."

• • •

After three weeks in Jackson, I was in melt down, "Does it ever cool off here?"

Bobbie Jean scolded me, "You've adjusted too well to Alaska, my Nanook of the North. August and September are Mississippi's hottest months. You were spoiled by the afternoon sea breeze."

"And I arrived after Christmas and left before mid August."

"Have you heard anything more from your friend, Bidwell."

"I was thinking about him in Omaha. Swore I saw Bonnie's pink and white Packard Caribbean in the headquarters parking lot. Have you heard anything?"

"Only that there was a federal raid on a floating casino in Austin. Someone floated a river boat loaded with gambling equipment on the Air Force Officer's Club Lake. And they found a race track nearby."

"Bidwell!"

"He went over the line."

"Why, the law in Texas?"

"Gambling on horses is against the law."

• • •

Not much I can say about the birth of our twins, except that we were so proud we could pop. Bobbie Jean was now able to walk without waddling, "Can't believe how uncomfortable it was carrying our boys. It was worth it, but I'm not about to travel that path again. If I knew you Yankee boys were so fertile, I would have married a southerner."

"I thought it was the woman who determined how many."

• • •

My mother raised her eyebrows when we named one of our boys, Randolph Livingston Langtry, after his deceased maternal grandfather and the other boy, John Ropp, after his great-great grandfather. She was understanding if not fully convinced. We immediately began calling our sons J. R. and R. L. That seemed to solve the dilemma, except I had to needle Bobbie Jean, "When our sons grow up and ask why they have two different names, you'll do the explaining."

"You're right! I didn't think about them when we picked their names."

"And our boys are identical."

"You know what?"

"I'll bite, what?"

"I'll worry about that until the time comes."

"Just thank our lucky stars your father wasn't named Calhoon or Beauregard."

"Can you stay a little longer?"

"With two grandmothers and a nanny? I only get to hold my sons when we feed them at two in the morning. My commander ordered me back to the Rock."

"Even without an airplane?"

"Crazy isn't it?"

• • •

Birdsill phoned the next day, "I've scheduled a KC-135. It'll to pick you up in Columbus, Mississippi. Call the command post tomorrow and get your exact departure time."

"Do I fly out to the Rock or stay in Fairbanks."

"After your crew arrives. Congratulations!"

"Why thank you. Bobbie Jean and our two sons are doing fine."

"That, too. You've been promoted to Major."

"I wasn't due for a couple of years."

"They changed the rules."

"Are you sure it's in our Air Force?"

Bobbie Jean asked, "Who was on the phone?"

"My ops officer from the Rock. He set up an airplane to fly me from Columbus, Mississippi to Alaska in the morning."

"Do you know when you'll return."

"In a month for training in Texas. Second honeymoon?"

"In Greenville? You're out of your mind. Are you sure you want to be promoted?"

"Yes, but I'm having second thoughts."

"Don't sign anything. Decide when you find out what your next assignment will be. The Air Force can't send you remote all of the time."

"Only when there is a war or when a President feels macho."

"Herbie is coming up later this morning. I'll have him drive you to Columbus."

"I hate to impose."

"He loves it. Won't be long before you and I are full partners in business as well as marriage. He wants to size you up."

• • •

I don't know if Herbie got my correct size, but he sure grilled me about everything from philosophy to business practices on our drive from Jackson to Columbus. Columbus, Mississippi? One look at all the good old boys lounging around the gas stations and I knew the true meaning of RC and a Moon Pie. And it was a good thing I stopped by base ops before checking into the VOQ. My flight had been moved up to this evening. I had just enough time to grab a snack and get to the airplane.

I arrived in Alaska with the mother of all jet lag headaches. C. Little met me at the airplane, "Get some sleep. We leave for the Rock tomorrow at eight."

"In the morning?"

"Roger that."

"Who else is going?"

"Just you and me. Everyone else extended their leave. How is the new father?"

"Proud as a peacock."

"I made captain!"

"Will wonders ever cease? They'll have to break the mold."

## Shemya Air Station

We arrived on the Rock in time to hear the good news. Mona Lisa was approaching with the toys promised by Alaskan Air Command for all of us good island boys. If she carried all the things AAC promised, the U.S. Naval Service's ocean going tug, and two barges would have to be as large as the Queen Mary. Birdsill met us at the airplane, "Sorry guys. Commander insisted you return."

I asked, "Is there work to do?"

"I tried to talk him into letting you stay south, but he would have none of it."

"Wake me up when this tour is over."

Birdsill smiled, "Well, its not a total waste. We can watch the Mona Lisa barges unload."

"Is it better than watching sea gulls disappear on a dead whale's back?"

• • •

The thump, thump, thump on my door woke me up from the sleep of the dead. C. Little couldn't contain himself, "Wake up, Johnny, it's our big day. Mona Lisa is sailing toward the dock."

I rolled out of bed and staggered toward the latrine, "How soon?"

"Not sure. Should be in this morning. Hurry up. We can stop at the headlands before breakfast and take a look." We parked at the top of Shemya's highest cliff and looked out through the lifting fog. "C. Little, either our ocean is very big or Mona Lisa is very small. This must be where the island gets the bat again. Let's eat breakfast."

"Birdsill wants us to pick him up on the way."

"Why?"

"We've got his truck."

Boozer wasn't on his throne this morning. He had joined our island throng, waiting at the dock by the harbor.

Lingering over breakfast coffee, Birdsill gave us a rundown on what Alaskan Air Command promised to provide SAC. "We're supposed to get a runway clearing snow blower to assist our current road grader and dump truck with a blade." I whistled, "It's about time. They have more of those than I can count at Elmendorf."

"And we're supposed to receive eight new pickups, a bus and a fire engine." I asked, "Have you seen the barges?"

"No."

"Well, if all the stuff they promised is on board, remember the little car in the circus? The one that all the clowns came out of. Mona Lisa will have to duplicate that feat."

"Oh, oh. We need that equipment for our second airplane and crew."

We drove down to the dock and watched as the barges were tied down. Excitement rose to a fever pitch as Mona Lisa's barge crane lifted the first vehicle out of its hold. A bright blue Air Force pickup was suspended in air over the dock. As the barge rolled on a swell, the crane dropped our new pickup five feet above the dock with a thump! When the "new" pickup finished bouncing, all of the new blue paint flaked off onto the dock. What was left said, "U.S. Navy" through gray paint and rust. Another pickup followed and as if by magic, all of its blue paint scattered about the dock. And that was it. All that was left to unload were sundries and foodstuffs. And these items were loaded into our one dump truck and driven to the warehouse at the composite building. We were not shorted on food. Our dump truck nearly wore itself out on one too many round trips. As we walked back to the pickup, I asked Birdsill, "Who was the supply troop that promised gold and sent lead?"

"Can't believe the hosing we got. They even spray painted over rust. And the supply guy? Haven't the foggiest."

• • •

I cornered our SAC supply sergeant and asked, "Who is your contact at Alaskan Air Command?"

The sergeant replied, "You want to know who shoved the bat up our ass. Captain Tucker Tubbs is the troop that took our orders, but it wasn't him that did us in. He's long gone out of the service. Left almost nine months back. My contact at Elmendorf says he's working as a reporter on a newspaper in Washington DC."

"Hope he knew enough to ship his household goods."

"That's how I found out about him. Tubbs must be a real flake. He left all of his stuff stacked in his BOQ room. They had to ship it to Washington DC two months after he left Alaska."

"Then who stuck the bat up our ass?"

"Someone higher up in Alaskan Air Command diverted our vehicles to Elmendorf. Not much we can do out here. We're just a tenant. Alaskan Air Command owns the rock. And they do damn well what they please. Looks to me like we need an IG visit."

"What good will that do?"

"They'll write an official report on the screwing we got and send it on to Washington. Even self serving generals don't care for that kind of recognition."

"Do you think it will happen."

He smiled, "You never know. If you don't tell, you can't ask."

• • •

Mona Lisa stayed at the dock another week before casting off to its home port in Seattle. This was a quiet visit. There weren't more than six fights at the NCO' Club and none of them amounted to much. Most of the merchant mariners were too long in tooth to fight and our rock citizens to remote to care.

After two weeks of twiddling our thumbs, Birdsill had good news, "I'm sending you off island. Have a KC-135 circling the high cone as we speak. You'll fly to Eielson and return with them to their home base in Fort Worth. Stay at the Carswell VOQ until you finish your training at the factory and return with our bird."

"I feel like a yo-yo. Why are you moving us on? We haven't been here long enough to satisfy our boss."

"I don't know if you've noticed, but our commander has taken to running around our empty hanger naked after midnight."

"You're kidding?"

"No I'm not, but it's the pamphlets he's been reading on theosophy that make me nervous. I may need an oversized net to capture this cuckoo. Get packed and get moving before he notices you're gone."

• • •

Birdsill and the KC-135 arrived at the end of the Rock's runway together. The airplane turned around and stood, ready for takeoff. As soon as it stopped, the hatch opened. We scrambled up the ladder and strapped in. We looked out the window at an island shrouded in fog as the KC-135 rolled down the runway.

C. Little shouted over the engine "That was fast. Feel like I'm on the wrong end of a shotgun wedding. What do you make of our travels?"

"Motion is work. We've got to show movement."

"Even if nothing is happening?"

"The faster we move, the more important our motion becomes. Nothing will become something. Move fast enough and all tracks will be covered. Our airplane won't be ready, but we will. And in the land of motion, that's as good as make-work can get."

## Fort Worth, Texas

Fort Worth in October? It was darn near paradise. Warm sunny days on the base golf course followed by cool fall nights filled with barbecue and beer. Doesn't get any better than that. Bobbie Jean flew over and stayed for three weeks until she couldn't stand being away from our twins any longer. Her Nanny wouldn't let them travel. Not yet. Said they were too young. I spent a few weekends in Jackson, but all that did was wet my appetite for a return to the world.

She asked, "Will it always be like this—living out of suitcases all over the world, not knowing when you'll leave or return?"

"It could be worse. Southeast Asia is beginning to heat up. They're talking about sending B-52s over. Doesn't look good. You know what's really crazy?"

"No."

"Majors up to colonels are worried about it being over before they get their chance to go. We've got a lot of crazy folks hungry for a wartime promotion. I don't think it being over is going to be a problem."

"You think it will last over a year?"

"Dien Bien Phu."

"Isn't that the place where the French surrendered?"

"And with their best Foreign Legion troops. Fighting on Vietnam's turf is like being a British Grenadier in our American Revolution—wearing red, marching down the center of a road, while the enemy is wearing green, shooting from behind trees. We'll get mired down in this one."

"Is there anything we can do?"

"Talk to your congressman."

"Can't, his hearing aid is turned off."

As I helped her on the plane for the last time, Bobbie Jean gave me a kiss, "Keep me posted."

"Should be Greenville, then back to the rock."

"Greenville?"

"Is it that bad?"

"Remember Columbus, Mississippi?"

"Right, RC and Moon Pies."

"Ralph wanted to build a casino in Texas. Greenville is closed to liquor and the overly religious."

• • •

C. Little helped me stack my gear into our shared VOQ room, "Only have one night remaining in Fort Worth. The factory airplane is scheduled to pick us up tomorrow and fly us and our gear to Greenville."

"And I almost got on the plane with Bobbie Jean. What's the schedule?"

"A week of ground training on the new collection gear and one or two training flights, depending."

"Depending on what?"

"All of our gear isn't installed. Can't test what we don't have."

"What if it doesn't work?"

"They're sending engineers along with the plane."

"Wonderful, friggin' wonderful. The same people who watched two bicycle repairmen design and fly an airplane, said it couldn't be done and built a profession around it."

"Tooth Fairy time?"

"Not as bad as that. At least we'll know why it won't work."

"You're worrying about nothing—the factory engineers promised to stay with us until everything is working, installed, or repaired."

"Or three weeks."

"Whichever comes first."

## Shemya Air Station

We returned to the Rock with equipment that worked at the factory, but not on the airplane. We had holes in our equipment racks where other equipment was promised, but not yet available for installation. The factory engineers watched our maintenance folks make the non-working equipment function and then drew diagrams to explain why. After three weeks of diagram drawing, interspersed with engineering incantations, they boarded an Alaskan Airline flight and flew away, never to be seen again.

Not much I can say about flying missions day after day with unsure equipment and teenage killers circling our airplane in Russian MiGs. Tempers grew short and our Arctic winter nights grew longer and longer. Like those who had gone before, we slowly withdrew into our own individual protective shells. Living out of a suitcase was taking its toll. Lack of mission success didn't help either. But if it doesn't happen you can't see it. And we couldn't force it either. Thanksgiving dinner was eaten in silence. I stared at C. Little and he stared back. We had nothing left to say. Thanksgiving dinner at the mess hall was wonderful, but hard to eat on bitter stomachs.

• • •

Bobbie Jean's telephone calls were a daisy a day and the one at Thanksgiving, a breath of spring, "We missed you at dinner. Mother and I had family and friends over. The twins were little angels. Cooed at everyone."

"They must take after my side of the family."

"How are you getting along? Are the squirrels still gathering nuts where there are no trees?"

"Japanese fishing boat pulled up to our dock and off loaded a crew member with appendicitis. C. Little tried to climb on board and surrender, but they took off. Their crew member is recovering in our infirmary. Don't know what we'll do with him. His boat vanished, no one here speaks Japanese and he doesn't speak English. Looks like he beat C. Little to it."

"To what?"

"He surrendered before C. Little could."

"It looks to me like Captain Little has missed the boat again."

"How are you holding up?"

"Great, Mother is busy with her new grandchildren. We're all fine. Get done what you must and hurry on home."

"Are you going to stay in Jackson?"
"Until you return."

• • •

C. Little was becoming an irritant. To get work done without adequate resources or manpower, we had to cut through regulations. Not C. Little, he warned, "When the IG comes, they're going to tear you guys a new ass hole."

C. Little would have been right under normal circumstances, but out on a Rock, at the end of a tenuous supply chain, he was wrong. As we passed the three quarter pole and turned on the home stretch, our back end crew was coming apart at the seams. The chief seam splitter was our commander. The good news is, he stopped his midnight run, naked around the hanger. The bad news is, he was running naked in the snow around the composite building flagpole. The only one who liked it was Boozer, he loved a good romp through the snow. When the Air Police brought the commander back to the hanger, Birdsill put him on a flight back to Fairbanks. I wondered, "What will they do with him? He's gone off the deep end."

Birdsill smiled, "Don't worry—he's now qualified to become a flag officer or president."

• • •

Tucker's letter arrived like a bolt out of the past. It was the first that didn't ask a favor.

> *Johnny*
> *The* Post *is sending me to Vietnam on a short assignment to report on the war. Thought I'd write a short note to give you a heads up. My contact at the Pentagon says they're shipping you to SAC headquarters in February. I have another project that includes SAC headquarters. We'll see each other there. Did your new snow blower arrive on Mona Lisa? Keep 'em flying,*
> *Tuck*

Birdsill confirmed Tucker's letter, so I phoned Bobbie Jean, "Hope you like good steaks and friendly people."

"We're going to Omaha."

"You guessed right."

"How is the hunting and fishing?"

"Excellent."

"Then you will still be in SAC."

"Right."

"I vote you stay with it. Nebraska is a good place to raise our twins. When you get orders, let me know. I'll fly over and house hunt."

"Our head squirrel has found his tree. He left the Rock for good."

"I can understand that. It's Christmas, the time for nuts and candy. Where is he?"

"They're keeping him in Fairbanks until his tour is up."

• • •

C. Little wasn't entirely off base with his concern about an IG inspection. We had the administrative responsibilities of a large organization, like a squadron, or wing, without people or equipment. We used our one and only typewriter for mission reporting. We didn't have a barber, so our clerk spent most of his time cutting hair. We all doubled up with additional duties and filled the administrative squares. My extra duties were safety officer and instructor/evaluator. And others had similar chores. Preparing to fly, flying, processing our take and reporting took twelve hours a day, seven days a week. When we did have time to spare, we were without forms, procedures, or adult guidance.

• • •

Like a thunderclap in a snow storm, days of tedium and nights of chaos on our mushroom shaped volcanic outhouse exploded. The day was normal. Our mission was uneventful—another empty-handed flight. Our landing was smooth as silk. It was the night of the full Beaver moon, without a whisper of wind. The runway was clear of snow as was the tarmac and taxi way. The centerline stuck out like a wide stripe on a skunk's back. In short, it was a perfect night—one lovers could only dream about, but was wasted on an Arctic outpost like Shemya. I've heard of folks going sun-blind and snow-blind, but not moon-blind. Our temporary pilot forgot to watch where he was going and taxied thirty feet off the centerline climbing the tarmac to Hanger One. As a result, the left wing's leading edge was imbedded in a lonely telephone pole. Unlike the near miss of the RB-47, as Safety Officer, I had an accident that must be reported and I was without forms or books to follow.

The wing Safety Officer from Eielson solved my dilemma with: "No report unless the airplane can't be repaired. A sheet metal and a wing spar expert is flying out tomorrow. Don't write about it, don't call about it, don't do anything about it until you hear from me."

"You mean don't ask, don't tell?"

"What?"

"Nothing important."

C. Little had a pot of black paint and a brush in his hand before anyone could interfere. Before breakfast, on the left front nose, next to the entrance hatch, he painted a telephone pole with a gouge in it, like a fighter pilot paints the flags of the vanquished. We took a few happy snaps to save this moment for posterity. It was well that we did. As soon as the Wing flock arrived from Eielson, their first repair was to erase C. Little's art work.

Took a few days, but the repair work turned out to be satisfactory. When the weather turned so bad we couldn't land on the Rock, we flew to Eielson. X-rays were taken and no damage was found. C. Little was a mite upset, "Damn it Johnny, you're the only one who made out on this affair. You didn't have to write a report which would have shown your ignorance. Since no one asked and you didn't tell, the wing commander thinks you're aces."

"Remember what we talked about after the RB-47 dove off our cliff?"

"No, what?"

"It's not what you do, but the wake you leave that counts."

"If we had taken some real damage, we'd all be home by Christmas."

"No such luck. We represent an investment of an enormous amount of money and people. Jobs will be lost if we disappear. Our bird would be repaired, regardless. Are we going to stand down over Christmas?"

"Always have. Did you hear about our Japanese fisherman?"

"Is he still here?"

"Not after tomorrow. His embassy is sending an airline ticket. He flies out tomorrow to Anchorage and then straight home to Hokkaido. They must live an austere life. He calls our island Disneyland."

• • •

A week before Christmas the sky fell. C. Little's prophecy came to pass. On a cold blustery winter's day, the tower called, "We have a SAC KC-135 inbound from Japan. Are you expecting visitors?"

Birdsill was as hung over as the rest of us. Last night was our first chance to stand down in over a month so I purchased enough beer and liquor for a promotion party. Bodies were scattered around the day room this morning, like limp dolls after a birthday.

Birdsill sprang into action, "What a hell of a way to wake up after a bender. That plane is carrying the SAC IG. We're getting a no-notice inspection. Johnny, get to cleaning the bottles and trash out of the day room. C. Little, roust everybody out of bed. We have less than thirty minutes to clean up the mess and get ready."

C. Little thumped on all the doors. He was in Cassandra heaven, "The IG is coming, the IG is coming. To arms! To arms! The IG is coming!"

Birdsill entered the day room, "What are we going to do about our latrine? Three out of five toilets are still backed up from the last earthquake."

Our clerk reassured him, "Alaskan Air Command gets the write-up. We've had emergency work orders in for the last two months."

I pulled Birdsill aside. I remembered our supply sergeant's comments about needing an IG visit to straighten things out, "Relax, the bat is heading elsewhere."

"A setup?"

"We need vehicles and beds for Hanger Two."

• • •

Birdsill is what they used to call a man's man. If a war was to be fought, he would rise to the top, take charge and win. But wars weren't being fought to win. And spit and polish soldiers of the barracks were in charge, ready to lose, but looking good. Smarter than your average pilot, he arranged to have the SAC IG's 135 parked at base ops. And then arranged an around the island tour in our crew bus while we finished cleaning our facility. When they arrived we were all lined up, decked out in clean flight suits and scarves with shiny shoes and combed hair. Would have made Little Lord Fauntleroy proud.

The colonel in charge attempted to place us at ease, "We've been sent to help you. To make sure you're getting what you deserve."

When we broke formation to show off our airplane, I whispered to Birdsill, "We're all in our places with sunshiny faces."

He laughed, "Handling you funny wings is like being in charge of kindergarten."

We gave the IG team a cook's tour of our airplane while administrators and safety types went looking for our records. After the first group was satisfied we knew what we were supposed to do, C. Little came charging down the aisle, "Johnny, get your ass upstairs to the commander's office. The Safety colonel wants to talk to you."

"What happened?"

"He slipped and fell on the stairs climbing up to our day room."

"Go back and tell him to watch his step."

"No way. They're looking for the SAC shield. The one that's supposed to be on our airplane. Do you know where it is?"

I knew, but had been sworn to secrecy, "Must have gone out the back door of Big Shaky the Crowd Killer with our booze."

"Aren't you going to speak to the Safety colonel."

I had it up to my ears with this Mickey Mouse business, "Tell him to place his head where the sun doesn't shine. I'm needed here. Can't be in two places at the same time."

"You're messing with the SAC IG. No one ever denies their request."

"Well, this is their lucky day. They're going to be denied three times before the cock crows."

"Three times?"

"The first was to park them out of the way. The second was to delay their visit and the third is they'll be out of here in less than an hour."

"Can't be, won't be finished by then."

"Watch our ops officer and learn."

· · ·

I knew better than to let C. Little know where our SAC shield was. He'd blurt it out and our NCOs would be in deep trouble. They had glued all of them to their day room wall and painted over each one. They didn't want to rile up a teenage Russian fighter pilot by flaunting the SAC shield in his face. He just might shoot first and ask questions later. My second tour group was called out of the airplane before we could finish showing off the gear and explain our mission. By the time we climbed down out of the hatch door, the SAC IG team was on their way out of the hanger. Birdsill shook each hand as they walked out the door.

He walked up the stairs to our day room, relieved, "It worked."

I laughed and asked, "Because you were shaking hands with them like a southern politician?"

"Only courtesy, doesn't pay to rile them up. Had base ops call and tell them a storm was coming in and they might not make it out of here today."

"We always have a storm coming in."

"Right and sometimes twice a day, but they don't know that. One look at this place and they were ready to leave. That Safety colonel would have been hopping mad if he could hop after spraining his ankle on your stairs. You owe our clerk a six-pack. He saved your ass. Had a work order in for non-slip stair covers for over a year."

"Did they ask where the new trucks and buses were?"

"Yes and they're going to tear Alaskan Air Command a new ass hole. Our island commander has his people coming down to fix your toilets and your stairs."

"They're not mine."

"They are now."

"Did they ask where our commander was?"

"That was sticky. I told them he was back in Eielson working on a special project for the wing commander."

"Did they buy it?"

"Think so, but I didn't tell them that our commander was the project. Did you know he's been promoted to colonel?"

"Are you serious?"

"Yes."

"How did that happen?"

"It's his reward doing such an outstanding job here."

• • •

Christmas arrived with the usual dual stand down for us and the Russians, who were drinking their fuel instead of lighting it. The Wing at Eielson decided we needed to be home for the holidays. Not ours, theirs. C. Little was not a happy camper, "Wonderful, Johnny, friggin' wonderful! What the hell are we going to do in Fairbanks over Christmas? The whole place will be shut down. Might as well put us in a lockup. After we freeze our butts off at forty below we'll be farmed out for Christmas dinner like poor relatives who are allowed to dine once a year, but not allowed to stay after the meal."

Birdsill smiled, "Sorry fellows, I can't go, someone has to watch the store. Not to worry, you'll be back in time for our annual USO show."

C. Little bit, "I didn't know that. We get a USO show? Bob Hope?"

"He flew over once and talked over a radio hookup, but that's as close as the big names get. Shemya isn't a good photo-op for big time entertainers."

I tried to see the up side, "At least we get a show. All those Navy guys on Attu get to see is an occasional botanist, our priest once a year and their replacements."

Birdsill added, with a knowing smile, "And two weeks of R&R on the sunny beaches of fun filled Shemya. Have a merry Christmas my funny wings."

• • •

We flew our bird to Eielson the day before Christmas, landing at forty-four below. This bus ride was the last transport we saw until the day after Christmas. Eielson Air Force base was locked down for the holiday. The O' Club was closed for Christmas Eve, the mess hall was seven miles away through blowing snow and the candy machines in the VOQ were empty. We were left to forage on our own, abandoned and starving. With temperatures hovering at fifty below, our morning trek to the mess hall turned into a survival hike.

C. Little was so cold he shook all over, "I'm so cold my feet are numb and I'm hungry enough to become a cannibal. Now I know what motivated the Donner party. How far is it now to the mess hall?"

"Must have four more miles to go. Our VOQ rooms are the last buildings on the north side of the base and the mess hall is on the other side."

"Wonder who thought up this arrangement?"

"Has to be the same folks who support us from Alaskan Air Command. I have come to the conclusion that the general in charge must have been a prison warden in civilian life."

"And we've been shipped to his Siberian Gulag."

"Do you notice we're the only ones out and about?"

"God, this place has to be the second loneliest place on earth."

"And the other?"

"Our island at the end of this chain."

We made it to the mess hall twenty minutes before it closed. Eggs were cold and pancakes half cooked, but it was gourmet food to our starving stomachs. First time I'd ever cleaned up a morning mess hall tray. The walk back to our VOQ was just as cold, but on full stomachs.

• • •

My Christmas dinner began at noon and ended at one. It was friendly enough, but to my host, I was an assigned duty, not a guest. I barely knew him and he didn't care for me. His wife held up well, considering a stranger was thrust in their midst on a family holiday. I'd just as soon have eaten at the mess hall where I could bring back leftovers. I left as soon as dinner was out of the way. Christmas is a magic time for children and theirs had presents to open. Back at the VOQ, I kicked the candy machine, but was out of luck. Wasn't any food stuck inside its sheet metal columns. Christmas night? Eielson was in absolute lock down. Without transport, foraging for food in Fairbanks was out of the question. I called Bobbie Jean, but all lines to the world were tied up. Nothing left to do but nap.

Bobbie Jean was asleep by the time my call got through. "Johnny, it's one in the morning here. Have you been out partying?"

"No such luck. A moose would die here if it had to forage for food. Even the candy machines are empty, but I can survive missing one meal. Lines back to the lower forty-eight have been tied up. Merry Christmas. Hope yours was better than mine."

"Except for missing you, it was the happiest ever. Your sons spent the whole day watching the reflections off the Christmas decorations, and playing with the wrappings, quiet as little mice."

"Did you get my package?"

"Yes and I appreciate everything except the moose pooplets. Not the kind of ear rings I'd wear to a ball. How was dinner with the major's family?"

"Harder on them than on me. I miss you."

"Do you know when you'll return ?"

"Mid-February was all they would say. Depends on when the new crew is checked out. Oh, the SAC IG took one look at our furniture. And they're sending new stuff to replace it."

"What type?"

"Ranch oak."

"The alert barracks's furniture."

"We buy in quantity. Don't ever furnish our home with it."

"Why not? Too expensive?"

"No. Ranch oak reminds me of lonely nights away from you."

• • •

We left too early for breakfast, so an in-flight lunch box fed a starving crew. C. Little was still mad, "Christmas here was like being caught in a restaurant after closing hours with the food lockers padlocked."

I asked, "How was your Christmas dinner?"

"Fastest meal I've ever eaten. When I placed my fork down after the pumpkin pie, they whisked me out the door."

"Out the door?"

"As soon as I stood up they had my parka out of the hall closet and door open."

"Must be a well practiced ritual, another set of good intentions dashed on the rocks of every day reality. Even the damn candy machine was empty."

"And mess hall closed. I'm starved to death."

"You know what I find hard to believe?"

"No, what?"

"I'll be glad to be back on the Rock."

• • •

The Rock's USO show arrived via Alaskan Air Lines the next day and was scheduled to leave the morning after, one hour of live entertainment after three months of anticipation. Even Birdsill couldn't hide his disappointment, "We waited all this time for an accordion player, a burlesque comic and an overweight lady tap dancer. My heart is singing!" He said it all. In true hermit-like fashion, C. Little and I hunched our shoulders and followed him to his truck. The show was so bad it was funny. Boozer was the star for the tenth year in a row. It was as if he waited for the yearly USO show with baited breath. His first trick was to amble across the stage, lift his leg and piss on the accordion player's leg. That always brought the house down. The comic made a big mistake this year. He kicked at Boozer, trying to get him off the stage. Boozer took a big bite out of his ass, the comic lost his pants and closed the show.

I really enjoyed Boozer's effort, "Got to admit, our Alaskan Husky has taste. Didn't he try to hump the lady singer's leg last year?"

Birdsill laughed, "Either Boozer doesn't care for tap dancers or he's getting long in the tooth. Let's drive to the NCO' Club for a beer. Russians are celebrating New Year. There'll be no mission tonight."

• • •

Birdsill set his can of beer down. His eyes lit up as the tap dancer entered the NCO Club with the USO players. He had that hungry dog look, "Think I'll invite her over for a drink."

I wondered, "Isn't she a bit on the heavy side for you?"

"Oh my no, pleasingly plump is the one to hump."

"Are you buying?"

"One round and I'll be tap dancing. Can you walk back?"

"Not a problem."

When I entered the hanger, I had a phone call waiting in the commander's office. Bobbie Jean bubbled, "I just had to find out how your USO show went. Did you get Bob Hope?"

"Even he won't come here. It was awful, but short."

"Who were the players?"

"A comic, an accordion player and a tap dancer."

"Did your dog approve?"

"I don't think so, he bit one on the ass, pissed on the other's leg, but didn't try to hump the tap dancer. He was never one to enjoy the human comedy. What's new on your end?"

"Your sons have learned to crawl. And Herbie paid off his loan. What should I invest in?"

"The way we're running up phone bills, I'd recommend AT&T, but Herbie would be at the top of my list. It's late and I'm bushed. Love you and see you soon."

"I'm counting the days."

• • •

In the world, New Year's Eve arrived with merrymakers, toasting and blowing into cardboard horns. On Shemya, our eve arrived with the sound of a Klaxon vibrating inside the cubby hole walls of our Station Exchange. C. Little and I ran from the composite building to our truck. He floored it to hanger one.

He mumbled, "Taking time off here is like taking vacation in a prison."

"Don't you wonder why we wander the aisles of the exchange? We've been here so long we must have every item memorized."

"Like you said, it's something to do when there's nothing to do."

The hanger doors were opening as we pulled up. One thing that's great about having a dedicated airplane, we could and did leave all of our gear on board. We scrambled up the entrance hatch as number one engine began to turn. By the time we were strapped in, our bird was rolling toward the runway. And another thing about flying off the Rock, there wasn't any traffic to interfere with departure. We were airborne less than twelve minutes after hearing the *aooga* sound of our klaxon.

This weeks front end crew was captained by the Red Baron. He was not one to wait around. His idea of a successful mission was a fast takeoff, a long flight and aerobatics. It was rumored he had shot a touch and go on an aircraft carrier in a RB-47. I wasn't sure about that until he shot a touch and go on Attu's earthquake shortened runway, at the end of one of our equipment test flights. Attu's only usable runway couldn't have been any longer than four thousand feet. And it ended in a box canyon. Climbing out of there with all four engines screaming was more a pucker than a thrill. I was left with the impression that their runway was the only flat spot on Attu.

I checked my equipment, turned on radios and listened to our radio for instructions. It was the only warning we received. In this area of the Arctic, radio signals arrived like visitors from another world, attracted by a warp in the earth's magnetic field. We were in an electronic sump, the black hole of radio waves. Attempting to tune in a frequency that was half way clear was like winning at roulette. Still waiting for a message from Garcia, I was startled as C. Little shouted over intercom, "Incoming." Within ten seconds, thousands of dollars worth of expensive film and tape wound their way through recording devices and cameras. C. Little was celebrating, giving high five's to the rest of his optical mates, when over the intercom came a voice of reason. The Red Baron, speaking in his best right stuff voice chided us, "Funny wings, listen up. Are we wasting our time and hard earned federal dollars collecting against ourselves? Please look out your windows. The collection side of your airplane is pointed toward Alaska."

Needing to reload film and tapes and with fuel running low, the Red Baron turned toward the Rock, carrying a subdued, silent and chagrined back-end crew of embarrassed funny wings.

• • •

It was several days before I said anything to C. Little about his error. I waited until he became feisty again, "You're leading a charmed life."

"Nothing happened on the mission and it was time to empty out our old tapes and film anyway. You know what pains me the most?"

"Go ahead."

"It was the best tracking I've done this year and it turns out to be a meteor."

• • •

By mid-January activity picked up, but it was much too late, our crew was in hermitage. It happened to those who had gone before and it was happening to us. As our time on the rock dwindled down, tempers grew short, nerve endings snapped, doors closed and our conversation consisted of grunts and nods. Our anticipation of leaving had reached its peak. Laughter became snarls, idiosyncrasies that were overlooked when we arrived became unbearable. Two of our crew members could take it no longer and were whisked away. Another was given a hardship transfer because he had family problems at home. Leaving early saved him, but it didn't save his marriage. Isolation wasn't the cause of everyone going Rock happy, but it contributed. It was the runway with commercial flights coming and going. Airplanes flew in and out at will, but the inhabitants had to stay on. The last straw was one prisoners knew. As freedom nears, confinement becomes unbearable.

The end was in sight when Birdsill called me into his office during the first week of February, "Our new crew is arriving tomorrow. I can't leave until they're trained and checked out."

"I just hope we don't scare the hell out of them."

"You will. You funny wings look as bad as the crew you replaced."

"Crazy as loons?"

"Yes, but none of you were crazy enough to grab the throttles."

"Wonder what ever happened to Plager?"

"The great impostor? He's out of the service. Lied on his academic records. Even falsified his combat experience. What a character. He disappeared after Air University called him on the carpet to explain how he received a Doctorate in Education when he didn't finish college. And you know what is really funny? Plager was one of their best, most highly regarded instructors."

"Looks like doers do and impostors teach. I wonder if he really attended EW school at Keesler."

"That he did. He pulled off another whopper there. Claimed he was in charge of the presidential inaugural committee for the military. Conned the base commander out of an airplane to fly to DC. Even had it stand by for him while he partied. He screwed up when he billed his stay to the inaugural committee. They never heard of him. That triggered an investigation into his records."

"Took a long time."

"He moved around from assignment to assignment before they could catch up with him. Wasn't one to let grass grow under his feet. If you need surgery or dental work, make sure Plager isn't doing it under a false name."

"I need a cup of coffee."

"Let's go to the day room and you can fill me in on your plans for the new crew of funny wings."

"Greet 'em, train 'em, leave 'em."

Birdsill poured, "Do you have everything you need for training?"

"Yes and we better get it over quick or the Medics may run out of straight jackets."

"I'll schedule an orientation flight the day after they arrive and you can have two training flights after that."

"How about missions."

"They can take the place of training flights. How much ground training will they require?"

"Not much. They've all flown recon. before. Equipment will be new, though. If everything goes right, two days max."

"How about emergency procedures."

"As long as they know the Lord's Prayer, they'll be fine."

"Is this something new?"

"Not for this part of the world. If they have to bail out or ditch in the Bearing Sea, he'll be the first person they shake hands with."

"I'm going to miss you, Johnny, but I've been given a squadron in a real airplane wing."

"That means you've been promoted."

"Mistakes were made. Do me a favor?"

"Your wish is my command."

"You're going to SAC headquarters, so don't ever recommend me for staff."

• • •

The new crew arrived at ten the next morning. Birdsill, with me and C. Little at his side, took charge of the ritual of greeting, "You're going to hit the ground running. C. Little will teach optical stuff and Johnny will teach electronics. We only have eight empty rooms. Some of you will have to double up until the old crew leaves. Training begins this afternoon at one. Your orientation flight will be tomorrow morning and after that you'll train on live missions. Two should do it. When the klaxon clangs, you've got five minutes to climb on board. Spark chasers follow Johnny and you four-eyed folks, follow C. Little."

I showed my five replacements to their rooms, let them unpack and took them on a tour of the island before lunch. Manicotti spoke for the new guys, "Don't take this wrong, but you guys really look weird."

"Takes one year here to become certifiable. But, don't worry, it's your turn in the barrel."

• • •

Their orientation flight was well done, but not without problems. When I looked out at clear blue skies and calm winds, I knew we were in for it. The Red Baron is the pilot who flew our new crew to the Rock. Manicotti noticed my concern after we completed our in-flight orientation. "What's wrong, Johnny? You look like you've seen a ghost."

"Wait a few minutes. I'll give you five to one that the Red Baron tours Agatu and Attu after we reach the high cone. And tour we did, flying around Agatu, below its cliff tops. As we flew to Attu, our bird came so close to the waves, the engines made four wakes. The baron lined up on Attu's runway and dropped the landing gear. We saw the whites of the Island Commander's eyes as he tried to wave us off. He ran to the side of the runway as we touched down with barely a bounce. This time the Baron turned, as soon as he had full power, on our climb out. We cleared the box canyon wall by at least two hundred feet instead of almost scraping bottom like the last time. He buzzed a Russian fishing trawler on the way back to the Rock, flying so low we snapped photos up while they were snapping theirs down.

• • •

In less than two days of ground training, the new crew mastered what took us weeks. Their experience outweighed our training efforts. Late on the fourth day after their arrival, the klaxon's electronic *aooga* interrupted my afternoon practice nap. When we met the new crew at the airplane, Manicotti asked, "Is this the real thing?"

"Won't know until we reach the mission area, but if you want to know if it's training, it is, but this is not a planned flight."

We had a live event and the new guys efforts were as good as could be expected. Except for a few glitches, they performed well. I pulled Manicotti aside after the flight, "Our Tech Rep will show you how we process the take. Pick out two guys to help him and get out of the way. Too many cooks spoil the broth."

"Did we pass?"

"With flying colors. You are now full fledged citizens of the Rock."

"I thought Birdsill said we would fly two training missions."

"Waste naught, want naught."

"What does that mean?"

"You've got it and we're out of here!"

• • •

It was the day of departure and here I was, sitting on the metal springs of a stripped down bed, waiting to board an Alaskan Airlines plane to return to the world. I looked at my wrist watch. The minute hand was frozen in place. I walked down the hall to the day room and paced the floor. Nothing worked, time was standing still. I walked gingerly down the newly rubber coated stairs. Instead of slipping, now our feet would stick and more that one of us had fallen. I strolled around the airplane and across the hanger to C. Little's room. I pounded on his door, "Open up!"

"Go away. I gave all I'm going to give at the office." He opened the door, "Didn't sleep a wink last night and when I finally get a little, you wake me up. What is it?"

"Time is passing slower than molasses flows in winter."

"You, too?"

"I can't concentrate on anything at all. Are you going to fly out of Anchorage to California in the morning?"

"Can't. We have to turn in our Arctic gear."

"Forgot all about that. Want to drive up to the composite building? I want to bid our friend Boozer a fond farewell."

"Me, too. How many hours before we board Alaskan?"

"Three."

• • •

Boozer! It was almost as if he was trying to honor our departure. He stood at the top of the entrance stairs, with a wide canine grin and a patch of torn khaki between his teeth. I wondered who the offender was this time. He accepted my pat on his head and offered up the cloth clenched between his teeth. I turned it over in my hands, "Damn, he got the whole pocket, billfold and all."

"Who does it belong to?"

I opened it and looked at the ID, "Our boy Boozer has stepped in it again. This belongs to the island commander."

We dropped it off at his office. The clerk couldn't hide his delight, "Good for our Mutt, he deserved it."

"Can someone hide him until this blows over?"

"The radar guys are on their way."

"Why did Boozer bite?"

"My commander is a squirrel without a tree. Boozer was on his throne and he tried to kick him out of the way."

"Take good care of our pooch."

"We will."

We wandered through our cubby hole BX for the last time, looking, but not seeing. I bought a James Bond novel to read on our flight out of here. After experiencing the real world, fantasy spies had lost all their glitter, but it was something to do. The klaxon sounded. We were out the door and halfway to the hanger before realizing its *aooga* was for them and not for us. Birdsill joined us on the hill over the runway. He poured each of us a drink from our commander's last bottle of the Source of all Knowledge. We raised our plastic glasses high and saluted the bird as it took wing. He poured the remains on the ground as a gift to the volcanic rock gods and handed me the empty bottle.

I threw it over the cliff, "From this day forward, let this no longer be the Source of all Knowledge!"

Birdsill turned away, no tears in his eyes, "Let's pack up and get the flock out of here. I'm returning with you to the world."

• • •

We boarded our flight, lifting off Shemya's runway for the last time. We left our tight little island in blowing snow and fog, both visual and mental. Didn't read much of the novel I purchased. After a night without sleep, I made up for it on our flight to Adak. Our Alaskan Airline Connie didn't hang around long. The second time here was not a charm. Fog was closing in and seats were occupied with sullen Navy wives and children. Our group of expatriates from the Rock were as effervescent as well-aged apple cider. The Adak wives had long since passed the effervescent stage on their descent into cider vinegar silence. White knuckles clenched tightly, well worn airplane armrests. One look and I knew why our schoolhouse on Shemya stood empty all these years. We flew on to Anchorage, our spirits dampened by melancholy penetrating through the cabin. When we touched down on the mainland, an involuntary cheer rose from our lips, only to be dampened by a sullen atmosphere of the Adak wives. We waited until the ladies debarked before gathering our possessions from the overhead storage bins.

## Anchorage, Alaska

Birdsill was all smiles, "Perk up funny wings. We're free at last!" He called for base taxi. By the time we retrieved our luggage from the carousel, a station wagon stood outside the terminal, waiting.

• • •

As we checked into the Elmendorf VOQ, I spotted the first good news I had, outside of leaving the rock. Supply had a drop box for our Arctic gear. I placed my gear in it and then placed a call to Alaskan Airlines. The next available flight south was to Seattle, early in the morning. I booked a seat and requested routing to New Orleans. My next call was to Bobbie Jean, "Free at last, thank God Almighty I'm free at last!"

"You made it out with half your wits. When will you be here."

"Sometime tomorrow."

"Rest, but if I know you, you'll be out celebrating with your Rock friends."

"Steak, beer and bed. Did you decide on a house?"

"Yes, but I want you to see it first."

"Is it close to the base?"

"Close, but far away. I think you'll like it."

"Is Nanny coming along?"

"Of course! I'm a southern lady."

• • •

Birdsill hustled us out the door, "We're going downtown and toast those we've left behind." C. Little asked, "Where?"

"Stew told me about a bar on top the tallest building in town, Anchorage's Top of the Mark. After that, we're going to sink our teeth into the biggest steak we can find."

On our ride downtown Birdsill remarked, "Phoned my relief on the island to wish him well."

"How's Boozer doing?"

"Air Police are scouring the island for him. Turned both of our hangers upside down. Radar guys have him hidden in the abandoned school house. That dog must have nine lives."

I laughed, "Like Tucker!"

"Who?"

"The Alaskan Air Command Supply Officer."

C. Little offered, "We've got to get together for a reunion after the dust settles."

Birdsill laughed, "That's the funniest thing I've heard all this year. You funny wings might want to get together, but you'll never see me again. I'm going back to the land of throttles and rudders. I've had enough of you tech guys to last me a lifetime. Here's our building. Bar's on the top floor. I'll buy the first round and you the next two. It takes three drinks for a complete closure."

I added, "And that completes a ring, my Wagnerian pilot friend."

From the bar high atop Anchorage's premier building, we looked out on fog, more fog and a harbor half empty at ebb tide, shrouding in obscurity, our view of the sea. After the third round and our third toast to our tight little island, Birdsill excused himself, "You'll have to eat my steak, I'm off on the town. Stew's waiting and as much as I like your company, I prefer hers."

As Birdsill foresaw, only a portion of our crew remained in contact. Reunions are for happy times, long past. We never saw him again.

• • •

Lonely island nights slipped into a distant memory except for one, our island Lancelot. Boozer died in pursuit of his holy grail. His liver and kidneys aged well beyond dog years, could function no more. Laid to final rest with full island honors, he was given a posthumous promotion to five stars for his effort to bring chaos out of order. But his greatest honor was that well chewed chunk of khaki cloth, placed gently between his canines.

*This seemed to Alice a good opportunity for making her escape: so she set off at once, and ran till she was quite tired and out of breath, and till the puppy's bark sounded quite faint in the distance. "And yet what a dear little puppy it was!" said Alice.*

# Chapter 13

## Biloxi, Mississippi

After hours and hours of climbing on and off airplanes from Fairbanks to Seattle to Chicago, I finally arrived in New Orleans. I stepped down the rolling stairs into the cool humid night of southern Louisiana, feeling again like I'd been rode hard and put away wet. Bobbie Jean, dressed in a light gray trench coat, open at the neck, revealing a white silk turtle neck and matching slacks, leaned against the arrival gate, right out of Casablanca, "Welcome home, my wandering soldier."

Her embrace and lingering kiss brought closure to my island prison. And a long, long trip across continental America, "I wasn't expecting you. How did you track me down?"

"Through feminine skill and cunning. How do you like our winter weather?" She placed her arm through mine and we walked, our bodies touching with each step. I sensed her warmth, a soft presence against my thigh, like Louisiana's mild weather, an unaccustomed, but pleasurable experience. "After the frozen north, you and your southern weather are a breath of spring to me."

"I've heard that line before from someone who looks a lot like you. How can our cold fifty-degree weather get your Yankee blood excited?"

"Fifty degrees warmer here than Anchorage and ninety-eight degrees warmer, with your body close to mine. Feels strange, but nice to be walking this close to real live woman. Going to take awhile to adjust to living with someone I share a bed with." I stood back and looked into her eyes and drew her close, "A real live woman. Will wonders ever cease?"

"After I get breakfast inside my Nanook of the north, you're going to find out just how alive I am. Do you want to drive?"

"Haven't been to bed for twenty-four hours. You drive. Your perfume should keep me awake until we get home, but not enough to handle a car. Breakfast? Will my stomach have to adjust to Louisiana hot sauces?"

"I'm not concerned about your stomach."

I held her close, not wanting to let go. She pushed me gently away, "If we hold each other any closer, we're going to give my Cajun cousins a thrill they won't normally see outside the French Quarter. We'll pick up your luggage and leave right away."

"Where did you park?"

"Outside the front entrance."

"Won't you get a ticket?"

"A policeman is watching it for me."

"I'll never learn."

• • •

Bobbie Jean pulled into a diner/bar on the outskirts of New Orleans. The type of place where night shift rednecks downed boilermakers with their omelets. She ordered thick steamy chicory coffee in lyrical Cajun French from a raven-haired waitress, as steamy as the mugs and coffee thermos she left on our table. Bobbie Jean smiled, "I see you can still appreciate a beautiful woman."

"Civilization is still a shock to my senses. A women not wearing a parka is like opening a centerfold."

We held hands and stared into each other's eyes for what seemed an eternity. She finally broke the spell, "How does it feel to be back?"

"Like someone lifted a five-hundred pound gorilla off my shoulders. Have you made arrangements for our move to Omaha?"

"I covered up what were not shipping. Not sending antiques. They're so used to gulf moisture, they'll shrivel up in the west. We can buy what we need at the Nebraska Furniture Mart."

"How soon do you want to leave?"

"Not until you have to report in. Nebraska is one great white sheet of ice and snow."

"Talk about absentminded, how are the twins?"

"Happiest little fellows you'll ever meet. They'll stay with Mother until we have our house set up."

"Tell me about the one you picked out."

"In a forest," she replied.

"On the prairie?"

Breakfast arrived and was it ever hot. I swallowed half a glass of water, "What's in this omelet?"

"Everything from sausage to peppers."

"I can taste the peppers. Really good. Glad you ordered beer to wash it down. How did you find this diner?"

"An old haunt of Ralph's, but don't come in after nine at night. This is Cajun country. If a fight is going to start, it will by then."

"You were going to tell me about our house."

"Located in a forest north of Bellevue and south of Omaha. A golf course home with a wonderful view."

"If you like it, buy it."

"Not until after you see it and approve. Do you know what your new job is?"

"Haven't the foggiest. All I know is that I'm assigned to the Estimates Directorate in Intelligence at SAC headquarters."

"Sounds like it is very bureaucratic."

"To me, too."

"Ready to drive to Biloxi?"

"Aren't the twins in Jackson?"

"I moved them down several days ago, when I knew you were on your way home. Mother was fit to be tied."

• • •

After driving for several hours, Bobbie Jean kissed my forehead and said gently, "Wake up soldier, we're home."

I shook the cobwebs out of my head and looked out on a vast gulf view, "Great to see salt water that won't kill you."

"You haven't lived through one of our hurricanes," she replied.

I carried my gear into the house, "Looks like an old movie set, with half the furniture covered up. Will Nanny be upset if I look in on our boys?"

"Not if you're quiet."

I whispered, "How do you tell them apart?"

"A mother can tell by smell, but just to make sure, I got them ID bracelets."

"What if we get the bracelets mixed up?"

"Don't even think of it. You look beat."

"You're right. With that Alaskan gorilla off my back, the wind has gone out of my sails. I'm going to undress, shower and sleep. Wake me if it looks like I'll miss dinner."

"We're going to the Broadwater. Herbie is running the bar again."

"Why?"

"To keep busy. When we sold his lounge he signed a clause that prevents him from opening a new one in this county for two years from the date of sale. The Broadwater jumped at the opportunity to have him manage their bar again. Don't even think of sleeping past five this afternoon."

• • •

I woke with the setting winter sun in my eyes and Bobby Jean at my side, "When did you hop into bed?"

"An hour ago. We southern ladies need beauty naps. And my body is still recovering from the birth of our two sons."

As we moved closer together our body temperatures began to rise, "Do you remember, or has it been too long."

Bobbie Jean propped her head in her hands and smiled, "I remember, life is short — eat desert first."

Our lips met and then our hands. Dinner would be late tonight.

• • •

Herbie's grin was as wide as the Broadwater Hotel's front entrance, "Welcome back to the sunny south, stranger. You look pale as Yankee of the Yukon."

I embraced Herbie, "Clean living and a celibate lifestyle, my Cajun friend from Arcadia. Bobbie Jean says you're an instant rich guy."

"And she is, too. We both did quite well."

Bobbie Jean placed her finger to her lips, "Shush, Johnny has his secrets and I have mine. Do you know what we want?"

"Before dinner? Two Irish coffee specials coming up."

Herbie motioned for a waiter, "How soon will you be leaving for Omaha."

"Not right away, Bobbie Jean says it's frozen over and we have a second honeymoon coming."

She laughed, "That's not true. This will be our first one. Where are you taking me?"

"Palm Beach."

"The Breakers?"

"Yes."

"When?"

"This weekend. Your mother has volunteered to take care of the twins."

"And she didn't say a word to me, that sneak!"

"She couldn't. It's her gift to us. All is forgiven, except . . ."

"A formal wedding at the Lee Mansion."

"With all those dead Yankees."

Herbie stood up, "Time to leave you two alone. Do you want to dine in the bar?"

Bobbie Jean answered, "Can we have a very private table in the dinning room? As much as we love you, we need to be alone. We have a lot of catching up to do. Is the new chef working tonight?"

"Yes and is he ever consistently excellent. It isn't on tonight's menu, but he'll fix you the best steak 'au poivre' you've ever had."

I asked, "Where did he come from?"

"Out of the French Quarter. Wanted to breath fresh air. Enjoy your coffee. I'll have a private window overlooking the gulf ready for you in the dining room. Stop back after dinner. I have a new business proposition."

After we were seated in the dining room, I pushed our chairs together and held Bobbie Jean close, "I can't believe I'm here with you. After a year of mess halls with nothing but crazies for company, this is overwhelming. A romantic table on the gulf, a beautiful woman . . . pinch me."

"For me, too. I have not been out since I left Fort Worth last fall."

"This is our winter of discontent."

"My, we've brushed up on our Shakespeare, my fair son of York."

"You didn't learn that at your Biloxi finishing school."

"My daddy read to me when I was a little girl."

"This is exactly why your mother pushed a honeymoon. We need some time alone. I'll have to reconsider my first impression of Mississippi's Grande Dame of Langtry Hall."

"And more, she gave us this honeymoon as her peace offering. I'm going to order blackened red snapper and I know what you want."

"Medium rare."

• • •

After the meal, I pushed my chair back from the table, "My pepper steak was incredible. Best I've ever had, anywhere, anytime. And your fish?"

"Let's stop in the bar and talk to Herbie. I believe our Cajun friend has uncovered the French Quarter's hidden treasure."

Herbie sat down at our table, "Well, what do you think?"

Bobbie Jean took his hand in hers, "Yes, we'll go in with you on your new restaurant."

"He's great, isn't he?"

"New Orleans's loss is our gain. Where do you want to build it?"

"Omaha, there will be nothing like it there."

I shook my head, "Not all true, you will have competition from the steak and potatoes people. There are several excellent steak houses and the Blackstone Hotel has a pretty fair French cuisine. Besides great food, you'll need a great location to make it a success."

Bobbie Jean stood up, "I can scout around for a location. We'll need a liquor license, zoning and I'll have to bone up on Nebraska law. Then there are politicians. We'll be newcomers. I almost forgot. What style of restaurant?"

"Simple. Mixed grill with prepared French sauces. And a small amount of Cajun. Limit the menu and concentrate on quality. Dinner first and add lunch if it looks profitable."

Bobbie Jean nodded, "Yes, I like the limited menu idea. Have you thought of the container?"

"Container?"

"Building, French Quarter style, Victorian, modern?"

"We may have to take what's available."

"Or build. How soon do you want to begin?"

"I'd like to begin operation by this time next year. I've taken up enough of your time. Another coffee?"

• • •

Our honeymoon began that night and continued until we arrived in Palm Beach. We strolled along Atlantic Ocean beaches in the late afternoon sun, dined under the stars and slept in until nine. Wearing formal attire for dinner is bit stuffy, but then, so is the Breakers. All in all, it was a honeymoon worth waiting for. We returned with sand in our hair, sun baked skin and happy songs in our hearts. True to her word, Bobbie Jean didn't ship her antiques, but she almost filled a medium sized moving van with all the furniture she considered modern.

"Where did you have all of this hidden?"

"You've seen my storage over the garage."

"How do you date an antique?"

"First you see if he has money."

"Touché!"

"My antiques are anything built before the War of Northern Aggression."

"A life of straight lines. Are you ready to travel west?"

"I don't want to drive two cars. Why don't we ride together in my Bentley?"

"We'll need two cars."

"Buy one in Omaha."

"What about my station wagon?"

"Herbie said the chef needs a better car."

• • •

It wasn't easy for either one of us to leave our twins, but we knew they were in the best of care. I survived, unscathed, a series of grillings by Bobbie Jean's mother and her aunts. Neither of us wanted to say good-bye, so we lingered until late in the morning on the day of our departure. As we drove west toward Memphis, Bobbie Jean asked, "Do you want to stay at the Peabody Hotel?"

"Do I have a choice?"

"No."

## Mississippi to Nebraska

We arrived in Memphis long after the Peabody's famous ducks were asleep inside their roost on the rooftop. Bobbie Jean rushed us to our room and followed me into the shower, "Four-star restaurant, Johnny. We must hurry before the kitchen closes. I don't want you to miss the experience. Careful, don't you dare get my hair wet."

"I don't suppose it pays to discuss dessert first."

"Not this evening. We have less than two hours before the kitchen closes. Scrub my back?"

• • •

As we walked down the corridor, returning to our room from a late dinner, Bobbie Jean gave my hand a squeeze, "Why did you order pepper steak again?"

"Business, to compare our soon to be chef with his four-star competition."

"I don't believe you, but how was it?"

"You can't go wrong. This was excellent, but there is no comparison."

"I'll invest with Herbie if the figures work out, but I'm not sure about his chef. I'm having second thoughts. The jury is still out."

"Is there a problem?"

"Not with his cooking. New Orleans chefs can't stay away from their city. It won't be long before he wants to return home."

"Sell before he does. What do you think of Tennessee?"

"Arkansas without red dirt."

"I agree. Hard scrabble, but not as mean. What time do you want to leave in the morning?"

"When we get up. Dessert?"

"Without whipped cream?"

• • •

We watched with amusement as the Peabody's ducks waddled from the elevator to the lobby fountain. Breakfast was well prepared, though I danced around the grits without comment. We were packed and on the road, heading west by nine. Bobbie Jean checked the weather and recommended we cross Arkansas and the Ozarks before ice formed on the road in the late afternoon. She drove the first leg through Marked Tree, Hoxie and Hardy, Arkansas, not stopping until we reached Thayer, over the Missouri border.

She woke me, "Coffee and a stretch, soldier? I had the Peabody fill our thermos. I've driven this way before. I would have stopped earlier, but I didn't want to park off the road in Arkansas's red mud."

"I'll take over and you can rest. Next stop, Springfield for a late Missouri lunch?"

"Wake me," and she curled up by my side.

We drove into the eastern outskirts of Kansas City, Missouri before dark. I nudged Bobbie Jean. She awoke with her arms pressed outward, stretching, "Kansas City?"

"Where everything is up to date. Where do you want to stay?"

"Find an expensive motel and pull in."

"We're almost to Omaha. Maybe we should keep on driving."

"No, let's stop. There is an art museum here that I want to see. It is supposed to be very special. We can stop there in the morning and be in Omaha before dark."

"I haven't seen a motel worth stopping at."

"Drive through downtown and north on the Missouri side of the river."

We found a place to her liking, north out of town, on the outskirts, but close to the museum. Bobbie Jean unpacked while I undressed and ran water for a shower.

She asked, "What are you interested in?"

"Do you mean dinner?"

"I'm thumbing through the yellow pages."

"A little Italian?"

"Do you mean dinner?" and we both laughed.

• • •

As we drove north on a blustery February day, Bobbie Jean was all smiles, "Now wasn't the art museum worth staying over for?"

"So were the home fries. We finally made it out of the land of grits."

"Hush, the way you complain they must have served grits on your island."

"Every morning. Do you know what I can't get used to?"

"Not me, is it?"

"Never! I've been off alert for over a month and I'm still reluctant to be farther than twenty miles away from home."

"We're a thousand miles away."

"I know. Weird isn't it."

"You've become a fireman answering his bell when there is no bell."

"It no longer tolls for me."

"We are becoming literary. Where do you want to stop?"

"Do you want to look at temporary quarters on base?"

"No, but I'm willing to compromise. If we can find a suitable one, a motel near the base will do."

"If not?"

"The Blackstone."

## Omaha, Nebraska

We crossed over the toll bridge south of Omaha and north of Bellevue into our new home state, Nebraska. I turned south on I-75 and drove toward Bellevue.

Bobbie Jean tapped my arm, "I haven't seen anything I like, yet."

I knew when I was licked, "Blackstone?"

"You'll have to backtrack and I know how much you hate doing that. It's still light out. We can drive by the area I want you to see."

"Is it safe to go down to the woods today?"

"Only if we go in disguise."

• • •

Fontennelle Forest lived up to Bobbie Jean's sales pitch. Trees were scarce on this side of the Missouri and finding a home near one was like living on the beach in Biloxi. "I like it. A little hilly for winter driving, but worth it. Is it open or do we have to wait for the owners to leave?"

"Brand new, built on spec. We have to get back to I-75 to go into town."

Bobbie Jean hovered over the porter like a mother hen as he unpacked her Bentley. I asked, "Don't you want to leave everything we don't need right away in the car?"

"We may be here for awhile."

"But, you have our home picked out."

"Moving van won't be here for a week and negotiations may take a little time."

"I better leave the business end of moving up to you."

"That's why I get paid the big bucks" and we laughed together while the porter looked puzzled. The Blackstone was a little worn around the edges, but the service was still first rate and our suite very comfortable. I had to ask, "Hotel owner's courtesy?"

"Not free, but we only pay the regular room rate. Shower and dress for dinner."

"Coat and tie?"

"Like the Breakers, but not formal attire."

"You do like the grand life. Why did we get treated so well when we checked in."

"Professional courtesy and we are driving a Bentley."

"We look important, even though we aren't?"

"You are catching on. When you own a big boat, sail it close to the shore."

• • •

I almost stumbled into a table when I saw him sitting at the bar. His hair was a little thinner and he had put on a little weight, but the Alfred E. Neuman grin hadn't changed a bit. I pulled Bobbie Jean along, "Tuck, Tucker Tubbs. What in the world are you doing in the Blackstone bar? I thought you were still in Vietnam."

"That's why I'm a reporter and you're still marching to the beat of a different drummer. Got too cozy with the Vietcong and the military asked me to leave. Now I'm chasing another story. Who is this good looking young lady you're with?"

"Meet my bride, Bobbie Jean Langtry, the belle of Biloxi Mississippi."

"How long have you two been married?"

Bobbie Jean gave Tuck a kiss on the cheek, "Not long enough. Johnny has mentioned you often. You do have the look of the devil about you."

I laughed, "Believe it or not this young lady was my landlady when I was wandering through Electronic Warfare training in Biloxi."

"You and I were threatened with extinction if we chose an assignment beginning with an E or R."

"It's too long a tale, I'll fill you in, later. What story are you chasing down?"

"I'm doing an in-depth piece on SAC headquarters. Have you reported in?"

"We just drove into town today. Everyone on the Rock wanted to hang you for what wasn't on Mona Lisa."

"The ocean going tug? Don't blame them. My general diverted your stuff for his own use. Couldn't believe he'd stiff his main reason for being. Taught me several lessons about organizations."

"What were they?"

"Stick around too long and all the feathers will go to your nest. His detachments were on one year tours and his people were on three to four. By the time the detachment folks figured out what was going down, they had moved on. Your Island was lucky to get food. What were you doing on the Rock?"

"Flying with the SAC detachment."

"Did you ever get your vehicles for the second airplane?"

"Not until SAC, IG pulled a no-notice inspection and tore Alaskan Air Command a new asshole. Even after that, your boss told our commander to shove it. When our four star pulled his head out of the ceiling, he flew right by Alaskan Air Command. A week later a flock of C-141s arrived with trucks, buses and ranch oak furniture for the alert hangers. SAC might work our butts off, but they know how to take care of their troops."

"I feel better. Didn't set well, leaving the service and not doing my job. At least that explains why no one here will bad mouth the organization. I can't pry anything negative out of your troops."

"Pays to have a mission."

Bobbie Jean tugged at my arm, "I'm starved. I hate to interrupt war stories from two long lost military waifs, but I'd like to eat dinner before the restaurant closes. Would you care to dine with us, Mr. Tubbs?"

"Love to. Hard for me to figure out how someone as ugly as Johnny wound up with the belle of the ball."

Bobbie Jean tugged on my arm again, "I have poor eyesight and bad hearing."

• • •

We followed Tucker into the dining room. Instead of walking through the main entrance, he forced open two locked French doors and ambled through the string quartet. And continued to the maitre d's desk as if entering this way was the right thing to do. The string quartet continued playing Mozart, but with open mouths.

The maitre d' greeted Bobbie Jean with a smile and Tucker with a scowl, "Mrs. Langtry?"

She nodded, "Yes."

"I was informed that you were staying with us. We are honored. Tonight you will be our guest. Our chef is the brother of your chef at the Broadwater Beach, follow me. I have a table reserved for you near our string quartet."

He frowned at Tucker, "Have you met all of our violin section?"

Tucker kept right on smiling, following the maitre d' and waving to the violin section.

Bobbie Jean whispered, "He is everything you said he was and more."

Our waiter asked, "Do you care for a before dinner drink?"

Tucker ordered a beer and Bobbie Jean ordered a bottle of California Chablis. After he delivered our drinks he explained, "Our chef would like to prepare his Nebraska version of steak 'au poivre' medium rare for you. If you would care for a different dish, he will prepare one, but he has an exceptional pepper sauce he wants you to taste."

Bobbie Jean was pleased, "It's my husbands favorite meat dish. We are honored by the chef's choice and delighted to be in his hands."

Tucker rolled his eyes upward, "Do you guys always get this royal treatment?"

"Bobbie Jean does. She owned the Broadwater Beach hotel in Biloxi. Sold it a few years back. Hotel owners have a union."

She added, "We may start a business venture here with a friend of mine and the chef's brother. I think the chef is sending us a message, I'm not certain what it is. How do you like living in our nations capitol?"

"Great! Bought a two bedroom condo in a new building on the Potomac River called the Watergate."

I asked, "And how do you like being a civilian again?"

"Never left it, as you well know. Love working for the *Post*. It's a muckraker's dream. My job is to look for the dark side of the Department of Defense."

"What if it's all sweetness and light?"

"Won't print it. If I did, I'm out on the street looking for work."

"I thought newspapers were supposed to seek truth, set it in print and protect our freedom."

"Not in today's world. We seek liberal causes, print what sells and pocket the money."

Conversation ceased as our salad plates were removed and the main course served. Bobbie Jean asked Tucker, "Does it bother you?"

"The newspaper business? Not as long as I get a paycheck. With a little luck, I may work my way up to an inside the beltway guru."

"What is a beltway?"

"A road that circles Washington DC."

"Tell me, Mr. Tubbs, are you married?"

"No, I'm not. Haven't been where there are enough eligible ladies. Not since Houston. Alaska was fun, but it's hard to get romantic when your girl is bundled up in a parka. Washington may change that. It's a bachelor's paradise."

"Do you plan to settle down?"

"If I find the right lady."

I interrupted Bobbie Jean's interrogation, "This steak is wonderful. Even better than his brother's. Has to be the meat. The sauce is identical."

Tucker asked, "Something I should know about?"

Bobbie Jean set her fork down, "It's very good. My bar manager and his chef asked us to look into building a New Orleans style restaurant here. The Blackstone will be stiff competition."

"Just how many businesses are you involved in."

I laughed, "Even I don't know, but I do know she owns a piece of the Sands in Las Vegas."

"Now, don't bother Mr. Tubbs with our business affairs. I think reporting for the *Post* is much more interesting than working for a living." Tucker turned a new shade of bleached white, before joining in our laughter. "I should have warned you about Bobbie Jean. She feasts on straight lines."

Our waiter cleared the dishes and poured coffee, New Orleans style. He was joined by the chef. "Our chef would like to introduce himself."

He bowed and shook hands all around, "Mrs. Langtry, I've heard so much about you."

"I hope it was all positive. My husband and I are honored by your generosity. Your sauces are Cordon Bleu. Did your brother tell you we were coming?"

"Yes. He asked that I provide any assistance you might need in your new venture." I asked, "He must have briefed you. What do you think?"

"Most of your competition will be on 72nd Street or tucked away in Omaha's ethnic neighborhoods. Not much down Bellevue way."

"How about outside of 72nd Street?"

He laughed, "Not much, Boys Town and farms."

Bobbie Jean whispered to him, "I'll be in touch after we are settled in."

He gave her his card, bowed and walked quickly away. Tucker pushed his chair back, "How about a drink on the *Washington Post*?"

I agreed, but Bobbie Jean hesitated, "After a meal like this one, all I want to do is curl up in the corner. Maybe just one and then its off to bed."

Bobbie Jean and I ordered a glass of Port and Tucker asked for another beer.

I opened, "I'm going to pry into your business, Tuck. SAC headquarters is too big a whale to swallow. Which piece are you interested in?"

"O' Clubs."

"What do you expect to find there?"

"Remember our cadet mess hall officer?"

"Isn't he the one that followed you to supply school."

"Right. Washed out and was assigned back into food service. This time it was O' Clubs. After two years he had enough funds to pay cash for his own restaurant."

"I didn't think he was smart enough to steal."

"If what I think, but can't prove is real, there's a whole lot of it going on. Don't know where my investigation will take me, but I'm enjoying the trip."

"Have you found a source? One that will spill the beans?"

"Yes, but only one. I'd like to have at least two or at a minimum, a wink and a nod."

Bobbie Jean gave my arm a second tug, "Say goodnight Johnny. You and Tucker can finish your war stories over breakfast."

"Meet you at seven-thirty for breakfast, Tuck? We can pick up where we left off."

"First one down orders coffee."

• • •

As we entered the elevator, Bobbie Jean poked me in my ribs, "I thought you would never leave the bar. I'm bushed. We have a house to purchase and furniture to buy in the morning."

"Sorry, haven't seen Tuck since Nav school. He sure can land on his feet."

"You always described Mr. Tubbs as a klutz, but he appears to possess a few cat like moves."

"Tucker used all of his nine lives in Nav Training."

"I mean, he seems to know what he's doing."

"As long as it isn't technical. Maybe he's found a job that suites his talents."

"Walking through string quartets?"

"Had all I could do to keep from laughing."

"He carried it off well."

"That he did."

As she undressed, Bobbie Jean mentioned, "We may have several problems if we must live south of Omaha."

"Don't tell me, stockyards and feeder lots?"

"Yes. I don't believe it's the location where Omaha's movers and shakers live."

"If Uncle Sam built an air base there, it must have been a swamp at one time. Although I believe it was an Army post, Fort Crook."

"Does that describe the inhabitants?"

"No, it was named after the general who fought the Indian Wars out here. At least Omaha has more than one TV station."

Bobbie Jean took my hand and led me to our bed, "I'm getting a second wind," she said.

"And we didn't have dessert."

• • •

I tiptoed around our suite like a mouse in front of a sleeping cat, but wild elephants on a rampage wouldn't wake up Bobbie Jean. I was on my second cup of coffee before Tucker entered the Blackstone's restaurant for breakfast.

He pulled up a chair, "Where is Bobbie Jean?"

"Out like a light. Takes awhile to recover from birthing twins."

"You have twins?"

"Identical boys last fall "

"And she kept her maiden name?"

"It's an old southern family tradition she asked me to uphold. Her family has no sons."

"Rich?"

"She spills more than I make as a major."

"Major? You're on a fast track."

"Ignorance and superstition will always win out over science and fact," and we both laughed. "We were married in Reno. She promised her father on his death bed that she would not change her name without her mother's permission."

"And her mother wouldn't give it?"

"Right. Hates Yankees. The twins changed all that, but it has been many cold years. She wants us to have another wedding at the Lee Mansion."

"Overlooking Arlington Cemetery?"

"And all those dead Yankees. Will you stand up for me when the time comes?"

"I will stand and deliver. You are a lucky man, Johnny. Rich, witty and beautiful. You couldn't find a better wife. I hope I'm as lucky."

"And you're the Romeo that broke the hearts of an entire airline."

Tucker looked surprised, "Which one? There's more than one?"

"TTA."

"I never did understand that electronic stuff. How soon do you have to report in?"

"In a week. If all goes right, we'll move into our new house before then."

"Take my card. Drop me a line after you settle in. We need to stay in touch. Won't be long before you'll wind up at the Pentagon.

"Don't count on it. When are you heading back?"

"At the end of the week. Bought a car here. A real collector's item. Finish your coffee and we'll step outside. I want to show it to you."

• • •

The rocker panels had been filled in and rust scraped away. It was either Bonnie the Body Beautiful's bright pink and white Packard Caribbean convertible or its twin.

"Leaving it at a body shop this morning. Should have a new paint job and new top on her by the time I'm ready to leave. Don't build them like this anymore. Even has its original leather seats and torsion bar suspension," he said.

"Who did you buy it from?"

"Chief master sergeant in SAC personnel. Drove a hard bargain."

"Are you going to drive it back?"

"Sure am. Wouldn't trust this beauty to anyone else."

"Better have a mechanic check it over."

"Do you know something about this car that I should know?"

"Only two of its past owners. It was because of your Packard that I was sent to the Rock."

"The chief master sergeant?"

"Yes."

"I'll have it wrung out before I leave."

• • •

Bobbie Jean stepped out of the shower as I entered the bedroom with a pot of coffee, "Just what I needed. How is your friend, Mr. Tubbs."

"Just bought Bonnie's pink and white Packard Caribbean convertible from a sergeant at SAC headquarters."

"Bonnie's?"

"Looks like it. Gave me a dump on how to cheat a restaurant and bar."

"Second cash register?"

"And several more."

"We can look at the house this morning and close this afternoon."

"That's impossible."

"We're buying from the builder and we are paying cash."

"What if we find something wrong after we move in?"

"We hold out ten thousand, until it's fixed."

"Will he do that?"

"Anxious to sell and get his money out. With a little luck we can have our furniture in place by the end of the week, fly back to Jackson and pick up our boys. Pour me a cup of coffee and find out when the Nebraska Furniture Mart opens. You can help me pick out furniture."

• • •

Our moving van arrived early Wednesday morning and the Nebraska Furniture Mart truck arrived Thursday afternoon. I helped unpack and assemble, until all our items were together, if not in their proper place. We flew to New Orleans Friday night, drove to Jackson and returned to New Orleans for our flight out, Sunday morning. Our twins were snugly tucked in bed in their new home by Sunday evening. Bobbie Jean and Nanny gave notice that I was to stay out of their way. They didn't need a male's help to decorate and arrange. Knowing when to leave well enough alone, I reported in to SAC headquarters early Monday morning.

• • •

Reporting into headquarters, any headquarters, is a one body operation. The system decreed that a body was needed for a particular slot and a body was requisitioned to fill it. If it was a command position, politics came into play. If it was a technical position, papers were shuffled until a matching body was found. I walked my matching body through incoming personnel and received identification tags not unlike ones coroners attach to toes. When I arrived on the doorstep of my director's office, he nodded knowingly and inspected the body he requisitioned to make sure it matched. He instructed his sergeant to escort me to the office and desk it was to fill. In less than a day my body had received its stamp of approval, all except a bar code. Introduced to my immediate boss, a moody lieutenant colonel by the name of D. D. Dripper, I didn't have to ask what the D. D. stood for. After a ten minute lecture on "do the right thing," I knew. I settled my body into a job it matched on paper not knowing what the paper said. Knowing mind over matter might work, I dug into the matter at hand.

• • •

Bobbie Jean settled in quite nicely, becoming a first-rate homemaker. After she selected a two story cross-home, between modern and Victorian, business ventures were placed on hold. We nestled in quite comfortably on a hillside drive at the edge of Fontinelle Forest. As spring drew near and the trees began to bloom, I admired her canny ability to choose the right location, be it house or business. There are damn few trees in Nebraska and she had planted us in the middle of a forest, on rolling hills, alongside the mighty Missouri. Our forest provided a sanctuary and our home an oasis from the searing competitive heat at SAC headquarters. All was well until the ground thawed in mid-March and warm western breezes swept in.

Bobbie Jean opened the windows to let in the breeze and was greeted by an unfamiliar odor. She closed the window and asked, "What's that smell? It's awful."

"You must not have had cattle on your plantation. That, my dear, is the odor of manure thawing at the first sign of spring. We must have a feeder lot to the west of us."

"Smells like a stockyard."

"Can't be. We're ten miles to the south of it."

"Three months of ice and snow, the first spring thaw and our place smells like an overturned outhouse. Find out how long it will last and call me."

"When you pick a place to live in a primeval setting, you've got to expect primeval smells."

"Spoken like a true farm boy."

• • •

I phoned after I arrived at work, "Troops say as soon as the ground dries out, or your odor will go away with the spring rains."

"I certainly hope so. I'm going to look at property along the Missouri for Herbie's restaurant this morning. I'll stop at the Officer's Club for lunch, meet me?"

"First one there reserves a table."

She arrived in the parking lot as I walked across the street from headquarters. "Did you find a spot up out of the flood plain?"

"Located several nice parcels, this side of the river."

"How far south did you drive?"

"Quite aways. Turned around when I saw a chemical plant on the horizon."

"Is it the location you've been looking for?"

"Maybe, it's pretty far out of the way."

"Not around here. Not much else to do but dine out. If it's good enough, you'll have more customers than you can handle. Give folks someplace to go and they will come."

"I still need to check north of here and across the river."

"You'll run into zoning problems north and folks don't like to cross the river on a toll bridge."

• • •

We ordered lunch. Today was Friday and clam chowder was the special. Bobbie Jean said, "I think I'll try the clam chowder."

"Depends."

"Depends on what?"

"If the clam has survived."

"What do you mean?"

"Last time I had chowder here, the soup was so thin, the cook must have dragged it through the pot with a string."

I ordered a reuben sandwich. After Bobbie Jean tasted her soup she made a face, "Someone murdered the clam. How is your job coming along? Have you found out what it is you're supposed to do?"

"Not really. All my boss keeps saying is, 'do the right thing.' I spend most of my time learning about what we used to do, not what needs to be done. And it's all classified beyond belief."

"Classified? Classified what?"

"Military speak, like Classified Secret or Top Secret."

"Jargon, Johnny. Can't you folks speak English"

"It's like Latin to a lawyer—except we don't charge a fortune for the interpretation."

"I'll have to get used to it. Something is on your mind."

I hesitated, knowing Bobbie Jean did not care for surprises, "My directorate is holding a steak fry out at the base lake tomorrow night."

"Why such short notice?" she asked.

"It's nothing sinister. My colonel forgot we belonged to his directorate."

"How could that happen?"

"His office is underground and we're on the top floor."

"That sounds inverted, the boss is supposed to be on top. That doesn't sound right, never mind."

"Never asked. My offices always seem to be out of the way. In case of attack, they'll be safe."

"Or the first ones out. I'm going to call around and find out what everyone is wearing to your steak fry. And when you get home, you can tell me about the people I'll meet tomorrow. And Johnny? Please, no more surprises. Do you want me to drive you back to work?"

"It's just up the hill, past the statue in honor of government workers."

"Isn't that a SAC missile?"

"It is, but it doesn't have propellant, so it can't be fired and it doesn't work."

• • •

When I arrived home that evening, Bobbie Jean met me at the door with a glass of red wine and a smile, "And I thought I had a bad day. You look like someone who needs a hug."

Our kiss would have become more than passionate if she had not wiggled out from under my embrace, "I have dinner in the oven and it's your turn to feed the boys. Nanny has the night off."

"Where are they?"

"Swinging and giggling with me in the kitchen. Keep me company while I cut up greens for our salad. You can tell me about the people I'll meet tomorrow night."

I wound up both swings, "Tucker and Oliver T. would both feel at home here. We have a major down the hall with a wall full of signed photos dedicated to him from generals. Don't know who's the vainest, our major or the generals. Most of the guys I work with are elusive—won't give a straight answer to any of my questions. Guard their information like it is gold. Information is the key to advancement, so the folks I work with won't share what they know with anyone that can't help them. They all tend to be on the defensive, like I'm Brutus with a knife hidden in my toga. So don't be surprised if they're not friendly. Did you find out what the other ladies are going to wear?"

"I made a few phone calls. We'll see."

"I asked D. D. Dripper and he said casual."

"That's a big help. What does that mean to you?"

"No coat or tie."

"For men, but for women that can mean anything from shorts to formal dress. I can't believe your colonel forgot that you worked for him."

"I'm the new guy. I believe it's an honest mistake."

"I hope you don't mind if I wait and judge later."

I wound the swings again. Our boys smiled with the motion, staring out the kitchen windows at the trees , "Going to change out of this uniform. I'll feed the boys after I get into something comfortable."

"And so they won't spit up food on your clean uniform."

"You broke the code."

After I fed the boys, we placed them in their oversized playpen in the kitchen. Bobbie Jean finished preparing our meal while they played with balls, bells, stared at each other and out the window at the trees. My eyes wandered to the same view, my boys were on to something, buds were popping out. Winter had stayed on far beyond its welcome. It was mid-April before Omaha's earth finally warmed up after a long winter's freeze. Temperatures soared, Mother Nature brought her climate back to balance. Spring arrives in Omaha like dawn in Mandalay, with thunder.

• • •

My work in Intelligence changed from chaotic to routine. Took me awhile to learn how to fly a big wooden desk, but I finally got the hang of it. Everyone I met seemed to know what their job was but me. I was still filled with self doubt. All I could get out of D. D. Dripper was, "Do the right thing, don't ever go around me to the colonel and we'll get along fine."

As long as I had to wait on special security clearances, I decided I might as well read through the files and see what my predecessor did. I found out he compared our collection assets against Intelligence requirements and recommended new systems. However, now that the war in Vietnam was heating up, there weren't any funds available for new systems. So, I decided to evaluate what we had against what was needed and recommend improvements. Finally, guidance floated down from above.

My directorate colonel requested a survey of all of our reconnaissance systems, other service systems and national systems to ascertain success rate per mission, versus cost—how long would they would be of value, and if they flew in range of enemy defensive systems, when would they become vulnerable. This dovetailed with the work I had all ready begun. My data gathering was almost complete. Analysis would take another week or two and writing the report another month, if the creek didn't rise.

• • •

Bobbie Jean broke into my mental world, "You and our boys have been staring at the trees in our backyard for five minutes. Do you want to eat dinner in the kitchen or dining room?"

"Sorry, my mind was on my work. I'm wrapping up a survey on our collection systems. Why don't we eat at the counter. The boys have fallen asleep in their playpen. We won't have to move them."

"And I won't have to carry our dinner to the dining room. Wasn't a survey done before you arrived here."

"Can't find one. SAC recently purchased a fleet of new airplanes. Our four star wants to know how they are doing in comparison to other systems and the ones they replaced."

"Sounds reasonable. Oh, I've narrowed down my search to two parcels south of here and one on the other side of the river."

"Council Bluffs?"

"To the south of town."

"Which way are you leaning?"

"One of the parcels south of here. You were right about the toll bridge. No one uses it. Might as well put up a fence."

"Did you decide what you're going to wear tomorrow night?"

"Blouse and slacks. If it's cool, I'll carry a sweater."

• • •

A cold spring wind whipped through the trees. Saturday afternoon's heat had changed to a damp chill. Early evening thunder storms bore down on Omaha from the northwest. The wind and approaching thunder sounded like garbage cans full of boulders, rolling down a hillside. Bobbie Jean and I ran from her car to the Base Lake pavilion, dodging raindrops the size of nickels splattering in the dust. As I lowered our umbrella, she gave me a nudge, "I was right."

"About what?"

"All the ladies are wearing what I am."

"Isn't that what you were told?"

"No, I was told everyone would wear shorts. I was going to be put in my place."

"Petty if you ask me.

"Not nice."

What is it you flyers say when you warn someone about watching their behind?"

"Watch your six."

"If this is any indication, watch yours at work. Now that the ladies know I have brains, they'll be more careful. Who is that waving?"

"The major I told you about. The one with the I love me photos on his wall, Major Christy."

Christy walked quickly, to where we were standing and before I could introduce Bobbie Jean asked, "Do you know who added a photo of Christ to my wall?"

"Haven't the foggiest. Was there a dedication?"

"Someone wrote, 'To Major Michael Christy, Come Visit Soon, Love JC.'"

I turned away, so he wouldn't see my widening smile and attempted to choke in my uncontrollable laughter. Out of the corner of my eye, I noticed Charlie Big Hands, doubled over in a convulsion of giggles. I introduced Bobbie Jean, but Christy was all ready moving, "Pleased to meet you. If you'll excuse me, Captain Hands is talking to my date. I don't trust him. Do you think he is the one who nailed the photo to my wall?"

Before I could answer, he was gone. Bobbie Jean had that look, one that spoke volumes, "So that's who Oliver Tugwattle would be if he stayed in. Buy me a drink, soldier and one for yourself. We'll need one if there are any more Tugwattles around."

"This group has premeditation instead of spontaneity and all of them, except Christy, have a sense of humor. Want to meet the gang of four?"

"Not now, buy me a drink and keep me company."

I carried Bobbie Jean's drink to her as the skies opened. Rain poured down in sheets into the pavilion's northwest side, driving everyone to shelter on the southeast side. As lightning danced across the sky, we found a seat in the middle of one of the semidry picnic benches, made small talk to folks we didn't know, or would care to remember. When we dug into our steaks, they were cooked cowboy tough and boot leather thin. Bobbie Jean whispered, "A dollar ninety-nine in Sacramento," and we both laughed. "Will I ever meet anyone from your office?"

"There will be other parties. Look at my boss over there, D. D. Dripper. He's so busy licking the colonel's boots, he doesn't have time for peasants. And my peers, the gang of four, have circled their wagons."

"I think it's time to leave."

"Charlie Big Hands has left the inner circle. At least you'll meet one." I introduced Bobbie Jean, but all Charlie did was nod in her direction and grab my arm, "You didn't squeal on me to Christy, did you?"

"About what?"

"The photo of Christ I added to his wall."

"Didn't know it was there."

"Neither did he. Had it up over a year and he just noticed."

He turned away laughing quietly to himself. And we turned away from a sea of backs and said good-bye to my boss, the colonel and their wives, as military protocol demanded.

Bobbie Jean snuggled close to my side for protection as we strolled on wet blossoms, scattered about by the storm across the parking lot.

She whispered, "We've just been ignored by the in-crowd."

"I'm the new guy that came from outside and took over a plum branch. We won't have many friends. Smell the air?"

"No more feeder lot odor. The rain must have washed it out of the air."

"Wait 'till the sun comes out and begins to bake the manure dry. What do you think of the folks I work for?"

"First group of military people I've met who are as political as our politicians in Biloxi. They must train SAC headquarters' people at the county courthouse."

"That's the down side. The up side is, I'm not a briefcase staff type."

"How about D. D. Dripper?"

"There is always an exception made for incompetent pilots.

"Want to stop for an after dinner drink in Bellevue?"

"After all the crow we've been offered, I'd rather stop for a sandwich and beer."

• • •

Springtime in Omaha flew by faster than a New Jersey minute. Nebraska's brisk westerly wind changed to summer slow, southwestern breezes. And my reconnaissance survey slowly ground down. I required more data as grist for our computers to calculate. And accurate cost and collection results from national systems were not available to me or to anyone outside of Washington DC. And my preliminary results were not ones my bosses expected, casting an unfavorable light on our new aircraft reconnaissance system. My two month project was in danger of stretching out to more than a year. While work was stagnating, our family wasn't. Summer trips to Jackson and Biloxi helped break the monotony of dust devils on the prairie. Spring and fall, Nebraska is a great place to be. Winter, those with money flew south to Arizona or Acapulco. Summer they baked with the rest of Omaha's citizens. Bobbie Jean, accustomed to steady warm temperatures of Biloxi's marine climate, could not adjust to Nebraska's extreme summer temperatures. So she didn't. While I fought the paper crush, she and the twins summered in Biloxi.

Fall arrived with a early winter cold snap. Leaves on the trees didn't have time to turn to red and gold. Instead, they froze into dark browns and greens. Like the weather, my collection survey was frozen in time. No matter how I ran the figures through our computer, results remained the same. The aircraft we replaced produced better collection data with fewer flights, than our new one. And Bobbie Jean's restaurant search froze in Nebraska politics. She purchased the parcel she wanted, but wasn't able to get a liquor license. Nebraska had a set number and like New York City taxi medallions, didn't grow with need or population.

• • •

Spring arrived with our twins standing and stepping out. And my survey moved from dead center to fast forward. While D. D. Dripper was off on an orientation course in San Antonio, a call came from our directorate colonel for me to stand and deliver. When I finished briefing, he asked that I give the same one to his fellow directors. This time I was to add why we had purchased a set number of airplanes and what was the criteria for selecting that number. That was easy. Our four star wanted the set number, so he doubled the request knowing that Washington would cut his request in half. I now had two answers that were unacceptable. And to make matters worse, D. D. Dripper returned from his orientation course as disoriented as ever. I had violated his guidance, speaking to our colonel without going through him. As a result, in his eyes I had done the wrong thing. He would not accept the results of my survey, but could not refute them. All he could do was mumble, "Consider the source," which meant he didn't agree, but had no answer. He directed that my study show our collection had doubled and we had arrived at the number of airplanes through science and fact, neither of which was true. So, being a consummate briefcase colonel, he sat on it, hoping it would go away.

His boss smelled a rat. So, he dispatched D. D. Dripper to another orientation course. While he was away, I was given an hours notice to present my briefing to the other directors. I explained the survey and results to a roomful of colonels who remained silent. Not a single question was asked.

When the lights came up my colonel took me aside, "Good pitch Johnny. Tell me, when did you come to your conclusion we had a turkey on our hands?"

"Last May."

"And when did you have this briefing ready to go?"

"Last summer."

He had that look of Caesar, as Brutus pulled a knife out of his back, "Interesting, take a couple of weeks off. If you don't have leave, I'll give you a pass. When you return, see me first."

Bobbie Jean was ready to go, "Good, we can go to Biloxi before it gets hot in Omaha. Why were you asked to take two weeks off?"

"Remember my collection survey? I briefed it to our decision makers."

"How did they like it."

"I was greeted with the sound of silence."

"Not even one polite question?"

"Not one."

"Should I call a van line?"

"Not yet. We'll see how it plays out."

"Now that you are persona non grate, do we have to attend your office party tomorrow night? Draft beer and hot dogs are not my idea of a night out on the town."

"It should be better than the last one."

"Watered down beer and pizza on the kiddies side of the pizza parlor? My stomach churned for three days."

"How is the liquor license coming along?"

"Have preliminary approval. We'll get full status in ninety days."

"Is this a good time to leave?"

"Can't do anything more until I have our license in hand."

"The twins?"

"I can have the twins ready to go in the morning. Do we have to go to the party?"

"Duty calls, I want to find out how far I've fallen from grace."

• • •

Wasn't much of a brewery, only one kettle. Bobbie Jean and I trailed along at the tail end. As we entered the breweries' party room, we were given a wide berth by my office mates. Bobbie Jean took one look at a sea of backs and said, "We're leaving. Will they lighten up on you when we return?"

"Don't know, but I've been here long enough to know messengers carrying bad news don't stay around."

"But you're only halfway through your tour here."

"Doesn't look good, does it?"

*"At any rate I'll never go there again!" said Alice, as she picked her way though the wood. "It's the stupidest tea party I ever was at in all my life!"*

# Chapter 14

## Biloxi, Mississippi

June in Biloxi is my concept of what an ideal vacation should be. The sea breeze cools down a normally very hot afternoon and the four o'clock thunder storm finishes the job. Almost perfect, except Bobbie Jean's apartments badly needed tending too. I pounded and plumbed, scraped and painted, but still needed professional help to finish the job. Her apartments were plumbed and wired before 1940. Salt air had damaged both beyond the capability of a shade tree mechanic. Chlorine mixed with water and brush removed the mildew covering my last paint job. And a mid-vacation stay at the Roosevelt Hotel in New Orleans renewed our courtship. Blueberry muffins, thick rich New Orleans coffee, romantic horse drawn carriage rides in the evening and Bobbie Jean's favorite restaurants added cement to our wedding vows.

On our last night in New Orleans, dining on pompano and white wine, Bobbie Jean turned wistful, "I wish we could carry this city back with us to Omaha."

"Isn't that what you're attempting to do with your restaurant?"

"I don't think it's possible to duplicate an attitude. Mississippi flows past New Orleans in a ribbon of rich brown molasses. The Missouri rushes past Omaha in a muddy frenzy, hurrying on its way."

"You can't duplicate the scene, but if I know you, you'll find a way to replicate New Orleans's ambiance."

"I see what you mean, maybe we can teach her laid back, friendly attitude to our wait staff. Can't we spend another week? I could use another trip to New Orleans before we return to your prairie."

"If things don't work out at work, we may have all the time in the world. A lot of powerful people invested their careers in the billion dollar project I called a turkey. And no one wants to hear their pet project didn't live up to expectations."

"Can you tell me what caused it to fail?"

"Can't give you a complete data dump."

"Without going into classified information?" I waited until our waiter finished pouring coffee.

"You asked why it failed. Without going into details, the system failed because our electrical engineers tried to stretch computer technology beyond its current limits. By the time the collection systems were installed in the airplanes, technology had progressed from transistors to miniature semiconductors. What once filled an airplane could be placed by a medium sized box. They also tried to defy several laws of physics, but I can't go into what."

"Won't they take that into consideration?"

"The colonel will. He's pretty sharp, but not D. D. Dripper and he's the one who writes my efficiency report. Dripper hung his chances of being promoted to full colonel on the success of these airplanes."

"Ignorance and superstition will always win out over science and fact."

"You're stealing my act. Do you want to drop by the Coffee Stand before we return to our hotel?"

"Of course."

"And when we return to our room I'm going to cover your body with powdered sugar."

Bobbie Jean motioned for our waiter to come over and whispered in his ear. He returned with a brown paper sack.

"What did you ask for?"

"Powdered sugar."

"Life is short."

"Eat dessert first."

• • •

After completing the architectural plans for her restaurant, Bobbie Jean was reluctant, but ready to return to Omaha, bubbling over with energy for her new project. "Our license may come in any day. Herbie and I have decided to go ahead and break ground. See if you can stay on at SAC for another six months—so I'll have my part completed."

"You're going to hang around during the summer heat?"

"Have too, if we want to be up and operating before winter sets in. At least we should have the walls up."

## Omaha, Nebraska

I walked in the kitchen door after my first day back at work relaxed with a perplexed smile. Bobbie Jean looked up from the sink, wiped her hands on a towel and gave me a hug, "Our twins are getting more mobile every day. I've spent all day trying to corral them. I'll pour you a glass of wine. You don't even look like you had a saddle on your back today. I'm dying to find out what happened on your first day back at work."

• • •

"I stopped by my office first thing this morning and it wasn't there."

"Your office disappeared? Is this the twilight zone?"

"The room was there, but folks from JSTPS had moved in."

"Jargon time again."

"Joint Strategic Target Planning Staff. They select targets for all three services. Believe it or not, they work for a three star admiral."

Bobbie Jean broke out in laughter, "Nebraska really does have a navy! What happened next?"

"I asked where everyone had gone too. No one in my old office knew. Then I remembered—my colonel requested I report to him after I returned from vacation. So I moseyed on down to his underground office and made an appointment with his secretary. I asked her if she knew where my office was and she said, "It isn't."

"Stop right there. I have to tend to dinner on the stove. Change out of your uniform and keep me company while I cook. I'm dying to find out where your Lieutenant Colonel Dripper was transferred to and what you're going to do."

When I returned to the kitchen I asked, "Where are the boys?"

"Nanny has them out for a stroll. Tell me where your boss wound up."

"Dripper was transferred to Eglin Air Force base in Florida."

"Was it a promotion? Do you know what he will be doing?"

"For a pilot, his new job is lower than a cat's hair ball. He's going to be a test pilot who doesn't test airplanes. He'll chase after experimental target drones after they're launched and shoot them down if they go out of control."

"What's a drone? Are they connected with a queen bee?"

"It's an Air Force version of a remote controlled model airplane. Not one of your more challenging jobs, but Dripper won't have to carry a briefcase."

"Why? Don't you?"

"No, I'm not allowed to carry work out of the building."

"So, Dripper has been put out to pasture. That's a shame. He worked hard at military politics. When he leaves the service, I bet he becomes a full fledged knife wielding politician."

"If he does, he'll soon discover mastering technique and knowledge are, in his case, an oxymoron. His problem is, he's ninety percent absolutely right and ten percent absolutely wrong."

"Is that bad?"

"Only when you fail to recognize the difference." Nanny brought the boys in. I had my hands full. I placed them in their playpen and helped Bobbie Jean set the table.

As we sat down, she asked, "Why didn't you call and tell me what was going on?"

"Don't have a phone, an office and when I found a phone I could use, your line was busy."

"I was chasing down the status of our liquor license."

"Is it on schedule?"

"We have a slight problem, but fixable. Finish your story. What did the colonel say to you?"

"He saw me standing outside talking to his secretary and asked me to come in. He apologized for not having a desk for me. I asked where my workers were and he said they had returned to crew duty."

"Why not you?"

"Might be because I'm too new. Anyway, he thanked me for being straight up with him and implied it was the only reason I was still around."

"They still shoot messengers, don't they?"

"I'll be waiting for that shot to be fired as long as I remain at headquarters. If I read the tea leaves correctly, we better be prepared to move on within a year."

"How are you going to keep busy?"

"That's a hard one. Can't fly a big wooden desk when mine has crashed. Guess I'll set up office in the cafeteria and wait until something better comes along."

"Would you do it again?"

"I thought about it. The easy way out is to fudge the figures, but we owe it to the guys who fly in harms way to provide them equipment that works."

• • •

Nanny arrived, sat down at the table and our dinner began.

I helped Bobbie Jean clean up and asked, "Coffee outside on the patio? Cool enough under the trees."

"I have to powder my nose. Can you carry it out?"

"Fetch and carry are the number one item in a navigator's job description."

When Bobbie Jean joined me, she strolled aimlessly around our patio, warming her coffee mug in her hands. She turned, "Think I should go slow on our restaurant?"

"No, press on. After it's up, it'll be Herbie's nickel. I may be reading the tea leaves wrong, but we should be here at least a year. Your restaurant should be up and running by then."

"I'll sleep on it. Another glass of wine?" Bobbie Jean returned with two glasses of red, "What will SAC do with their airplanes?"

"Modify them with new collection gear that does the same job and takes up one tenth the space. And add on gear for a new mission. SAC will kill two birds with one stone and everyone looks good."

"Can you tell me what the new mission is?"

"You know I can't give specifics."

"Before I forget, we're dining out tomorrow night."

"On a Tuesday?"

"Business. I want to check a steak house on 72nd Street."

"Does it have a name?"

"Angelo 's. Our Chef's brother at the Blackstone says they have a great pepper steak."

"My God, a little Italian and a pepper steak?"

"You'll be in heaven."

"Come on over here and I will be."

• • •

Angelo's Italian pepper steak was incredible, better than Herbie's brother advertised. Covered with green and red peppers and marinated in a sauce we could not place. Bobbie Jean was impressed, "Now I know why Johnny Carson sends for a case of these each month."

"Won't Angelo give you stiff competition?"

"No, too far away to have an impact and the cooking style isn't the same. And he is adding a show room."

"They do well in Las Vegas."

"Only as a loss leader to attract gamblers. None of the New York clubs are doing well and the Blue Room at the Roosevelt is closing."

"What happened?"

"Television. Show rooms are going the same way as vaudeville."

"What are you planning for yours?"

"Trio—piano, bass and drums."

"What, no Dixieland?"

"Not in Nebraska. But that's something we can do to establish our New Orleans style when we open. Have to restrict it to the bar. Dixieland is too loud and fast for fine dining. What would you like to hear?"

"Same as you, but add a good sound system for when someone shoots the piano player. No piano bar."

"Why not?"

"You'll get singers who can't sing and drinkers who won't drink. Light classical background music is my cup of tea."

"I'll put you down for elevator music. After dinner drink?"

"In the lounge."

• • •

Bobbie Jean wrinkled her nose, "We won't have to worry about competition from this Irish coffee. What will you do at work without an office or job?"

"I'm frozen in time and without friends. When Mike Christy gave me the cold shoulder, I knew I was in trouble."

"You're not going to stay around for make-work are you."

"If that happens, I'll resign my commission and help you with the restaurant."

"I don't know if I want a known loser associated with my project."

"Then I just might drive to Biloxi and wait for you there."

"That's the best news I've heard tonight. I'll go with you and we'll let Herbie bring our restaurant in."

• • •

I wandered the halls for two more weeks, spending most of my time at a rear table in the cafeteria. On a late Friday afternoon, I was joined by a colonel, new to me and to headquarters. He sat down beside me and introduced himself, "I'm Colonel Black Bird. I'd rather fly than be stuck in headquarters, but I'm here and we'll both have to make the best of it. As far as I'm concerned, staff work sucks. You're the fellow they call Johnny Ropp?"

"Yes Sir. Welcome to my office. Can I buy you a cup of coffee?"

"I'll take black and hurry back. I have business to conduct and damn little time." I carried two mugs back to my table.

He smiled a sly Irish smile, "I heard you had an unusual office. Makes more sense than most of the ones I've been to. I'm setting up a new reconnaissance office. When I found out about how you tugged on superman's cape and stuck with it, I figured you're the one for my outfit. I've absorbed all the functions of your old branch. I want you to focus on intelligence requirements for current SAC aircraft systems. Work directly with the analysts. Find out what they need and go after it."

"With our aircraft or by other means?"

"Try us first. If we can't do it, use other means."

"Shouldn't be a conflict. When do I start?"

"Now. Make tracks to the rear basement. Your desk is waiting."

"Anything else?"

"Work hard, play hard and don't hang around when you have nothing to do."

• • •

My new office was located in the SAC Reconnaissance Center. Unlike Gaul, the center was divided in two parts—Operations and Intelligence. Intelligence provided the requirements and tasks and Operations planned the missions. With the Vietnam War in high G, the reconnaissance center was manned around the clock. I was in good spirits when I arrived home from work. I walked in the kitchen door and breathed a sigh of relief. Bobbie Jean had not begun dinner, but she had poured a glass of red wine. I picked it up and wandered into her office. She was busy going over revised architectural drawings. The twins were playing with old blueprints on the floor.

She looked up, "I know. You have a new job."

"How did the information get here before me?"

"Mrs. Bird called. She invited us to dine with them at the Officer's Club tonight. That is the first invitation I've ever received from one of your boss's wives. We'll meet them in the bar at six-thirty. What is your colonel's name? Is he a nice guy?"

"Colonel Black Bird. He is a refreshing change, a job doer not a job stopper."

"Is he a pilot?"

"Flew the Blackbird, the SR-71."

"Is it a jet fighter or bomber?"

"Neither, it's the highest and fastest."

"Herbie phoned. He and the chef are flying in the last of July. They want to look at our site and go over the revised drawings."

"Are they going to stay with us?"

"No, the chef's brother has reservations for them at the Blackstone."

"Looks like you might be serving meals by Thanksgiving."

"I have my fingers crossed."

• • •

The Officer's Club looked like it had been designed by Holiday Inn, complete with a drive-through entrance and reception desk, lacking only a bellhop. The cocktail lounge, bar and dining room were side by side and open to each other. When the drapes were open, the nine hole golf course provided a view, which couldn't be seen after dark or when the sun set through the windows, which happened every evening. The previous SAC commander's wife had new carpet installed. It was thick, luxurious and was wearing like iron, which was a great misfortune. It reminded Bobbie Jean of early carnival with its bright, fluorescent colors. We were paying for it with higher dues. Still, the O' Club's ribeye steak was as good as any in town.

Colonel Black Bird and his wife were waiting as we entered the lounge. He introduced his wife, "Johnny, you didn't tell me you had a beautiful wife. Bobbie Jean, you're gorgeous. Don't tell me, is she rich, too?"

I laughed, "And she is about to build a restaurant south of here."

He helped Mrs. Bird to her feet, "Service here isn't worth a damn. Let's go to the dining room. We can order cocktails at the table. Me and the Mrs. are from Las Vegas Nevada."

"Bobbie Jean is from Biloxi, Mississippi and I'm from Bellpoint, Ohio."

"Hope it doesn't seem like I'm prying, but your last names aren't the same."

I let Bobbie Jean explain. When she finished, Colonel Bird laughed, "My first name is Bart, but I use my middle name because it fits where I came from and where I want to return. Riding herd over a bunch of funny wings is not my idea of a good assignment. Mrs. and I are sticking with bourbon and branch."

Bobbie Jean ordered a bottle of Medoc for us, "We began our evening with a glass of red wine at home and we'll stay with it."

As our ladies chatted away. Colonel Bird took me aside.

"One of the reasons I wanted to get together with you is because of my boss. When I told him I wanted you, he gave you a good report, but . . ."

"SAC shoots messengers."

"I wouldn't put your house up for sale, but I wouldn't add a recreation room either. He appreciates your hard work and honesty, but you and I both know that sometimes two rights make a wrong. He's bringing in a silver tongue to defend our airplane's new configuration. And he is removing you from that portion of your work."

"I can understand that. He lost a flock of birds the last time I worked on the project."

"Don't be so hard on yourself. We haven't really lost a single one. They're just changing missions. It would have happened eventually, you sped it up."

"System requirements are a no win situation. I'm glad to be rid of that task. Silver tongue can have it."

• • •

Our waiter appeared, "Our special tonight is ribeye steak and lobster tails, or you may wish the broiled trout."

Black Bird's interest had been stimulated, "Systems requirements, a no-win situation? I tend to agree. Why are you convinced?"

"Technology drives Air Force procurement, not requirements. The engineers come up with bells and whistles and we have to come up with the need. It doesn't always work that way, but it happens often in electronics."

"Computers are supposed to be the wave of the future."

"Most times they are nothing but adding machines with a cult formed around blinking lights. When we can't do it on the collection end, we try to make computers solve our problems on the processing end. You've heard of garbage in, garbage out?"

"I see what you're driving at. Can you give me more on the problems with system requirements?"

"It's really an artificial field. All began back in World War II by accountants, like that guy from Ford, Robert MacNamara. Problem is, requirements are historical. And because we create new things that don't have a history, we spend all of our time working backwards to find requirements that will fit. As a result, paperwork winds up costing ten times more than the product."

Black Bird stirred his drink, "Sad, but true. Kelly Johnson can create a system in his Skunk Works and have it flying while the normal procurement system is mired down in paper. The only thing that flies out of MacNamara's system is paper airplanes."

• • •

Our dinner arrived. Bobbie Jean changed the subject to Las Vegas and how fast it was growing. Mrs. Bird knew some of the same people, Bobbie Jean did. As we adjourned for an after dinner drink in the lounge, Bird whispered, "remember what I told you."

"Don't add on a recreation room?"

"Right."

• • •

After we arrived home, Bobbie Jean asked, "What did Colonel Bird say to you that made you so upset? You hardly touched your steak."

"I'm not on my General's 'A list.' He wasn't happy with the message I carried, even though it was correct. Did you mention to Mrs. Bird that you owned a piece of the Sands?"

"Not good for your career to have an independent wife. My Bentley raises enough eyebrows. And your boss may not care for my associates in Vegas. He knows where all the bodies are buried. Your colonel grew up there when it was Biloxi's size. Are you sure we'll leave?"

"Bird couldn't have been more direct. It's only a matter of time."

"Our restaurant is on hold, unless Herbie agrees to take over when we leave."

"Don't slow down for me. If your concept is a winner, you'll have a valuable property."

"Do you think we should put our house up for sale?"

"Bird said don't, but added, don't build a recreation room."

"That certainly gives me a lot of confidence."

As we undressed, Bobbie Jean gave me a hug, "Thought you needed one. How do you feel, inside?"

"Like I've been hit in the stomach by a two-by-four."

• • •

I settled into my new job, satisfied, knowing for the first time in two years what it was I was supposed to do. As soon as he walked in the door Colonel Bird took control. Watching him in action is the equivalent of a postdoctoral degree in management. He guided without interfering, accepting what he didn't fully understand and pressed on. Black Bird wasn't afraid to delegate work and retain the responsibility. The same as proper handling of draft horses, firm control with light reins. With horses and people— trust works, both ways. He took me aside during my first week, "I don't expect you to be able to fly an airplane at Mach three-point-two, you shouldn't expect me to understand how your electrons dance around the way they do. However, if you can explain what you're doing so I can understand, our general will and we'll both be winners."

He spent most his time studying what we did, how we did it and who was doing it. Black Bird was like a symphony conductor taking unlike instruments, making them work in harmony for the best overall performance.

• • •

Bobbie Jean bubbled over with excitement when she called Monday morning, "Herbie and the chef are still flying in next week."

"Did you tell Herbie about our eminent departure?"

"Yes, they're planning to go ahead with or without us."

"Are we going to stay in for a piece of the action?"

"Of course. My only hang-up was our chef might leave before we could sell."

"What changed your mind?"

"His brother will join us if our chef decides to return to New Orleans."

"It will be another absentee investment."

"My intuition says it will be a money maker."

"Follow it, you haven't been wrong yet. How much is it going to cost us."

"Between two-hundred and three-hundred thousand. Worst scenario, we'll lose no more than thirty thousand."

"Average and best?"

"A gain of three hundred to six-hundred thousand."

"Did you settle on a design?"

"Three story riverboat."

"On the Missouri?"

"No silly, on dry land."

• • •

Herbie and the chef flew in and out on a whirlwind tour. With their approval, Bobbie Jean had the foundation poured and walls up in record time. Her roof would be on before the first leaf turned gold. And her liquor license came through two weeks after Herbie flew back to Biloxi. While she spent part of each day on the construction site, making sure their specifications were met, Colonel Black Bird drew up a new set of specifications for us. He took his time, visiting each desk and listening, as each cubicle occupant explained what it was he did. On the first Monday of October, Bird called us into the briefing room we shared with ops, "We have shift workers who are required to monitor missions from five o'clock in the evening to seven o'clock in the morning. And I still find most of you working from five in the morning to seven at night. I want this overtime to cease. We have more than enough manpower to accomplish our mission. I have only one rule, if you can't accomplish your work between seven and five you're either incompetent or stupid. Either way, I don't want you around here. Listen up funny wings, don't waste your time or mine. Are there any questions?"

Captain Schweig, who sat next to me whistling *Deutschland Uber Alles*, under his breath, raised his hand, "What if we have to work a special collection mission or finish a rush project for the Pentagon?"

"Use your head, rules are meant to be broken when they interfere with getting the job done. I'm eliminating make-work."

I raised my hand and asked, "You play ball with me and I'll play ball with you?"

He broke out in laughter, "And if you don't, I'll shove the bat up your ass."

Tucker had been served.

• • •

I was greeted with a kiss and a glass of red wine when I walked through the kitchen door, "You're certainly chipper this evening."

"Roof is up and the plumbing is in. Before I forget, don't forget to read your mail."

"Anything of interest?"

"You have a letter from your friend, Mr. Tubbs of the *Washington Post*."

"Wonder what Tucker wants now. He hasn't written in two years." I opened the letter and almost choked on my wine. Bobbie Jean pounded on my back and my throat cleared, "Christ all Friday!" I gasped.

"What does Mr. Tubbs have to say?"

"We're going to Washington."

"How would he know?"

"He's the *Post*'s military reporter."

"I thought he was a foreign correspondent covering Vietnam."

"He was, but he kept getting lost in Saigon and shot at by our troops in the Delta. Only thing that saved him was his *Mad* comic book cover grin. Even the Vietcong wouldn't waste a bullet on an innocent like him."

I sat down on a stool at our pass-through counter and read Tucker's letter.

*Johnny,*

*Don't ask me how I know, but you're being transferred to Washington, DC They want you to report in by the last of November. You'll be on the Air Staff. Got to go. I'll phone in a couple of weeks and fill you in.*

*Tuck*

"We report to DC the last of November."

"I'll put our house up for sale in the morning."

"You can stay here and see the construction through to completion."

"Too many single women in Washington to let you go alone. Herbie is ready to move here."

"You should ask him if he wants to buy our house."

"I'll speak with him before I list it. It'll save us commission and a lower the price for him. How did Mr. Tubbs find out about our move before we were notified?"

"I have no idea."

"Your friend must be well connected."

• • •

Herbie jumped at the chance to buy our house. If we weren't transferred, I had decided to resign so Bobbie Jean rushed through the paperwork. Two weeks later, Tucker phoned as promised, "Congratulations, Colonel. You're being assigned to Air Force Intelligence and you have just been promoted to lieutenant colonel."

"And I thought SAC shoots messengers."

"What does that mean?"

"Nothing, just a local joke."

"I have two Realtors sending information to you."

"I hope you're right. We just sold our house. We'll be house hunting the last week in October. Can you make reservations at a central location for us?"

"Call before you leave and I'll make all the arrangements. I'd have you stay with me, but I use the second bedroom as an office."

"If I know you, it's more like a landfill for sporting goods."

After more small talk, Tucker excused himself, "Gotta go, have a deadline to meet."

Bobbie Jean asked, "What did smiley face have to say for himself?"

"He says I've been promoted to lieutenant colonel and assigned to Air Force Intelligence at the Pentagon. And he's having two Realtors send along house and area information."

"You're not due for promotion."

"I know, but Tucker has been right so far."

"Has anyone at work talked to you about promotion?"

"Not a soul."

"I wouldn't speak about this with anyone."

"It's hard to keep it in, but I haven't said a word to anyone about our move."

"Including your colonel?"

"Yes."

• • •

The following Monday, Colonel Black Bird called me into his office and closed the door. "Johnny, don't know how you did it, but you've been promoted to lieutenant colonel and assigned to the Air Staff at the Pentagon. Only the general and I know about your promotion. It won't be announced until after you leave. He has requested that you not mention it to anyone except your wife. You can begin clearing out today. Turn all of your work over to Silver Tongue. Don't rat hole any of your information. And I want you to write an end of tour report for my eyes only. Tell it like it is. Don't sugar coat anything."

I tried to appear overwhelmed, but I knew I couldn't, "Any advice for the soon to be dearly departed?"

"Outside of watch your six? Be careful up there. You're being assigned to an advanced course for military politicians. Remember, in peacetime it's the politicians who get promoted. But, when a war comes along they look for warriors. You can make it to colonel on your brains and talent, but after that it's strictly politics. Neither Eisenhower or Patton would have made it past colonel in peacetime. You'll have to make a choice one of these days. Do what's good for the country or for yourself. You've all ready come up against that decision here and you got lucky. You did what was right and it worked for you. No matter what you've experienced in SAC, Washington is not a society that rewards achievement."

"For you pilots that may be true, but for funny wings anything above major is a miracle."

Bird laughed, "That's probably why you survived your first test. You'll do fine in DC as long as you keep that attitude."

"Will you and your wife be our guests at the Blackstone Hotel tonight. As long as I have to keep my promotion close hold, I'd at least like to have a small promotion party."

"Monday night shouldn't be a problem."

"I'll have Bobbie Jean make reservations for seven. Pick you up at six-thirty?"

• • •

Bobbie Jean added the general and his wife to our small party, "A promotion party should include more than one couple. And the only one who influenced your promotion has to be your general. Black Bird hasn't written an efficiency report on you, has he?"

"Your right. We'll have to use your Bentley if we're going to drive six people."

"I phoned ahead to make sure the chef's brother is working tonight. We set up a special menu."

"I shouldn't ask, but did you ask the ladies if they preferred fish or steak."

"I did and you shouldn't have. That's your last glass of wine."

"I've only had one glass."

"You're driving and we have to be on our best behavior."

"Dessert?"

"Not first, later."

• • •

Bobbie Jean's Bentley raised a few eyebrows. When we stopped by the brick quarters to pick up the general and his wife, Mrs. Bird asked, "How can you afford this limo on a Major's salary?"

"I can't. Now that we're on our way out of here, I'll let you in on one of Bobbie Jean's secrets. She owns a small piece of the Sands."

"In Las Vegas?"

Bobbie Jean nodded, "Yes. I didn't think it was wise to mention it before, but now that we're leaving it shouldn't matter."

She changed the subject, "A friend of mine from Biloxi, a New Orleans chef and I are opening the River Boat restaurant south of the base. The New Orleans chef's brother is the chef at the Blackstone. I asked him to prepare several items we'll have on our menu. If you don't mind, we'll have a Chinese style meal, so we can share the dishes. I'd like to have your opinion."

• • •

Bobbie Jean's interest in what they thought and discussion about her new venture was another stroke of genius. It took the pressure off me and eliminated any need for competition between wives. She was genuinely interested in their opinions about the menu. They liked it.

The general asked, "How much of the restaurant will you have. I have never had better blackened snapper and the shrimp in garlic. Well, I'll be back."

Bobbie Jean was pleased, "My friends will each have thirty five percent and I have thirty. I plan to sell my piece back to them after the restaurant is established. My part was planning, designing, construction and obtaining licenses. My work is almost complete. Oh, the chef won't prepare this menu here again. He has his own specialties.

These are his brother's. I'll make sure you are treated with first class accommodations when our River Boat opens."

• • •

I had to admire Silver Tongue. He not only was the spokesman for all SAC's fast pacers, his gift of oratory was also matched by a better than average intelligence. He was able to absorb my work and files in the week allotted. I sat down with him at the O' Club bar Friday evening after work.

I couldn't help but put a little needle into his balloon, "Tell me, how do you sugar coat manure?"

"Logic, Johnny, logic. No matter what I'm given, I try to always find the sunny side. And if you build a logical positive case, brick by brick, it will be accepted."

"And if it can't be done on a computer?"

"That's where the sugar comes in, when a computer can't handle a job, have a human do it and print out the results with the computer's printer."

"You're dealing in smoke and mirrors."

"Johnny, you and I are trained technical funny wings. Pilots and ground pounders are dreamers. They believe in Camelot and the Holy Grail."

"And the Holy Grail is?"

"Computers."

"Computers?"

"Now you've got it. The powers that be are looking for a Wizard to solve all of their problems. If it comes out of the computer's printer, they believe God has spoken and they are happy."

"You've become the man behind the curtains. The one that pulls the levers and runs."

"You ain't in Kansas anymore, Dorothy."

• • •

Monday and Tuesday Bobbie Jean made her last inspection trips. She gave her general contractor a long list of items that had to be completed before she would release the third of five payments.

I thought we were going to fly east, but she surprised me, "We'll drive your car and when we leave for good, we'll take mine."

"And the boys."

"Nanny and they will fly to Jackson in the morning. They'll stay with Mother until we're settled in Washington."

"They're getting pretty rambunctious. Think she can handle them?"

"Your mother is visiting. She'll help. They both need grandma time, and it has been a year."

"Who is going to watch the store."

"No one is needed for two weeks and by then, we'll be back. Which way are we going to drive?"

"Not much choice. We drive on interstate all the way. With Mother going south do we scrub our stop at the farm?"

"No. She won't fly to Jackson until after we leave. And I want to find out how she won Mother over. They're like old school chums now."

"The Lee Mansion will be receiving a call."

"You're right. They must be in cahoots. You know, they're planning our wedding!"

## Nebraska to Washington, DC

We ate breakfast in Des Moines, lunch outside of Champagne and a late dinner at my Concord Township farm. Bobbie Jean helped Mother clean up after dinner. She was direct, "How did you win Mother over? You two are like old friends."

"I looked for common ground."

"Almost impossible. My mother is Past President of Daughters of the Confederacy."

"Johnny's father's family owned a plantation in Alabama before the war. But it was Daughters of the American Revolution that established our common bond. Your mother is quite a history buff."

"Has she mentioned the Lee Mansion?"

"We're going to plan the wedding as soon as I arrive."

"Do I have to wear white?"

"She said your grandmother's dress is now more of a winter white. I can't wait to see the boys. When do you think it will be all right for the twins to stay with us on the farm?"

"Not until Nanny decides they can manage on their own."

"She's set in her ways?"

"She was the same with me and her children. We were five before she turned us loose."

"A nanny, my goodness. Southern folks certainly live a different lifestyle."

• • •

An early frost painted the southern Ohio hills shades of red, green, brown and gold. The pleasant, but acrid aroma of decaying leaves was softened by autumn's cool dry air. As we crossed over the Ohio River into Wheeling, West Virginia, Bobbie Jean leaned forward and turned off the radio, "If I have to listen to John Denver singing *Mountain Momma* one more time, I'll pull the knobs off your radio. It must be the national anthem for West Virginia."

"I kind of like the song. Where do we join the Pennsylvania turnpike?"

"Outside of Washington, Pennsylvania. Your mother packed enough food for an Army, but I still need to powder my nose. Find a clean gas station and pull in."

I turned the radio back on after we traveled into the mountains of Pennsylvania on the turnpike. After picking up static and evangelical radio preachers and being unable to tell the difference, I turned it off. As I dodged another pothole, "Remind me not to use this turnpike again. This road has so many holes, it looks like the craters of the moon. The only cash Pennsylvania spends on this turnpike is for additional toll booths."

Bobbie Jean didn't respond. I glanced over. She was sound asleep. Bobbie Jean woke as I slowed down to pay our last toll at the turnoff north of Breezewood, "How long was I asleep?"

"You missed the entire turnpike and the mountains of southern Pennsylvania. About three hours."

"Lovely country. Looks like mountains to a Mississippi girl."

"Proves it's not how high the mountain is, but how steep the hill."

"If you were on my side of the car, it's how steep the cliff."

"I'd hate to go through Breezewood on a holiday weekend. Traffic must back up for miles. There's no way to bypass it."

"And you thought Mississippi was the queen of political pandering. Someone has a legislator in his pocket when a bypass isn't built and it's obvious that there is a desperate need for one. You Yankees make us Southerners look like pikers when it comes to buying politicians. We can get one for a jug of moonshine."

"At least ours are protecting local business."

"Who said they are local? Stop at Maryland's welcome center down the road. I need to use a rest room and we both need to stretch our legs."

"Touché!"

## Washington, DC

As we continued on, into the outskirts of Washington DC, Bobbie Jean asked, "Where is the motel Tucker booked for us?"

"Outside the main gate of Fort Myers. He said the price is right and we'll be in the center of where you want to look for housing."

"Washington DC is like a giant wheel with a lot of little hubs, but no central one. Don't miss the turn to the beltway."

"Where is our next turn after that?"

"After we cross the bridge into Virginia."

I passed by the Pentagon twice, going both directions before finding Route 50. I turned off at the Fort Myers exit and into the motel parking lot. Bobbie Jean frowned, "Don't sign in. I'll use the pay phone and call the Watergate Hotel."

"That's the same complex where Tucker lives. Why didn't he book us there?"

"Probably because it is very expensive."

I almost asked if we can we afford it, but didn't. She hung up the phone, "We have a suite overlooking the Potomac that is affordable."

"Only to members of the hotel Mafia."

That remark caused a sharper than normal dig to my ribs, "If I can find the Watergate in this evening traffic it will be a miracle."

"Cross over the Memorial Bridge to Rock Creek Parkway and take the first exit past where the new Kennedy Center is being constructed."

• • •

After battling late evening traffic on the bridge and parkway, I drove by the Watergate complex three times before finding the hotel entrance. The bellhop unloaded our luggage and a valet whisked away my station wagon, "Parking here is almost as much as the motel Tucker booked us into."

"Not for me. As they say the cost will be a wash."

"Same as the motel?"

"A little less. I remember when you used to say, 'Live fast, die young and leave a beautiful corpse.'"

"That was before I had the responsibility of a beautiful wife and two sons."

We followed the bellhop to our suite. As he opened the curtains for a view of the Potomac, Bobbie Jean sighed, "Now isn't that better than a view of Fort Myers and the odor of horse barns? We even have a sitting room and a desk."

I tipped the bellhop as she opened an oversized case. Inside were twelve bottles of wine, six red and six white, "No wonder that damn thing was so heavy. I suppose you want ice?"

"Of course. I think it's in the little room next to the elevator. The refrigerator has a tray, but I prefer the other. I'll open our wine while you fetch."

When I returned, Bobbie Jean was entering the shower, "Phone your friend, Mr. Tubbs and let him know of our change of plans."

• • •

Tucker answered his private office phone, "You're staying where? The Watergate? Talk about rich friends. You want to meet me for dinner tonight?"

"What time?"

"I'll meet you in the bar of good old reliable Nathan's for dinner at seven. I have to get back to work no later than nine. We work nights to get out a morning newspaper."

"Are you bringing a date?"

"Not enough time."

I opened the shower door. Bobbie Jean handed me her back brush, "And what did Mr. Tubbs say?"

"He wants to meet us for dinner at seven."

"Where?"

"A little Italian restaurant in Georgetown."

Her caress told me that we might not make it there by seven.

• • •

Bobbie Jean handed me a tie, "Hurry up or we'll be late."

"With Tucker it won't matter. Who were you on the phone with?"

"The hotel concierge. I gave him the type of place we're interested in and he is selecting areas and houses he thinks may be suitable. Saturday is open house day in Northern Virginia."

"Where are we interested in looking?"

"Arlington and McLean tomorrow and Mount Vernon on Sunday."

"How about the Watergate? This isn't a hovel."

"Twins—don't you remember. We need space for them to roam and grow up safely."

"It would make Washington DC livable."

"For us, but not for them. Is Nathan's a place I'd like to dine in or one of Mr. Tubb's surprises? After all he does own a pink Packard Caribbean convertible."

"He says it's pretty good, but if you know Tucker, he'll eat sawdust if it has catsup on it. Read the brochure to me while I finish dressing."

"You will find our Watergate complex is a city within itself. The Watergate consists of four buildings. We have private residences, hotel, offices, shops and restaurants."

"Does it mention how it got its name?"

"Watergate is a water regulating device located at the confluence of Rock Creek and the C&O Canal."

"Makes sense."

The phone rang. Bobbie Jean answered, "It's the concierge. He recommends we take a taxi to Georgetown."

"I'd rather walk. It's less than a mile as the crow flies."

"He doesn't recommend walking. Not safe after dark. He will have a taxi waiting for us at the entrance and has scheduled one to pick us up at nine from Nathan's."

I picked up towels and turned off lights as she finished her conversation. I locked the door and walked toward the elevator, "He kept you on the phone for quite awhile."

"The concierge is all ready working on real estate. He'll have several condos open for us here, tomorrow. Has a pretty good idea about values here, but he's not certain about Virginia. He found a small farm in McLean selling under distress. I'd like to look at it. Will you mind mowing grass?"

"No problem, we'll buy a small flock of sheep."

"Are you serious?"

"From the looks of the hillsides around here a mower wouldn't do any good."

"My own shepherd."

"Life does go in a circle. Did he mention taxes?"

"High."

• • •

It was a typical Georgetown Friday night. Nathan's was knee deep in singles hoping to find love, or true love, depending on which gender was looking. We found Tucker at the end of the bar, deep in hot and heavy conversation with a stunning blonde.

When Tuck finally noticed us, he stood and offered Bobbie Jean his stool, "Forgot about the Friday night crowd. This stool is all that I could get. Our table will be ready any minute."

Bobbie Jean was proper to a fault, "Introduce us to your friend, Mr. Tubbs."

"Oh, this is Ingrid. She's a stew with Scandinavian Airlines."

I tried to hide my laughter, "You've gone international, Tuck."

"Made editor last week, dinner tonight is on me."

"Which department?"

"Military. My exposé on military clubs was the clincher. Have you decided which area of the city you're interested in?"

"I like the Watergate, but Bobbie Jean wants room for the twins to roam."

"Watergate is a great address, but three bedrooms start at sixty thousand and DC's taxes are out of sight. The maitre d' is waving. I think our table is ready. Good thing you remembered to wear a tie."

"I know my eastern establishment rules, khakis, regimental tie and a dark blue sport coat. Form over substance. Let me pay for the drinks."

"No way, I owe you big time for your help. Tonight is on me."

Tucker led the way into the dining room.

Bobbie Jean chided Tucker, "You have come up in the world. We have the A table."

"Never underestimate the power of the press."

"Isn't Ingrid joining us?"

"Must be the crowd noise. I met her at the bar and didn't think to ask. I'll be right back."

"Mr. Tubbs never ceases to amaze me. How did he ever make editor at the *Post*."

"Eccentricity is highly valued in the east."

"And in the south, too. And will you look at how these folks are dressed? We'll have to throw away your white shoes, white belts and leisure suits."

"We're not in Kansas anymore, Dorothy?"

"Ingrid is coming with him. It has to be Tucker's boyish charm that attracts women."

"And his forever youthful sixteen year old mind."

Tucker pulled out Ingrid's chair, "She stopped by with her pilot, but he became ill and had to turn in."

I asked, "Airsickness?"

"Once a navigator always a navigator."

Ingrid added, "I'm staying with my sister. She is my twin."

Bobbie Jean wondered, "Does your sister work in DC?"

"Oh yes, Lisa is the protocol officer at our embassy."

Tucker opened his menu, "Pasta here is excellent and anything Italian."

Bobbie Jean raised her eyebrows, "I've never seen prices this high for Italian food."

"Wasn't always this way, but our restaurant editor gave Nathan's four stars and a great write-up. Within a month all the waiters were wearing tuxes and the prices doubled. It's still my favorite place to fish."

Ingrid, not fully understanding Tucker's meaning said, "I'll have the poached salmon over linguine."

Bobbie Jean didn't crack a smile, "I'll have the same."

Before I could say pepper steak, Tucker advised, "Order a chicken or veal dish. Our waiter is growing roots."

Dinner and wine were excellent, if a bit overpriced. Tucker ate everything that didn't move, including half of Ingrid's and Bobbie Jean's poached salmon. Over an after dinner coffee he asked, "Are you sure you know where to look for housing? You ought to consider the Watergate. Although it's pricey. it's an excellent buy. You won't lose any money if you have to sell."

Bobbie Jean was very diplomatic, "We're looking at two units, tomorrow. Is this area a good place for our twins to grow up?"

"Not if you let them roam. Arlington or McLean would be better."

"We're going to look now, think it over and buy in November."

"If you find something you like, better get a contract on it. Property is moving fast here. Johnny, I need to talk business with you, off line."

"Newspaper talk, not for attribution?"

"Right. How about dinner in your suite tomorrow evening? I'll bring Chinese."

Bobbie Jean cautioned, "We won't be back until after five."

"Six it is. Don't forget to call if you need help."

• • •

As we rode the elevator to our floor, Bobbie Jean took my hand, "Glass of wine on the balcony?"

I drew her close, "I'll take red."

"Why didn't Mr. Tubbs invite us for dinner at his condo? He must live close, in one of the buildings."

"Out of deference to you. I imagine his place looks like the aftermath of a Kansas cyclone. He's buying two meals in two days, so I'm impressed."

"Does he want to talk military business with you?"

"He mentioned that."

"Make sure he doesn't put our names down on his expense account. I learned long ago that there is no such thing as a confidential source."

"You must be talking from your Gulf Coast experience with a gambling investigation by a well known U.S. Senator."

"Not mine, but Ralph's."

"I'll be careful. Don't think Tucker would intentionally try to throw me in jail."

"It's not the intentional I'm worried about."

We walked down the corridor to our room, arm in arm like two lovers hurrying to a rendezvous.

I poured while Bobbie Jean opened up the drapes. We looked out over the lights of autos winding their way up and down on Rock Creek Parkway, almost blocking out the moonlight on the Potomac. She shivered and drew close, "What did you think of Ingrid?"

"She's a drop dead blonde, almost as pretty as you."

"While you and Mr. Tubbs were telling war stories, she asked a dozen questions about your friend. I'm certain she's interested."

"One thing about moving to Washington—we'll know the outcome. No complaints about Tucker coming over tomorrow night."

"None, but I'm not sure about Chinese food."

"We can always go downstairs for dessert."

"I thought you'd never ask."

I swept her into my arms and carried her into our suite. As I placed her on our bed, she gently pushed me toward the balcony, "Better close the doors and pull the drapes. Never know when someone may be watching."

"Or listening."

• • •

We woke to the ringing of the suite telephone. It was our Realtor, "I have three condos for you to view. I'll meet you in the lobby in an hour."

We showered together and almost missed dining on concierge coffee and breakfast rolls. Our tour took less than an hour. All three condos were open and vacant. Purchased as investments, none had been lived in. Their owner had fallen on lean times and had to sell. After the Realtor departed, Bobbie Jean asked, "What did you think of the last one?"

"Terrific view of the river, but did you notice the traffic noise when we opened the doors to the balcony?"

"It's the only one that is suitable for us."

"Should be with three bedrooms, an office and den. It will take me awhile to get over the sticker shock."

"Mr. Tubbs was right about Watergate condos being moneymakers."

"That doesn't make sense. Those three were new and never lived in."

"Timing and location. There isn't any land left near the seat of our government along the water to build a complex like this. I might buy the larger one and maybe one other and rent them out."

"You're out of my league."

"Silly, we will buy it with borrowed money through my corporation."

"That's why you make money and I serve. How about a late brunch in the hotel restaurant before we continue our house hunting expedition?"

Bobbie Jean waited quietly until after the waiter took our order, "If we buy here, where can I shop?"

"Fort Myer across the river, Georgetown and there are shops in the building. The Watergate has a convenience store for small items."

"Can't walk to a grocery store?"

"Not that I know of."

"We would really have to stock up."

Our waiter interrupted, handing Bobbie Jean a phone. Bobbie Jean placed her hand over the mouthpiece, "It's the concierge, McLean in an hour. Off Chain Bridge Road. And the two houses in Arlington."

She handed the phone back to the waiter, saying, "Can you expedite our order? We have to be in McLean in an hour."

He nodded and returned with our plates in less than five minutes. We nibbled half, signed the check and were on our way to the lobby.

I asked, "Are you sure we won't get lost?"

"The concierge provided a highlighted map and written instructions. If you work very hard at missing street signs, we can still get lost."

"Touché!"

• • •

All three places were expensive, nothing under one hundred thousand and all much larger than I expected. As we drove back to Watergate on George Washington Parkway at four in the afternoon, Bobbie Jean spoke with the authority of one who knows value, "The farm in McLean is our best buy."

"But, it was the most expensive and needs a lot of work. The stables will have to be rebuilt from the inside out."

"True, but it does have forty acres and if I know our government, the way it continues to grow by leaps and bounds, the land alone will be worth six times what we pay for it in less than ten years. Remember the Realtor that advertised on TV in Roswell?"

"Yes, he said, 'There will always be more people, but there'll never be more land?'"

"He might not have been right about New Mexico, but he is dead on about here. McLean will be the next hot address."

"It'll take a lot of upkeep."

"It has its original stone exterior and hardwood floors. I love the ceiling to floor fireplaces. There is even one in the stable."

"And ancient plumbing and wiring."

"Don't worry, I'll have a contractor look at it as soon as we sign a contract."

"I thought we were only looking."

"A woman has a right to change her mind."

"Who's buying—us or your corporation?"

"This one is on us."

"And the two at the Watergate?"

"I ran the numbers. They'll pay loan costs, upkeep and provide a small return. We'll buy all three. I'm glad you were transferred. Washington DC is certainly the land of opportunity."

"You've convinced me."

"And we'll have a stable for our boys' ponies."

• • •

While Bobbie Jean was on the phone with the real estate broker, I looked over the data sheet on the farm. It was still a working farm with a tractor for sale. When she hung up, I showed her the data, "We better buy the tractor. It comes with all the attachments. Can't buy an equivalent one for twice what they want. We'll have to plow the snow off the lane in winter and keep the weeds cut in summer."

"Reasonable. Can you have your sheep?"

"I don't see any zoning against them. The boys will go nuts over lambs."

"We may not be able to build a subdivision, but it can be split into half acre lots when the time is right."

"Do you want to see Mount Vernon tomorrow?"

"Might pay too, before we sign on the dotted line."

• • •

The knock on our door was like a sledge hammer blow. Our friend Tucker had arrived, bearing Chinese food.

I whistled under my breath, "How many do you have attending your banquet?"

Tucker kept right on trucking to the bar, "Just the four of us. Ingrid had to fly out, so she fixed me up with her sister, Lisa."

"Lisa?"

"Yes and they are identical twins in every way. They share a condo in my building."

"And you never met them?"

"Morning newspaper. We have weird hours. Give me a hand with the boxes while I retrieve the beer. Where is Bobbie Jean?"

"Downstairs getting her hair done."

Tucker came back with a case of beer, "Where do you want it?"

"Won't all fit in the refrigerator at the bar. We have ice near the elevator."

"I'll fetch some after we unpack the food." I whistled, "You brought enough for ten people."

"Where did all of these boxes come from."

I looked up, Bobbie Jean had returned and Tucker was gone. "Tucker delivered his Chinese banquet. You must have passed him in the hall. He went after ice for the beer. Wouldn't all fit in the fridge."

"Chinese and beer. I'm glad I remembered to bring wine. Is Ingrid coming?"

"She had to fly back to Europe. Tuck is bringing her sister, Lisa."

"Oh, the protocol lady."

Bobbie Jean unpacked the plates from under the bar, "And no chopsticks. No matter, we have silverware and bowls with the suite."

Tucker returned with two buckets of ice and another stunning blonde on his arm, "Lisa, these are my friends, Johnny and his wife, Bobbie Jean."

I took her hand, "Ingrid was right, you are a lovely copy of your sister."

Tucker interrupted, "I'm starved, let's get on with dinner. We can talk while we dine. Where do you want the food?"

Bobbie Jean handed Tucker bowls and me silverware and plates, "We'll dine out on the balcony. It's a lovely Indian summer evening." Lisa opened the French doors, "DC has too many hot summer days for me, but it does have lovely fall days and nights and that makes it livable."

Bobbie Jean and Lisa set the table. Tucker and I carried out ice, wine and beer.

Tucker looked out over the Potomac, "Great view. Can't see anything but lawn from my condo."

I poured four glasses of wine and offered a toast, "To two of the most beautiful women in Washington and to our new home."

As we sat down to dine, Tucker asked, "Where did you decide to buy, here or Virginia?"

Bobbie Jean nodded, "Yes to both places. We're negotiating for three condos here and a farm in McLean. We'll lease the condos and live on the farm."

I scanned the dishes, Chicken Lo Mein, Curried Shrimp, Mu Shu Pork, Fried Wontons, with spareribs as an appetizer and enough sticky rice to sink a small boat. Table talk was confined to real estate and Scandinavia. As Bobbie Jean and Lisa cleared away the dishes, Tucker pulled me aside. "I've paid the piper, now it's time to talk."

*"The time has come," the Walrus said, "To talk of many things: Of shoes, ships, and sealing wax—Of cabbages, and kings—And why the sea is boiling hot, and whether pigs have wings."*

# Chapter 15

I walked inside and whispered to Bobbie Jean, "Tucker wants to talk business. Do you want to sit in, or take Lisa aside?"

"We'll sit in as long as you keep it clean. Port or Cognac?"

"I'll stick with beer as long as Tucker does."

Back on the lanai, Tucker asked, "Do you know what your job is going to be on the Air Staff?"

"No, but by your smile it looks like you do."

"Intelligence Systems, but I'm not sure what that really means."

"What are you interested in"

"I'm interested in our tar baby, Vietnam."

"Tar baby?"

"We are sinking up to our knees in tar and if we keep adding troops we'll be stuck in it up to our neck."

"You're saying we didn't learn from the French experience?"

"Can't learn if you don't understand the past and we don't. When I was over there we had fifteen thousand troops called advisors."

"How many do we have now?"

"I don't really know, but the number is climbing. If Johnson keeps worrying about losing, we are going to lose big time. What do you think about our new hot spot?"

Bobbie Jean interrupted, "Tucker needs a beer and do you want another?"

"I'll have a beer, too."

I responded to Tucker's question, "You asked me what I think. My gut feeling is the same as yours. My field of expertise is Technical Intelligence. I look for threats to our airplanes and attempt to figure out how to counter them. From what I know about the Vietcong's Command and Control it isn't very modern. They're fighting the same guerrilla war against the South they fought against the Japanese and French. Can't counter someone who uses notes and hand signals with anything, but a bullet. So my area of expertise is not the solution. Looks to me like an Army war. If the South wants to win they'll have to control their own territory. And if we take it on, it'll take overwhelming force and most of our national budget."

"We're in agreement. The way I see it, we have two more choices, pull out and back the South with weapons and a pat on the back, or continue our current involvement and fight a war by proxy. The South can't win if they don't control their own territory. Trouble is, the Vietcong controls the countryside and the South controls the cities. A no-win situation."

"Looks like we can't win if we don't go all the way."

"And there's no support for that course of action. And it gets stickier, Johnson's afraid to pull out because he doesn't want to be labeled a loser."

"It's a tar baby."

Tucker stood up, "I need to go inside and see a man about a horse."

When he returned, I reminded him, "You asked for my help. Looks to me like you don't need any. You have a pretty good handle on what's going on."

"Intentions and actions are what I need. We have a Secretary of Defense who has tied our military's hands with a new concept called gradual escalation."

"Interesting how one can rise to the top making one error in judgment after another. I'm on the losing end of his Systems Analysis concept."

"And his tactical concept is to counter the Vietcong with slightly more force."

"I'm aware of it, but since I'm not directly involved, I haven't paid much attention. His tactic may be flawed, but we're equally at fault for allowing him to let us commit military suicide."

"No one in your Pentagon has the balls to stand up to Mr. book smart, life stupid."

"Curtis E. Lemay."

"Forgot about him. McNamara is doing a number on Lemay. He's being painted into a corner as a hot headed killer. He's been politically isolated. From where I sit at the *Post*, it looks like our civilians are playing the tune and the military is doing the dancing. I need to know who's driving the ship. If McNamara is playing the pipes, what's going wrong with our military leadership? Are they speaking out or are they kissing up, to keep their jobs?"

"McNamara has the mentality of a bean counter. That may account for some of the stupidity, but it doesn't excuse our generals. It's my turn to see a man about a horse."

Lisa asked, "Is he inside your bathroom?"

I left Tucker smiling, wondering how to answer her Scandinavian question.

I opened two more beers and carried them out to the patio, "For an ex-navigator who couldn't find west Texas from an airplane, you sure have come a long way at the *Post*."

"Simple logic, navigation is abstract. Military thought is closer to classical literature, an art, not a science."

"You've found the nut of the problem. McNamara tries to reduce military problems to mathematical solutions and wants his explanations in numbers."

"Can you help me?"

"Maybe, I won't give you any classified data and I'm not allowed to release official information. My hands are tied by my oath."

"I don't need classified information. The power structure in this town leaks classified data to my newspaper like water out of a broken sieve. The powers that be will do almost anything to get the *Post* on their side. Your Pentagon does its fair share of leaking, too. So we have to work overtime, to protect our government from itself. I want your opinion on people and personalities. And I'd like to know what the real movers and shakers inside the Pentagon think."

"At the top? I'm not connected."

"Action officers, the troops in the Pentagon trenches." The hair went up on the back of my neck, "You believe that we're going to take over the fight?"

"It's only a matter of time. Johnson doesn't want to lose and the South can't win. There is no other choice."

"But we don't have the will to stick it out, or funds."

"Congress gave Johnson carte blanche when they passed the Gulf of Tonkin Resolution. That Texan is all pride and you know what hubris can do to common sense."

"He bought off on McNamara's gradual escalation?"

"Had too, to control costs."

"Penny wise, dollar foolish."

"If it was my nickel, I'd back the South with weapons and a pat on the back. We could win a military victory with overwhelming force, but we'd be the new colonial power."

"Not a pleasant pickle to be in, is it?"

"You and I can't change the direction of the winds of war, but I'd like to know who's doing the puffing."

"I won't violate my oath, but I'll let you know what the troops think."

"I'd like your assessment of your leaders, too."

"I'm impressed. You have found your niche in life."

• • •

After our guests departed, I helped Bobbie Jean clean up. She had remained silent, except for small talk with Lisa.

As I stacked the last empty beer can in the waste basket, I asked, "Well, what do you think?"

"About the war?"

"And anything else we discussed."

"I won't believe what I read in the papers anymore. I hope you don't have to go over there. I thought you worked hard at preventing loss of life on foolish missions?"

"Would if I could, but this one is above my pay grade."

"I'm not sure you're in the right profession. It seems to me every military job you get comes with its own briar patch and tar baby."

"Keeps me from returning to tending sheep. We should have given Tucker the rest of his beer."

"To go with the remains of the Chinese banquet he left."

"I'll call him in the morning."

"We fly out tomorrow afternoon. What about our car."

"Leave it at the airport. We can pick it up when we return. Are we going to drive through Mount Vernon in the morning?"

"We have two Realtors stopping by with contracts. After we sign we can drive down the parkway, have lunch, look around and catch our flight out."

• • •

Cool, windless fall days create smooth air and smooth flying. We were on our way to New Orleans with an interim stop in Jackson. Bobbie Jean needed a twins fix. It would be at least two weeks before our farmhouse was ready.

When we stepped off the plane at the airport, Herbie was waiting at the exit gate. "Greetings my wandering friends. My spy told me of your change in plans."

Bobbie Jean asked, "How is our restaurant progressing?"

"I landed an hour ahead of you. Chef is overseeing installation of his kitchen and storage. Those folks in Nebraska really know how to work. We are four weeks ahead of schedule. I'm back in town to pack up. How soon are you moving out of my house?"

Bobbie Jean answered, "You can move in no later than two weeks from today. I'm having the walls painted and carpets cleaned as soon as we pack up and leave."

"Do you want a ride to Biloxi?"

"Not on this trip. We stopped to see our twins in Jackson. They're staying with Mother until we move. Keep me posted if we run into any glitches on construction. With the chef supervising, we could wind up with one table and all kitchen."

## Jackson, Mississippi

Our drive north to Jackson, under a full moon, brought back memories of romantic late fall Mississippi nights.

I nudged Bobbie Jean, "Wouldn't you rather be walking along the beach tonight."

"Under a full moon? It would be tempting, but I miss my children. Strolling under a Mississippi moon is how I trapped you last time."

"Fish always return to the same bait."

"I may not have the same bait, but I can show you the same hook. How about a walk in the moonlight under our magnolias when we reach my Jackson home."

She snuggled up, "How long will it be before we arrive?"

"Not soon enough."

"I really miss our boys."

When we arrived, the boys were in bed. Bobbie Jean peeked in, then tiptoed in and tucked them in, giving each a kiss on the cheek.

We gathered out in the solarium, sipping rich New Orleans coffee. Bobbie Jean asked our mothers, "What have you two been up to? From the way you're getting on, it looks like our Revolutionary War has won out over Johnny's War of Northern Aggression."

Her mother smiled, "Now Bobbie Jean, we don't have time to talk foolishness. Johnny's mother and I have worked day and night on your wedding."

"Lee Mansion?"

"Overlooking Arlington Cemetery. It will be lovely in June. I've all ready reserved it for the first weekend."

"I didn't know they allowed private parties."

"Don't you remember? You're a direct descendant from Light Horse Harry on your father's side."

"I hope you are holding it down to immediate family and a few friends."

"Johnny's mother and I are working on the list now. Your boys are certainly a handful. They have been everywhere, inside and outside."

"My old playroom?"

"They've had a few tiffs over your rocking horse, but have learned to share."

I whispered to my mother, "How many guest on the list?"

"Not more than two hundred, but it keeps growing."

"That's around four hundred. At least I won't have to hold a bachelor's party."

Bobbie Jean added, "And a shower would be ridiculous."

As she refilled her mother's cup, she added, "I insist you print, 'Renewing Their Wedding Vows' on our invitations. My God, we have two sons."

Both mother's blushed.

Her mother asked, "About your last name. Don't you think it is time to take Johnny's?"

I interrupted, "I'm quite comfortable with things staying the way they are. It adds a certain spice to our relationship."

• • •

We woke to a full press breakfast of waffles, eggs, thick country bacon, hot New Orleans' coffee and of course, grits. Bobbie Jean poured while I dug in, "I could get used to this life style."

"Maybe when we're older, but not now. It's too close to my childhood. Would you want to live on your farm?"

"Maybe when we get older, but not now." She squeezed my neck with her hand, "Now who is producing all of those straight lines."

"We may not have to worry about taking over our parents' homes. We have two boys. They may wish to carry on the tradition. Wouldn't it be funny if JR stayed here and RL liked my Concord Township farm?"

"I don't want to think about who's going where. We might all wind up in Florida. Our real estate lawyer phoned. Mother left a note."

"We have a lawyer?"

"All closings in Virginia are held in law offices."

"Guess who writes the laws. What was it about?"

"We have four signed contracts at the prices we offered."

"You are amazing. You offered ten percent less."

"The real price is always ten percent less. Mother is sending one of her cars around. We're going to drive her, your mother and the boys to our place in Biloxi. Your mother has never seen it."

## Omaha, Nebraska

Colonel Black Bird was waiting at the exit gate when we walked off the airplane in Omaha. I shook his hand, "Never had a full colonel drive a taxi for me."

"Don't count on it ever happening again. Are you carrying your luggage?"

"Yes, Bobbie Jean has clothing scattered from Jackson Mississippi to Virginia."

"Good, I have a staff car waiting out front." Colonel Bird took Bobbie Jean's hang-up bag, "Follow me. Guess what, I'm leaving, too. Taking an F-4 squadron over to Saigon."

"Is it heating up?"

"Only war we've got. I jumped at the opportunity."

"Why are you honoring us with a free ride to our house?"

"Not my idea. I was directed to by the general. He wants you to pack up and move out. I have all the necessary clearance papers ready for your signature."

"Why am I being given the VIP treatment."

"Air Force screwed up when they promoted you. You weren't in the zone or even eligible below the zone."

"Will they take it away?"

"Too late for that."

"How did it happen?"

"One of our personnel sergeants mistakenly sent your folder to the lieutenant colonel promotion board. The board promoted you on your record, so you made the cut below the zone."

"You said it will stick?"

"Like glue. A review board has all ready met and decided that you would make it next year, so they changed your line number."

"I'm in the last group to pin it on?"

"Right, but I'll let you in on a secret. The only reason you scooted through is no one at the top will ever admit to a mistake."

• • •

Nebraska's fall wind scattered leaves as Colonel Black Bird's staff car turned into our driveway. He opened the door for Bobbie Jean, "Keep your good fortune to yourself at the Pentagon. Don't go bragging about how young you were when you made it."

"If I don't go along?"

"How would you like to be my exec. in Saigon, flying in the back seat of an F-4 with a teenage killer up front?"

I laughed, "We have a contract on a farm in Virginia. I'll keep my mouth shut."

"Wife and I drove out to look at your new restaurant. Very impressive. General took some friends out to see it. He liked what he saw, too. Do you still have a chef?"

Bobbie Jean perked up, "Part owner. He's from New Orleans. I'm sure you'll like it, four star food at reasonable prices."

"Packers will arrive tomorrow and a van on Friday. Be out of here before Monday."

"The word will be passed among my peers that I've been sacked?"

"A time honored SAC tradition. It will keep those who stay behind on their toes."

"Let's keep in touch."

"Don't think I'll ever come your way. Pentagon? I'll quit before they haul me in there."

• • •

Black Bird was on target about our movers. A double shift of packers arrived at eight in the morning, but the van arrived a day early. Our house was cleaned and empty by six Thursday evening. VIP quarters had been reserved for us next to the O' Club, but following the general's wishes we made ourselves scarce, staying at the Blackstone and dining out downtown. Contract painters from her restaurant arrived at our house the following morning and carpet cleaners late Friday afternoon. We left the keys to Herbie's house with his chef and drove eastward, early in the morning on a cold windy Nebraska day. As we crossed over the Missouri into Council Bluffs I asked, "Do you think we'll miss Omaha?"

"I'll miss the people."

"Yes, they're friendly."

"I'm looking forward to fixing up our new home and of course, our wedding in June."

"Are you kidding?"

"Only about the wedding. Let's not stop at your farm. Drive on to Washington. I want to look around and see what I missed. We need our farmhouse wired and plumbed so your boys can move in. I have a contractor dropping by early Monday morning."

"Where do you want to stay? At the Watergate?"

"Not this time. I want to stay close to the farmhouse. We'll look for a place in Mclean or maybe Arlington. I want the house fixed in seven days."

"That's a mighty tall order and almost impossible in Virginia, Pilgrim."

## Washington, DC

Six days later, Bobbie Jean and I stood at the bottom of the farmhouse lane with our arms around each other, looking up at our partially remodeled farm home.

Bobbie Jean shook her head, "Even I didn't think it was possible."

"Only because the plumbing and wiring had been replaced by the last owners."

"I can live with it while we finish the interior."

"I thought we were done."

"All three bathrooms have to be brought up to my standards and I want a gourmet kitchen."

"Two of everything?"

"Yes, and I'd like to refinish the hardwood floors."

"I don't want to move our furniture again."

"First things first. I want to fix up the stables."

"Are we going to have horses?"

"Are you certain you really want sheep?"

"Forty acres is a lot to mow and it's too hilly for anything else. At least the grass is dormant until spring. What about the stables?"

"I want to bring them up to my standards. It will be a great place for our boys to play."

"If I know you, we'll be able to eat off the floor. Ours must be one of the last working farms in McLean."

"It's becoming suburbia."

"You purchased it as an investment."

"I know, but I'm growing attached to it."

"Glad the fall weather is warm enough to leave the windows open and air out the paint smell."

"Speaking of airing out, how about a night out. Buy me dinner at Harvey's in DC tonight?"

"Great and move out of our motel tomorrow. Paint smell should be bearable by then."

"I hope so. Nanny is flying in with our boys tomorrow afternoon."

"I'll call ahead. Reservations at six-thirty?"

"Excellent. When do you plan on reporting for your new job?"

"We're ahead of schedule. I'll spend a couple of weeks getting our grounds up to snuff."

• • •

Two weeks of work around the farm wasn't enough time. There were more than enough honey-dos to keep me busy and out of Bobbie Jean's hair. I cleaned out the ditches on our side of the road and rented a bushwhacker to chop down small trees, bramble and underbrush. Least that's what the guy called it when I rented it. Sort of like a huge lawn mower, but with long thick blades. Hooked it to the power takeoff on the back of my tractor. Only took four days to wipe out five years of neglect on our forty acre farm. On Monday of the second week, Bobbie Jean's contractor built a small shelter, open on three sides, on the southeast side of our stables for my sheep. We took delivery of one ram and five ewes on Friday, near the end of my vacation. Our lawn mowers were now in place. Bobbie Jean's contractor remodeled our farmhouse in stages, starting with the kitchen and master bathroom. The stable was the last item on her list of priorities and by the plans, looked more like a giant rec. room. I was more than ready to report into work. My body needed time to recuperate and Bobbie Jean wanted me out from under her feet, so she could redecorate in peace.

• • •

My orders were to report to Air Force incoming personnel on the fifth floor at the Pentagon. It was not an easy trip to get there. I parked in North Parking, at least a mile from the building and entered on the opposite side of where I should have, near the Pentagon Officer's Athletic Center. I soon discovered the Pentagon is a medieval maze of corridors and stairs, either blocked off or lead to nowhere. Figured it became so, as competing fiefdoms captured more territory. After failing to discover a shortcut to the other side of the building, I gave up and walked the long way, around E Ring. Thirty minutes later, after walking into more dead end stairwells than I could count, I found incoming personnel. There I discovered, too late, that a walk around A ring is the shortest route to circumnavigate the Pentagon. Processing into the Pentagon was uncommonly quick for one used to a military mind set. I reported to my new office conveniently located in a blocked off hall on the fourth floor, eighth corridor.

• • •

Discovered that my office was located inside a security vault. So I had to telephone my new boss, a Colonel Mac Muddle to get in.

He opened the vault door with a frown, "Welcome aboard, Major Ropp. The funny wing you replaced cashiered out of here two months ago. Major Black has your job for the interim. He's in the middle of a close hold project for Southeast Asia, so the turnover may take awhile. While your waiting I want you to inventory the safes."

I looked toward the interior of this blocked off corridor and saw cubicles and safes stretched out before me, along both sides of the wall and two deep at the back. "Did you have any trouble finding us?"

"Not after I found in-processing at personnel, but before that I must have been lost a dozen times. This building is made up of walled-off corridors just like this one."

"A funny wing getting lost? My-oh-my, what is this world coming too? Do you have any questions?"

"What am I supposed to do?"

"Why do the right thing, of course, do the right thing. My-oh-my, a funny wing getting lost. What is this world coming too?"

I walked along the row of cubicles until I found Major Black's desk and introduced myself. He looked up, "So you're the new guy who's replacing me at the agency. I'm Paddy Black. What did Muddle ask you to do?"

"Inventory the safes."

"You'll be at that for several months. Hasn't been done in years, long overdue. When it's appropriate, I'll have you follow along with me."

"When do I go solo?"

"We'll see, we'll see. Watch out for Muddle. He's a frustrated pilot trapped in a land of funny wings. Heed my warning—stay out of his way after lunch, he's a mean drunk."

"When do I start my inventory?"

"After I introduce you to the rest of the office."

We walked along a double row, twelve cubicles in all. Paddy introduced me to each occupant, all funny wings like myself. Somehow, I didn't envision myself winding up in this situation, but as long as I was here it was to my advantage to learn all I could. And as all the office files were in safes, an inventory was as good a place as any to start. So, I began with safe number one after spending an hour looking for the combination. I ended the day barely half way through the top drawer of a four drawer safe. The first lesson I learned was not to ask anyone to review a document. The delay would stretch my work into late winter or early spring.

● ● ●

When I drove up the lane to our farmhouse, Bobbie Jean strolled out on the front porch, "Welcome home my Pentagon warrior. Did you find your way around the building on your first day in the fray?"

"Just barely. What a maze."

"Did you discover what you were sent here to do?"

"Not yet, in a couple of months, maybe. But I will know what my office does."

"Going through the files again?"

"That's why I get the big bucks. Only found things that no one has thrown away since the office opened. I'll destroy lot of outdated classified information by the time I'm through."

"Will you eliminate the need for safes?"

"By the time I finish, at least a third of them. I am a little down though, feel like my wings have been clipped."

"My poor soldier, knocked off his perch by his peers again."

"Has to be our military's way of training staff officers."

"Let me show you our new kitchen."

"Is it finished?"

"No, but the cabinets are in. Notice the fireplace?"

"Looks new."

"Won't have to re-brick it. All it needed was a good cleaning. Appliances are coming tomorrow and the floor will be tiled next week."

"Why didn't you tile first."

"Couldn't get anyone to tile until next week. Tell me about your boss."

"Colonel Mac Muddle is his name. Don't worry about inviting him over. He won't be around long. He spends his lunch hour tapping the source of all knowledge."

"At work?"

"Came back from lunch smelling like one of your Mississippi stills. Then there is Major Paddy Black."

"Nick Nack Paddy Black, give the frog a loan?"

"Another straight line delivered."

"And accepted."

"Major Black is temporarily occupying my job."

"Doesn't sound promising."

"It isn't, but reading through all of the files should be. How is Nanny adjusting to her new home?"

"We don't have to worry about monitoring contractors. She's making sure the job is done right. Mother may have a hard time getting her to come back."

"How so?"

"I've been bringing her up to speed on my corporation. She's all ready taken over bookkeeping and taxes and is doing a better job than my former accountant."

•　•　•

After a week of wandering the Pentagon corridors in silence, passing by one eyes to the floor denizen after another, I decided to smile and say hello to every person I passed. The first two folks I greeted almost jumped out of their shoes, "This is going to be a fun way to pass my time in hell." During the second week, I went looking for my operations counterparts in the land of a purple water fountain, in the bowels of the Pentagon. I wandered around the ground floor looking for a staircase that would lead down. Had to give up and use a non-working narrow escalator, the only way I found to go down two floors to the basement. After passing by the purple water fountain for the third time, I stopped and asked for directions to the reconnaissance office. When I finally found it, no one was in. I did find an Army map storage area, by mistake, so far underground that its denizens were losing their eyesight. The brochure said that any location inside the Pentagon is within a twenty minutes walk from any other location. I soon discovered this was only true if you knew your location and knew where the hidden stairs were and which corridors were blocked off, which I didn't. Most of its 26,000 inhabitants never left their area of influence, staying within their own fiefdom. Lunch with Bobbie Jean was out of the question. Walking to my car in north parking took half-an-hour and a drive to a decent restaurant another thirty minutes.

•　•　•

Three weeks of shuffling papers and I had worked my way up to safe number ten, gaining a vast knowledge about my office, but not knowing anything about my new job. I soon discovered a number of letters signed by generals who had long since retired. Almost half of the documents were over five years old and of no historical value. Still, I had great difficulty getting the current holder of a particular file to let go. Persistence finally won out, or it may have been that no one else wanted to join me in bottom feeding. Inventory of classified data was looked upon the same as an officer pulling latrine duty. Since I had gone through this drill in Nebraska, I looked upon it as an opportunity to excel. And as in all staff work, knowledge is power. I learned not to worry about not knowing the background of actions taken in the past. No one knew. Wasn't long before I was up to speed on Intelligence programs and systems, keeping what was necessary and throwing out the extraneous. I was anxious to complete my work. Southeast Asia was heating up and I wanted to be in on the decisions about which reconnaissance system would do the best job. And I still had twenty-four safes to be inventoried.

• • •

Monday morning, two weeks and fifteen safes later, my call to duty came through. Bobbie Jean rubbed her eyes as she entered the kitchen, "What are you doing here? You should be at work by now. It's almost eight o'clock."

"Coffee? Right out of a shepherd's pot."

"Yes, but why?"

"Free at last, thank God almighty, I'm free at last."

"Dr. King's birthday is in January."

"I have an appointment at CIA in an hour. Finally get to do real work."

"Is this a permanent thing?"

"Oh, no. I'm not being assigned to CIA. I'm still in the Air Force. I'm being assigned to a U.S.I.B. committee."

"U.S.I.B.?"

"United States Intelligence Board."

"A committee? You'll go crazy. Pour me a cup of coffee and I'll fix you a Virginia breakfast."

"The whole U.S. government is run by committee. What kind of breakfast?"

"Ham so salty you'll have drink water all day. Eggs that are round in the middle, like potholes. Grits that stick to your ribs like marine clay and whole wheat toast, which is what you'll be if you don't start coming home before seven at night."

I had to learn to eat grits, if only to keep Bobbie Jean happy, but I still didn't care for them.

• • •

Still smiling from Bobbie Jean's punch lines, I drove north from Chain Bridge Road on the George Washington Parkway and turned at the Fairbanks Highway Research Station exit sign. I located visitor parking near the geodesic dome and entered the visitor's reception area. After several photos were taken and my identification verified, I was escorted to my committee office and introduced to the Secretary, the only permanent member. In less than an hour, I was back on the Parkway, driving south to the Pentagon. The parkway between Chain Bridge Road and the 14th Street bridge was almost empty this time of day, except for empty headed congressional staffers, senators and congressmen. Just past the Memorial Bridge stood the five sided swamp, its sandstone stained brindle by the fumes from Shirley Highway and the Pentagon power plant. Inside, the floors shined from years of wax on top of wax. And the walls mirrored the exterior, with yellowed white paint stained rust, brindle and brown, like a limestone cave in Kentucky. Knowing that my inventory had to be complete before I could take over my new job, I worked through lunch.

At half past one, I walked to the fourth floor snack bar, just in time to get a deli sandwich before the line closed down. Paddy Black wandered in and sat down with a cup of Pentagon coffee. Now, the only thing remarkable about Pentagon coffee is it is too boiling hot to drink, takes five minutes to cool down and tastes like dishwater when it does. Paddy Black looked like the cat with a canary—me—in its mouth, "How's your inventory coming along?"

"I'll be finished in another week, if I'm lucky. Have seventeen empty safes when It's completed."

"That much trash?"

"We've got pack rats."

"Be careful, you never know when an old document can cover your backside."

"The documents I'm throwing out aren't useful enough to replace corn cobs in an outhouse. I wouldn't be surprised if I ran into a message from President Wilson to General Pershing."

I excused myself to get a refill.

When I returned, Paddy offered to do something to help me that was a two months late, "If you find something you're not sure about, run it through me. Did you clear in at the Fairbanks Highway Station?"

"Cleared in, met the Secretary this morning."

"Have you been called up to the general's office?"

"No, why?"

"Air Force is looking for volunteers."

"Southeast Asia?"

"Looks like we're going in. Must be anticipating a buildup."

"If we had any sense, it would be to build down. Mucking around in that swamp was a lost cause for the French, we won't fare any better."

"You need to go there if you want your ticket punched for promotion. It's the only war we've got."

"Ticket punched or body punched into a plastic body bag. Not a very good choice. Do you think we'll go in with guns blazing?"

"Not with McNamara's policy of gradual escalation. Shouldn't be too bad if we tiptoe in around the edges."

"Two steps forward and one step back? We're in for a long walk if we follow his policy. Did you see the general?"

"Have a security problem. Know too much. Can't afford to be captured."

"Does that include me, too?"

"As soon as you signed in at the agency."

"If we really do get involved, this war is going to last a long time and our clearances won't keep us out of it. Not if we continue to use one year rotations and back fill with TDY—temporary duty personnel."

"We're too smart to fight wars with personnel on temporary assignment."

"Hope your right."

I checked my watch, "Need to get back to the vault if I'm going to complete my inventory."

• • •

As we walked down A corridor to the vault, I invited Major Black and his wife to our farmhouse for dinner Saturday evening. "Should be able to make it. Have to check with the wife." After I returned, I decided to take time out. If the Air Force was hot after volunteers, something important had to be going down. Several phone calls later I had to admit, "Paddy was right, they are looking for volunteers. And our chief of staff, General LeMay is in hot water for not giving McNamara's policies his full support."

I found what Tucker would call a reliable source, in the basement. Another expatriate from SAC reconnaissance with his ear tuned into Pentagon politics. Lieutenant Colonel Wilson Wrangle had flown high and fast in a photo-recon bird under my old boss, Colonel Black Bird. He was a kick the tires, light the fires type, "You worked for Black Bird, too. Hell of a boss. What do you want to know about my hero, LeMay?"

"Need to know what's going down in Southeast Asia. Where does he stand?"

"Rather not talk here. Let's go upstairs to the cafeteria for a cup of coffee."

We sat down in the front of the cafeteria, just up the ramp from the Concourse, where all the shops are. Wrangle asked, "Where is Black Bird these days?"

"He was at SAC headquarters, but he's leading a squadron of F-4s to Saigon sometime soon."

"The recon office will let me know where he is. I volunteered when my ops general called me in. Rather fight under someone who wants to do the job, not just fill squares. You asked about LeMay. Rumor has it that McNamara tried to get rid of him, not once, but twice. LeMay advocated that we destroy the North's port of Haiphong. Also wanted to take out the dikes. Figured if they couldn't get supplies shipped in and their fields were flooded, they'd be too busy to support the Vietcong. He's right. That war would come to a screeching halt. The *Post* misquoted him as saying he wanted to bomb them back to the stone age. I carry a copy of the full text in my billfold." He handed it to me.

*My solution to the problem would be to tell them frankly that they've got to stop their aggression, or we're going to bomb them back into the Stone Age.*

I handed it back, "They did a number on our boss. Problem is, he's right, but it isn't politically popular."

"And it goes against McNamara's policies. He didn't endure himself to McNamara when he didn't go along with the F-111 and fought cancellation of the B-70. If our bird is so bad, why are the English and French copying it for a commercial airliner?"

"You don't think he's long for the Pentagon?"

"Only a matter of time before LeMay retires."

"Wouldn't blame him if he did. Can you imagine, we're going to fight a war wearing red coats and march down the middle of the road."

Wrangle laughed, "And the Vietcong will wear brown, hide behind the trees and pick us off, one at a time."

• • •

As I spun the combination lock on the safe, securing it for the night. Paddy came over, "Did you find out who is pushing us into the Southeast Asia quagmire?"

"According to the guys in plans its the civilians at State, the National Security Council and Robert Strange McNamara. And our Army has discovered a new way to fight. They're going to scatter out in small cavalry units to counter the guerrillas in the countryside."

"Isn't that how Custer got clobbered at Little Bighorn?"

"Absolutely, and when the Cong mass enough troops, our units will be picked off one by one."

• • •

I polished off my last remaining safe inventory by five-thirty Friday evening and arrived home, late again.

Bobbie Jean was waiting, standing out in the cold on the front porch, hands on hips, "You were supposed to leave early. You should have been home an hour ago. We have guests arriving in a few minutes."

"Forget about Paddy Black and his wife. They won't be able to make it."

"That leaves only Mr. Tubbs and Lisa."

"And don't worry about Tucker arriving early. He won't find his way here without stopping and asking for directions."

"You sent him a very detailed map."

"Mark my words, thirty minutes after he's scheduled to arrive, Tuck will call from the corner gas station and ask for directions. What are you serving our guests tonight?"

"Nothing special, an easy meal to prepare. With the Blacks canceling, I'm glad I didn't hire a caterer."

"You cook better than the last one we had."

"Hurry and change out of your uniform. I want you to greet our guests and keep them entertained while I finish preparing dinner."

At exactly six-thirty Tucker phoned from the corner gas station and asked for directions, "I have the map you sent, but it's flat and I see nothing but rolling hills and forest along these roads."

"Which way are you pointed?"

"Don't know. We've been driving around in circles."

"Drive north from the gas station, turn left, count three hills and turn right at the bottom of the next valley. I've marked the entrance to our drive with a wooden sign, JRL Ranch."

"What does JRL stand for?"

"First letters of my boy's names, JR and RL."

"Which way is north?"

"Can you see the afterglow of the setting sun?"

"Yes."

"Put it on your left shoulder and you'll be facing north. Watch out for my sheep when you turn in. They tend to wander."

"You have sheep in the middle of McLean?"

"Have to do something to keep the grass short. Bobbie Jean purchased forty acres of rolling hills."

"Sheep in Mclean? Which way is north?"

I watched Tucker's pink and white Packard Caribbean convertible weave up our lane, dodging a ewe and stopping when my ram decided to challenge his radiator. We met on my front porch, "See you just missed one of my sheep."

"You weren't kidding about your woolly lawn mowers. Where's Bo Peep?"

"In the kitchen fixing your dinner. How do you like our little home on the range?"

Before Tucker could answer, Bobbie Jean opened the door and ushered us all into her kitchen, "We're going to dine in here tonight. What do you think of my farm?"

Tucker grinned, "Picturesque, but you can't plow rocks and trees. Outside of Johnny's sheep, what are your plans for it?"

Bobbie Jean couldn't resist, "Why we'll do what every red blooded Virginian does with his land."

"Plant tobacco?"

"Of course not. We'll subdivide it when we're ready, sell it to Yankees for ten times more than it's worth and move south. But for now, this farm will be a wonderful place for our twins to grow up."

"Can we see the boys?"

"Johnny, take our guests to the play room while I garnish our hors d'oeuvres."

• • •

When we returned, Bobbie Jean motioned for us to sit at the counter overlooking the cooking area, separating it from the fireplace and dining area. She served smoked salmon and a Chinese style barbecue ribs, "Johnny, pour Lisa a glass of white wine. I'll show her the rest of the house while you two armchair generals spin your war stories."

I poured Tucker a mug of English Stout and Lisa a glass of white wine.

Tucker took a sip, "This is good stuff."

"Only the best for our muckraking friend."

"What's the latest news from the Pentagon?"

"The brass have asked for volunteers to go to Southeast Asia. Are we escalating?"

"Gradual, gradual."

"Stupid."

"Any word on the status of LeMay?"

"Rumor has it he isn't long for his job as Chief of Staff. Is McNamara going to can him?"

"Can't, too much grass roots support or he would have been gone by now. Know he's crosswise with the secretary. Anyone else?"

"Understand he has serious problems with the JCS Chairman."

"That figures. MACV, General Harkins in Saigon, and Maxwell Taylor are both active supporters of McNamara's tit for tat gradual escalation policy. Your rumor is probably right. LeMay is too much of an iron ass to stick around when State, DOD and Johnson freeze him out of the decision making process."

"From what I understand at the Pentagon, the thorn in LeMay's paw is civilian control of bombing policy. McNamara's band wants to pick nonessential targets to get the North's attention. LeMay says that's how politicians lose wars. He wants to destroy the North's ability to support the Vietcong, not drop a few bombs on the jungle."

I refilled Tucker's mug and poured another glass of wine for myself. Tucker polished off the last of Bobbie Jean's Chinese spareribs. I never ceased to be amazed at his incredible appetite. Tucker wiped his hands on a napkin and asked, "What do you think the solution is?"

"I haven't changed my mind. There isn't any. We can't win friends and influence the natives with bullets."

"What do the troops think?"

"Majors and below aren't keen about taking a year-long vacation in the jungles of Southeast Asia. Lieutenant colonels and up are blinded by an opportunity for promotion."

"Do you have a feel for what the other service chiefs think?"

"I believe Shoup and McDonald have the same feelings as LeMay, but they're all outvoted by McNamara. I'm not certain about the rest of our Air Force generals. Everyone below the Chief keeps their mouths closed. Who do you feed my thoughts to at the *Post*?"

"Phil Graham."

"You go to the top?"

"Don't worry. Even if he doesn't agree with LeMay on this issue, Phil still believes he is our number one warrior. Did I here you right? Three of the chiefs oppose McNamara's policy?"

"Yes, however your boss supports McNamara."

"Not everyone is perfect."

"Can you change his mind?"

"Not on this one."

"If this war keeps growing, we'll wind up with a lot of dead soldiers."

"I know my history, the Vietnamese won't fold under the pressure of gradual escalation. Those folks can read and understand"

"LeMay is right. If we threaten to eliminate their economy, they'll arrive at an accommodation, even if it is temporary."

"To the Vietnamese, temporary means decades. They survived occupation by the Chinese, Japanese and French and they'll outlast us."

Bobbie Jean and Lisa returned from their walkabout, "I see my ribs were a hit. I'm glad you saved some smoked salmon for Lisa. Now, no more of your war talk until after dinner. Johnny, throw another log on the fire and Mr. Tubbs, you can help Lisa carry dinner to the table. On our farm we dine family style. We'll pass the serving plates."

• • •

Dinner was superb, as usual. Bobbie Jean had supervised several of the countries best Chefs and her sauces showed the results. Tucker ate everything in sight and more. While our ladies cleaned up, I poured coffee and cognac and we sat around kitchen table.

I chided Tucker, "Now you know where the phrase Kitchen Cabinet came from."

"Discussions around the table? But, we don't make things happen."

"I don't, but you can influence them."

"Even an editor gets edited. What do you think of the Vietnamese countryside?"

"Not an expert. You know more about it than I do. I haven't been there, but I've tasked reconnaissance missions. It's almost impossible to see into a jungle from the air. The books say never to get involved in a guerrilla war between religious factions, but we've gone over that time and again."

Bobbie Jean asked Tucker, "What about dominoes? Will all of Southeast Asia collapse if we pull out?"

"That's a load of crap from State. I don't trust those guys. They see the world through Ivy League eyes. We should look at the Vietnamese world through their eyes, not ours. Hurt their economy, LeMay's way, may be the only way out, but it will never sell. So, we're back to square one. Supply the South Vietnamese and get out of the way. Let them win or lose on their own. Bottom line, get our troops out of there. When I was over there covering the war, I traveled extensively outside of Saigon. It's a different story from the one we're being fed by State and the White House. Our officials in Saigon are feeding our folks bad data, distorting the information they send here."

I added, "And once we've been given a mission and its constraints, we'll find a way to make it a success, even if it isn't."

Bobbie Jean asked Tucker, "What do you think will happen?"

"McNamara's ego won't let him admit there isn't a solution to winning, so he won't let go. And Johnson doesn't want to be labeled as a loser."

I interrupted, "You and I are beating a dead horse. We're back to where square one. We began this discussion at the Watergate."

"Speaking of dead horses, I have to see a man who owns one. Which way is it?"

When Tucker returned he changed the subject from Vietnam to systems policy, "You really raked McNamara's Systems Analysis concept over the coals. Congress thinks it's the greatest thing since sliced bread. If it's as bad as you say it is, why does it have so much support?"

"Most of our lawmakers are lawyers, or accountants who believe filling out a sheet of paper is doing real work. At the peak of World War II the Air Corps had five people approving hundreds of thousands of airplanes. Mark my words, if we keep on piling up paper as we're doing today, we'll have hundreds of thousands of people approving five airplanes. It looks like Calvin Coolidge will finally get his wish."

"And he wished for?"

"Coolidge told his War Department to buy only one airplane and let the fliers take turns."

"If I understand you, you're saying the Defense Department will spend all of its funds on studies and none will be left to buy airplanes."

"Or damn little. We can build paper factories or we can build hardware. Looks like we've chosen paper."

"I forgot to ask you what our troops are thinking about Vietnam."

"I don't think they've decided one way or the other. Most of them are not involved and could care less."

"Will they support a war over there?"

"They'll fight if told too, but support? We'll do our duty, but might not care for the conditions."

"One year rotations and temporary assignments?"

"One way to prevent a mutiny. Our minds will be on getting home, not the futility of it. With gradual escalation, we'll be so busy fighting snakes and crocodiles we'll forget our mission was to drain the swamp. There will be no corporate memory of pitfalls and minefields. All our troops will care about is surviving and coming home. My turn to visit the man who owns a horse."

I returned as Bobbie Jean served dessert. Tucker gave me his best *Mad* magazine smile, "That wasn't so bad, was it? All I'm interested in is scuttlebutt, not classified."

"And I'm the Tooth Fairy."

"I play by the rules. If I need classified data I have official sources to go to."

"If the *Post* was in a horse race, your editors would cut across the infield to win."

"We won't sacrifice National Security on the altar of journalism. I don't need too. Like I said, the executive branch plays I've got a secret with us daily."

"Your boss is hard over to support the administration."

"Yes, but if their policies fail we'll be all over them like a blanket."

"Right, if it works it's on page one."

Tucker laughed, "And if it doesn't it's next to the Obits. Bobbie Jean, tell me about your Watergate condos. Do you have them leased?"

"Long term to diplomats. Lisa gave me the idea."

She whispered, "Are you and Lisa an item?" Tucker blushed, but didn't answer.

As Tucker got up to leave, he pulled me aside, "I report direct to Phil. He knows I'm opposed to our increased involvement. That's why my assignment to Saigon was cut short."

"And I thought it was because you kept getting lost in the Delta."

"MACV wouldn't let me out of town without an escort and a driver."

"Managed news?"

"They tried."

"You didn't answer Bobbie Jean's question."

Tucker grinned as he whispered, "Double your pleasure, double your fun."

Bobbie Jean asked, "What are you two doing for Christmas?"

Tucker looked at Lisa and they both shrugged. "Why don't you spend Christmas Eve with us? You can watch our boys tear wrappings off their packages in the morning."

"Best offer we've had this year. After tonight's meal, I'm looking forward to another one at Christmas. Now, so I won't get lost, will you give me directions to Watergate?"

• • •

After we watched Tucker turn the wrong way onto the main road, Bobbie Jean closed the door and gave me a full body squeeze. After a lingering kiss, she led me to the kitchen. "I'll make you Herbie's Irish coffee, if you tell me what you know about Tucker and Lisa."

"Not certain if Tucker is serious."

"Lisa says Tucker proposed and she has accepted."

"That rascal danced all around my question."

"Mine, too. Do you think he has a tapeworm? I've never seen anyone as thin as he is eat so much."

"Metabolism and nerves."

The phone rang. Tucker was at a pay phone in Great Falls, "You can't give directions worth a damn. I'm at a closed gas station."

"How did you get there?"

"Followed a roundabout route."

"Can you see a road sign?"

"Georgetown Pike."

"Follow it southeast. It runs into Chain Bridge Road and that runs into George Washington Parkway."

"Where did I make my mistake?"

"When you drove the wrong way out of our lane."

Bobbie Jean laughed, "Lisa will have to learn navigation."

"She all ready knows how. Tucker will have to learn how to listen."

"What was Tucker interested in?"

"The Pentagon gossip mill."

"And they say women can't keep a secret."

• • •

Tucker gave Lisa a rock large enough to cut glass at our farmhouse on Christmas Eve. Lisa and he were now more than an item, but had not set a wedding date. She was concerned that the *Post* might send him back to Saigon. The battle for Ben Hoa Air Base, eighteen miles from Saigon, in November brought the war home to the Pentagon. We were seeing a sharp upward turn in the number of troops and an equivalent degree upward on McNamara's gradual escalation curve. Things didn't bode well for our Vietnamese venture. Right after New Year's, I began a new career as Major Black's caddie. I carried his briefcase, riding shotgun on classified data, to our committee meetings at the agency. Bobbie Jean was right, I was not cut out to sit and listen to drivel. Our meetings droned on, hour after hour, without much of anything being accomplished.

A long expected event occurred in mid-January. Paddy Black and I returned late on a Monday afternoon from the agency to an office in turmoil. Colonel Mac Muddle had been canned after returning to the office from a liquid lunch dead drunk. Before anyone could coral him, he was on his way to the general's office, swearing and yelling. His voice carried all the way to the snack bar. The Air Police escorted him to Andrews Air Force Base. After he dried out, he was given an offer he couldn't refuse, retirement our else. Everyone, except me, moved up a slot.

I was still carrying Major Black's bag. And because of the stellar work I had performed on the branch classified inventory, my reward was to inventory all of the classified documents in the general's office. Paddy Black was all heart, "Busy hands get all the good jobs."

"Thanks for the vote of confidence. When do I go solo at the agency?"

"Soon."

"Will you sign off on my inventory sheets for the general's office?"

"No, have someone from his office do it. I'll give you the combination to my safe so you can get up to speed on your new job, but don't destroy any documents." I was moving up. His was the only safe out of bounds on my last inventory. I dug into Paddy's safe and boned up. It was just as dull as our committee meetings.

• • •

On a cold winter's day late in January, Tucker left a message for me to call him at the *Post*. I dialed his private number, "What's up?"

"Need to talk to someone who isn't in my business."

"You need a sounding board?"

"Right. Can you get away for lunch?"

"I'm on another make-work project. Where and when?"

"You know where the Market Inn is?"

"DC near the railroad track by the old market."

"See you there at noon."

"How's Lisa?"

"Getting anxious about living together and not being married. Wants me to fly to her home and meet her folks."

"It is serious."

• • •

I handed the parking lot attendant my keys. Tucker was inside at the bar.

"Care for a drink?" he said.

"Make mine coffee. My office has a very low tolerance for drinking on the job."

"Have you been here before?"

I looked around at photos of naval ships adorning the walls and furniture that looked like early prohibition and said, "No, it's the first time I've seen a parking lot attendant with a shotgun. Must be a rough neighborhood."

"Wouldn't walk around here at night without an armed escort. Clam chowder is to die for here."

"What did you want to discuss?"

"Remember Diem's overthrow and the chaos that followed?"

"Four new governments in less than a year. Kennedy's folks really screwed the pup. That got us up to our ankles in the swamp. Are we having problems?"

"No one will talk openly about it, but the war is going badly for the South. We have over twenty thousand advisors now."

"Wow, the number is going up?"

"Big time."

"Sending in more advisors won't do us any good. We'll have more troops than our allies."

"Lost cause time. The peasants will be so busy chasing after us with pitchforks, they won't have time to listen to our political message."

The bartender interrupted, "Are you ready to order?"

Tucker continued, "The South Vietnamese Army is fighting a guerrilla Army supported by peasants. We're joining a fight with both hands tied behind our back. The joint chiefs are the key. If they oppose sending more troops, McNamara will have to throw in the towel."

"If they don't?"

"We will be in a war longer than any in memory. I want you to keep your ears tuned to the rumor mill. If LeMay retires, you know what I'm thinking."

"Phil doesn't pay attention to you."

"History. If this war goes into the toilet, we need to know who flushed us into the sewer."

"The handle has been pulled. LeMay is on a tour, visiting Air Force units all over the world."

"What does that mean?"

"He's retiring soon. Our chiefs visit when they take over and when they leave."

Our lunch arrived. We dined in silence with an occasional, "Damn!"

As we walked to our cars I asked Tucker, "Set a date for the wedding?"

"Middle of March. Are you and Bobbie Jean still going to stand up for us?"

"Sure, but you should know the last time we did, the couple separated after a year."

"Bonnie the Body Beautiful."

"How did you know?"

"I have her car. Lisa and Bobbie Jean tell their own war stories while we're spinning ours. Is Bonnie that good?"

"The best there is, not one blemish."

"I'll see you a week from Saturday. Bobbie Jean will fill you in."

"Are you going out of town?"

"Lisa and I are flying to Denmark to meet her family."

"Ingrid, too?"

"I hope so."

"You are living on the edge."

"Hands off time since Lisa captured me."

*"What do you know about this business?" the King said to Alice.*

*"Nothing," said Alice.*

*"Nothing whatever?" persisted the King.*

*"Nothing whatever," said Alice.*

# Chapter 16

Major Black's note was short and to the point.

*Meet me at the POAC if you're back before two. I'll sign you up. I'm on racquetball court three.*

*Paddy*

I checked my watch, it was one-thirty. If I walked fast, I'd make it before two. I was going to join the Pentagon Officer's Athletic Center, but hadn't gotten around to it. Besides a gym, swimming pool, weight room, courts for all the ball games, lockers and showers, the POAC had three distinct advantages, check cashing for out of town banks, barbers that knew how to cut hair and a cafeteria that served beer. I stopped by the office to join up.

While filling out the form, I felt a tap on my left shoulder and turned around, "Bidwell, Sergeant Bidup Bidwell, how long has it been and what the hell are you doing here?"

"Same old Johnny. See that you made Major."

"And lieutenant colonel."

"When do you pin on your silver leaves?"

"First of April. Your fingerprints are all over both my promotions."

"That's why I'm an NCO and you're not. We're capable of anything."

"And crafty enough to bear watching."

"That's why we have officers. Finish filling out your application and stop by my office."

"You run this place?"

"Lucky me, I'm the Army's manager."

"An Air Force sergeant running an Army facility?" I handed in my application with the required twenty-five dollar deposit and looked for Bidwell's office.

I found it in the entrance corridor behind an unmarked door. It made my general's office look shabby. Bidwell motioned for me to sit down and wait while he finished a phone call. He hung up, "Poker game at a hotel in Middleburg tomorrow night. Have you settled in yet?"

"Why didn't you give me a call?"

"You were getting settled and my schedule got backed up."

"How did you get this assignment?"

"Skill and cunning. Got crossways with a member of the Texas Legislature when I was stationed in Austin. Seems he got shot in the foot at one of my poker games."

"That happens a lot when you open a deck of cards. Where did you have the game?"

"On my houseboat in the middle of the base lake. Couple of skin divers boarded my boat and tried to rob the game."

"Why were you holding a poker game in the middle of a lake?"

"Had too, they closed my racetrack down."

"Horse racing is illegal in Texas."

"So I found out. There's a lot of itch down there that needs scratching. Texans would just as soon race quarter horses as eat."

"How did you wind up here."

"Not just me, it's how we wound up here. I arranged the sale of that pink and white Packard Caribbean convertible for my NCO friend at SAC personnel and he got lucky in a poker game. When I called he hauled."

"And me?"

"Let's just say we accelerated your career. You were heading this way, anyway."

"That promotion raised a few eyebrows."

"Don't ask."

"Don't tell."

Paddy Black knocked on the door and walked in, his hair still wet from the shower. I introduced him to Bidwell, "Meet the second richest NCO in the Air Force."

Bidwell laughed, "What do you mean, second?"

"Did you move up a notch to first?"

"My poker playing buddy from Roswell is out of the service."

"The one that owned all those laundries in New York City? Why? He loved it."

"Served in Southeast Asia during the second World War. Voted with his feet when he discovered we were going to be more than advisors."

"I've been chasing that rumor down. Are you sure?"

"Our president is a big risk taker. Played a few games of chance with him in Austin. Has an ego as big as Texas."

"So, you think we're going to do more than advise?"

"We all ready are. You need a full sized locker. I'll put you in next to the movers and shakers. Most of them don't come down anymore. You'll have an area all to yourself."

"Will you be free a week from Saturday?"

"Should be back by then. Have to set up a poker game at Homestead Air Force base outside of Miami this weekend. Four stars are having their annual meeting next week. Where did you buy?"

"We have a forty acre farm in McLean."

"Almost next store neighbors. I live across the river in Potomac. How is Bobbie Jean Langtry?"

"Getting domesticated. Out of the hotel business."

"Still have a piece of the Sands?"

"As far as I know she does and a restaurant in Omaha."

"Heard about it from my friends at SAC. Getting rave reviews. Is she going to hang onto it?"

"Bobbie Jean doesn't care for absentee ownership, but if she sells, it will be to the Manager and their chef."

• • •

As we rode the escalator up to the fourth floor, Paddy whistled under his breath, "Took me two years to get a full length locker. Where did you meet Bidwell?"

"Roswell, New Mexico. He was my Gunner. Great troop. Only one in town with his own federal gambling stamp." As we walked along corridor eight, a line drawing, of the Air Force art collection lining the wall, caught my eye. The inscription caught my eye. I stopped and read: *Gus, a fighter pilot and Lieutenant General, former Vice Commander of Air Force Systems Command.* It was an artfully done line drawing of the first chimpanzee to fly in space.

Paddy said, "Someone is going to get into trouble."

"Don't think so. Most pilots I know have bad near vision and are too proud to wear glasses. Whoever changed the caption knew his pilots."

"What do you mean?"

"It doesn't say former fighter pilot. None of them will ever admit they're over the hill."

"But this is a chimp."

"Not even an astronaut chimpanzee."

• • •

Dull work had fogged my mind, but I remembered to talk about our get together when I arrived home. I asked Bobbie Jean, "Have you decided what to serve Tucker and Lisa next Saturday?"

"Your friend, Mr. Tubbs never said one word to me about getting together. Lisa mentioned that we should talk, but didn't say when. I'll give her a call."

"You better do it tonight. They're flying to Denmark to meet her parents. Tucker said the wedding will be in March. Wants us to stand up for them."

"Where?"

"Don't know, could be here or Denmark."

"This is all news to me. Do you have any other surprises?"

"I joined the athletic center today. Guess who I ran into."

"There can only be one person that can make you smile like that, Sergeant Bidwell. Did you invite them over next Saturday?"

"Yes, and I apologize for not telling you about it earlier."

"Your punishment will be to barbecue steaks out in our stable "

"Almost finished?"

"Good enough to hold a party there. Why don't you phone Tucker at work while I finish cooking dinner."

I changed out of my uniform and dialed Tucker's private *Washington Post* phone number. "Who is this?"

"Johnny."

"Make it quick, I'm on a deadline."

"LeMay's retiring."

"Is it official?"

"No, but as you say, I found a reliable source. You'll meet him at my house next Saturday. Be there at six-thirty."

"I am getting depressed. We are heading into hell in a hand basket."

"Have Lisa phone Bobbie Jean before you fly away to Denmark."

"Oops, I forgot to tell Lisa to call earlier."

"Anything you can do about Vietnam?"

"Keep score. I'll bring wine."

"Screw cap or corks?"

"They have corks?"

After Tucker hung up, Bobbie Jean asked, "What's that about screw caps or corks?"

"The good news is that dinner is on for a week from Saturday. The bad news is that Tucker is bringing the wine."

"While you're up, I'll take white."

After dinner, as we huddled by the fire, Bobbie Jean wondered, "How can it feel so cold here when the temperature is above forty degrees?"

"Somewhere in Virginia in the rain."

"Is that why?"

"Humidity and it's also a song title. Chill goes right through to your bones."

"Aren't your sheep cold?"

"Just their noses. They huddle up in the lean-to we built for them. Should be more than enough shelter for this climate."

"Don't lambs arrive in the spring?"

"Don't worry, if the weather turns bad, we have a large farm kitchen and two boys who would love to feed them."

"Lambs in the kitchen!"

"Only poor little lambs that have gone astray."

"Baa! Yaa! Baa!"

"I'll spend my life feeding you straight lines."

"Father read me to sleep with Kipling."

• • •

Bidwell phoned from his POAC office Monday afternoon, "Back sooner than I expected."

"What happened?"

"Four stars cut their winter meeting short."

"Any news about LeMay?"

"He made a short speech and they all packed up and went home."

"No poker game?"

"Night before with the early birds. You were right. He is retiring. Hate to see a real leader go, but all things must pass."

"The passing of an age of warriors. Wonder how long it will take the fighter pilots to eliminate strategic bombers and SAC?"

"Can't be anyone around that crazy."

"You're right. McNamara's system analysis will do it for them."

"How so?"

"Drive up the cost so we won't have more than a hundred or so bombers left." Speaking of fighter pilots, are you the one who promoted our astronaut Chimpanzee to three stars?"

"You mean our new three star, Gus?"

"I read the caption on the line drawing last week."

"Is it still up on the wall?"

"Sure is."

"I have a three star that's dogging me here. Figured he wouldn't carry his glasses with him."

"Are you behind it?"

"Don't ask."

"Don't tell. Did they mention his replacement?"

"Gus or LeMay?"

"LeMay, you sly dog."

"No one knows. They're all jockeying for position. How do you like your locker?"

"Raised a few eyebrows of several generals and admirals when they saw a major amongst them."

"I know, complaints came straight to me. Had to inform them that there is supposed to be no rank on the playing fields."

"Try getting a tee time at Andrews on Saturday morning."

"I can take care of that."

"You won another pro shop?"

"Sold it back to the Pro at one third of retail. What time Saturday night?"

"Six-thirty. Hope your wife is coming, too."

"Of course. She can't wait to give you a hard time."

• • •

I completed my inventory of the general's classified files late Thursday evening. Outside, a slate gray Ohio-type winter day had turned into a Nebraska pitch black night. I noticed the beginning of a winter storm, snow flakes falling outside, through the inner courtyard windows. I crunched through new fallen snow to my car in North Parking. It stood waiting, lonely as the Blue Ridge Mountain's fabled lonesome pine. Turning north onto George Washington Parkway, snow driven by a noreast wind stuck to my windshield in soap sud clumps. My wipers moved the snow about like a stick through kindergarten paste. A twenty-five minute drive turned into an hour of stop and go, reminiscent of bumper cars at a carnival. I must have sidestepped a dozen wrecks and stopped a dozen times to clean my windshield.

Bobbie Jean met me on the front porch with a broom and a smile, "Where is your car?"

I brushed off the snow and replied, "Had to park at the bottom of the lane."

"Change into your work clothes. Not all of your sheep are in the lean-to."

"Our ram?"

"Sacked out, chewing his cud."

"On a night like this we need a Border collie. Before I play Nanook of the North, how many are missing?"

"Two."

"How many are pregnant?"

"All five ewes." I changed, bundled up and began my search.

It didn't take long. Both ewes were huddled, sheltered from wind and snow in a grove of trees not far from the lane. "Come on ladies. We need to get you under the lean-to and out of this storm." Herding them uphill, into wind-driven snow made up my mind, "I have to buy a Border collie."

I bedded them down with their kin, inside the lean-to. Each received a salt tablet treat. I chucked the ram under his chin, "Old fellow, you might as well be on welfare. A Border collie will get you in shape."

I peeked inside the stables to check on Bobbie Jean's project. The stalls were gone. Large yellow Mexican tiles covered the floor. Two bathrooms had been installed. Besides a floor to ceiling fireplace, two pot-bellied stoves decorated both ends. She could entertain a large group, if they didn't sit down. She had installed a barbecue on the side of the fireplace, using the chimney for ventilation. "So that's where I'm cooking steaks Saturday."

I entered the farmhouse through the mud room attached to the kitchen, hung up my outer garments and removed my boots. Bobbie Jean handed me a mug of hot coffee, "Find your sheep?"

"In the south pasture near the lane. They're all bedded down in the lean-to, including the ram."

"All he wants to do is eat, sleep and chase after our ewes."

"It's my fault. He was so frisky and obedient when he arrived, I changed his name from copilot to pilot and now all he wants to do is sit on his ass and 'Baa! Yaa! Baa!'"

"You stole my punch line. What took you so long?"

"I would have been in earlier, but I stopped to see how the stables are coming along. Will those pot-bellied stoves keep the pipes from freezing?"

"Lisa gave me the idea. They're made in Denmark. One or two good sized pieces of wood will burn all night."

"Just to make sure, I better add a piece before we go to bed. Did you hear the weather forecast?"

"We're in for at least a foot of snow. When it clears, the temperature is supposed to drop into the teens."

"See the barbecue is in. What's left to do?"

"We'll add a bar and refrigerator. I may stain the interior wood. What do you think?"

"The interior walls look good the way they are. Gives it a rustic look. I've lived in worse looking places. Besides, smoke leaking from the fireplace and barbecue will stain the wood. I wouldn't do anything until spring."

"You sure have learned how to dance around with your answers."

"Pentagon training and the survival tools of a male in marriage."

"Is everyone still coming?"

"They're looking forward to it."

"Has Lisa phoned?"

"This afternoon. Boys are bathed and ready for bed. Why don't you tuck them in while I serve dinner."

Bobbie Jean smiled, "Hope you like soup and salad. Cold weather makes me hungry for a big pot of beef vegetable with lots of noodles."

"You didn't answer when I mentioned buying a Border collie. A good dog will offer protection when I'm not around."

"You'll have to take care of him."

"Me and the boys. A barking dog will keep intruders away."

"And herd your sheep to shelter when it's snowing. Major Black phoned before you arrived home. He wants you to call him before ten tonight. I was so worried about your missing sheep and your driving through the storm, it slipped my mind."

"Did he mention a subject?"

"No, but he lives in Springfield and the snow is getting deeper."

"Probably wants me to cover for him at the committee meeting tomorrow."

"As long as you don't have to work another Saturday."

"Soup is delicious. Family recipe?"

"Whatever is left over and stock."

• • •

Paddy Black was worried, "Can you believe this snow?"

"After three years in Nebraska, yes. What's up?"

"Roads are blocked. I barely made it home. Can you take my place at the committee meeting tomorrow? I'll never make it there through this snow."

"What time?"

"Nine o'clock. I'll phone ahead and let them know you're my replacement."

"Any special instructions?"

"Make like a recorder and ask for a time out if anyone attempts to pull a fast one on us."

"Do the right thing."

"What do you mean by that."

"Nothing—just an old saying that popped into my mind."

As I hung up, Bobbie Jean asked, "Are you going to check on your sheep?"

"I'll wait awhile and throw another log into your pot-bellied stove fires. Don't want our pipes to freeze."

"What did Major Black say to you?"

"Wants me to take his place at the agency tomorrow. He doesn't think he'll be able to make it there."

"The way the snow is blowing, you'll need a four-wheel drive to get out of our lane."

"We should buy one."

"We'll talk about it after you try another variation of my Irish coffee."

"Not Herbie's?"

"See if you like it?"

"Creamy and very smooth."

"What's the difference."

"Lighter beans and our favorite moonshine. How about a four-wheel drive Jeep station wagon?"

"Have you gone eastern."

"Of course not. We don't own horses. What do you want to cook for our friends Saturday night?"

"Barbecue ribs and beans?"

"To messy. I'll marinate steak and you can prepare beans."

"Beans, beans what a wonderful fruit."

"The more you eat, the more you toot."

"The more you toot, the better you feel."

"Why can't we have beans for every meal?"

• • •

Bobbie Jean nudged my arm with her elbow, "Wake up. We both fell asleep in front of the fire. It's late. You check on your sheep while I turn down our bed."

"Forgot to ask. Does the vent work in the stable?"

"Fan was wired Monday. It will take out the excess smoke from your barbecue or the fireplace. Look outside, it's really coming down. We may not have to worry about what to cook Saturday."

"Don't know about Saturday, tomorrow is the problem."

"You'll get to try out the snow blade on our tractor. Make sure you don't dig into the packed stone."

• • •

I bundled up in outer garments still damp from my last trip outside. Snow was now blowing horizontal as the noreaster cranked up. For a minute I felt like I was back in the Aleutians. It was difficult to tell if this was new snow or snow that had all ready fallen. I searched for the stables. Finally found them when I was less than ten feet away. My sheep were huddled together, warm as toast under the lean-to. They were covered with only a light skiff of the white stuff. Our Scandinavian stoves were living up to their billing, but I added one more log to fire anyway. All was secure.

Bobbie Jean called out, "Close the door to the mud room. The cold air is whistling up our chimney. How are the sheep?"

"Huddled together under the lean-to and warm as toast."

"Come to bed, my toes are cold."

"I was afraid of that. Right after I bank our fire and secure the screen." I knew, when the fire went out we'd lose heat as interior air flowed up the chimney.

I undressed and hung up my clothes to Bobbie Jean's laughter, "Dry your hair. It's covered with snow."

"Now you know what I'll look like when I'm old and gray. Set the alarm for six. I have a lot of clearing to do if I want to get out of our lane."

"Don't you remember, you left your car at the bottom of the hill"

"I'll have to be careful not to cover it up."

• • •

After making coffee, checking on my sheep and stoking the pot-bellied stoves, I started the tractor and attached the blade. While it was warming up, I ducked back into the stables and warmed my fingers around a mug of hot coffee I had warming on top of one of the pot-bellied stoves. "Damn it's cold. And I left the farm so I wouldn't have to work outside in this kind of weather."

I hopped back up on the tractor under stars blinking brightly on a cold, crystal clear morning sky. The noreaster had roared through and now snow was blowing into frozen drifts. A razor sharp wind from the northwest cut through my jacket like frozen glass. Snow drifted back as soon as my blade pushed it away. I made three unsuccessful round trips before returning the tractor to the barn. I poured fresh water for our sheep and retrieved my coffee mug from the top of a pot-bellied stove. Shivering through the snow, I entered the mud room.

Bobbie Jean took the coffee mug out of my frozen fingers and refilled it, "You look like Jack Frost."

"I feel like Scott."

"Who is that, Sir Walter?"

"No, the Scott who froze to death on his way back from the South Pole."

"How did our Scandinavian stoves do last night?"

"Still hot this morning, but the room temperature was down to fifty degrees."

"We can either be rustic or insulate. Are you going to try plowing snow again?"

"Not unless the wind slows down. Like plowing water out there. Looks like I'm going to miss the committee meeting."

"How about breakfast?"

"Bacon and eggs?"

"And I have pancakes on the way."

"You are becoming a Yankee wife."

"I draw the line at home fries. Peek in on the boys and see if they're awake."

"Will do. Have they given the weather forecast."

"Look outside. It's freezing."

Both boys were sound asleep. Nanny shooed me away when I lingered too long in the doorway watching them. Bobbie Jean asked, "Are you going to be underfoot all day?"

"More snow on the way?"

"No, but the town is shut down. All government offices are closed until Monday morning."

"That takes care of my meeting. The boys are asleep, but Nanny is awake."

"I'll set three plates on the table while you throw another log on the fire."

• • •

It was midday Saturday before most of Virginia's main roads were cleared. Heavy frozen snow and ice, tossed by snow plows, blocked the entrance to my lane. I almost flipped my tractor, pushing snow away from the entrance into the ditch. As the tractor rotated backward on its wheels, I pushed the clutch in. The front end dropped down and the tractor slid sideways into the ditch. I eased it out slowly, creeping upward in low gear. Once warned twice cautious—I pushed snow to the sides and over the road into the opposite drainage ditch. After parking the tractor back in the barn—I freed my car from the snow.

Bobbie Jean helped me out of my coat, "I watched you try to make a sled out of your tractor. Be careful out there."

"Almost flipped it over on top of me. Been awhile since I've handled those big back wheels under these conditions. Can our guests make it up the lane tonight?"

"Not without four-wheel drive. I'll phone and tell them to park at the bottom of the hill. The surface will freeze solid before the sun sets."

"Are you going to build a fire in the fireplace to warm up the stables"

"I restoked the stoves. I'll set a fire about thirty minutes before they arrive."

"We're going to dine there. Better start it at five. Do you want to invite Major Black?"

"Not with this group. I'd rather not talk office politics. Let's keep it friendly."

• • •

Tucker and Lisa were the first to arrive, almost. He failed to take my instructions and attempted to drive up the hill. As a result, he stuck the rear end of his Packard convertible into the snow bank I made clearing the lane. I slid down hill on shoe leather to help, but was too late. Tucker stuck his convertible's rear end deeper into the snow bank, trying to break free.

"Tucker, hold on while I get my tractor out. Lisa, take my arm and I'll help you up the hill.

When I returned, Tucker had his car's rear end stuck even deeper into the bank, his Packard looked like a cork in a bottle.

He leaned out the window, "Pull me to the top. I should be able to navigate my way down hill when we leave."

"If you could navigate, you'd still be in the Air Force."

I attached my log chain to his front axle, "Put it in low and don't gun it. My tractor will act as an anchor. Use idle speed and try not to brake. If you begin to slide, steer in the direction of your slide." His pink Packard convertible popped out of the snow bank like a champagne cork under pressure. Reminiscent of a Hal Roach silent movie comedy, Tucker gunned his engine instead of using idle. He alternated driving up the chain and sliding backwards, turning in the opposite direction of his slide. Tuckers trip uphill on my icy lane was like a sidewinder slithering over hot desert sand, careening off the snow banks on both sides of my lane.

Bidwell and his wife drove into our lane as Tucker's stuttering stop and go climb up the hill was in progress. He waited until Tucker turned off his engine before engaging four-wheel drive and climbing the hill. As Bidwell helped his wife out of his Jeep station wagon, he called over, "Has your friend ever thought of driving a cab. He'd do great driving in downtown DC."

"Do you recognize the pink Packard convertible?"

Bidwell stopped in his tracks, "Is that Bonnie's pink and white psychedelic cloud?"

"Fully restored by an ardent lover of antique autos."

Tucker retrieved two gallon bottles of wine from his trunk, "Just shorten that to lover. Is this the previous owner?"

"No, Bidwell is more like a used car dealer."

"No way, I won it fair and square in a poker game."

"And like Ali Babba, thirty-nine more used cars, an entire lot in New Mexico. Mr. and Mrs. Bidwell meet Tucker Tubbs of the *Washington Post*. Come on inside and get warm. What kind of wine is that, Tuck?"

"The type we serve at weddings and funerals. It has a cork in it."

"In a gallon jug?"

"On sale in DC."

As is always the case, we adjourned to the kitchen. I poured while introductions were made by Bobbie Jean. I handed the ladies a glass of white wine and mugs of

English ale to Tucker and Bidwell, "We're going to have a cookout in our stable. Bobbie Jean wants to show it off. She just had it remodeled."

Bidwell grinned, "Can't you afford dining room furniture?"

"Wait until you see her stable."

Tucker feigned shock, "My God we're cooking horse meet."

I needled right back, "Tonight we're all going to eat a little crow."

Tucker laughed, "Touché! Now I remember Bidwell. I met him in Omaha. He introduced me to the sergeant in personnel that sold me my pink Packard cloud, a real collector's item. Did you know it's worth five time more than what I paid for it?"

Bidwell breathed a sigh of relief, barely audible under his breath. "When you purchased it, Johnny's and my stock in the Air Force shot up five-hundred percent. It was a win-win deal for all three of us. Nice place you have here, Johnny. Are you going to show off your twins?"

Bobbie Jean broke in, "Johnny, take the steaks out to the stable and start the fire. I'll show our guests to the boy's playroom."

After the flames were almost out, I adjusted the coals, tenting them so they would all catch on. Bobbie Jean opened the stable door, leading a pack train of guests each carrying a portion of our evening meal.

She whispered to me, "Do you know where I stored the wine out here?"

I nodded, "No" and she pointed to a storage locker, which at one time held grooming equipment, "We'll use Mr. Tubbs' wine for cooking."

Tucker accepted a refill, "You didn't tell me that Bidwell is the world's greatest card player. Winning an entire used car lot is quite a feat."

"I wouldn't be one if I admitted it. I really like your spread, Johnny. Forty acres in McLean, Bobbie Jean hasn't lost her business touch. I purchased several farms over in Potomac. Do you know where the Gore Mansion is?"

"Senator Gore's place? North of Congressional Country Club on Potomac Road?"

"Right, in that area. Good place to raise kids and it should be a good investment."

"How about your Roswell real estate?"

"I sold everything except my ranch near Riudoso before Walker closed. Got lucky, even I didn't expect Senator Chavez would die. Losing the Armed Services Committee Chairman was Walker's death knell."

"Coals are ready. I better start cooking steaks or we won't have solid food tonight."

• • •

After dinner, the ladies adjourned to the kitchen in the farmhouse while we pulled our chairs in a semicircle in front of the stable fireplace. I poured cognac and Bidwell offered us each a cigar. Tucker declined, but I didn't, "Not often I have a chance to smoke a gourmet cigar. These look like they're from Cuba. Isn't that against the law?"

Bidwell leaned over, "Don't ask."

"Don't tell."

We lit up and stared at the fire for what seemed like an hour, but was more like five minutes.

Tucker broke our silence, "Well, troops, how does it feel to know what the power structure is doing in Washington and not being able to do anything about it?"

I nodded, "And we're middle managers. Imagine how LeMay and the Joint Chiefs feel. They have an accountant for a boss, who is attempting to reduce their job to numbers."

Bidwell asked Tucker, "Where did you meet Johnny?"

"On his first day at Nav training, south of Houston. He made it through by the skin of his teeth while I was fortunate enough to depart early and avoid the rush."

I added, "The bums rush."

"Johnny mentioned that you're well connected with the brass, even played poker with our president."

"Mostly when he was with Mr. Sam. Met Lyndon in Dallas a few times at Mr. Sam's game. Later in Austin when he came by himself. This cognac is top drawer."

"Thank Bobbie Jean. She stocks our liquor locker. You'll have to try some of her moonshine."

"I still remember the bottle she gave me in New Mexico."

Bidwell blew a smoke ring toward the embers, "Mr. Sam held his cards close to the chest. Lyndon, well he was a risk taker."

Tucker asked, "Have you been paying attention to the war in Southeast Asia?"

"Hard not too. All of the brass I play poker with are involved."

"What do you think about it?"

"It's like a boulder rolling downhill, gaining momentum and out of control. We'll be crushed big time if we don't get out of the way."

"Are we going to stay out?"

"Doesn't look like it. Most of the wheels I know spend all of their time trying to figure out how to find and fight an elusive force. Outside of LeMay, I don't think a one of them has looked into whether we should be there or not. They leave that up to the civilians."

"What do you think?"

"Only way we can win is with our troops. If we use just a little more force each time the enemy attacks, we'll be in that jungle forever. A stupid way to fight. If it were me I'd either kick ass or get out."

"Is LeMay going to retire?"

"All the signs say Iron Ass will be gone in sixty days, maybe sooner."

"Iron Ass?"

"A nickname he picked up early in World War II. LeMay could sit in the left seat and fly an airplane for hours without getting up. That war has been over for twenty years. Looks to me like LeMay is the only one who hasn't forgotten how to win. Troops today call him one tough son of a bitch, but not to his face."

"What do you think of him?"

"I always thought he was ten feet tall, until I met him in person. He's barely over five feet, but when he enters a room the walls part. He has that much charisma. Have you met him?"

"Interviewed him a few times and you're-right about his charisma. How about you, Johnny?"

"The only thing LeMay and I have in common is graduating from ROTC at Ohio State. How about a refill?" Tucker nodded, "No, have to navigate back to the Watergate."

"Coffee, then?"

I pulled on an oven mitt and lifted my Grandmother's granite-ware coffee pot off the charcoal grill. The coffee came out steaming hot, "Even bad coffee tastes good brewed over an open grill. Must be the residual smoke."

Tucker took a sip, "You're right, but is it ever hot. What about CINCSAC?"

I looked up, "General Powers? He retired in November. Didn't three fingered Jack take over? He's a warrior, but lacks LeMay's clout."

Bidwell nodded in agreement, "Plays a pretty mean game of poker, too."

Tucker was in his question mode, "Lots of turmoil in the Air Force, guys. Any reason for it?"

I answered, "LeMay was given a new term as chief. Powers didn't have anywhere to go except out."

Bidwell added, "And when McNamara canceled SAC's supersonic bomber, the B-70, Powers was miffed. Air Force is losing funding for new planes."

I offered, "McNamara is doing his Coolidge imitation. More coffee?"

Tucker held out his cup, "What does LeMay think about Vietnam?"

"You all ready know that."

"From official documents, yes, but Bidwell may have some off the cuff remarks."

He looked at me, "Can I speak freely?"

"As long as it isn't classified or official data."

"He believes we're going to hell in a hand basket. His thoughts mirror mine."

"What about the rest of your fearless leaders?" Bidwell looked down at the embers, "I'm leaving the service after this hitch. I've seen too much and know too much. We're going to have a whole new generation of book smart, life stupid bosses. Maybe it's the aphrodisiac of power here in Washington. Did you two ever read *The Devil and Daniel Webster*? Well, this town is like that. Some folks would rather sell their souls than give up being near the center of power."

Tucker nodded, "And it's especially true over at the White House. What about our foreign policy?"

Bidwell shook his head, "I'm in serious disagreement over the way it is heading. We'll go broke trying to police the world. I don't mind dying in another country if we're helping defend it from barbarians, but a civil war? Not my cup of tea."

"Can it be turned around?"

"You're asking a sergeant who manages an athletic center and plays a little poker with the brass some very tough questions. Look, if we continue to let whiz kids experiment with live soldiers we're going to wind up with a lot of dead ones. And I do mind dying if I'm being led by commanders who fail to learn from history. It's your turn in the barrel. How about the *Post*?"

Tucker stood up, "Pour me another cup of coffee while I see a man about a horse. I'll answer your question when I return."

Tucker placed another log on the fire, "Coffee's great, but in cold weather, goes right through me. My newspaper supports the president and his policy. We're democratic and so is he. I call it our head in the sand editorial policy, but I'm in the minority. If and when we run into trouble, we'll make like a weather vane and go in a new direction. Johnny, are you going to hang it up?"

"I've thought about it. I will when I can't do my job, tell the truth or keep the troops I support from being sent on fool's missions. Even if we don't agree with our current policy, someone has to stand watch. But I know sheep and I won't be one. If the guy at the top leads us to pasture, water and safety, I'll follow. If he leads us off a cliff, I'll watch. So far Vietnam isn't our war, but if we do go in, someone will have to warn our folks where the enemy is. That's where I come in."

"How about his plans?"

"Intentions? If we could collect intentions there'd be no wars."

"Only if we believe what we see. Our state department has a tendency to see what they believe."

"Time to adjourn before we all decide to fall on our swords.

As we stood up to leave, the door to the stable opened. Bobbie Jean entered, shivering, "Are you going to join us or stay out here all night?"

Like three lost sheep, we followed her back to the farmhouse. She asked Bidwell, "Do you still have a federal gambling stamp?"

"Never can tell when a game will get busted. That stamp has saved me more than a few times. When I hold a high stakes game and the local law drops by, my stamp and a few dollars usually will do the trick. But you know more about local law than me, you own a casino."

"We may make and sell whiskey in a dry state today, but after Estes Kefauver's committee persecuted the Gulf Coast, our casinos were closed. I have dessert waiting for you in the kitchen and real New Orleans coffee, not that dishwater Johnny has been serving you."

We entered the kitchen through the mud room, stomping snow off our feet. Tucker warmed his hands around a mug of Bobbie Jean's coffee, "This is smooth. What did you put in it?"

"A little bit of this and a little bit of that." I handed him a bottle of her Mississippi moonshine, "This is a little bit of that."

"Moonshine? With a black Mississippi State liquor stamp on the bottle?" Bobbie Jean smiled, "Now, don't you pick on us poor Southerners. After your Yankee Reconstruction, we only had a limited number of ways to make money. Do you like the taste of our limited effort?"

"This whiskey is better than any I've ever tasted."

"I can give each of you several bottles, but that is all. It's a limited run." Bidwell asked, "How old is it?"

"Over twelve years, I think. What does the stamp say?"

"Fifteen."

She took Bidwell's hand, "You look down. Did Mr. Tubbs pick on you?"

"Tucker? He sure did, but that's not the reason. I have to give up poker games at the NCO' Club on payday."

I couldn't let that pass, "You can still belong after you retire."

"I'll be an entrepreneur, no longer a sergeant. It wouldn't be right."

Bobbie Jean asked, "Can't you find another place to play?"

"Congressional Country Club, but it won't be the same."

"Do you have a membership?"

"Family and a single membership at Burning Tree. It's restricted to men, only."

"Is it a complete club?"

"Strictly golf. The clubhouse looks like an old Civilian Conservation Corps mess hall. Your stable would make a great place for a game."

"It would, wouldn't it, but I think not. You would be too close to home. You mentioned your farms in Potomac. Why not there?"

"Same reason, too close to home. We better get on the road. It's getting late. I'll follow Tucker down the hill. After what I saw of his driving when we arrived, I don't want to be in front of his Packard."

I turned away, so I wouldn't have to see carnage, as Tucker's Packard slid sideways down the hill. By some miracle of Physics, he was able to do a two hundred and seventy degree sliding turn and exit our lane onto the road head first. Luckily there was no one coming. This time Tucker turned the right way and sped off with a wave, tires spinning on ice. Bidwell followed after Tucker, creeping slowly down the hill. Bobbie Jean huddled close as we watched the last of our guests exit the lane.

She was still shivering as we entered the house, "I like Bidwell, but stay away from his gambling activity."

"That's why we're good friends, neither one of us believes in gambling."

"Does he manipulate the cards?"

"Only to help a loser win, but never for himself. Doesn't have to. After the Black Jack lesson he gave on our way up to Wichita, I'll never even think about playing a serious game of chance again."

"With that much skill, he must be a mechanic."

"Only to be able to spot those who are."

• • •

LeMay retired quietly, on a cold blustery winter day in late January. America's military was prepared to willingly accept civilian micro-management of a war lost before it began. Longing to be near the center and overcome by the aphrodisiac of power, translucent generals were now in charge, but McNamara was in command.

*"How the creatures order one about, and make one repeat lessons!" thought Alice. "I might as well be at school at once."*

# Chapter 17

I wondered, "Am I the only one who noticed unusual activity at the gazebo refreshment stand in the Pentagon's center courtyard?" It closed in November and wouldn't open again until spring. I had to ask myself, "Then why all the apparent activity?"

I tried one of their hamburgers last fall, soon after I arrived. Hockey puck is what comes to mind when I recall that unpleasant dining experience. As we walked to the POAC, I mentioned this activity to Paddy Black. His response was, "Haven't noticed anything unusual. Maybe they're doing repairs."

"I hope it's to the cook. If DC ever gets a hockey team, I've found a source for inexpensive pucks."

"Got to admit, it's in a great location."

"In our gazebo's case, location isn't everything."

"Do you think you're ready to take over at the agency?"

"I'm going to fly solo?"

"It's time. I'll brief you in when we get back to the office."

Bidwell looked up when I knocked on his door, "You're finally getting with it."

"You were right. Exercise is the only way to stay sane around here. What do you know about the gazebo in the center courtyard?"

"Great location, lousy food. Hear they're remodeling. How about our friend Gus, the chimp astronaut—is he still hangin' in there?"

"I check everyday, he's still up on the eighth corridor wall. Are you admitting to being the mischievous Pentagon mad art bandit?"

"Knowing you won't turn me in, yes, and knowing how vain pilots are, it won't come down until they paint the walls."

"Speaking of coming down, Have you put in your papers?"

"I retire in August. I am now officially a lame duck."

"I'll buy the lame part. What do you plan to do?"

"Might go into the restaurant business. Tell Bobbie Jean to keep her eyes open for a suitable location."

"What will your theme be?"

"Can't decide if it'll be western or eastern. Have you tried to get a good steak around here?"

"Only ones worth while are at the Jolly Ox."

"Not enough of them around to compete."

"You're on to something."

• • •

Paddy Black was waiting, "What kept you? I've been here for ten minutes."

"Bidwell bent my ear. What did you want to talk about?"

"Your guidance."

"Fire away."

"Do the right thing, carry a briefcase and walk fast."

"I can handle that. So, I'm being thrown to the committee wolves."

"You'll do all right. You know our systems better than most. You won't need to haul along an engineer."

"Knowledge is power."

"That's only your entry. It'll keep you in the game, but politics is your trump card."

"Then I'm a babe in the woods."

"Remember, Chairman and Secretary are both agency."

"And they have a member, too."

"They're all honest brokers, but watch out for NSA, Navy and keep an eye on White House and State. They'll push their own agendas."

"Which is?"

"Navy is only interested in support of the fleet. Damn the torpedoes, full speed ahead mentality. NSA wants to take over our business and freeze everyone else out."

"Is that bad?"

"Damn right it is. Right now they control our collection resources. We do the work, they control the take."

"But, don't we get the information?"

"By the time we do it's history. If they take over, we'll be reading hot off the press documents about British marching on Concord."

"And the White House member?"

"He plays fair except when his people need something from NSA and then he's been known to make a deal."

"Who's the enemy, the Soviets or NSA?"

"Sometimes both. NSA wants to play I've got a secret."

"How did we get in this fix?"

"Consolidation of intelligence resources in Washington under the banner of effective management."

"What about Army?"

"Not organized. They tend to listen and support whomever they can cut a deal with."

"State?"

"They sold out to NSA when they cut back on their internal Intelligence staff."

"What are you going to do now?"

"General is sending me out to take a look at our resources in Germany and Japan."

"Southeast Asia?"

"Can't go there because of our security clearances. Anything I can do for you, let me know."

• • •

With the weather warming up, I could take the shortcut across the center courtyard to get to North Parking. Tonight, I noticed smoke rising from the gazebo chimney.

As I passed by I heard, "Place your bets" and the sound of a roulette wheel spinning. I thought to myself, "Bidwell! Is he trying to commit suicide?" I stopped and listened. I could hear muffled voices and the sound of cards shuffled, "Blackjack, too? In the middle of the Pentagon courtyard? Who would be playing here?" I hurried on. Luckily, no one else seemed to be paying attention.

I didn't wait to change out of my uniform. I found Bobbie Jean in the kitchen, "Roulette, Bobbie Jean, and Blackjack in the courtyard gazebo! Our friend Bidwell is up to something big."

"Did you say a casino in the middle of the Pentagon courtyard?"

"Dead center. Looks like he's trying to hide his game out in the open."

"Why doesn't he take up cliff diving in Acapulco. It's safer. Can't believe he would ask to be raided. How did your day go?"

"I'm on my own at the agency."

"What happened to Major Black?"

"The general is sending him overseas on an inspection tour."

"Are you nervous?"

"Not anymore. Most of the committee members don't have a clue about what's going on, I have a leg up. How was your day?"

"Boys are doing fine. Lisa phoned. She wants to use our stable for their wedding."

"Did she say when it will be?"

"Spring."

"Is right around the corner. Oh, almost forgot, Bidwell is retiring in August. He wants to talk to you about the restaurant business."

"And I almost forgot. Tucker wants you to phone him. He'll be at his work number until eleven tonight."

"Did he say what he wants to talk about?"

"Something about weather vanes."

• • •

Tucker answered his phone, "Johnny?"

"What's up at the *Post*, Tuck?"

"Our weather vane has switched one hundred and eighty degrees. The winds of war are changing our editorial board's opinion about Vietnam. They're sending me back to Saigon. Flying out in the morning. Tell Bobble Jean the wedding will have to go on hold until I return." I figured now was not the time to tell Tucker that she had just found out we were holding it and didn't know when, "How long will you be gone?"

"Two, three months at the most."

"Why is the *Post*'s military editor pulling up stakes and folding his tent?"

"My Vietnamese and Vietcong connections. Our editorial board wants to know who we'll be up against if we take over the war."

"You could tell them that today."

"I've all ready got it written, but don't you remember?"

"What?"

"My third law. Motion is work." I had to laugh, "We're living proof of that."

"Paddy Black may be in Japan if you stop by on your way over."

"Black? Air Force Intelligence?"

"Right, do you know him?"

"I'll contact him through his detachment commander at Ben Hoa Air Base."

"Don't you mean Fuchu Air Station in Japan?"

"No, you really do have a lot to learn."

"If you need help back here, you know who to call."

"I have Bidwell's phone number. Got to go. Take care of Lisa."

• • •

Tucker was right, I was learning more than I needed too.

Bobbie Jean shooed me out of the kitchen, "Change out of that dreadful uniform for dinner. Hurry back and tell me what smiley face wanted."

"Not to be called smiley face."

I returned in more comfortable attire, "As I was saying," and gave her a hug, "Tucker is being sent to Saigon by the *Post*. He'll be over there for two to three months. Said to tell you the wedding will be delayed."

"So far, all I know is where it will be held, not when, so it won't interfere with any of our plans."

"What about your mother's plans for our wedding at the Lee Mansion in June?"

"You won't believe this, it slipped my mind. I've been married to a sweet Yankee boy long enough not to be enthused by mother's foolishness."

I held her in my arms, "Are we having fun, yet?" She gently pushed me away, "Not until after dinner. It will get cold."

"I hope not."

She scolded me, "I mean dinner."

"I have tamed a Southern lady."

"Lucky for you, you didn't say shrew. But, you're right about being a homebody. I've learned to appreciate caring for someone I love."

• • •

All through March the gazebo chimney stood silent, cold as the slate gray days. I looked in when I had time, which wasn't often. Day after day of mind numbing committee meetings at the agency occupied most of my time.

The last Friday in March, when dogwoods were in full bloom, I confided in Bobbie Jean, "Now I understand why Paddy gave this job away. By Friday afternoon, I'd rather jump off a building than sit through another committee meeting."

"Why don't you resign. We don't need the money."

"What can I do? I've had on the job training to be a shepherd or what I'm doing now. And I've seen enough sheep to last a lifetime."

"Why don't we open a restaurant here or in Biloxi?"

"From what I've seen of that life, it's twelve hour days, seven days a week. While we're on the subject, you ought to sell our share of the River Boat to Herbie and the Chef."

"You must have second sight. Herbie phoned this afternoon and made an offer hard for us to refuse."

"Call him back and take him up on it. It was fair, wasn't it?"

"More than fair, but we'll have to reinvest or be stuck with a large tax bill."

"Remember what I said about Bidwell? He would like to open a steak house and asked for your help."

"What does he need?"

"He said location, but I imagine he could use your advice on every aspect. What is our profit from the Omaha venture?"

"Two dollars on every dollar we invested."

"Why so high?"

"Business has been gangbusters since they opened their doors. They began serving lunch last week and had to start taking reservations. The Omaha bank we use did an extensive financial survey on its prospects and is eager to lend money on the buyout."

"As conservative as those folks are, it must be doing well. I'll check on the boys if you'll pour me another glass of red wine."

"Your favorite!"

"And with a cork!"

Bobbie Jean handed me a platter, "Speaking of steaks. The coals in our stable grill should be about right by now. I'll bring the salad and bread."

I had the steaks on the grill when she lightly kicked the stable door with her foot and I opened it for her.

She was carrying a basket, "It's heavy."

I lifted it, "It is. Where do you want it?"

"On the bar."

"I was wondering when you would mention it. Must be antique. Where did you find it?"

"Came out of an older hotel in Washington. Lisa found it on one of her antique rounds."

"It's huge, must have room for thirty stools. Are you going to open a restaurant in our stable?"

"Of course not. Not that I didn't think about it, but it's too close to home."

"And too far away from the center of town."

"It won't be in twenty years. Do you think we should go into business with Bidwell?"

"We can do that. He needs more help than he thinks he does."

"I think he'll be a good manager, but we must insist on a no gambling clause. If he isn't interested in a partnership, I can get backers from New Orleans."

"Why not go it alone?"

"You have a lot to learn about business, Johnny. It's prudent to spread the risk among at least two, maybe three owners."

"Speaking of risk, our steaks need to be turned over."

I liked what I saw, "Steaks smell good."

"I used lemon, soy, Worcestershire sauce, garlic and ground pepper in my marinade. What do you like in a steak house?"

I didn't hesitate, "Remember the one on the way to Hondo, New Mexico?"

"The Silver Dollar bar?"

"That's the one. All they served was steak or lobster on the grill. We should keep it simple, with reasonable prices."

"You are ready to fly solo."

"I was thinking of a little Italian."

"Dinner first, dessert second."

"We are getting to be old married folks."

"Better check on your steaks."

"They're ready, are you?"

"Bring them over here. We'll eat at the bar. Need a refill?"

"Does a duck need wings?"

"Have you heard from Major Black?"

"He returned from Europe last week and left for Japan Monday. He almost went ballistic when I asked him what he knew about our Saigon Detachment."

"The one at the Air Base?"

"Yes. He refused to answer my question."

"Did you tell him Tucker is on his way to Saigon?"

"Didn't get a chance."

As we sat down to eat Bobbie Jean asked, "Have you given any more thought to resigning?"

"Checked into it. Can't. Not until I serve the two year commitment they levied on me when we accepted this assignment and I might have another year after I pin on my promotion."

"When will you know?"

"Sometime next week."

"The witching hour is nigh."

"And our steaks are getting cold."

"Will you see Bidwell?"

"Monday noon when I go to the POAC."

"If he brings it up, offer to go in on his restaurant."

• • •

Bidwell called before ten Monday morning, "If you're not busy, come on down."

"Anything important?"

"We need to talk."

He met me at the POAC door, "They're going to have another cattle call."

"Is this about Southeast Asia?"

"Yes, can you get word to your friend Tucker?"

"He's in Saigon, but before he left, he said you have his phone number. I'm in the dark. What's going on?"

"My poker playing friends say we're going to take over the fight."

"Tucker said the same thing before he left. That's why the *Post* sent him to Saigon."

"Then he doesn't need me."

"Tucker likes to have as many sources as possible. If it's heating up over there, he may need you're connections."

"Maybe, planning is for officers, execution is for sergeants."

"What about the cattle call?"

"Everyone of our Commanders is going to poll his troops for volunteers to go to Vietnam."

"Are you going to pull your retirement papers and volunteer?"

"You still have a lot to learn, Johnny. Sergeants run this man's Air Force. I talk weekly with my counterparts at Ben Hoa."

"And what do they say?"

"It is not a healthy place to visit. The Vietcong is everywhere and everybody. They not only own the countryside, they're the real estate agents in the cities. Our State Department is propping up a piss-ant government. Let me get you a cup of coffee. I need one, badly."

When Bidwell returned I asked, "Fess up. What's going on at the gazebo in the center courtyard?"

"Just a little going away present for a three star who's after me."

"Is that why I heard a roulette wheel and card noise?"

"I'll have to improve security. How did you find out?"

"I must be the only one in the Pentagon that doesn't walk around with my head in the clouds and my eyes on my shoes. You have smoke coming out of the chimney, be careful. This is federal property."

"My prints are wiped clean. Don't worry, this one is a set up. Nothing illegal is going on. Did you ask Bobbie Jean about my restaurant idea?"

"She's got you one better. Would you like a partner?"

"I was afraid to ask. With your twins, she has to be very busy. How much control does she want?"

"Forty-nine percent and the right to sell out to you or your designee after one year. You can use her expertise in design, construction and set up. Can you get the liquor license and zoning wavers if they're needed?"

"Piece of cake. That's a load off my mind."

"How soon do you want to start?"

"Now, I'll take terminal leave the first of July and give it my full attention. Tell her it's a deal."

"Where do you think you should build?"

"Not in DC. Even I don't have any clout, there."

"Maryland?"

"Too many trees and almost as crooked as DC."

"That leaves Virginia and the nations largest good old boy network."

When I returned to my cubicle, a note was on my desk.

*Major Paddy Black is missing. While traveling with a* Washington Post *reporter from Ben Hoa Air Base to Saigon, his vehicle was attacked by unknown assailants. Bodies were not found. Search and rescue efforts are underway.*

"Bidwell, this is Johnny. Bad news, Paddy Black's vehicle was ambushed between Ben Hoa and Saigon. Tucker may have been riding with him."

"Are they alive?"

"Don't know. Paddy is listed as missing. Can you help?"

"Tall order for someone in the basement of the Pentagon. I'll phone my contact at Ben Hoa and get the details, but search and rescue missions are too hard from here."

"I apologize for asking a stupid question. I should know better. I'm out of pocket this afternoon. See what you can find out. I'll phone you at home, tonight."

"What if I need to contact you?"

"Can't, have a meeting up river."

"You spooks talk in code."

"At the agency north of here."

"Understand. I'll get you the real skinny, but any action by me to retrieve them is out of the question. Your boys may be in over their ears. The Vietcong have wild eyed ideologue spear carriers."

• • •

The drive north on the George Washington Parkway cleared my mind of worry about my friend. The dogwoods were in full bloom. Virginia was enjoying a spectacular spring. More so, along the Potomac River. Winter's cold lingered on west of the Blue Ridge, but spring was in full bloom here. I returned to the real world after turning off of the Parkway at the Fairbanks Highway Research Station sign and stepping off the elevator on the seventh floor, the last committee member to arrive. The Secretary nodded in my direction and placed a check mark next to my name. Our Chairman motioned for me to sit next to him.

He whispered, "Major Black is missing in Vietnam. Our director is very concerned. Paddy should not have gone there. Not with the sensitive data he has handled. Our director has talked to your general. We are going to take extreme action to insure that Paddy is not interrogated or transferred North. Don't speak about this with anyone, not even our committee."

"Rescue?"

"If possible."

"If not?"

"Don't ask."

"Don't tell."

• • •

Bobbie Jean sat rocking, in one of our rocking chairs on the front porch, tapping her foot. As I walked up the steps, I knew I was married when she greeted me with, "You're late."

"Sorry, had to haul my classified back to the Pentagon. Got held up by a wreck in the southbound lane on the parkway. Bad news, Paddy Black's vehicle was ambushed outside of Saigon."

"Is he alive?"

"Missing along with a *Washington Post* reporter who was with him."

"My God, not our Mr. Tubbs."

"Tucker has friends among the Vietcong. If it was him, he'll have to spend a chip to get free. Bidwell is checking on their status with a contact at Ben Hoa."

"He phoned an hour ago. Call him at home."

• • •

"Got your message. What did you find out?"

"The *Post* reporter is Tucker. He's in the hospital at Ben Hoa."

"Was he injured."

"No, standard procedure to make sure he's okay."

"And give the medics something to do. Did you talk with him?"

"Roger that. Is your friend more than a little off center?"

"That's normal for Tucker. What did he have to say."

"That he was lucky this was a high level job and not a random one by Vietcong peasants. They recognized him and let him go."

"How about Paddy?"

"He got nicked."

"Nicked?"

"Nack Paddy Black."

"Bobbie Jean is training you. Where did he get nicked?"

"Bullet creased the top of his head. Tucker said Paddy was alive when they hauled him away. The ambush was a case of mistaken identity. They were after a South Vietnamese colonel who was supposed to be on the road at about the same time."

"How did they make that mistake?"

"Tucker had the colonel's driver. He got the colonel drunk when he was pumping him for information at a bar near our embassy. Tucker used the colonel's staff car to pick up Paddy at Ben Hoa."

"Can you hold for a minute. I want to let Bobbie Jean know Tucker is okay."

"Thanks for waiting. She wants you to know you can have any percentage you want, your deal is sealed. Is there anything else?"

"Tucker made an arrangement with the Vietcong to get Paddy Black back."

"Did he have to pay ransom?"

"No, not even the Vietcong will screw around with the *Post*. They don't want bad press."

"Is Paddy okay?"

"The bullet probably saved him. You spooks are lucky. It scrambled his brain. Doesn't know who he is or where he is. So he's of no value to the Vietcong. Can you get in touch with anyone high up in the agency?"

"My committee chairman is connected."

"Tucker said the next twenty-four hours are critical. He doesn't want anyone to show any more interest in Paddy than normal. If they do, the deal will go south. Tucker will be in harms way and Paddy will be on a plane to the Soviet Union."

"Did Tucker say when he's returning?"

"No, but he wants Bobbie Jean to tell Lisa the wedding is on for mid-May."

"Is he certain Paddy will be returned in good shape?"

"Returned, yes. In good shape is a problem."

• • •

I phoned Ops at the agency and got a phone patch to the committee chairman at his home. I was carrying coals to Newcastle. He knew the details, but twenty-four hours was all the agency was willing to wait. "I'll phone my contact."

"We would rather that you didn't. Our people will cooperate with your friend. Come in tomorrow."

"I have a meeting at eight. I can be there by ten."

"Stop at the front desk. They'll give you directions. Johnny?"

"Yes, sir."

"The director wants you to keep all of this close hold."

That was easy to do. I didn't know any more than the extraneous data we discussed,

"Will do. I have to let my boss know about Paddy's status."

"Keep it to that."

•  •  •

My immediate boss wasn't happy about receiving a phone call at home. His only response was, "How did you get involved?"

I couldn't say how, so I answered, "I'm not. I'm just the messenger."

"Who did you get the message from?"

"I'm not free to say."

"Our general shoots messengers. Come directly to my office when you arrive tomorrow."

"What about my eight o'clock?"

"It's canceled."

•  •  •

Bobbie Jean knocked on the doorway, "Are you finished? I'm starved. Change your clothes, we're going to try a steakhouse in Arlington."

"Roger that, looks like I'm finished in more ways than one."

"When you're given a hot potato, pass it on before you get burnt."

"This one came with handcuffs. Is it coat and tie or casual?"

"Coat, tie is optional. Hurry."

•  •  •

Our morning *Post* arrived early, in the ditch by the side of our lane, as usual. I opened it to page one with one hand and poured coffee with the other. I almost dropped the pot. The story of Tucker's capture and release was on page one with his byline. I scanned it. Tucker kept his word. He didn't mention Paddy.

Bobbie Jean wandered into the kitchen rubbing her eyes, "I thought you would be on the road by now. Is that a story about Mr. Tubbs on the front page?"

"And written by him. Doesn't mention Paddy Black. I'm in no hurry. They canceled my eight o'clock meeting."

"Can they force you out of the service?"

"Not that lucky, I haven't done anything."

"Except have two very eccentric friends. What did you think of the steak house last night?"

"Not very good. You won't have much competition. You and Bidwell have found a niche."

"Can you stay awhile? I'll cook your breakfast?"

"The condemned man's last meal?"

"More like my brave warriors send-off."

•  •  •

I made a mental note to leave for work earlier or later. At seven o'clock, the traffic south on the George Washington Parkway is close to gridlock. And the only parking space was at the far end of North Parking. Far enough away from the POAC entrance to qualify as an aerobic walk. I checked on Gus, our chimpanzee astronaut on my way down corridor eight. He was still hanging in there, in his place of honor with the rest of the Air Force art collection.

As I turned onto A ring, I ran into my boss on his way to the general's office, "Where have you been Ropp? The general's exec. called four times." Before I could say I was stuck in traffic or I could care less, he said, "Stuff your excuses. Come along with me."

We were ushered in, to the front of the general's desk. He laid his copy of the *Post* aside, "So you're the one who arranged for Major Black's release in Vietnam, and from the Pentagon, no less. I don't have to remind you that no good deed goes unpunished." While he took another sip of coffee I attempted to control my fight or flight response.

"I'm in hot water with the CIA director because of your meddling. You're in the military. We play by the rules and you didn't."

I wasn't about to get run over without putting up a fight, "Excuse me, Sir. What am I accused of?"

"None of your damn business. Damned *Washington Post* would screw up a wet dream. You're confined to quarters until I find out who blew the whistle on my operation at Ben Hoa. If I find out it's you, you'll be out of uniform in a week. You're dismissed."

I saluted and did a smart about face. My mind was racing. It was hard to control my fight or flight response and I wasn't doing a very good job of it. My face was as red as a beet. I knew it wouldn't do any good to mention my ten o'clock meeting at the agency to my boss—so I didn't.

"Should I clean out my desk?" I asked.

"Drive your car to the POAC entrance. You'll find my sergeant waiting with your personal items, and Major Ropp?"

"Yes, Sir." I was saying a lot of that this morning.

"Don't bother to return for a visit. We're changing the combination on the vault door."

This certainly was beginning to be a strange day. I was canned before I could reach my cubicle. I drove along the old railroad tracks to the POAC basement door. My personal items were outside in a box. The sergeant who was supposed to be guarding it, wasn't.

• • •

I drove north on the Parkway, enjoying a spectacular spring day, wondering what happened to Paddy Black and what this was all about. Driving off the parkway to the agency is like going from a technicolor movie to a black and white one.

An escort waited for me at the reception desk, "Put your badge on and follow me."

He led me to a special elevator and we descended into the bowels of CIA. I was led through a maze of corridors to a debriefing room. He motioned for me to sit down at a student desk and left me alone. A studious looking lady attached wires and leads to various pressure points on my body.

She checked her equipment, "Relax and answer all of our questions to the best of your ability."

Three hours later, she unhooked the wires, "Thank you Mr. Ropp. That will be all."

"Did I pass?"

She turned away. My escort opened the door, "Follow me." We retraced our steps through the maze and entered a different elevator, one that went from the basement to the seventh floor.

My escort knocked on the door of the deputy director, "Come on in, Colonel Ropp. I've been waiting for you. What do you know about the Paddock in Middleburg?"

"I'm an old farm boy. Isn't that where racehorses are saddled?"

"You have a lot to learn, but from your dossier you look like a quick study."

"You said 'Colonel.'"

"As of this moment you are now a lieutenant colonel and commander of the Air Force detachment at the Paddock."

"Any guidance?"

"Continue as you have."

"Do the right thing."

He looked puzzled so I replied, "It's an old inside joke. When do I report?"

"Monday. Follow your general's orders until then. The director wants to thank you personally. Follow me."

I was as puzzled as I had ever been. I had been threatened with court martial, fired from my job, given a command, promoted and commended, all in the span of one morning and half an afternoon. Tucker's second law—screw up and move up—had to be in play.

The director shook my hand, "Good job, son," and I was out the door. I drove onto the parkway from the black and white world of the agency into technicolor spring.

• • •

Bobbie Jean looked up from her account books, "What are you doing home at this hour of the day?"

I almost said don't ask, "I was fired by the general and hired by the agency."

"Are you still in the Air Force?"

"Must be, I was just promoted to lieutenant colonel and commended by the director."

"What did you do?"

"I don't know."

"Don't ask?"

"Don't tell. That's what the deputy director said."

"Did you hear anything about Major Black, or Mr. Tubbs?"

"Nothing and I'm not supposed to ask."

"Where is your new job."

"I'm commander of a spook outfit called the Paddock in Middleburg, Virginia."

"Out Route 50."

"I guess so. I'm to stay home on vacation until told otherwise. What's really weird is that my general has me under house arrest and the agency has me on paid vacation."

"You must have some idea about what's going on."

"Paddy Black was sent by our general to an Air Force detachment in Vietnam that doesn't exist and without agency clearance. He was captured while riding along with a reporter from the *Washington Post*. I guess my general was caught with his hands in the cookie jar."

"Looks like he has designated you as the stuckee and the agency, a hero. You need insurance."

"In case my general wins out?"

"You are learning."

"I'll call Bidwell."

• • •

Bidwell answered, "Good afternoon, Colonel."

"How did you know?"

"You forget, Sergeants run this man's Air Force. Understand your general is giving you trouble."

"How did you know?"

"Don't ask."

"Don't tell."

"I called in another chip. Don't worry about me burning bridges. I have more than I can spend before I retire. You'll be back to work in the Pentagon tomorrow morning and leaving for Middleburg with honors. Your general won't be around long enough to write your report."

"Political influence?"

"Is there any other kind? I need a favor in return."

"Name it and you have it."

"I want to borrow three of your sheep."

"You've got them. When?"

"Not certain. When you notice they're gone, report them as missing."

"You're not going to use them as part of a Greek festival are you?"

"Of course not and not in a nativity scene, either. I want to keep you in the clear if this goes project goes south."

"Just give me your word that no harm will come to them?"

"Safe as babes in their mothers' arms."

"Don't ask?"

"Don't tell."

• • •

The general's exec called after dinner, "Your security clearances are restored. Report back to work in the morning. The general apologizes for any inconvenience he may have caused."

"Any word on Paddy Black?"

"He's safe, but has no memory. Flying out on medivac. If you have more questions, call me in the morning. Its been a long day and I'm heading home. Let me give you a piece of advice. Keep checking your six."

"Thanks for the warning."

Bobbie Jean asked, "Who was that?"

"The general's exec. All is forgiven. My vacation is over before it began. I report to work in the morning."

"Any word on Major Black?"

"He's safe, but doesn't know who, or where he is."

"He'll fit right in with the rest of your friends."

"I'm going to check on our sheep."

"The lambs are doing fine. Your flock has almost doubled."

• • •

"Sheep are watered and bedded down. Lambs sure are frisky. Is the ram still chasing our boys?"

"And they chase after him. They're both getting a workout. Oh, Herbie phoned from Omaha. Our check is in the mail along with release forms for our signatures. We now have a hefty down payment."

"Have you found a location?"

"In town Arlington."

"Any difficulty with licenses and zoning."

"Bidwell said he'd take care of that. I have to call about the location and see if he approves, anyway."

"Is Virginia a good old boys network?"

"Almost a closed shop. They haven't forgiven you Yankees for stealing West Virginia from them."

• • •

The next morning, my cubicle mates were cordial enough, but that was as far as they went. No one wanted to stand next to a condemned man or building, a stray brick may fall on them. I smiled and said hello to one wave and received barely a grunt of recognition on my way back to my cubicle. I sat down at an empty desk. Everything I didn't take home in the box, except the phone was gone. Fortunately it worked.

It was Bidwell, "Tucker is on his way back."

"He's a month early."

"Lucky to get out alive. The North jumped all over the Cong for giving away Paddy Black. They came after Tucker. Blew his apartment up at the same time he was making a run for Ben Hoa. Hitched a ride out on a transport to Guam."

"Do you know where he is now?"

"Somewhere between Guam and Saudi Arabia."

"He never was one to navigate in a straight line. My sheep are still mowing away. When are you going to borrow them?"

"Soon. Let Bobbie Jean know her Arlington location for our steak house is perfect. Zoning was easy. Licenses are tough to get, but we'll have them before we open."

"How are you going to get them?"

"Don't ask."

"Don't tell."

I leaned back in my chair, looked over a clean, empty desk. I would have looked out a window, if I had one. My new job had not begun and my old one was over. My mates weren't interested in talking to a condemned man and I had nothing to do. I wandered up cubicle row. Most didn't look up and those that did looked away.

My boss stormed out of his office, "Where are you going?"

"Snack bar for a cup of coffee."

"No! come along with me. The general wants to see you." A row of heads popped out of every single cubicle. All eyes were on me, now. Everyone likes to witness a crash, as long as blood doesn't splatter on them.

• • •

The general was all smiles when I entered his office, "You're out of uniform Lieutenant Colonel Ropp. He came around his desk and shook my hand. He pinned one silver leaf on my shoulder while my boss pinned on the other. He sat back down and shuffled through some papers on his desk before looking up, "Oh, don't bother returning to your office. I want you to report to your new job this morning."

Even though I knew, I asked, "Where do I report?"

"I have a staff car waiting for you at River Entrance."

"What about my car?"

"A staff car will bring you back here this afternoon. For now you will simply disappear."

"Can I let my cubicle mates know. I'd like to hold a promotion party."

"I'm afraid not."

"Don't ask."

"Don't tell. That's the spirit. Tell no one in your office about your promotion or your new job."

"Who writes my report."

He looked up and smiled, "I do."

I walked out of his office alone. The general's exec. handed me my hat, "Remember what I said?"

"Watch my six?"

"And seven and eight and nine."

"I'm not long for the Air Force?"

"Worse, he'll keep you with him."

"And get even?"

"Good luck on your new job at the Paddock."

• • •

I walked down the River entrance steps. A driver held the staff car door open. I asked, "Where?"

"West of Middleburg. Nice day for drive."

"Are you going to wait for me?"

"I work for you, Sir."

"Then drive me to my car in North Parking. I'll follow you to the detachment. We'll save you a trip back to the five sided swamp this afternoon."

• • •

Bobbie Jean noticed the silver leaves on my shoulders, "I didn't know you were that old," and gave me a kiss. "How was the Pentagon today?"

"No longer there. Reported to my new job this morning."

"Why didn't you phone?"

"No personal phone calls over long distance lines."

"Not even to the *Washington Post*."

"I didn't think of that, there is method in their madness."

"But we can call in."

"We'll establish a time."

"Tell me about your office."

"The general really did a number on me. I've been moved so far away from the center of power, you couldn't find me with a Boy Scout as a guide. I can't tell anyone what I do or where. Had to sign my life away. Having said that, it's going to be a great place to work. I can see the Blue Ridge and we're almost out of the smog."

"Is this going to be one of those jobs where you can't tell me where you've been or where your going?"

"Worse. Not even supposed to tell you where I am."

"Lisa phoned. Tucker Tubbs will be in Friday morning. Wants you to pick him up at Dulles."

"What time?"

"Plane lands at six-thirty. We already had plans to have the Bidwells over Friday evening, so I invited Lisa and Tucker. Tell Mr. Tubbs we expect to see them at six when you pick him up."

"So he'll be here at six-thirty."

• • •

One of the bennies of being a commander and having a boss that doesn't ever want to see you again is the only person I had to notify where I'd be is my Secretary and she wasn't all that interested. I waited for Tucker's people mover to slowly arrive at Dulles main terminal. The decision to use motorized ramps to move people from airplanes to the terminal was not an all time bright idea. Another decision that looked good on paper, but bad in practice. If I had worried about missing Tucker, I shouldn't have. He wandered off the vehicle into the terminal wearing a multi-pocketed khaki costume, reminiscent of Stanley in Africa searching for Livinston.

He approached with his famous gapped tooth smile, "Hello, Johnny. What are you doing here? Where's Lisa?"

"Had to work. I'm your taxi driver. You look like that famous African explorer."

"Livingston?"

"No, Groucho Marx's Dr. Spaulding. Where did you get the plantation hat."

"Like it? In Egypt. How is Paddy Black?"

"Paddy Black has cracked."

"From his nick?"

"Nack Paddy Black. Our foggy friend is undergoing treatment in San Antonio. Lucky guy—still can't remember a thing. Other than that, he is healing good. You look pretty chipper for a guy who flew all night from London. Do you want to go home and change, or go to your office?"

"This is my reporter outfit. Style over substance, don't you remember?"

"Is this rule the one right after motion is work?"

"You may make it in the spy business, after all. I'm wearing this to impress my boss."

"Did you discover a war on your jungle vacation?"

"It's briar patch time for Uncle Sam."

"Did you know the Vietcong bombed your apartment?"

"Yes, I made it out just in time."

"You must have a whole new set of nine lives. Let's motor, Pravda on the Potomac is many miles away."

• • •

I waited, rocking on the front porch. Tucker was the first to arrive, followed almost immediately by Bidwell. I greeted my problematical friends, "We're having cocktails in the stables. Wait 'till you see the bar Lisa found for Bobbie Jean." Lisa added, "And we can see how many people we can invite to our wedding. We're holding it in Bobbie Jean's stable." Bidwell shook his head, "And your first born will arrive in Johnny's manger?"

"My nativity scene is back. The sheep you borrowed returned this afternoon."

"I'll take one of your English ales. My God you have it on tap."

"Told you Bobbie Jean had one hell of a bar."

"You must have thirty stools."

"Thirty-three. Tell me what you did with my sheep."

"After you pour Tucker another ale and he tells us about his visit to the jungle. I'm anxious to hear how he survived the ambush." Tucker drained his glass, "It's unreal to be back in the world. Vietnam has faded from my memory like a bad dream." I asked, "What does the war look like up close?"

"It's a dirty little war. There are no fronts, or organized fighting, it's all around. We're going to wind up in the same mess the British were in when they fought farmers and merchants in Massachusetts." Bobbie Jean interrupted, "Can you open another bottle of wine, Johnny?"

"White and three glasses coming up. There are three types in your fridge. Which one?"

"Chablis."

"Go ahead with your adventure, Tuck."

"Same old story. Hasn't changed since we last talked. We look upon this fight as containment of Communism and the peasants look on it as a patriotic war of liberation. To the peasants, America is propping up another French puppet government. Remember Kipling's poem about fools who hustle the east?"

"Roger that. It went:

*'And the end of the fight is a tombstone white with the name of the late deceased,' And the epitaph drear: 'A Fool lies here who tried to hustle the East.'"*

"We're going to be the fools he wrote about. We'll fight a war of attrition and lose." I asked, "No matter what we do—we lose?"

"You broke the code. Short of using Vietnam as a nuclear test ground, there is no way we can win."

Bobbie Jean interrupted, "Dinner will be buffet style. Serving plates are on the other end of the bar. Help yourselves when you're ready. Informal seating around our table."

Serious conversation was replaced by dinner banter as we filled our plates. Southeast Asia took a back seat to Lisa and Tucker's wedding plans at the dinner table.

Tucker's eyes were still glazed over from his trip, but after dinner coffee perked him up. We adjourned to the bar.

Bidwell spoke with authority, "Enough about wedding plans. I'm still waiting for Tucker to tell us about the ambush."

"Wasn't a big deal to the Vietcong until they found out that Paddy Black was a keeper. Our driver was Vietcong and not all that bright. When I used him to pick up Paddy Black at Ben Hoa, he forgot to tell his buddies. He stayed with the plan even though he wasn't transporting his colonel. When he pulled off the road into the brush. The Vietcong colonel recognized the fowl-up right away. Would have let us both go, but Paddy lost it, bolted for the trees, running away in zig-zag crouch. Colonel fired a warning shot over Paddy's head at the same time Paddy came out of his crouch and nicked Paddy's noggin with a single shot. Paddy fell like a giant redwood tree. If he hadn't run, I could have saved him on the spot. Vietcong realized he was a walking zombie, so they released him in the morning."

My curiosity got the better of me, "How did you find out they changed their minds and decided to come after you?"

Tucker didn't answer, not right away. He pointed at his cup and I got up to refill it with coffee, "This information stays with the three of us. I haven't sworn an oath to protect data like you two, but there are times when it's prudent to do so. The CIA Station Chief made sure Paddy was on a Medivac airplane the same morning he was returned. When the North Vietnamese colonel reported the incident, his folks checked with the Soviets and all hell broke loose."

I shook my head, "Pieces of this puzzle are falling in place. We have a mole somewhere." Tucker wasn't certain, "A mole in Saigon? Don't think so. How about the Pentagon?"

"It's possible, but not likely. Paddy's folder is held at the agency. Who is your CIA contact in Saigon?"

"Colbie, Kolby, or something like that. A quiet studious type. Wears glasses and looks more like a State Department accountant than an agency cowboy."

"That leaves the agency." They both looked at me. "I'm a new guy on the block. I can only hazard a guess. It would have to be someone in CI—Counter Intelligence. If it was someone on the substantive side, they wouldn't give a damn about Paddy. Who warned you?"

"My Vietcong contact in Saigon. She gave me a heads up that I had lost my immunity as a reporter. I didn't return to my apartment. Hitched a ride on the back of a motor scooter to Ben Hoa. If you have to go over, take a cab, you can get killed on one of their scooters. Didn't have time to return for my things. When they're after you, it's serious business. However, they did me a favor when they blew up my apartment. The *Post* won't reimburse me for abandoned property."

I asked, "Has your Vietcong source been turned?"

"Fat chance. Our agency boys are supporting the establishment. Really weird. When they were OSS back in 1944, they supported the Vietcong."

• • •

I looked at Bidwell, "Your turn in the barrel. What did you do with my sheep?"

"I'll come clean after Tucker tells us about his trip home. How in the world did you wind up in Egypt?"

"Wasn't easy, I flew out of Guam to Calcutta. Now that's a place that I don't recommend for a vacation. One trip there and the Pope would endorse birth control. Hot and humid, the stench was unbelievable. I've never seen so many poor people. At night the streets are lined with sleeping peasants. The privileged ones were allowed to sleep under the overhangs. From Calcutta I flew to Saudi Arabia. Dust storms! Not where I'll go again. Egypt after that. I don't blame the Israelis for giving the Sinai back. Everywhere I stopped, wall to wall people." I added, "There'll always be more people, but there'll never be more land."

Bidwell laughed, "The real estate guy on TV in Roswell! When did you finally reach civilization?"

"London. Now it's your turn. What did you do with Johnny's sheep."

"Not until he pours us a glass of cognac and after we step outside so I can smoke a cigar. No fireplace draft to evacuate my smoke."

• • •

Bidwell offered me a cigar, but I refused. He lit his and took several drags, blowing smoke rings into the cool night air, "Got crossways with a vindictive three star at the Pentagon. Seems he didn't like a sergeant hobnobbing with the brass at poker and golf. So, he took after me, trying to nail me for anything illegal. You know me, I decided to give him a helping hand. I dropped a few hints that I'd set up a casino inside the center courtyard refreshment stand."

Tucker grinned, "You mean the gazebo in the middle of the Pentagon that sells hockey pucks for hamburgers?"

"That's the one."

"I rigged it so smoke was coming out the chimney and made it sound like a Las Vegas casino. General triggered my tape recorder when he walked by. Had it set to turn on by a motion detector. When the time was ripe and I was tipped off that a raid was on the way, I borrowed three of Johnny's sheep and herded them inside."

I had to ask, "How did you get them inside the Pentagon?"

"You forget, sergeants not only run the Air Force, we run the Pentagon. My three star thought he had me for sure. He was leader of the pack. Had his GSA marshals kick in the gazebo door. As he was going in, Johnny's ram came charging out with two ewes following. The ram butted the three star in the midsection, doubled him over and the ewes knocked him backwards out the door. My three star went ass over teakettle and Johnny's sheep went to pasture."

Bidwell reached inside his coat pocket, "Had the Air Force photographer take happy snaps of the whole event."

I looked at the photos and handed them to Tucker, "Don't ask."

Tucker laughed, "Don't tell."

*"But I don't want to go among mad people," Alice remarked.*
*"Oh you can't help that," said the Cat, "we're all mad here."*

*Pentagon*

*White sandstone turned dingy brown*
*With soot, from Washingtown*
*Five buildings, wrapped in one—*
*Pentagon*

*Each building, five stories high*
*A center courtyard, open to sky*
*And, closed to the sun—*
*Pentagun*

*Divided by four*
*Army, Navy, Air Force*
*And, Marine corps—*
*Pentagore*

*Could have stopped a war*
*Planning McNamara's gore*
*All you had to say*
*Can't win it that way—*
*Pentasway*

*Blue suits and khaki*
*Politician's lackey*
*Dancin' on a string*
*To an executive wing—*
*Pentalacky*

*What, no promotion?*
*This side of the ocean*
*Five sided square*
*Why didn't you care—*
*Pentagrief*

*Career and opportunities*
*Open up, so take a stand*
*Better sign up for Vietnam*
*Now, ain't war grand—*
*Pentaband*

*Got a new way to fight*
*Pockets of men separated*
*But, connected by air*
*All alone, out there—*
*Pentaplan*

*Damn you, five sided swamp*
*We got mired on the ground*
*Waiting for your air*
*To come around—*
*Pentabog*

*Your plan's not new*
*It's over a century old*
*The British did the same*
*In Afghanistan I'm told—*
*Pentacopy*

*Ten thousand marched*
*Over the Khyber Pass*
*Only one soul came out*
*With his pack and ass—*
*Pentadumb*

*Afghans saw supplies*
*Set apart from tents*
*Like the Vietcong*
*Came between*
*Men and munitions*
*And won—*
*Pentadone*

*Five sided enigma*
*With parking lots full*
*Should-a used*
*Your head*
*Your heart*
*Not your—*
*Pentabull*